The Black Sheep

Peter Darman

Contents

3

4

It is over 800 years since Rome fell to the barbarians

But in the eastern Mediterranean, a Roman emperor still rules an empire founded 1000 years before, from the city of Constantinople

Western Europe is riven by incessant warfare between jealous and greedy kings and princes

All Christendom is under threat from the followers of Islam, who have conquered Arabia, North Africa, the Holy Land and parts of Anatolia

And in Sicily, a 20-year conflict called the War of the Sicilian Vespers has come to an end

List of characters

Those marked with a dagger † are known to history.

Byzantine Empire (called Roman Empire by contemporaries)
†Andronicus: Roman emperor
Arabates: Alan mercenary in the service of Emperor Andronicus
Arcadius Drogon: Governor of Magnesia
†Athanasius: Patriarch of Constantinople
†Ioannes Komnenos: Count of the Thrakesion Theme, Governor of Philadelphia
Leo Diogenes: commander of the Paramonai
†Maria: Byzantine/Roman princess, sister of Emperor Andronicus
†Michael: Co-Emperor of the Byzantine/Roman Empire, son of Emperor Andronicus
†Michael Cosses: Count of the Opsikion Theme, Governor of Artake
Timothy the Forest Dweller: eunuch, imperial treasurer

Catalan Company
(a band of Spanish mercenaries made up of horsemen and foot soldiers called Almogavars)
Angel: Almogavar captain
Ayna: Persian, former ghazi warrior
†Bernat de Rocafort: commander of the Catalan Company's horsemen
Carla Rey: wife of Sancho Rey
Chana: Jew, former Turkish slave
Hector: Almogavar captain
Jordi Rey: friend of Luca Baldi, only son of Sancho Rey
Luca Baldi: former Italian shepherd
Marc: Almogavar captain
†Roger de Flor: Commander of the Catalan Company
Sancho Rey: Almogavar captain, head of the Almogavar council

Turkish warlords
Izzeddin Arslan: Sufi fanatic, leader of the ghazi army
†Karesi Bey: emir of the Karesi Emirate
Mahmud of Caesarea: Karesi Bey's commander of horsemen
†Mehmed Bey: emir of the Aydin Emirate
†Saruhan Bey: emir of the Saruhan Emirate
†Sasa Bey: emir of the Germiyanid Emirate

6

Preface

Constantinople, 1302

The great city still looked impressive, if one did not peer too closely. It had been nearly a hundred years since the Latin Frank crusaders from the west had sacked the city, emptying it of most of its treasures, damaging and burning its buildings, raping its women and girls and desecrating its holy places. For nearly a thousand years the city named after the Roman Emperor Constantine had been a beacon of light in a dark and uncivilised world. At its height, the city's population had totalled half a million souls, but barely seventy thousand now lived within its impressive and still intact walls. It was still a great city of marble, stone and red-tile roofs when many towns and cities in the rest of the world were filled with drab buildings of wood and thatch.

Constantinople was surrounded on three sides by water, and on the landward side were strong fortifications that had resisted the attacks of barbarians, such as Persians and Muslims, but not the Latin crusaders who had so basely betrayed fellow Christians. The crusaders had breached the walls of Constantinople in the northwestern section of the city defences, in the so-called Blachernae area, from where they launched attacks into the city itself. And it was to the Blachernae area, specifically the palace of the same name, that General George Mouzalon headed, riding through the district containing the houses of Constantinople's wealthiest aristocrats, which clustered around the palace. The latter was sited on a hill overlooking the city walls and beyond them to the west the Philopation, a large park used for hunting. To the north were the sea walls of the Golden Horn, the narrow bay that was one of the finest natural harbours in the world.

The Roman emperors who ruled from Constantinople used to live in the Grand Palace, an impressive, sprawling complex built as an equivalent to the Palatine Palace in Rome. At its height it was a vast collection of individual palaces built on terraces overlooking the Sea of Marmara. But they had been so thoroughly looted and vandalised by the Franks that there was no longer a Grand Palace. Instead, reflecting the diminished status of both the emperor and the empire he ruled over, the imperial throne was located in the much more functional Blachernae Palace, in reality a palace-citadel surrounded by walls and towers.

The general rode through the gates into the huge courtyard where chariot races, gymnastics and military parades took place, though only on celebratory occasions. He looked around the largely empty space and smiled. There would be no celebrations for a long while, if ever. Guards on the walls observed him as he rode up the hill to the palace itself, burly soldiers with axes stepping forward to block his path. Then stepping aside and bowing their heads when they recognised him. He dismounted and handed the reins of his horse to one.

'Take him to the stables.'

'Yes, general,' answered the soldier in a foreign accent.

They were Varangians, the 'axe-bearing barbarians' who were the emperor's personal bodyguard. Originally from Kiev-Rus, they now comprised mostly Norsemen and Danes, with a smattering of Englishmen. How he would have loved to lead a whole army of Varangians – men superbly equipped with chainmail armour, helmets, large axes, swords and shields. Soldiers who could cut through enemy formations like a hot knife through butter. Alas, the Varangians never left the palace, the emperor keeping them close to him at all times. Once they had numbered a corps of six thousand men; now only a few hundred remained. It cut him to the quick to know, despite their depleted numbers, they were still the best soldiers the empire could muster.

He walked up the steps leading to the palace and caught sight of a familiar figure. Obese, bald, a double chin threatening to obscure the solid gold torc around his neck, Timothy the Forest Dweller stood smiling at him like an oversized toad. His nickname derived from his place of birth in a densely forested area in Cappadocia, a region now lost to the enemy. The derogatory term was due to his immense power at the court of the emperor, for Timothy was not only a eunuch but also the imperial treasurer. Dressed in an apricot-coloured robe called a *kabbadion*, a kaftan-like garment with full sleeves and fastened at the front, it was richly decorated with gold on the cuffs and hem. A multitude of pearls had also been stitched on the garment but the most expensive item Timothy wore was the gold torc. The church denounced such 'pagan' items but such was the influence of the chief treasurer with the emperor that he ignored its denunciations.

'Welcome, general, the emperor is expecting you.'

George Mouzalon was always surprised by the deep voice of the eunuch, that and his great size, but then he found the whole concept of eunuchs bizarre and slightly unnerving.

'It is good to see you are unharmed, general,' remarked Timothy as they both walked through one of the long, colonnaded corridors that filled the Blachernae. Though the palace was a functional, three-storey building, attempts had been made to decorate it in a style to make the emperor and his family feel at home. Thus, corridors were adorned with gold mosaics portraying imperial military victories, their floors paved with different-coloured marble tiles.

Varangians stood guard at every doorway, round scarlet shields decorated with a double-headed eagle in gold slung on their backs. In the throne room itself, more Varangians stood along the walls and around the platform on which the emperor sat on a throne of gold inlaid with precious stones. Occupying it was Emperor Andronicus, a man in his early forties but who looked twenty years older. His hair was greying and his cheeks were sunken, accentuated by his narrow face and long nose. His brown eyes were pools of weariness and the gold crown suspended by a gold chain above his head resembled a Sword of Damocles rather than a bejewelled orb of power. A deeply religious man, he wore a forked beard to signify his moderation, reverence and graveness. He lifted a hand to Mouzalon.

'Welcome, general, we are glad to see you.'

The general doubted that, but he thanked God his emperor was indeed a man of moderation and religion, else his head would most likely already be decorating Constantinople's walls.

'How many men did we lose, general?'

Michael, the emperor's son, was not so moderate or pious. A man in his mid-twenties whom his father had made co-emperor, his eyes bored into the general. He was the future of the empire of Constantine and he did not look favourably on anyone who jeopardised that future. The recent defeat of an imperial army at Bapheus, a plain east of the city of Nicomedia, in the province of Bithnyia, near to Constantinople, had resulted in yet more territory being lost to the Muslims.

'A couple of hundred, highness,' replied the general.

'Then you will be retaking the field against these infidels,' snapped Michael.

The general sighed. 'Alas, no, highness. Half the army, the Alan contingent, deserted before the battle began, which makes attacking the Muslims foolhardy in the extreme.'

The Alans, originally an ancient Iranian tribe, had occupied the areas north of the Caspian and Black Seas, before the Huns had forced them west into Europe, though others ventured south into the Caucasus. Famed horse soldiers, they had been hired as mercenaries by Roman emperors for centuries. However, like all mercenaries they quit their service when their pay ran out.

Andronicus looked at the general. 'Deserted?'

'They were paid for three months' service, highness,' said Mouzalon, 'which unfortunately expired the day before the battle.'

'If we lose Anatolia,' stated Michael, 'the empire loses all its recruiting grounds, and our army will wither and die. We must retake the lands the Muslimss have captured, otherwise they will be hammering on the gates of Constantinople itself.'

Mouzalon nodded. 'I agree, highness.'

He glanced at the Varangian Guards standing around the emperor's platform.

'Perhaps I could have the Varangian Guardsmen as a cadre, around which I could build a new army.'

The emperor's eyes opened wide in alarm.

'The Varangian Guard? They exist to defend the imperial family, general. Would you rob me of the only thing that stands between me and ruination?'

It was a fair point, especially as the only things standing between Andronicus and the victors of Bapheus were the Varangian

11

Guard, another indigenous guard unit called the *Paramonai*, the city garrison and the empire's navy anchored in the Golden Horn, though many of the ships were manned by Genoese mercenaries.

Andronicus shook his head. 'For a thousand years, this city and the empire it built has stood as a beacon of light and hope in a dark and uncivilised world. God will not abandon Constantinople in its hour of need, general. But I will not allow the Varangian Guard to leave the city.'

The emperor turned to his son and co-emperor.

'What of the counts in Thrace and Greece? They must surely be able to raise an army between them to fight the Muslims?'

Each province of the empire was ruled by a count, who commanded all the military resources his province could muster. And any force raised by a count was made up of natives rather than foreign mercenaries, which in theory made it more reliable on the battlefield. But, as with so many things in the empire, the provinces had shrunk in number following the contraction of the empire's borders. And just as provinces in Anatolia had been lost to the Muslims, those on the western side of the Bosporus, the narrow strait that divided Europe from Asia, were under threat from the Serbs and Bulgars.

'Alas, father,' said Michael, 'if we strip the western provinces of troops, our enemies will seek to take advantage and we may lose Greece altogether. A blow from which we may never recover.'

'There must be some soldiers somewhere we can use to reclaim our territories in the east,' wailed Andronicus pathetically. 'The march of the Muslims on our eastern frontier is an affront not only to God, but also to me.'

His tired eyes looked at George Mouzalon and Michael in turn, though neither had an answer to his miserable plea. The emperor's gaze eventually turned to Timothy, who was smiling in a self-satisfied manner.

'Something amuses you, lord treasurer?' asked the emperor icily.

In Rome, eunuchs had been classed as lower than beggars, but in Constantinople they had always been accorded high status, aristocrats often having their sons castrated so they could more easily become governors, ambassadors, generals, admirals and other important posts in the empire. The Orthodox Church regarded eunuchs as 'angels on earth', and emperors saw them as being reliable and free of the vice of sexual desire, which was far from the truth. They could thus be trusted to carry out duties in the women's quarters, as well as being relied upon to undertake the education of royal princes and princesses. For centuries, the rulers of Constantinople had surrounded themselves with high-ranking eunuchs to provide them with loyal service and valued advice. Timothy the Forest Dweller did not disappoint his master.

'This is God's city, highness, which as you say has stood for a thousand years and will stand for a thousand more,' began the eunuch. 'He who loves this city, its emperor and its people will not allow the infidel to foul its holy precincts or indeed approach its sacred walls.'

'Get to the meat of it,' snapped Michael.

Timothy remained unflustered. 'You will have heard of the War of the Sicilian Vespers, my lord?'

Michael wracked his brain. 'No?'

Timothy fought the urge to laugh in Michael's face. The emperor, though, was not so ignorant.

'The conflict between the Angevin French and the Aragonese Spanish over control of the island of Sicily?'

Timothy bowed his porcine head. 'Indeed, majesty.'

'What of it?' asked Andronicus.

'The war has recently ended, highness,' said Timothy. 'The brother of the Spanish King James, King Frederick, has been recognised by the Angevins and the false Bishop of Rome, the so-called pope, as the legitimate ruler of Sicily, thus bringing hostilities to an end.'

'I thank God for bringing this about,' reflected Andronicus. 'The people of Sicily have been subjected to the cruelties that war brings for twenty years. Glad as we are for this miracle, lord treasurer, I fail to see how this benefits Constantinople.'

'There are mercenaries in the pay of King Frederick, highness,' said Timothy, 'who are now without employment. Mercenaries, moreover, who have proved themselves to be ferocious soldiers. We should look to bringing these mercenaries to Constantinople, highness, to fight against the Muslims.'

'They are Catholics,' said Michael. 'Why would apostates fight for the true church?'

'Money, lord,' sighed Mouzalon. 'If they are paid, they will fight. They have, after all, been happily fighting and killing their fellow Catholics for twenty years.'

Andronicus was unsure. 'The empire has a long history of hiring mercenaries, which has cost the imperial treasury much money, often for little success. We currently employ Alans and Genoese, and in the past have hired Cilicians, Cumans, Georgians and Hungarians

14

to fight our enemies. Why should I pay for yet *more* mercenaries who might run away from the enemy, just as the Alans did?'

'Two reasons, highness,' answered Timothy. 'First, and to be blunt, we have little choice. General Mouzalon has valiantly endeavoured to hold back the Muslim tide, but without additional resources he cannot withstand them.'

Mouzalon was nodding his head in agreement, which was noted by the emperor.

'And the second?' asked Andronicus.

'These mercenaries,' said Timothy, 'comprise a self-contained army, an army moreover that has tasted victory after victory in Sicily, against the flower of Frankish chivalry.'

'Is there such a thing?' sneered Michael.

The emperor ignored his son. 'You are certain these mercenaries are no longer employed, lord treasurer?'

'My spies inform me King Frederick desires to be rid of them as speedily as possible, highness.'

'Even if they are willing to fight for us,' said Mouzalon, 'Sicily is hundreds of miles from Constantinople, which means weeks of marching. By the time they arrive, the Muslims will be knocking at the gates of this city.'

'I am reliably informed that the commander of these mercenaries has his own fleet of ships,' replied Timothy. 'Transportation will not be a problem, general.'

Andronicus brought his hands together, rested his chin on his thumbs and closed his eyes. Silence filled the chamber as all eyes looked at the emperor, the heir of Constantine and the man responsible for defending the true Christian faith. Andronicus opened his eyes and looked at Timothy.

'Very well, lord treasurer, use your spies to make an approach to the commander of these Catholic mercenaries. They are to relay a message from the Roman emperor that he has selected them to defend the city of Christ from the infidel Muslims.'

So it was that the Emperor of Constantinople, on the suggestion of a eunuch, took a decision that would have profound consequences for the empire he was desperately trying to preserve.

Chapter 1

Luca Baldi considered himself luckier than most. For one thing, he was still alive. For twenty years armies had criss-crossed Sicily fighting a war to control the island. In that time many villages, farms and towns had been destroyed, along with their populations. The great island still looked the same, with its woods of pine, oak, beech, willow, elm and poplars, and Sicily was still the main granary for Italy, just as it had been for over a thousand years. But the shipments of grain to the mainland were not what they were, a consequence of the war that had blighted the land, destroyed crops and conscripted peasants into armies, from which a great many did not return.

Sicily now contained many large and mostly empty expanses of land, which were either barren wastes or were given over to cattle and sheep farming. In theory, all the island's land outside the towns was divided between the crown and powerful barons whose estates were administered from a large manor house called a *casalis*, around which were stretches of grassland and pasturage dotted with villages. But even the manor houses lay abandoned and derelict, their masters having been either killed or left together with their families for the mainland.

Luca neither cared about the causes of the war or who had been fighting it. He was a simple shepherd, though as a child his first job had been herding geese and goslings. He had then moved on to pigs, spending most days enduring their squealing and grunting, and sharing the filth they lived in. His father, also a shepherd, had insisted he also learn about the care of cows and horses, and a for a while he had even assisted one of the town's blacksmiths in his forge, learning to make and fit horseshoes. But his purpose in life was to care for his family's flock of sheep. To look after the lambs in the spring, and to shear the rams, ewes and yearlings. A shepherd's life was idyllic in summer among the wildflowers and fresh air, and unceasingly bleak in winter when being lashed by wind and rain on the hillsides.

His hometown – Rometta – was a quaint place built on a hill a short distance from the port of Messina, around which were cultivated terraces growing lemons, oranges, grapes and olives, as well as accommodating grazing sheep.

The fierce heat of summer was a memory now, the autumn bringing more pleasant daytime temperatures and cooler nights. There was still the occasional hot wind but rains now replenished the streams and lakes so the hillsides around Rometta were green instead of brown. Like Luca, the town had been lucky during the war, its walls, which had been built by Arabs, had withstood numerous attacks and even helped beat off an army of French knights and soldiers. Luca had been a boy when he had thrown stones from the walls and had hurled a spear at a soldier scrambling from a scaling ladder trying to clamber on to the battlements. Even as a boy Luca had strength in his arms and shoulders and the spear had struck the man in the chest, the point going through his mail armour to penetrate his ribcage. He had seen the man grimace before he fell to the ground below. In the horror and chaos of that summer's day, he had not given the fact he had killed a man much thought. He was just glad the attack had been beaten off, that his family had survived, and he was briefly feted as a hero afterwards. But the reality was he was lucky, as was his town, for which he gave thanks to God. He had seen the face of war and survived.

Now there was no more war.

'If I was a wolf I would have eaten half your flock by now.'

Luca stopped his daydreaming to turn and see a beaming Jordi Rey creeping up on him. The dark-skinned Spaniard was crouching low but drew himself up to his full height when his friend faced him. They were roughly the same height, barring an inch or two, Jordi broader shouldered and more powerful in appearance than the sinewy Luca. His skin was darker in hue, though both had thick black hair and calloused hands, Luca's through hard work, Jordi's through war.

They had known each other for only a short time, but in that time had become friends. Jordi was a soldier in an army of mercenaries raised in far-away Catalonia, a region of northeast Spain, though Jordi had never seen his homeland. The mercenary army was made up of two parts, one of horsemen and the other, larger part made up of foot soldiers called Almogavars. They were given that odd name because they were the descendants of Spanish shepherds who had fought the Muslim Moors decades before. So effective were the Almogavars that the Spanish king offered their services, together with hundreds of Spanish horsemen, to the King of Sicily in his war against the French, though they did not come cheap. The mercenaries had travelled to Sicily twenty years before to fight against the French, a task they had excelled at. They were now led by a military adventurer named Roger de Flor, a part-Italian, part-German larger-than-life character and veteran commander. His deputy and second-in-command of the mercenary army was Jordi's father, Sancho Rey.

Now there was peace, the Spanish Almogavars and horsemen had no one to fight and nothing to do. Jordi placed a sack on the ground.

'I have brought you food and wine to stop you starving,' he grinned, pulling bread, cheese, olives and a wineskin from the sack. 'No wolves today?'

'Only Spanish ones,' answered Luca, accepting the wineskin and taking a swig before handing it back to Jordi.

He flopped down on the grass, his friend doing likewise, in front of them the flock of sheep in Luca's care grazing on the hillside. Above them Rometta basked in autumn sunlight. Jordi drank some wine, tore off a chunk of bread from the large loaf he had brought and handed it to Luca.

'How do you do it?' he asked.

Luca looked surprised. 'What?'

Jordi gave a lazy sweep of his arm. 'This. Sitting on a hillside all day staring at sheep.'

'It is not all idleness and relaxation, my friend. The winter is a bad time. In the summer, a shepherd replenishes his stock of stamina in preparation for the tests to come.'

He broke off a piece of cheese and stuffed it into his mouth, then washed it down with more wine.

'What will you do now the war has ended?'

Jordi shrugged. 'Return to Spain with the others, I suppose, though there seems some doubt regarding whether we will be welcome in Catalonia. One thing is certain, King Frederick wants us gone.'

Frederick, the third son of King Peter of Aragon, was beloved by the Almogavars, even though he wanted his kingdom of Sicily to be rid of the Spanish soldiers who had helped him win his throne. Generations before they had been shepherds like Luca, but now they lived and breathed war. They also retained a strong identity to their homeland. Jordi spoke excellent Italian, but he had told Luca that the Almogavars spoke in their native Catalan when conversing among themselves.

'I will miss you, my friend,' said Luca, now feeling the pleasant effects of the wine.

'When we leave Sicily, you could come with us,' retorted Jordi.

Luca was shocked. 'Leave Rometta?'

Like the vast majority of peasants, his world comprised his hometown and the surrounding area. Travel was rarely undertaken, and the idea of leaving Sicily filled him with trepidation. He had never even visited the city of Messina, a mere eight miles to the east.

'Why not?' smiled Jordi. 'You would make a good Almogavar, and you have already proved yourself in battle.'

Luca shuddered. 'I was fighting for my life like a cornered animal. I have no wish to repeat the experience.'

Jordi ate some more cheese. 'I could have a word with my father. He is always looking for new recruits.'

Luca had never met Sancho Rey but had heard stories of the Catalan who had a quick temper and a formidable reputation as a fighter.

'I will think about it,' answered Luca, evasively.

Jordi, like his friend, had seen only eighteen summers, but he had grown up among soldiers who had been fighting a bloody war; and his instincts were already finely honed when it came to sensing danger. His black eyes were following four riders trotting along the western road leading to Rometta, which would take them right past him, Luca, and the latter's herd of sheep. Some of the animals had stopped their grazing to lift their heads to watch the horsemen.

'Who's this?' asked Jordi, jumping to his feet.

Luca, now slightly light-headed, followed, squinting at the approaching horsemen. He saw the banner carried by one of the riders and nodded. He had seen the same colours flying from the town walls when the French had assaulted Rometta. They showed rows of horizontal red and white bands – the coat of arms of the Carafa family.

The riders slowed as they approached the flock, which began to move away from the four horses, further up the grassy slope. Luca recognised the type of mount the soldiers were riding. They were coursers: fast, light and strong beasts imported from North Africa and bred specifically to carry soldiers. Knights rode warhorses called destriers in battle, but while attending to their day-to-day business they also used a riding horse called a palfrey, which had a very smooth gait, and coursers. The lead rider slowed his horse and drew level to the shepherd and his Catalan friend.

Luca had seen the young lord several times in Rometta in recent months. If there was ever a man who resembled what a knight should look like it was Fabrizio Carafa. Tall, handsome with a strong jaw and piercing brown eyes, he also possessed the arrogance and rashness that characterised his social group. He peered at the two peasants and then pointed at a black sheep among the flock.

'Is that your flock?'

'Yes, lord,' answered Luca.

'Why is there a black sheep among it? Are you not aware of the town rules?'

Luca was indeed aware that shepherds were supposed to kill black lambs when they were born. Black sheep were believed to be unlucky and were linked to the devil. More practically, black wool could not by dyed and was thus almost worthless. More importantly, in a land that had been ravaged by war and where superstition was rife, such totems of misfortune and witchcraft were frowned upon. And Rometta's rules clearly specified that black sheep were to be killed to avoid encouraging Satan 'taking an interest' in the town. But Luca liked his black sheep, and since he had for a short while been the hero of Rometta, no town official had raised the matter with him.

'I'm waiting,' snapped Fabrizio impatiently.

'What business is it of yours?' asked Jordi.

The noble's top lip curled into a sneer.

'What did you say, peasant?' demanded the knight.

Jordi certainly looked like a commoner, with his sheepskin coat, called a *zamarra*, and his shoes comprising one piece of coarse leather tied on the soles of his feet by wool laces around his lower legs. They were called *abarka* and were worn by all the Almogavars, though Fabrizio probably did not know that. His three companions stared disbelievingly at the oaf who had just spoken to their liege lord in such a disrespectful manner.

'I am no peasant,' said Jordi defiantly. 'Be on your way before I teach you a lesson you will not forget.'

Luca, appalled his friend had spoken to an anointed knight in such a way, jumped between them, holding up his hands to Fabrizio.

'Too much wine loosens the tongue, lord. He meant no disrespect.'

Fabrizio's noble nostrils flared. To a knight, respect was closely tied to honour, and honour was everything. To be spoken to in such a disrespectful manner could not go unanswered, even if there were no witnesses to the insult. But Fabrizio was accompanied by three of his men, who would report back to their comrades and anyone else with ears to listen that their lord had been insulted. Next

23

to religion, honour was the most important aspect of knighthood. It was like a delicate flower that required nurturing and protecting. Fabrizio ignored Luca's pleadings and focused on his companion.

Luca was alarmed, and rightly so. The man on the fine brown horse was not only well armed and equipped, he was also a knight. A man whose life was dedicated to war. Whereas Luca had spent his childhood years attending to animals, Fabrizio would have been a page – a boy servant to a lord. A glorified servant but one who nevertheless learned to ride a horse and whose character, manners and sense of loyalty were moulded by his master to direct him to follow the knightly path. At the age of fifteen he became a squire, a knight's personal apprentice. He was taught not only how to care for weapons and armour but to put them on and use them. His master practised fighting techniques with his squire and the latter followed the knight into battle. And when he had fully mastered the skills to do so, the squire became a knight himself. And this knight was freshly made and brimming with the virtues of his order.

Fabrizio drew his expensive sword and pointed it at Jordi.

'Arrest him, and the shepherd.'

His men began dismounting but before they had done so, Jordi hurled the wineskin at Fabrizio, who reacted instinctively to cut the leather container in half with a deft sideways cut of his sword. Jordi also reacted quickly, launching himself at the knight, grabbing his sword arm with his left hand, yanking it towards him prior to slamming his fist into Fabrizio's handsome face. The head was the only part of the lord's body that could safely be struck with a fist as his torso and limbs were heavily protected. Under his red surcoat he wore a long-sleeved mail hauberk and his legs were protected by

24

quilted cuisses over his thighs and knees. Domed iron poleyns covered his knees and hardened leather greaves shielded his shins.

The knight, dazed, dropped his sword and toppled from his saddle when Jordi punched him again, this time in the windpipe. He fell heavily on his back, winding him and rendering him unable to rise. A triumphant Jordi stood over him, laughing impiously at the crestfallen young lord.

Luca's jaw dropped as he stared in horror at the scene, and was rendered unconscious when the blunt end of a spear was struck against the side of his head. When he regained consciousness, he discovered his wrists had been shackled and his head throbbed from a splitting headache. He was also aware of being in a cold room with stone walls, a closed thick wooden door and iron bars over a single window in one of the walls. His mouth was dry and he found it difficult to focus his mind.

'The hero awakes.'

He heard Jordi's mocking voice and felt comforted, his friend helping him to raise himself up and rest his back against the cold stone wall.

'Where are we?' asked Luca, looking around the bare room.

'In prison,' said an angry Jordi.

Luca glanced at his friend beside him and saw his left eye was closed and his face was cut and bruised. Jordi saw his friend's reaction to his wounds.

'It took three of them to subdue me,' he said, 'plus the idiot knight when he had regained his senses.'

'You should not have done that, Jordi, you could have killed him.'

His friend sighed. 'Sadly, he still lives.'

Luca's head dropped. 'They will hang us both.'

Jordi spat out a mouthful of blood. 'No, they will not.'

But Luca's prediction looked set to become a terrifying reality when the cell door opened and two guards entered, hauling the pair to their feet, one striking Jordi across the face when the Catalan made a disparaging remark about his large gut. Grinning, blood showing between his teeth and apparently without a care in the world, Jordi marched proudly from the cell to face the town's magistrate.

Called a *podestá*, he was a noble with extensive knowledge of the law who administered both civil and criminal justice in Rometta. Unfortunately for the two defendants, he was also a close friend of the Carafa family.

The ashen faces of Luca's parents affected him deeply when he was led into the courtroom, a rather drab chamber with peeling walls adjacent to the town jail. It smelt of musty leather and did nothing to raise his spirits. Luca's father, a man worn out by years of hard work for little reward, tried to speak to his son but was rudely forced back by the fat guard.

On a raised platform sat the three judges: the *podestá* himself, Roger Fontana, the bruised and fuming Fabrizio Carafa, and a bored abbot from Messina who had the misfortune of passing through Rometta when he was stopped by the *podestá* and asked to sit in judgement on the two peasants that had assaulted an anointed knight.

The charge was read out to the court to the accompaniment of the sobbing of Luca's mother, a wizened woman in her late thirties who looked closer to sixty, the bench taking no notice of her obvious distress. On the face of it, the charge did not warrant a death sentence. An assault on a knight was a serious offence, but usually incurred a fine, perhaps the loss of a hand, a flogging and a short spell in prison. Capital punishment was reserved for the most serious crimes, such as murder, robbery, counterfeiting and sodomy. Even rape, which was considered a serious offence, was usually punished with a fine. But Luca saw the stern faces of the judges facing him and a chill went down his spine.

The three men talked in whispers to each other for a few minutes before Sir Roger pointed at him and Jordi.

'According to the decree of Pope Innocent, now sitting beside our Lord in heaven, *rei publicae interest, ne criminal remaneant impunita*, that is to say it is in the public interest that crimes do not go unpunished.'

Fabrizio and the abbot flanking Sir Roger were nodding their heads.

'When you assault one of the king's knights, you assault the king himself. And as the king has been chosen by God to rule over his subjects, I interpret your heinous act to be an assault on God himself.'

'No. Have mercy,' cried Luca's mother, her plea being ignored by the bench.

'Luca Baldi,' continued Sir Roger, 'you are found guilty of attempting to murder a Christian knight, for which you will hang.'

Luca's mother cried out in anguish and fainted.

'Silence in court,' shouted Sir Roger. 'Your flock of sheep is given to Sir Fabrizio in compensation.'

The abbot leaned over to whisper into his ear. Sir Roger nodded.

'Ah, yes. This will not include the black sheep, the spawn of Satan, which will be destroyed forthwith.'

'You will regret this,' seethed Jordi, an outburst that earned him another slap across his face from the fat guard.

Not being a native of Rometta, no one knew who the broad-shouldered young man with the seditious tongue was.

'Who are you?' demanded Sir Roger.

'Jordi Rey,' came the answer.

The clerk sitting at a small desk at right angles to the bench made a note of the name.

'You too will hang in the morning,' said Sir Roger, 'and may God have mercy on your soul.'

Luca's knees nearly buckled beneath him but Jordi had not finished, turning his head to the bench as he and his friend were led away.

'I give you one last chance to change your minds. If not, I cannot vouch for your safety.'

Sir Roger jumped up and pointed at him. 'Before you are hanged, your tongue will be cut out and fed to pigs, and afterwards your head will be cut off and mounted above the town gates as a warning to others.'

Jordi laughed. To him it made no sense to hang someone and then cut off their head. But he was forgetting that beheading was viewed as a nobleman's death, which was deprived to lowborn peasants. The peasant had to be first dead before his head was removed from his body.

Luca, distraught, caught a fleeting glimpse of his father helping his mother to her feet before he was bundled from the courtroom. The next few hours were a confused blur. He and Jordi were taken back to their cell where they were given water and slop not fit for pigs. Luca was angry and upset that his pleas to see his parents were

28

denied. He was also angry his friend was so blasé in what would be their last hours on earth. Then anger gave way to fear. Fear of the unknown, fear he would disgrace himself on the scaffold in the morning, and fear God would cast him into hell after he had left this life. How he wanted the presence of a priest, which they had also been denied. To hear the soothing words of one more enlightened than he, telling him there was nothing to worry about. But all he heard was the venom of his friend.

Jordi spent most of the night pacing up and down the cell.

'You worry too much, Luca. Tomorrow we will be free and there will be nothing to worry about.'

'We are going to be hanged in the morning, Jordi. You should make your peace with God.'

Jordi laughed, walked over to the door and began hammering on it.

'Are you there, fat guard? Tomorrow you are going to die. You hear me?'

'Keep your noise down,' came the reply, 'otherwise we will cut out your tongue now rather than in the morning.'

Luca slumped to the floor and reflected on his life, such as it was. He had been born in Rometta and he would die in Rometta. He had been to markets in neighbouring towns and villages but had never seen Messina, except from afar. He had never experienced the love of a woman, or indeed had had even the friendship of a member of the opposite sex. His life was, or rather had been, tending to sheep on the slopes around Rometta, and he would have traded his soul for the chance for that meaningless existence to continue.

Jordi crouched in front of him and grabbed his shoulders.

'Try to get some sleep.'

'I don't want to spend my last hours on earth asleep,' Luca told him, 'not that I could sleep, anyway.'

Jordi winked with his one good eye.

'Do you believe in God, Luca?'

Luca was shocked he would even ask. 'Of course.'

'Then have faith that the Lord will keep us safe. Tomorrow is a new day.'

He believed Jordi might have gone mad, for why else would he have been so carefree, even happy? How he wished he could escape to a make-believe world instead of the brutal reality that was creeping ever closer.

'I will pray for us both,' said Luca, pathetically.

He did pray, long and hard, holding his hands together in front of him so tightly they became numb after a while. It did not help. He did not hear the voice of God and there was no visit from an angel to tell him all would be well. The only sound was Jordi snoring. Snoring! His mind had clearly gone, which meant he was alone in the cold, dark cell. Then it was dark no longer as the dawn broke to herald another sunny day in Rometta. His heart began to race and he started to shiver. He told himself it was because of the cold but he suspected it was really fear. He felt shame. He had heard stories of men walking calmly to their executions and meeting death with honour. But they were aristocrats who had been trained since childhood to ensure they met their ends in a manly fashion. His heart began to beat faster when he heard a key turning in the lock to the door.

'Out you both come, your public awaits,' came a gruff voice.

Luca gave the slumbering Jordi a gentle tap with his shoe to wake him, his friend stretching out his limbs in a leisurely fashion.

'Now!' shouted the guard.

30

The fat guard was one of the four detailed to escort the prisoners to the town square where they would be executed, and afterwards their corpses would be hung in gibbets until they rotted as a warning to others. Jordi's corpse would be headless: the missing part of his body would be decorating one of the entrances to the town.

After they were manacled, they were led out into the sunlight where a small crowd had gathered. No one spoke as the pair were prodded along the main street towards the square. Luca began to pray but stopped when someone, a woman, spat in his face.

'Devil worshipper.'

He looked at her in amazement, the fat guard shoving her aside and then grabbing Luca's tunic to bundle him forward.

'Keep moving.'

He and Jordi shuffled along, their manacles making a jangling sound as they trudged towards their fate. It required a mighty effort from Luca to stay on his feet and not collapse when they entered the square and saw the gallows in the dead centre, around which was a sizeable crowd. He glanced at Jordi, who was smiling! How he wished he too was insane. He also caught sight of another man, more sinewy than his friend, but who was dressed in exactly the same manner as Jordi, in a sheepskin coat and coarse leather shoes. He nodded at Jordi, who nodded back, before disappearing into the crowd.

Luca's attention was brought back to the gallows when he saw something hanging from one of the three nooses. He screwed up his face in horror when he saw it was the black sheep from his flock. The fat guard grabbed his hair tightly and pulled his head towards his face.

'Don't worry, boy, you will soon be joining your evil familiar.'

His breath was pungent, causing Luca's eyes to water.

He and Jordi were manhandled to the gallows, around them a sea of expectant faces, some very young, all eager to see justice meted out to Luca, the devil-worshipping shepherd, and his foreign accomplice.

'Make way, make way.'

His head dropped when Fabrizio and Sir Roger, with an armed escort, appeared in front of the gallows. It was a simple structure, comprising a thick crossbeam supported at both ends by A-frames. Beneath the two empty nooses were wooden boxes, on which Luca and Jordi would stand prior to having the nooses placed around their necks. The boxes would be kicked away, the pair would drop and slowly strangle to death. The drop would be insufficient to break their necks to kill them instantly. It was considered just they should endure a few minutes of agony before being judged by the Lord and sent to hell.

Two burly executioners, their heads and faces covered by black leather hoods, grabbed Luca and Jordi and marched them to stand behind the boxes. Their identities were masked to safeguard against the families of the condemned exacting vengeance on their executioners, should they have a mind to do so. Luca searched for his parents among the crowd in vain. He was glad. He did not want them to see him dangling on the end of rope, being slowly choked to death in an obscene spectacle.

He heard the words of the priest beside him but took no notice, his eyes focused on the noose suspended above him. His life expectancy was now a matter of minutes, seconds if the drop broke his neck. Please God let it be so. With great effort he was maintaining his dignity, though his body was now shaking with fear. The priest stopped talking, the executioner behind him seized his arms and he was aware of something flying past him.

'Stay still, Luca,' called Jordi.

The executioner was no longer holding his arms, and when he glanced to his right he saw the other executioner was staggering backwards, a spear lodged in his chest. Then the crowd started screaming. He stared directly at Fabrizio Carafa and saw him drawing his sword, the soldiers accompanying him collapsing on the cobbles as they were cut down. Pandemonium filled the square as panicking people scattered in all directions. The young knight froze when a knife was held to his throat, and then his sword was taken from him by another individual dressed in a sheepskin coat, who then punched him hard in the stomach. Fabrizio doubled up, coughing and retching as the square emptied.

A big man with broad shoulders and a mere fringe of black hair, an individual with dark brown eyes and an unforgiving face, walked over to Jordi and looked him up and down.

'Are you hurt?'

Jordi held up his manacled wrists. 'Only my pride, father.'

Another man, stouter and with a large round face, bounded up to Jordi and locked him in a bear hug.

'Did you think we would let you dangle, young pup?'

'Get these chains off my son,' commanded the big man.

Luca was being ignored as the Almogavars secured the square and examined the dead, one of whom was Sir Roger, a spear having been driven through the back of his neck, the point protruding from his windpipe. Two men with spears were standing over the spluttering Fabrizio, a woman, an attractive woman with a sultry expression and shapely figure, holding the knight's sword. He saw her

33

tuck a knife into a sheath attached to her belt and realised it must have been she who had held the blade to Fabrizio's throat.

The short man rummaged through the clothes of the dead guards and found the key to unlock the fettles binding Jordi. The young man grinned and nodded at Luka.

'Him too, Roc.'

Roc. It was an apt name for the man had a head like a large boulder. He moved towards Luca but Jordi's father stopped him.

'He is not an Almogavar.'

'He is my friend, father.'

Jordi's father ambled over to Luca and examined the shepherd. He had a long face covered with skin that had a tightness to it, giving the impression of simmering emotion about to explode.

'My name is Sancho Rey. Your name?'

'Luca Baldi, lord.'

'You are the shepherd with the black sheep?' he pointed at the carcass hanging from the third noose. 'That sheep?'

'Yes, lord.'

'Are you a devil worshipper?'

'No, lord.'

'Then why did you keep a black sheep?'

'I don't believe in killing something just because it is born with a different-coloured coat to the other sheep, lord.'

'The boy was nearly hanged, Sancho, and now you wish to interrogate him?'

Sancho turned when the sultry woman walked over to embrace Jordi, planting a delicate kiss on his forehead.

'You smell disgusting,' she smiled.

'Release him,' ordered Sancho.

34

A grinning Roc unlocked the chains and tossed them to the ground.

'You are blasphemers.'

The priest who had been saying prayers prior to the hanging was still standing near the gallows, holding up a wooden crucifix to Sancho Rey, as though warding off a demon.

'You dare to interrupt the Lord's work?' the priest accused Sancho. 'You have killed an anointed knight, have murdered his soldiers and…'

Sancho Rey carried a short sword in a scabbard attached to his belt. Similar in size and weight to the Roman *gladius* of old, it appeared smaller in his large hand when he whipped it from its scabbard and slashed it across the priest's throat in a blur. The priest was cut short in mid-sentence, his eyes filling with fear as he saw the fountain of blood spurting from his windpipe, before falling to the ground, dead. Blood continued to pump from the wound as the corpse lay on the ground, the Almogavars taking little notice of the dead priest. A shaken Luca noticed that the sultry woman with shining black hair did not bat an eyelid when her husband had killed the priest, and seemed at ease among the death and bloodshed.

Jordi slapped him on the back.

'I told you to have faith, Luca.'

'I must get back to my family,' said Luca.

Sancho barred his way. 'Your life here is over, shepherd. If you stay, they will hang you, or worse.'

'You will be one of us, Luca,' smiled Jordi, 'an Almogavar.'

'That remains to be seen,' said his father.

Roc pointed at the prostrate figure of Fabrizio. 'What about him?'

'Bring him along,' Sancho told the men guarding the knight. 'We will decide his fate later. And retrieve all our weapons.'

The knight was hauled to his feet, the spears wrenched from the corpses of Sir Roger and his soldiers by the Almogavars, who carefully wiped the blood and gore from the metal heads of the weapons. As far as Luca could ascertain, each Almogavar carried three or four spears, though if he had enquired they would have told him they were not spears, but javelins. Around four feet in length, they had steel heads incorporating an integral socket and a diamond cross-section. When thrown with force, they could go through mail armour with ease, as Sir Roger had discovered to his cost. Each man also carried a short sword, as well as a knife, even the women, of which there were more than one.

'Move,' ordered Sancho.

Luca had not eaten since the day before and the mental strain he had been under since his arrest had weakened him considerably. Nevertheless, when Jordi's father gave the order to leave the square he was forced to break into a run, the Almogavars setting a hard pace as they left Rometta and headed east, to Messina. Jordi next to him was beaming with delight, but Luca was filled with trepidation. Only the day before the course of his life had been mapped out precisely. But that life was now over. But what would now be the fate of a poor Sicilian shepherd who had lost his home, his family and seemingly his future?

Chapter 2

Despite twenty years of war, the port city of Messina was still a thriving commercial centre. Ships of all varieties filled its harbour, unloading and taking on board goods to be transported throughout the eastern Mediterranean. Inside the walled city itself, Greeks, Italians and Jews lived in reasonable harmony, conducting business with each other under the watchful eye of the city authorities. Messina enjoyed a unique position of having close contact not only with the hinterland outside its walls, but also with mainland Italy, from which it was separated only by the narrow Strait of Messina. Grain grown in Sicily was shipped to the mainland through Messina, and textiles, slaves and spices arrived at the port for sale throughout the rest of the island. Messina and its traders grew rich, and the foreign merchants who had homes and offices in the city – Genoese, Venetians and Pisans – rented great warehouses around the harbour from the city authorities for princely sums. Those authorities had maintained and strengthened Messina's defences to ensure no marauding army was tempted to seize the city. They had been grateful for the services rendered in its defence by the Catalans, now camped beyond the city walls. Indeed, a grateful Messina provided them with food and shelter. But with the war ended the question on everyone's lips was: when would they be going back to Spain?

The name Almogavar had derived from the Arabic word *al-mogauar*, meaning 'devastator'. Originally shepherds and forest dwellers, Almogavars had been fighting the Muslims in Spain for nearly a hundred years. Now, several thousand of them were sitting on their hands in Sicily, along with a few hundred Catalan horsemen that had journeyed with them. Enforced idleness did not sit well with the Almogavars, who were naturally restless, as well as being naturally

37

warlike. The incident at Rometta had at least been an interesting diversion from the monotony they now endured.

The Almogavar captains listened intently to Sancho Rey as he recounted in detail the events in the town, which had culminated in the rescue of his son and the capture of a young Sicilian nobleman.

'What are you going to do with him?' asked Marc, who unlike Sancho had a thick mop of hair.

'Kill him and have done with it,' suggested Hector, who wore a permanent frown when not engaged in battle and killing, activities that put a smile on his face.

'Exchange him for some slaves,' suggested Angel.

'Female slaves, presumably?' said Marc.

Angel flashed a smile. 'Naturally, all in their prime and who preferably know only two words of Catalan – "yes" and "more".'

'Don't you have enough whores, Angel?' asked Sancho.

'One can never have enough whores,' the handsome captain shot back.

'Ransom him,' suggested Marc, 'that is the usual custom of nobles and their like.'

The Almogavars revelled in the fact they were all, or mostly, low-born men who had no lands, titles or indeed income, save what they were paid and what they looted. Everything about them repulsed the nobility, from their threadbare clothing to their coarse manners and, the greatest crime in the eyes of those who inhabited the higher echelons of society, their democracy. The Almogavars took decisions by vote and popular choice. The men sitting in the tent outside Messina deciding the fate of Fabrizio Carafa were members of the Almogavar council, which had been elected by their fellow mercenaries to speak on their behalf. Normally, such a notion would be ruthlessly and bloodily quashed by kings and their nobles, but the Almogavars were first and foremost fighters, and after twenty years plying their trade, they were treated with a cautious respect.

'What about the shepherd?' asked Marc.

Sancho considered the matter for a few seconds.

'He will be handed back to the Sicilians. It is his fault my son was placed in danger.'

'And the young lord?' pressed Marc.

Sancho nodded. 'He will be ransomed, if no one has any objections.'

Hector shrugged, Angel beamed with delight, already thinking about fresh slaves to amuse his sexual appetite, while Marc nodded thoughtfully.

'I will send a rider to the Fabrizio estate.'

'How much will the ransom be?' enquired Angel, conscious that the price of female slaves had risen alarmingly in recent months.

The question took Sancho by surprise. 'Good point. Two hundred florins should be ample.'

The florin was a gold coin minted in the city of Florence and accepted as currency throughout Christendom. Two hundred was enough to purchase a decent-sized mansion.

'What do we need with money?' asked Hector. 'We always take what we want.'

'The war is over, my friend,' said Sancho. 'At the moment, Messina is paying for our food and other supplies. But with winter approaching, the city's generosity will fade, of that I am sure. We therefore need to think ahead. Having money buys us time.'

Marc grinned. 'That is why we made you the head of the council, Sancho.'

Their meeting was interrupted when one of the tent flaps opened and a man they all knew well sauntered in. Tall, handsome and attired in a hauberk beneath a black surcoat emblazoned with a white vulture, Roger de Flor, military adventurer, King Frederick's vice-admiral and supreme commander of the mercenary army, was flamboyant, ostentatious and affable. He was essentially a pirate made good, but his wit, charm and intelligence kept him one step away from calamity. It was so now.

He sat down at the wooden table the council were sitting at, poured himself some wine and toasted the other four men.

'Gentlemen, Count Carafa wants his son back, and is marching at the head of an army to retrieve him.'

Concern showed in the admiral's blue eyes. 'I trust he still lives?'

'He lives,' replied Sancho, 'though only by God's grace.'

Roger toasted his old friend. 'Then all's well that ends well.'

'We were going to ransom the little bastard,' said Hector.

Roger grimaced at his coarseness. 'It is probably best all round if we give him back, without ransoming him.'

Marc tipped his head at Sancho. 'He nearly killed Sancho's son. He should answer for that.'

Hector and Angel both nodded in agreement. But Roger was used to extricating himself from tight spots. He finished his wine.

'I have come with news that will make you forget all about petty squabbles, my friends. God smiles on us. The Emperor of Constantinople has need of our services and will pay handsomely for them. We are going to the promised land, my friends.'

The council was underwhelmed by the pronouncement, not least because they had never heard of the Emperor of

Constantinople. But Roger was nothing if not determined, and his next words pricked their interest.

'The emperor has promised to pay us in advance for our services, and has also promised that what we take while fighting for him, we keep.'

'Who will we be fighting?' enquired a now interested Hector.

'Muslims,' said Roger.

He looked at their blank faces. 'Muslims, my friends. The enemies of Christ. They have overrun most of Anatolia, the land east of the city of Constantinople, and will keep on conquering unless someone stops them.'

'This emperor has no army to do his fighting?' asked Sancho.

'It has been beaten many times,' Roger told him. 'It is a broken reed. Anatolia is ripe for the taking, and much plunder will be ours when we defeat the Muslims.'

Angel rubbed his hands together. 'Sounds good to me.'

Roger studied each one of the council.

'So, we can give Count Carafa his son back?'

The others looked at Sancho, who shrugged.

'Very well. We give him the shepherd as well.'

Roger was intrigued. 'The shepherd?'

'A friend of my son, whose foolishness nearly got Jordi killed.'

'What foolishness?' enquired Roger.

'He kept a black sheep, which prompted the ire of Fabrizio Carafa. A quarrel ensued, which led us to the current situation.'

'Black sheep are regarded as unlucky,' agreed Roger.

'Unlucky for the shepherd, certainly,' said Marc. 'He thought he had escaped the noose.'

'Count Carafa will want to make an example of him, to keep face and uphold the family name,' said Sancho.

'The count can fetch his son, and the shepherd,' said Hector, 'but tell him to keep his army away. If he thinks he can intimidate us, he is mistaken.'

But Count Carafa had no intention of arriving at the sizeable camp of the Catalans like some impoverished hawker selling his wares. A man who was high in King Frederick's favour, who owned great estates and held lordship over dozens of villages, and whose son had been taken by low-born Catalans, was intent on presenting an intimidating spectacle to both affirm his determination to get his son back, and also behave in a manner befitting his superior social position.

The Catalan camp outside Messina was a messy sprawl: cows, chickens, pigs and sheep being kept in pens among the tents, to provide milk, wool and meat. Barefoot children ran between tents, which were far from the magnificent pavilions used by great lords, with their two or more central poles, ridge poles, roofs, sidewalls and interiors divided by curtains. These travelling displays of wealth and power were decorated with pennants, merlons and ornamental valances. There were a few smaller pavilions where the Catalan knights were housed, though most of Sir Roger's horsemen were adventurers, poor sons of impoverished Catalan knights and mercenaries who had managed to acquire a horse during their campaigns in Sicily. The vast majority of tents were either the cone variety or simple linen structures with two sectional upright poles supporting a ridge pole, over which was a fabric covering.

The camp reverberated with the sounds of horns and whistles warning of the approach of the count's army, prompting Almogavars to arm themselves and rally to their captains and horsemen to run to their mounts. Luca roused himself from his pit of self-pity when Jordi appeared at the tent he had been given until his fate was determined.

'Luca, come quickly, Giovanni Carafa approaches with his army.'

Luca was surprised to see his friend wearing a strange helmet comprising vertical metal strips secured to a horizontal metal band, with a leather neck guard. He was also carrying a spear and three javelins slung on his shoulder. Jordi kicked his friend.

'Move, Luca.'

The camp was a bustle of activity, men rallying to their units, which numbered between five and fifteen men. Jordi led Luca to where his father was standing with the sultry Carla, his wife, the large-headed Roc, and ten other men, all sporting beards and armed in a similar fashion to Jordi.

'You took your time,' growled Sancho to his son, ignoring Luca.

Most of the women stayed behind in camp to guard their children, but Luca noticed several dozen females among the large body of soldiers assembling to the immediate west of the camp, ready to face the approaching Carafa army. Among the ranks of the Catalan army, which now numbered several thousand, were many banners comprising alternating horizontal red and yellow bands. The flag was called the *Senyera* and was the ancient standard of Catalonia.

From the northern part of the camp came the Catalan horsemen, all wearing iron helmets of one shape or another, and a variety of body armour from mail hauberks to boiled leather. Every rider carried a shield, a lance and a sword. Luca also saw

43

crossbowmen among the foot soldiers, and a small group of horsemen wearing black surcoats sporting white vultures and mail hauberks, their horses covered in black caparisons on which were stitched white vultures. They trotted over to where Sancho Rey stood in the centre of the Almogavar battle line.

Sancho's jaw was set rigid as he stared at the oncoming army, which was led by a host of horsemen. The man in the black surcoat smiled at the Almogavar's wife.

'It is good to see you, Carla, and looking so beautiful.'

She gave him a dazzlingly smile. 'You flatter me, lord.'

Roger continued to smile at her as he spoke to Sancho.

'Where is Sir Fabrizio?'

Sancho turned, clicked his fingers and one of his men marched the young noble forward. He had a face like thunder, which the words of Sir Roger did nothing to change.

'We will soon have you back with your family. Where is the shepherd?'

Sancho walked over to his son and grabbed Luca by the scruff of the neck, hauling him forward. Fabrizio curled a lip at the shepherd.

'Well,' said Roger, 'better let me do the talking. The sooner we get this over with, the sooner we can put this sorry episode behind us all.'

Roger turned his horse and began trotting towards the Carafa force now filling the ground to the west of Messina. The authorities had ordered the city gates to be closed, but the walls were lined with curious onlookers eager to see the unfolding drama from the safety of thick, well-maintained walls. Sancho looked left and right to see his fellow commanders and council members – Marc, Hector and Angel

– standing in front of the battle line. He saw Hector practising a stabbing motion with his spear and hoped the negotiations between Roger and Count Carafa woùld conclude quickly.

The count's army was now leisurely spreading into a line to match the extent of the Catalans. It was perhaps inferior in numbers to the thousands of Almogavars and hundreds of horsemen, but better armed and equipped. The élite were the knights who surrounded the count, all wearing gleaming one-piece iron helmets, long-sleeved mail hauberks over a quilted gambeson, and red surcoats, the upper part of which were lined with scales secured by gilded rivets. Their legs were protected by leather armour and each rider carried a shield emblazoned with red and white stripes. It was difficult to be precise, but Luca estimated their number to be between two and three hundred.

Outnumbering them were the count's foot soldiers. The best wore iron helmets and red, knee-length, long-sleeved tunics worn over short-sleeved mail hauberks. The rest, the majority, wore their peasant costumes – light woollen tunics beneath heavy smocks secured down both sides by loops and wooden toggles – being commoners temporarily impressed into the count's army. They all had spears, knives and small wooden shields. None had any head protection. There was also a square of crossbowmen superbly equipped in padded coifs beneath mail equivalents, and quilted outer garments worn over short-sleeved, short-hemmed mail shirts.

The drums had stopped beating and no trumpets sounded while Roger spoke with the count, the latter pointing at his son around a hundred yards away. Roger kept nodding and spinning in the saddle, looking at Fabrizio and then Luca. After a tense few

45

minutes, he turned his horse and walked it back to where Sancho, who was still holding Luca's tunic, was standing.

'It is agreed,' Roger said to the Almogavar commander. 'When you have finished, we will thrash out the details of how we are getting to Constantinople.'

Carla's ears pricked up. 'We are leaving Sicily?'

Roger smiled at her once more. 'No more living in a tent for you, Carla. We are travelling to a land of riches where your husband can win you a lifestyle you deserve.'

Sancho handed his spear to one of his men, grabbed a mortified Fabrizio by the scruff of his neck and bundled him and Luca forward.

'What are you doing, father?' asked Jordi.

'Silence!' commanded Sancho.

Luca, momentarily alarmed, was then relieved when he saw his parents appear from the horde of spearmen around the count's mounted knights. He grinned like an idiot, expecting a happy family reunion in the no-man's land between the two armies. Only to have his hopes cruelly dashed when the throats of his mother and father were slit by grinning, knife-wielding assassins.

Luca stared in disbelief as the bodies of his parents flopped down on the sun-bleached ground, lifeless corpses watering the earth with their blood. Luca knew nothing of the chivalric code that was supposed to regulate the behaviour of knights, even in battle. He would have perhaps been more familiar with the code of vendetta, which was rife throughout Italy and especially Sicily. But even the code of vendetta had its own strict rules. Vengeance, for example, had to be both proportionate and appropriate. Luca saw murder but Count Carafa viewed the two deaths as justifiable retribution for the insult done to his son and his family name. Then Luca saw nothing but white-hot fury.

He grabbed Sancho's spear and ran forward, one thought in his mind – kill Giovanni Carafa. He was unaware of the thousands of Sicilians and Catalans observing him, or the crossbowmen opposite who brought their weapons up to their shoulders, ready to unleash a blizzard of bolts to cut him down.

'Come on, then.'

Sancho heard Hector's call and cried out in anger. Then he heard a thousand war cries and knew the die was cast. The Almogavars surged forward, following the foolish shepherd into battle, taking great strides to get to grips with the enemy. Their charge was reckless, brave, contrary to the rules of war, and wholly irresistible.

The Sicilian crossbowmen got off one volley that cut down several dozen Almogavars. But then they, the spearmen and mounted knights were assailed by a storm of javelins as the Almogavars hurled their deadly darts at the enemy. The air was filled with thousands of light spears that fell among the Sicilians, causing chaos. Those that had them raised their shields to deflect or stop the javelins, concentrating on the first, second and third volley of javelins lancing through the air towards them. High-pitched screams rent the air as iron heads pierced mail, flesh and bone. And then the Almogavars were among them.

Luca hurled his spear at Giovanni Carafa and saw the shaft fly straight and true, past the count and into one of his men immediately behind. He raised his arms and roared in triumph, then stared in disbelief at the hundreds of men passing him by.

47

At first glance it looked chaotic and doomed to failure, for how could ill-armed shepherds and foresters triumph against the cream of Sicilian chivalry? But the Almogavar way of war had been honed over decades, and to brutal effect. Frontal charges were risky affairs, but if one was going to be mounted then it had to be conducted as quickly as possible. There was no bulky armour or clothing to get in the way or slow them down. No large shield to worry about, and no long sword in a scabbard to get entangled in the legs. Hit the enemy fast and hard. The spear was carried in the left hand, the shaft resting on the shoulder when rushing forward. The javelins, heads pointed up, were carried in a special quiver slung on the back, which allowed them to be plucked and thrown with the right hand. And when all three had been hurled, the spear shaft was gripped with both hands and driven into the nearest enemy belly. The small round shield favoured by the Almogavars was slung on the back, on the left-hand side, to be used with the short sword when the javelins and spears had been used up.

Assailed by volleys of javelins and then assaulted by screaming Almogavars gripping spears, the Sicilian battle line buckled and then disintegrated as the Catalans carved their way into it. They pulled their short swords from their scabbards and went to work, stabbing and slashing with gusto with spear and sword. But by then it was all over. Only those with nerves of steel and total faith in their comrades will stand and fight such a merciless and unrelenting foe, and the Sicilian foot soldiers, those still living, were for the most part garrison troops and impressed peasants. They were already running before the Almogavars went to work with their swords.

The knights were a different proposition, but they were few in comparison to the bearded horde sweeping around them, and they

48

and their horse were still vulnerable to expertly thrown javelins. Count Carafa led a phalanx of knights into the maelstrom to rescue his son, whom everyone had forgotten about, before heading back to his fortified home with his entourage. The Almogavars did not follow.

They may have given the impression of being a rabble, but their commanders had instilled in them the need to obey orders at all times, even in the thrilling moments when the enemy turned tail and ran. Pursuit was a temptation, but lightly armed soldiers spread out over the countryside would be vulnerable to mounted knights, and Count Carafa still had his horsemen with him. So, the Almogavars finished off the enemy wounded, rallied to their commanders, and waited for orders.

Luca stood in the centre of the carnage staring down at the bodies of his parents, the corpses having suffered the indignity of being trampled on in the Almogavar charge. Tears filled his eyes and they dripped on the corpse of his mother, a gentle woman who had lived a pious life. She had deserved better. He felt an arm around his shoulder and saw his friend beside him.

'I grieve for you, Luca,' said Jordi, unhurt though his face was beaded with sweat.

Jordi slapped him on the back. 'You did this my friend. You have avenged the murder of your parents a hundredfold.'

Luca did not care about vengeance, nor did he notice the dozens of Sicilian bodies lying on the ground, most with javelins sticking in them, others with hideous belly wounds resulting from Almogavar spear thrusts. A screen of Catalans had been established beyond where the brief battle had taken place to guard against them being surprised should the count and his men return; others were

49

going among the dead to retrieve their javelins, prising the steel heads from corpses.

Luca was still staring disconsolately at the bodies of his parents and Jordi stepped away to leave his friend alone with his grief. He changed his mind when he saw the figure of his father marching towards Luca, fury etched on his face, his anger-filled eyes focused on his friend, his sword gripped in his right hand. He knew his father well enough and was certain he was going to kill his friend, if only for stealing his spear. His father did not become de facto leader of the Almogavars by tolerating his authority being undermined.

Jordi grabbed Luca's right arm and hoisted it aloft.

'*L'ovella Negra,*' he shouted, prompting those around him to desist their activities and look in his direction.

They understood the words of Catalan, meaning the 'Black Sheep', and after a few seconds recognised the insane young man who had charged the mighty enemy army alone.

'*L'ovella Negra,*' shouted Jordi a second time, to be enthusiastically repeated seconds later by those within earshot.

Sancho stopped and looked around as more and more Almogavars took up the call and began chanting '*L'ovella Negra*', walking towards a surprised and embarrassed Luca, his arm still being held aloft by Jordi. Sancho squinted at his son with a look of resignation. He had no wish to see his authority undermined a second time, which would surely happen if he took any action against the Almogavars' new hero. The chants grew louder as more and more men joined in acclaiming Luca Baldi, the shepherd from Rometta who had just entered Almogavar folklore.

Chapter 3

Sancho Rey and Roger de Flor felt like small boys as the Archbishop of Messina, Raniero Lentini, chastised them. He alone of the nobles and prelates in the city had dared to leave Messina in the immediate aftermath of the bloodbath that had taken place outside its walls. Tall, imposing and from a long line of senior Papal prelates, his power rivalled the king he served. And that king wanted the Spaniards gone. King Frederick and his court were located in the city of Palermo to the west. But a courier had reached the archbishop from the king the day after the unfortunate battle, demanding he usher the mercenaries on their way.

'Do you know what you have done?' asked Lentini, towering over Sancho and Roger as they sat at the table. 'You have insulted a close friend of the king himself, and in doing so have insulted King Frederick.'

'It was unfortunate,' agreed Sancho.

'Unfortunate?' roared the archbishop. 'Not far from this tent, hundreds of bodies lie on the ground, men who were your allies during the war only recently ended.'

'Your excellency,' said Roger, 'I can only apologise for the behaviour of my men and assure you it will not happen again.'

The archbishop, dressed in a jewel-encrusted mitre and holding his crosier – a tall, hooked walking stick symbolising him being a shepherd of his people – slowly took his seat at the table, a young novice rushing forward to fill his goblet with the wine he had brought with him from his palace. He knew the Almogavar predilection for austerity and pious living, and had no wish to share their meagre living, however briefly. He sipped at the goblet and observed what had become the bane of his life. The flamboyant

51

Roger de Flor contrasted sharply with the severe Sancho Rey. How he would have liked to have had them both arrested and thrown into jail for their gross insubordination. Unfortunately, they had just worsted the best soldiers at King Frederick's disposal. He stroked the pallium around his shoulders – a circular band of lamb's wool with long streamers decorated with red and black crosses – and smiled at the two.

'My friends, God sent you to Sicily to aid the king to rid the island of the French. That task has now been accomplished, but soldiers without a war to fight are like fish out of water. The king, anxious to allow you to fulfil your military obligations, has authorised me to make available ships to take you to Constantinople.'

'Your excellency is most generous,' smiled Roger, availing himself of a goblet of the archbishop's wine, 'but I already have ships at my disposal.'

'But not enough to transport all your soldiers in one voyage,' replied Lentini. 'The king is generous.'

'The king wants us gone as quickly as possible,' said Sancho.

The archbishop pointed a finger wearing a gaudy gold ring holding a large amethyst at him.

'Can you blame him? Sicily is crying out for peace after twenty years of war.'

'A war we helped to win,' Sancho reminded the archbishop.

Lentini sipped more wine. 'For which you were well paid. But understand that Count Carafa is a proud man who has the ear of the king. You have insulted and shamed him.'

'He shamed himself,' spat Sancho, 'thinking he could appear before our camp and intimidate us, making unreasonable demands.'

Sancho was not angry with Count Carafa, far from it, but he could not be seen backing the Sicilian against one of his own council members. The shepherd friend of his son would have died after launching his one-man assault against the count, but the intervention of Hector had provoked a general assault. The shepherd was still alive. Worse, he had become a hero among the Almogavars, who had nicknamed him 'the Black Sheep'.

The archbishop examined his ring admiringly.

'If we wish to talk about unreasonableness, Sancho, then what about your killing a priest in Rometta?'

'Sancho was rescuing his son, your excellency,' interrupted Roger. 'It was a tragic incident born of a misunderstanding.'

The archbishop looked at him. 'The misunderstanding is still alive?'

'The shepherd?' said Roger. 'Yes, excellency.'

'Perhaps if he is handed over to Count Carafa,' suggested the archbishop, 'then honour can still be saved and all parties appeased.'

'That is not possible,' said Sancho firmly. 'For good or ill, my men have adopted him, like a man adopts a stray dog. And they are in no mood to appease Count Carafa, I can tell you that.'

Lentini shook his head. 'Then I have to tell you, my son, that your stay in Sicily is fast approaching its end. The count will not tolerate the shepherd remaining at liberty, and he will be lobbying the king personally for the sentence passed on him to be carried out.'

Roger looked at Sancho but the big man's jaw was set rigid, his eyes unblinking. He knew it would be useless to argue with him. He sighed.

'If you could convey our gratitude to the king and assure him we will be leaving Sicily as soon as the ships have been assembled at Messina.'

The archbishop stood, prompting Roger and Sancho to do likewise. Lentini made the sign of the cross at them.

'May God give you the strength to defeat the infidels and remain uncorrupted by the heretics.'

Sancho raised an eyebrow. 'Heretics?'

'The Orthodox religion of Constantinople, my son. They have strayed from the true path, which is why they were excommunicated by His Holiness.'

'What would you prefer, excellency,' asked Roger, 'Orthodox Christians ruling Constantinople, or Muslims?'

Archbishop Lentini made the sign of the cross again, turned and walked from the tent to his waiting carriage without answering.

The pair followed, to run into the strutting figure of Hector, still buoyed by the spilling of blood when Giovanni Carafa had unwittingly appeared at the Catalan camp at the head of an army. Sancho waited until the archbishop was in his carriage before turning to confront the Almogavar captain. They were roughly equal in height but Hector was lean in stature, whereas Sancho was broad-shouldered and powerful. But Hector was like a viper: dangerous and quick and not to be underestimated. He tipped his head to Roger and watched the carriage and its escort leave camp.

'Who's that?'

Sancho jabbed a finger in his chest. 'That was Raniero Lentini, Archbishop of Messina and friend of King Frederick. He came with a message for you, Hector.'

Hector's black eyes lit up. 'For me? What message?'

'You are to leave Sicily immediately and never come back.'

Hector's visage changed instantly. 'Just as well he is scarpering back to Messina. Men have died for saying less.'

'If only the order was just for you, Hector,' lamented Sancho. 'Unfortunately, we are all leaving with you. You just couldn't help yourself, could you.'

Hector's hateful expression changed to one of smugness.

'That is our way, is it not? Attack first and ask questions later. Besides, I did not start the battle.'

Sancho rolled his eyes. 'The shepherd, you mean? Had you restrained yourself, he would have been quickly killed and the whole sorry business would have ended there and then. As it is, you have thrown tinder on the fire.'

Hector looked at Roger. 'We were leaving anyway, were we not?'

'True,' agreed Roger, 'but now we have to leave straight away, and I had hoped to arrange transport for all our horses. As it is, they will now all have to be sold.'

Sancho gave a semblance of a smile. 'That will displease the Bastard.'

Hector laughed. 'The day gets better and better.'

'Where is the new hero?' asked Roger.

'Digging graves,' answered Sancho. 'It is a pity one of them is not his own.'

'Are you upset he stole your spear, Sancho?' grinned Hector. 'I can understand that. After all, it might be Carla next. At least the lad can throw a spear.'

'He missed his target,' snapped Sancho.

'Training will rectify that.'

'He stays with us, then?' enquired Roger.

'Of course,' said Hector, answering for Sancho. 'The Black Sheep is an Almogavar now.'

The Almogavars, being the victors, usually left the dead following a battle. The corpses would be stripped of anything valuable before being left to rot in the sun, though the inhabitants of nearby towns and villages would often descend on the battlefield to loot the dead of anything useful, such as clothing and footwear. Under pressure from the church, local lords and town authorities would then organise the burial of the corpses, to save pestilence sweeping the area. However, because the brief but bloody battle had taken place near to their camp, the Catalans undertook burial duties themselves.

Luca had been hacking at the hard earth for days, helping to create burial pits in which the dead would be interred. In the immediate aftermath of the battle he had been hailed a hero, the adulation and wine blocking out the pain of losing his parents in such an abhorrent fashion. But then the Almogavar council had ordered that the dead be buried, and so he and dozens of others had been given the grisly task of hauling hundreds of naked bodies several miles from camp to the site of the burial pits. Bodies moreover that were covered in wounds, mostly as a result of spear thrusts and javelin strikes, but also belly and face injuries as a result of being stabbed and slashed by Almogavar short swords.

The facial wounds were the worse: visages made hideous by sliced-open eye sockets, cheekbones smashed by the points of javelins or swords rammed into them with force, and jaws nearly severed in the frenzy of battle. Faces looking barely human were made worse by the flies congregating on torn flesh and blood congealing and turning black in the heat. To complete the ghastly scene, the dead were smeared with faeces as bowels relaxed and opened, to add to the horror and nausea Luca had been plunged into.

Jordi offered his ashen-faced friend his water bottle. 'Here, drink.'

Luca accepted but the tepid liquid tasted of blood. He forced himself to drink it. Their clothes drenched in sweat and their hands calloused from digging, they and the others had been driven hard to remove the bodies from near the camp and dispose of them quickly. Their own priests and others from Messina had been saying prayers as the dead were being interred in the pits, before they were covered with earth. The pits had been dug deep to ensure the bodies would not be disinterred by wolves and other scavengers, including humans.

'Watch your heads.'

The voice from above made them look up and seconds later the handcart tipped its dreadful cargo into the pit – two corpses as stiff as boards and covered with flies. Luca and Jordi jumped out of the way as the corpses fell at their feet.

'It's deep enough now. Out you come.'

The Almogavar sergeant, an *Almogaten*, beckoned them from the pit, shouting at the other four with them to ascend the ladder so the grave could be filled with dead. Tired, dirty, their mouths filled with the nauseating stench of dead flesh, they gladly obeyed the order. A steady stream of handcarts was coming from the road to dump their cargoes into the pit, twenty paces away more Almogavars were furiously hacking at the ground with mattocks to loosen the soil so it could then be dug with spades.

Luca saw the pale priest making the sign of the cross at the edge of the pit, trying hard not to retch when fresh corpses were dumped into the grave. He was glad his own parents had been taken back to Rometta to be buried in the town cemetery, a gesture of kindness from the Almogavars who had taken him to their hearts. As he watched the grisly spectacle, he wondered if he would ever see his home again, Jordi having informed him he and the rest of the Catalans were leaving Sicily for Constantinople, wherever that was. And he would be going with them. He could stay, of course, but to do so would mean certain death when the hired assassins of Count Giovanni Carafa came looking for him.

The mood and lifestyle of the Almogavars suited his black mood. They may have been soldiers with a fearsome reputation, but like him they lived austere lives. His initial observations of the Catalans had revealed a people who rarely ate meat, preferring a diet of fish, eggplant, cheese and bread. Indeed, there were over seventy varieties of bread on the island, and it was not unusual for merchants to swear oaths on bread and salt, so integral was it to Sicilian life. To a man, the Almogavars were lean like him, and in the days following he found out why.

Luca was used to an outdoor life, with its attendant hardships, but he had never travelled great distances carrying a weapon, though weapons was the reality. He stood next to Jordi under a warm sun, though not excessively so since autumn was now coming to an end. His favourite seasons were spring and autumn, when the weather was still pleasant but temperatures never reached the furnace of summer. On his head was a helmet identical to the others worn by the hundred men standing in a semi-circle around their commander: Sancho Rey. Like them, he too now wore a *zamarra* and *abarka* on his feet. The clothing did not concern him. What bothered him was the spear he had been given, the three javelins slotted into the quiver slung on his back, the shield on the other side of his back, and the short sword in a scabbard dangling from his belt. He might be able to throw a spear and a javelin, but he had no notion when it came to using a sword, especially one that looked very different from the long-bladed items carried by the knights and foot soldiers he had seen during the war. A water bottle also dangled from his belt.

Sancho pointed at him. 'For the benefit of our newest recruit.'

He stopped when the others began banging the ends of their spears shafts on the ground in a display of admiration. When they had finished, he continued.

'The Almogavar way of war, which has proved so successful in decades of conflict, from fighting the Moors in Spain to defeating the French and their allies in Sicily, depends on individuals who are courageous, determined, self-disciplined, reliable and physically fit.'

The men raised their spears and cheered and Jordi slapped Luca on the back. For his part, the shepherd temporarily forgot about his grief and embraced the surge of positive emotion around him. Sancho held up a hand to still them.

'There is no point marching to a battlefield and arriving in a state of exhaustion. Our success is built around mental and physical stamina. We travel light and fast, over any terrain and in any weather. And when we reach our destination, we attack immediately, irrespective of the distance we have covered beforehand. That is the Almogavar way of war. It is unchanged since the first Aragon and Catalan shepherds and foresters descended from the hills of our homeland to battle the Moors, and will still be in existence when our bones lie under the earth.'

More cheering and rapping of spear shafts on the ground followed.

'Let's move,' commanded Sancho.

The first mile was easy enough, Jordi beside him and his father in front acting as a marker. Luca was lean and sinewy and his legs were used to hard usage. But he found the spear cumbersome to wield, notwithstanding it was resting on his left shoulder, and he was constantly aware of the shield and javelins on his back, the straps of the quiver rubbing on his shoulders as the march continued. Added to which, the scabbard and water bottle, attached to a leather strap slung over his shoulder, insignificant at the beginning of the march, seemed to gain weight with each passing mile.

They tramped along a dirt track with a surface made rock-hard after a long, hot summer, around them the greenery of the Sicilian countryside. It was quiet and no one made a sound, there was no encouragement from Sancho, only the relentless pounding of a hundred pairs of feet. Luca found the fast-paced walk a hindrance and wanted to break into a run.

'Do not run,' hissed Jordi, 'you will damage your shins, knees and lower back.'

After ten miles, the straps were biting into Luca's shoulders and his legs were on fire. Jordi tried to help by imparting tips – take short, fast steps, straighten the knee with each step to briefly relax the leg muscles, bend the knees when going downhill to absorb the shock of each step – but it did not help. It felt as though his legs were in a giant vice, which was tightened after every mile. He began to falter.

'Dig in the heels with each step,' said Jordi.

The pace was relentless both uphill and downhill. Luca lost track of the distance they had covered when Sancho at last called a halt, the shepherd nearly collapsing with relief, to be held up by his friend.

'Stay on your feet, Luca.'

'Horsemen,' shouted Sancho, pointing to the right, at a line of riders heading towards the Almogavars. 'It is Count Carafa and his men.'

Luca had had enough. His feet were on fire and his legs ached, but he had just enough energy to flee, dumping his spear and running, or trotting, away from the horsemen.

'Luca, come back,' implored Jordi, to no avail.

He did stop when he heard laughter, turning the see the others pointing and whistling at him in a derogatory fashion. Beyond them, the riders, all wearing leather armour and carrying a Catalan banner, had slowed their horses to approach the Almogavars in a leisurely fashion. Despite sweat pouring down his face he felt himself blushing. Shamefaced, he trudged back to the grinning and mocking soldiers, though one of them was far from amused.

Sancho grabbed his *zamarra* and dragged him back to the column.

'You run, you die, boy.'

He manhandled him to once again stand beside his friend.

'Pick up your spear.'

Luca did so. There was no sound coming from the ranks now, just an ominous silence.

Sancho held out a hand.

'Water bottle.'

Luca pulled the flask from his shoulder and handed it to Sancho. The commander grinned savagely, pulled the cork from the flask and poured the contents on the ground before Luca's eyes; eyes which opened wide in alarm. When it was empty, Sancho tossed it back to him. Rage welled up in Luca, which was the boost he needed

61

for the march back to camp. His eyes bored into the broad back of Jordi's father as the Almogavar council leader led the way back to the tent city, which was only five miles from the spot where they had been 'ambushed' by the horsemen.

His anger against Sancho Rey had not subsided by the time they reached camp, but it was rivalled by the sense of humiliation he felt over his reaction to the appearance of the horsemen. Jordi shrugged it off.

'A few days ago, you were a shepherd,' he told him as the two enjoyed an evening meal of fried onions, bread and cheese. 'You cannot become a soldier overnight.'

The pleasing aroma of campfires and food being cooked hung in the air, along with the excited chatter of men and their wives discussing their leaving Sicily to win fresh laurels in what was left of the Roman Empire. Luca would be going with them, and he was determined to become a soldier like Jordi, not the amusing pet, akin to an adopted stray dog, he felt like.

One advantage with being a pet dog was that some took an interest in him, unlike Jordi's father who made no attempt to hide his hostility towards Luca. Each day he was forced to undertake a gruelling march as part of Sancho Rey's formation. His life before he had joined the Almogavars had been a hard one, which meant his body soon became accustomed to marching, or fast walking as he was constantly reminded. What he found difficult to master was carrying and using the weapons he was forced to haul over the countryside around Messina.

For whatever reason, Hector, the lean, violent bearded thug who had been responsible for starting the battle against Count Carafa, took a keen interest in Luca's progress, which the shepherd never questioned but was glad of. If only because it provided a counterweight to the hostility of Sancho Rey. Every day, after his feet and legs had been tortured during Sancho's fast walk, Hector would provide insights and instruction on the weapons the Almogavars used. Around the camp were areas where targets – straw bales sitting on wooden frames topped with a piece of wood cut to resemble a human head – were located, and where units could be found practising throwing javelins. The crossbowmen had their own target areas, with banks of earth behind the targets to stop stray bolts.

Hector tossed Luca a javelin and picked up another. He held it in his right hand.

'First lesson. When you hold a javelin, hold it so it is balanced. If you hold it too far to the back, it will tip forward; too far to the front, it will tip backwards.

'And hold it strong, with your hand wrapped around the shaft, like you are throttling someone. Ever throttled someone, Luca?'

'No, lord.'

He pointed the tip of the javelin at the shepherd.

'I am not a lord, boy, though I've killed a fair few. None of us are lords. We hold rank because we have won it. You understand?'

Luca did not, really, but he nodded anyway. Hector turned back to the javelin.

'When you aim at a target, throw the javelin straight and true, and where you want it to land.'

He held up the javelin at the height of his ears, drawing it back before launching it at the target, around ten paces away. The steel point lodged fast in the straw. Luca was impressed.

'I showed you how to hold and throw the javelin but ignore everything else,' said Hector.

'But you hit the target, lord,' gushed Luca.

Hector ignored the praise.

'Now you.'

Luca stood square-on to the target, drew back the javelin and hurled it forward, the missile dropping alarmingly and harmlessly to the ground, beneath the target. Luca's head dropped.

'Where were you aiming?' asked Hector.

'At the straw, lord.'

Hector pointed at the target. 'Don't call me lord. Lesson number two. Never aim at the body. In battle, unless you are fighting peasants, you will be facing soldiers who will be wearing some sort of armour. At the very least they will have a shield that will be tucked nice and cosy to their torso. But even if he is wearing a helmet, an opponent's face will always be exposed.'

He picked up another javelin, retreated a few steps, walked forward and hurled it at the target. The point struck the centre point of the face, splitting the wood.

'You hit a man in the face, he will go down. He might not die, at least not immediately, but he will no longer be able to take part in the battle. And if he's lying on the ground screaming, all the better, because he will be having an adverse effect on those around him. Lesson number three. Never throw a javelin from a stationary position.'

Over the following days, Hector tutored Luca in the intricacies of javelin throwing. With persuasion and coercion, he imparted the principles of hurling the steel-tipped missiles.

'You have to have speed coming into the throw for both range and impact power. Launching a javelin is a reaction. In essence, it is not really a throw but a reaction to what the rest of your body is doing. Retain discipline at all times to keep the throwing arm both long and relaxed behind you during the whole movement. The force of the throw is generated by the lower body, through the guts and into the upper body. And finally practice, endless practice, which allied with the correct technique will make you an accomplished javelin thrower.'

The days passed, autumn turned into winter and Luca continued his transition from shepherd to soldier. His feet and legs got used to the endless marching, his shoulders and back healed, thanks to the delightful Carla, the wife of Sancho. She had great knowledge of medicine and applied fresh comfrey poultices to his chaffed and bruised body until it had healed. And he had the constant companionship of Jordi to keep up his spirits. When he had been a shepherd, Luca had asked his friend why the Almogavars and the Catalan horsemen, having helped to win the war against the French, did not travel back to Catalonia, a land Jordi had never seen. Indeed, a land the majority of the Spanish soldiers had not seen, those the same age or younger than Jordi having been born in Sicily. His friend did not know the answer, but Hector certainly did.

They sat on stools restoring the keen edges of the javelins with which they had been practising using whetstones of hard schist.

'King James don't want us back,' Hector told him. 'If we sailed back to Catalonia, he would have a few thousand soldiers with nothing to do on his hands. Better for him we are kept as far away as possible.'

'That seems ungrateful,' said Luca.

Hector gave an evil chuckle. 'Kings and lords are like that, boy. Always remember that. Priests as well, come to that. They all like

65

others to do their dirty work, but when that work is over, they want rid.'

'What about the Emperor of Constantinople?' asked Luca.

'He will welcome us with open arms, and as soon as we have killed his enemies, will clear us out of his lands quicker than evicting a leper colony.'

Two days later, Sir Roger informed the mercenaries all the ships to transport them to Constantinople had been assembled in the harbour at Messina.

Chapter 4

Luca had never been to Messina, had never seen its grand cathedral or the large harbour where the ships waited to take the mercenary army of Roger de Flor to Constantinople. Some of the eighteen galleys and eighteen other vessels were owned by Roger himself, having been used by him to both line his own purse and supply the city during the recent war. It was the first and last time the Almogavars and Catalan horsemen were allowed into Messina, to be greeted at the gates by the fawning Archbishop Lentini. The prelate spread his arms and smiled at Roger, who was flanked by Sancho and the other Almogavar council members, who did not smile. Behind them was a long column of soldiers, women, children and carts carrying the weapons, tents and supplies of the Catalan Company, the name Roger had chosen for what was his private army.

It was an impressive army – four thousand Almogavars, fifteen hundred horsemen – with an attendant two thousand seven hundred dependents. Sadly, the horsemen had been forced to surrender their mounts, there being no room on the ships to transport them. Roger had assured their captains fresh horses would be purchased once they reached Constantinople, but it left a bitter taste in the mouth to leave the beasts behind, especially as the individual who had purchased them on behalf of King Frederick had been none other than Count Carafa. Such are the exigencies of war.

Messina was beautiful that day, the city bathed in radiant winter sunlight, its streets clean and its skyline punctuated by many steeples. It was also empty. Streets were deserted, markets were closed and all windows were shuttered as the company made its way from the city gates to the harbour. But from behind those shutters a thousand pairs of eyes observed the fearsome Catalans making their last journey in Sicily. They followed in the footsteps of the crusaders who had embarked at Messina for the Holy Land, to reclaim Jerusalem from the Saracens. That had been two hundred years before and now no Christian soldiers departed for a land and a city that had long been lost to the infidels. Now the Catalans were going to prevent the Muslims from seizing Constantinople and sweeping west into Europe.

The Almogavars, clutching their spears, glanced left and right as they tramped along eerily quiet streets, only the soft thuds of their feet on the cobbles disturbing the silence.

'It's too quiet,' said a worried Jordi. 'I smell an ambush.'

His father turned to berate him.

'Keep your mouth shut. You know nothing, boy.'

Angel beside Sancho turned and flashed Jordi a grin.

'The boy might have a point, Sancho,' said the Catalan-cum-master of harems, pointing at the archbishop at the head of a coterie of priests a few paces ahead. 'He might be the equivalent of the Pied Piper.'

Sancho gave him a sideways sneer.

'Who?'

Angel rolled his hazel eyes.

'I sometimes think I am among barbarians. I heard the story a couple of years ago, though the event took place a quarter of a century ago.'

'Get to the point,' snapped Hector.

'I will,' smiled Angel, 'if you will allow me the courtesy of continuing uninterrupted. Heard of Hamelin, Hector?'

'No.'

A snigger. 'It's a town in Germany somewhere. Anyway, the town was infested with rats. I mean, really infested. They were scurrying around the streets in broad daylight, occupying homes and businesses and eating their way through the town's granaries. Well, one day this piper appeared dressed in a coat of many colours and offered to get rid of the rats.'

'Did not the town have rat-catchers?' asked Sancho.

'Please don't interrupt,' Angel scolded him. 'So, the piper agreed to get rid of all Hamelin's rats in exchange for a tidy sum of money.'

'How much?' asked Marc.

Angel frowned. 'I have no idea.'

'Then how do you know it was a tidy sum?'

'He has a point,' agreed Hector.

Angel sighed. 'For the sake of argument, just accept that the piper was promised a substantial amount for his services. So, the piper played his pipe and the rats followed him out of the town, never to be seen again.'

Hector was disappointed. 'Is that it?'

'Not quite,' said Angel. 'The good people of Hamelin reneged on their promise and refused to pay the piper when he returned. Vowing revenge, the piper returned a few days later and began playing his pipe once more, whereupon all the town's children followed him out of town, and like the rats were never seen again.'

He tipped his head to the archbishop, chatting away to Roger de Flor beside him.

'Just like we are being led away from Sicily.'

'The emperor of Constantinople should have hired this Pied Piper instead of us,' opined Marc.

69

'Why?' asked Sancho.

'One man with a pipe is cheaper than five and a half thousand soldiers, that's why.'

He gave Angel a sly glance. 'Perhaps you could hire him to lure away wives from their husbands.'

The others laughed, prompting Roger and the archbishop to turn and stare at them quizzically.

Luca was not smiling. He liked the Almogavars and was cheered by their ebullience and devil-may-care attitude. But his stomach was churning at the thought of leaving Sicily. Until a few weeks ago, Rometta and the surrounding countryside had literally been his world. But he had been wrenched from that life and plunged into an alien world of mercenaries, fighting and travel beyond seas. Like most peasants, he could expect a hard and short life in a small community of other peasants. His fate was to be buried a hundred yards from where he had been born. But now everything had changed. He even looked different in his Almogavar attire with weapons strapped to his back, dangling from his belt and carried in his hand. His sense of dread increased when they reached the harbour.

Messina had originally been named Zankle, or 'sickle', in ancient times on account of the shape of its harbour. Luca was preoccupied with his own fears but had he inspected the harbour more closely, he would have discovered the neck of land that gave the harbour its distinctive shape was strongly fortified, with a citadel erected on the spot where the neck joined the mainland. In addition, there were four smaller forts along the neck to defend the entrance to the harbour.

Roger left the bishop and returned to Sancho and his fellow commanders.

'Get everyone loaded. I want to be away as soon as possible.'

'What's this?' Hector was pointing at a line of carts pulling up on the quay beside the ships that would take the company to Constantinople.

Roger turned. 'A gift from the archbishop. A ration of biscuit, cheese, salted pork, garlic and onions for every man, woman and child travelling with us. To fortify our bodies for the fight against the Muslims.'

Sancho chuckled. 'He can't wait to get rid of us. Right, let's get everyone loaded.'

The Almogavars travelled lightly, so there were no chests filled with clothes or sumptuous pavilions to be loaded on the ships. Nevertheless, it took time to load just over eight thousand men, women and children, plus food, tents, weapons and equine equipment. The ships earmarked to take the people and their belongings to Constantinople were divided equally between impressive-looking galleys and more modest, though sturdier, merchant vessels.

Luca and Jordi helped to load one of the galleys, a magnificent vessel called a *dromon*, meaning 'runner'. Around one hundred and sixty feet in length with a beam of sixteen feet, it sat low in the water, its two lateen sails furled until the ship left harbour. Luca forgot his worries as he formed a human chain to shift the supplies from quay to ship. The *dromon* had a hull that was closed by a deck, though the small hold could be accessed through ten hatches along its length. Luca glanced at the stern of the vessel where an awning on a wooden framework protected the captain's berth.

71

'Where will we sleep?' he asked his friend.

'On land,' came the answer from one of the crew within earshot, a rough-looking individual in hardy linen breeches and a shirt, both heavily mended and patched.

He pointed out to sea, to the Italian mainland across the Strait of Messina.

'Tonight, you and your companions will be sleeping in Italy.'

Luca was confused. 'Ships float at night, surely?'

The sailor leaned over the gunwale and cleared one of his nostrils of phlegm.

'Yes, they do, but unless it is a clear night with a full moon, a captain cannot see where he is going, which means a ship can easily run aground or get smashed to pieces on rocks. So, no sailing in the dark.'

Luca was surprised, envisaging a non-stop voyage at sea with no sight of lands for days, perhaps weeks. The reality was very different, and for him very reassuring. The short uneventful journey from Messina to the Italian mainland was for him a gentle introduction to maritime travel. He actually enjoyed it. The sea was calm, the wind light and favourable, and it was reasonably comfortable for the two hundred Almogavars sitting on the deck observing the galley's crew row the vessel out of harbour and into open seas.

The *dromon* was propelled by two banks of oars along the sides of the hull, the distance between the gunnels and water short in order to generate maximum propulsion. But this made sailing in troubled seas dangerous, so galleys avoided rough water, hugged the shoreline and came ashore at night. Luca discovered that the oars were used for exiting and entering port and in conditions of dead calm. The rowers themselves, all free men and not the slaves of legend, stood while using their oars, stepping forward against a load-bearing beam on the floor in front of them.

The trepidation he felt over his first voyage at sea proved unfounded. The fleet of ships left Messina and sailed the two miles across the strait to land in Calabria, a region of southern Italy. Once there, the company disembarked for the night and slept on the sandy shore. In the morning, the ships put out to sea once more, though they hugged the shoreline as they sailed around the tip of Italy. For Luca, boredom replaced fear as the fleet inched its way along the Italian coast before reaching the port of Otranto, in the Principality of Taranto, or rather a strip of beach near the city. The ruler of the principality, Prince Philip, had recently been a captive of King Frederick of Sicily following his defeat in battle, a battle the Almogavars had helped to win on the king's behalf. In theory, the prince could have attacked the fleet in revenge, but he had neither the resources nor the desire to provoke the Catalans, and so instead sent them rations as a goodwill gesture, that and a letter to Sir Roger to urge speed in their departure.

Luca and the others ate well during the first part of their journey, the generosity of King Frederick and Prince Philip ensuring they feasted on salted pork, cheese and wine daily. Occasionally the weather would prevent that day's journey, so the Almogavars stayed onshore and practised their drills. Constant practise to maintain the skills that had been used to devastating effect in Spain and then in Sicily. Luca, his body now accustomed to carrying weapons and covering long distances on foot, found the training invigorating and absorbing, which meant he had little time to think of his dead parents.

The fleet loitered in the principality for a few days until the sea was calm and the winds favourable, before striking out for the coast of Epiros, a self-governing kingdom allied to Constantinople. The only incident of note during the five-hour dash across the sea was one of Angel's whores falling into the sea. The Almogavar captain was distraught but was reunited with the missing member of his harem when the fleet dropped anchor in a beautiful sheltered bay fringed by a semi-circle of luscious white sand. The courtesan had been picked up by another galley after a short time thrashing around in the turquoise Ionian Sea. Their reunion on the white sand was truly touching and was reckoned a good omen for the rest of the journey.

Roger had planned the journey to Constantinople thoroughly, mapping out with precision the spots where the fleet would anchor each night. Epiros was selected because its ruler, Regent Anna, niece of Co-Emperor Michael, was well disposed towards efforts to restore the Roman Empire in the east to its former glory. She had therefore wholeheartedly endorsed the voyage of the Catalan Company and ordered any locals who encountered the mercenaries to supply them with food and other supplies.

The day after they had arrived at the sheltered bay, scouts reported to Roger that horsemen were approaching the anchorage, and he gave orders for the Almogavar captains to accompany him to welcome what he believed would be a reception party sent by Regent Anna herself.

Sancho ordered his son to accompany him, and Hector commanded Luca to also join the party as part of his overall education in Almogavar diplomacy. The day was overcast with spits of rain in the air, a fresh breeze blowing off the sea. Everyone wore long-sleeved woollen tunics beneath their sheepskin coats and woollen caps now it was winter, though Luca felt no cold as he tramped across the dunes to welcome Regent Anna. Only Roger de Flor among them resembled a knight, though he looked awkward not being on a horse. The rest resembled poor shepherds, which is what they had originally been and why he felt at ease in their company, notwithstanding Sancho's frostiness towards him.

'Try to remember you are in the presence of royalty,' Roger reminded them.

'They shit like the rest of us,' said Marc crudely.

'You have just illustrated my point,' sighed Roger. 'Don't say anything, unless you are asked, of course.'

Hector stopped. 'Damn!'

The others likewise halted.

'What is it?' asked Angel.

'I forgot to bring my knee pads,' said Hector. 'I will need them, seeing as we are going to be grovelling to this woman.'

'We are guests in her land, and should behave accordingly,' Roger reminded them.

Angel turned to Luca.

'What do you think, Black Sheep, shall we abase ourselves at the feet of a woman we have never met, just because Roger says so?'

He felt all their eyes on him, waiting for his answer. He swallowed.

'I, I think we should be grateful for the lady's hospitality, lord.'

Hector slapped him on the back. 'We should send him to grovel at her ladyship's feet.'

Sancho pointed his spear ahead. 'Here she is.'

The land they stood on had once belonged to the Roman Emperor who sat in Constantinople, but a hundred years before Latin crusaders sent by Rome's Pope had sacked the city. In the aftermath of that calamity, the Roman Eastern Empire had fractured and the territory opposite the eastern shore of the 'boot of Italy' had been seized by a rebel Roman family from Constantinople, which established the so-called Despotate of Epiros. For the next hundred years the rulers of Epiros held absolute power in their lands, while paying lip service to the emperor in Constantinople who had no way of bringing the empire's former territory back under his control.

The small group stood and watched horsemen and foot soldiers fill the horizon, the land adjacent to the beach being largely flat until it ran into the hills in the distance. The wind made the plethora of blue banners billow, the uniforms of the foot soldiers and riders matching the colour of the standard of the rulers of Epiros. That banner was a rampant golden lion with red claws on a blue background. The rulers of Epiros had deliberately chosen the lion as their symbol because the beast stood for courage, loyalty, nobility and strength. And the army of Epiros was certainly strong, or at least that was the view of the man who had moulded it into the instrument marching towards Roger de Flor and his senior commanders.

Thomas Komnenos Doukas was not a handsome man, being rather short and stout with large eyes and a mouth shaped in such a way as to give its owner a permanent disapproving scowl. Surrounded by a large number of lancers kitted out in knee-length blue tunics, helmets, grey leggings, short-sleeved mail hauberks and almond-shaped shields, he trotted up to Roger and his officers, halting his impressive stallion a few paces from them. There was an awkward silence before a shrewish individual leapt from a smaller horse and

76

scurried over to stand in front of his lord. He stood to attention and addressed Roger and the Almogavars in a slightly high-pitched voice.

'You stand in the presence of Thomas Komnenos Doukas, by the grace of God Great Despot of Romania, Prince of Vlachia, Lord of Archangelos, Duke of Vagenetia, Count of Acheloos, and Naupaktos and Lord of the royal castle of Ioannina.'

Silence followed the announcement, neither Roger nor his commanders knowing what any of those titles meant. But Roger knew a prince was higher in rank than a count or duke. He bowed his head.

'Lord prince, we had expected your mother but are pleased to see you.'

'My mother has retired from official duties,' snapped the prince. 'I am responsible for the security of Epiros.'

He spoke in Italian out of courtesy to the Almogavars, the mercenaries he had heard so much about. But he was underwhelmed by the ragged bunch of individuals standing before him. Were these really the men who had defeated the cream of French chivalry in Sicily?

'We thank you for allowing us to beach on your land, lord,' said Roger.

Thomas Doukas examined his manicured fingernails.

'I did not, my mother did. I assume you have availed yourself of fresh water for your onward journey?'

'Yes, lord,' smiled Roger, 'this area is abundant in fresh water.'

'There is a fee,' the prince smiled back.

Sancho was unimpressed. 'What?'

Roger held up a hand to him.

'I do not understand, lord.'

77

The prince leaned forward. 'It is quite simple. I require payment for the supplies you are extracting from my land. Failure to do so will result in grave consequences for both you and your mercenaries.'

'Arrogant bastard,' hissed Hector, an insult heard by the ears of the prince, who smarted, his eyes bulging.

'Arrogant? How dare you! I demand immediate payment or I will unleash my army to teach you a lesson.'

That army was now forming up behind their prince, who had decided to seek a confrontation with the Catalans. He cared nothing about the water or indeed anything else they had taken from the land. He was thinking ahead. He knew the Muslims were pressing Emperor Andronicus hard, which was the reason he had hired the Spaniards. And if the so-called Catalan Company was successful against the Muslims, then the emperor would be free to turn his attention to reclaiming the territories lost by his predecessors, including Epiros. That he certainly did not desire. And if he destroyed the mercenaries, it would not only remove a future threat to his reign but would also test the army he had lavished much money on.

Sancho and the other Almogavars abruptly turned and began striding back to the beach, leaving Roger alone with the smirking Thomas Doukas. Roger's next words wiped the smirk off the prince's face.

'I would advise you to turn your army around and march it back to your palace, lord.'

He bowed his head, turned around and followed his captains, leaving Thomas Doukas fuming.

'Deploy the army for battle,' he shouted at his commanders.

The army of the Despotate of Epiros was certainly an impressive sight: thousands of foot soldiers in identical uniforms marching perfectly in step. For this was a force trained in the same way as Rome's imperial legions, though designated by Greek names. So, the army was called a *tagma*, which was divided into several *tourmai*. Each *tourmai* was in turn divided into three *droungoi*, which were sub-divided into 'banners' – *vandon* – each one commanded by a count. The old Roman century still existed, called a *kentarkhion* and commanded by a *kentêrion* – centurion – being the final sub-division of each *vandon*.

Sadly, neither Epiros nor Constantinople had the money or manpower to field large *tagmas*. Indeed, the army currently deploying into battle formation numbered barely five thousand men. The cream of Epiros' army were the horsemen, though the beasts themselves wore no caparisons or the expensive scale armour worn by the élite horsemen of Constantinople's guard. Three hundred horsemen attended the prince, deployed behind the foot soldiers to be the instrument that would strike the final blow once the mercenaries had been fatally weakened by the foot soldiers.

Those foot soldiers – three thousand men organised in three *droungoi* – all wore iron helmets and blue, heavily padded coats with sleeves slit at the elbow and turned back to the shoulder for freedom of movement, underneath which they wore long-sleeved red tunics. The coats were padded with raw cotton wadding, which could defeat glancing blows, though not direct strikes with a pointed weapon. Extra defence was supplied by teardrop-shaped shields made of soft, light wood edged in iron and faced with leather painted with white and blue squares.

79

Much expense had been lavished on their footwear, each man having been issued with a pair of thigh-length leather boots, which were folded down onto the shin for ease of marching. As the separate *droungoi* halted to dress their ranks, the men folded the tops of their boots back up over their knees to provide protection in the coming battle. They rammed their eight-foot-long spears into the sand as they did so.

Sancho ground his heel into the soft sand.

'We can't move fast over this ground.'

Hector nodded. 'We burrow, then?'

The others nodded. Luca was none the wiser but had no time to ponder Hector's words when Sancho pointed at him.

'You find the commander of our horsemen and tell him to get the women and children on board the ships.'

Marc laughed and pointed at the blue-uniformed mass around four hundred paces away.

'You think that can beat us?'

Sancho tapped his nose. 'I think if they see us trying to evacuate the beach, they will become over-confident.'

He turned on Luca. 'Move, boy.'

He sprinted through the dunes to reach the beach, around two hundred paces from where Roger and his commanders stood. Around him, fully armed Almogavars were forming into their units on the fringe of the beach, drums beating as they did so. The few crossbowmen were also assembling around their officers. He found the commander of the Catalan horsemen with a knot of his officers near one of the galleys, a standard bearer holding his banner behind him. Luca fell to his knees at the feet of the tall, imposing Spaniard attired in mail armour and helmet.

80

'My lord, Commander Sancho requests you begin evacuating the women and children, so as to encourage the enemy to be reckless.'

The knight nodded. 'Makes sense. Get up.'

Luca did so. The handsome noble examined him closely.

'You are the one they call the Black Sheep?'

'Yes, lord.'

'Well, you had better run back to your commander if you don't want to miss the battle. Tell Sancho we will clean up if his men get overrun.'

'Yes, lord.'

He ran back to where Sancho and Roger stood with the others, except when he retraced his steps he discovered they had disappeared. He was shoved roughly aside.

'Out of the way.'

A line of Almogavar crossbowmen passed him, perhaps around a hundred, all with loaded weapons in their hands. There were more crossbowmen to their left and right, forming a long line walking slowly towards the blue and white shields of the enemy.

'Luca.'

He heard Jordi's voice and looked right, to see a hand appear above the marram grass on the lip of a nearby dune.

'Over here.'

He scampered over to where Jordi, his father and around twenty other Almogavars were crouching in a sand dune. He slid down the bank to rest beside his friend.

'The commander of horsemen says he will take care of things if we are overrun, lord,' he said to Sancho.

The others guffawed. Sancho did not laugh but pointed at his spear.

'You touch that and I will kill you myself. Understand?'

Luca nodded, 'Yes, lord.'

He gripped his own spear and checked the three javelins strapped to his back were still in place. They were. He glanced at the sword in its scabbard at his hip. He had had only rudimentary training in its use, and he viewed it as something to be used only in an emergency. Jordi slapped his arm.

'When the enemy is close, we will spring a trap on them. Look.'

He was pointing behind them where hundreds of crouching Almogavars were moving forward before disappearing.

Into sand dunes.

Sancho and the other captains had a keen eye when it came to ground to fight on. Beyond the beach was a wide belt of sand dunes – shallow, semi-circular-shaped hollows that had developed as a result of wind and the relatively flat terrain. They were surrounded by clumps of marram grass – vegetation with dense, spiky tufts with matted roots that acted as stabilisers for the dunes.

Thud, thud, thud.

The crossbowmen were now shooting at the enemy and Luca could see no more Almogavars. The sandy terrain appeared empty.

Thud, thud, thud.

The crossbowmen had shot a second volley. Then there was silence, only the sound of the wind blowing off the sea breaking the tension. Luca became aware of his heart pounding in his chest. He gripped his spear with his left hand and pulled a javelin with his right.

Around him, everyone had a javelin in their throwing hand, ready to rise up and hurl them at the enemy.

Then he saw the Almogavar crossbowmen beating a hasty retreat, keeping low to avoid the arrows of the enemy archers, threading a way between the dunes at speed. He knew the foot soldiers of the enemy would be close behind, buoyed by the apparent flight of the crossbowmen, and enticed by the sight of women and children being frantically marshalled back on the ships in the bay. A beach seemingly within touching distance.

Sancho was peering over the top of the dune, whistle in his mouth. Luca thought his heart would burst from his chest.

He did not hear the enemy, their boots being muffled by the sand they were marching across, and he believed they must be some way off so quiet was it. Then the air was rent with a shrill whistle blast and Sancho clambered up the last few feet of the dune. He screamed a war cry in Catalan and hurled the javelin he had been clutching in his right hand. Hundreds of 'hurrahs' filled the air as the men in the other dunes emerged from their hiding places. Luca clawed his way up the inside of the dune with the others, stood and froze.

In front of him, a mere ten or less paces away, was what looked like hundreds of heavily armed soldiers, all looking at him! Or at least it seemed that way. He saw an impenetrable wall of blue and white teardrop-shaped shields, helmets and dozens of spears with lethal points levelled at him. Time seemed to slow as he beheld the fearsome spectacle, but that was because the soldiers of Epiros were being slowed by the soft ground underfoot. Luca hesitated for what seemed like an eternity but was in reality only a second or two before his training kicked in.

83

The weeks spent hurling javelins at targets and thrusting spears into tightly packed straw paid off. He had been pushed hard by Hector, day after day, week after week, and now his instincts kicked in. Without thinking, he focused on a face and threw his javelin at it. The shaft was in the air for a second before the steel point embedded itself in the neck of the target.

It was the second time he had hurt another human, the second time he had drawn the blood of an enemy. Perhaps he should have felt a solemn remorse for taking the life of another person, for that would surely be the result as the spearman collapsed with the javelin lodged in his throat, blood shooting from the wound.

All he felt was elation.

Elation that he had proved his worth to his peers, the men around him who were unleashing a hailstorm of javelins at the only target that presented itself – the faces of the enemy. Supreme joy that he had not faltered in the face of peril, that he had stood his ground and fought back. Elation and a strange relief as he finally threw off the shackles of his former peasant life. A life of grinding servitude. A short, humiliating life now washed away by the blood of the man he had just killed. And he was not alone in dying on the stretch of sand dunes in a nameless place near the shoreline of Epiros.

Luca had thrown one javelin but either side of him, extending left and right, veteran mercenaries hurled three javelins in under a minute. Not wild, inaccurate volleys but targeted throws, each missile finding a target. And those targets were faces and necks. Steel points shattered teeth, split eye sockets and severed windpipes in a frenzy of killing that destroyed the cohesion of the soldiers of Thomas Doukas, and dealt a death blow to his army.

The soldiers of Epiros had been trained well. As soon as the Almogavars had risen up from their sandy hollows they had instinctively locked shields and levelled their spears, before shuffling forward to take the sting out of the Catalan attack. But the assault was made by javelins thrown at their faces from close range, and within seconds the front-line centuries had been decimated. The first volley scythed down most of the front ranks, the second the remainder of the first rank and much of the second in each century. The third volley was followed by the Almogavars rushing forward to plunge their spears into the now demoralised, disorganised and depleted centuries.

Luca followed, the bliss he felt making his steps feel effortless as he closed on the faltering enemy unit in front of him. Either side of him screaming Almogavars were gripping the shafts of their spears with both hands, the points having been driven through the blue padded coats of the enemy, some having pierced shields first. Enemy soldiers went down. Others turned to beat a hasty retreat. And it was one of the latter Luca reached first, the soldier having abandoned his spear to unburden himself. But in turning he wasted valuable seconds, and in that short space of time Luca reached him and drove the point of his spear into the man's back.

He heard Hector's voice in his head, the result of endless hours of the older man emphasising the crucial elements when fighting with a spear.

'A spear is long, pointy and heavier than a sword. It travels in a straight line, which means a lot of power can be put into a thrust. A spear moves fast and they have tremendous penetrative power. But beware.'

85

He thrust the point into the man's back and yanked it back. The soldier momentarily froze before pitching forward face-first in the sand. The spear felt as light as a feather as iron determination flowed through his veins. He swung left and stabbed its point into the side of a soldier who had spotted him and was swinging left to plunge his own spear into his body. Too late. He heard Hector's voice once more.

'Don't penetrate an enemy deeper than you have to. Most people are only about ten inches thick, the fat bastards excepted. You only need to drive the point into them a maximum of six inches to kill them, or at the very least incapacitate them.

'Don't bury your spear into an enemy, no matter how great the temptation. It takes an age to extract it. And on the battlefield, you don't have time to loiter.'

The spearman went down, wounded, falling to his knees and then toppling over when another spear thrust from Jordi killed him. Luca, his jaw set rigid, moved on. But there was no one else to fight.

Unbeknown to the former shepherd, Thomas Doukas was already galloping away from the dunes. He had witnessed his *droungoi* moving forward in perfect step, only to see them ambushed by the Almogavars and put to flight. He could have tried to rally his now fleeing foot soldiers. He could have led his horsemen against the Catalans to put fresh heart into his *tagma*. But instead, he decided his life was worth more than three thousand lowly foot soldiers and quit the field.

Luca saw the backs of the fleeing blue-uniformed soldiers and made to follow them. Only to be grabbed roughly from behind.

'Where are you going?'

86

Angry he had been denied the chance to add fresh kills to his tally of one and a half, he spun round, ready to fight whoever had dared to manhandle him. To see Hector daring him to challenge him. And with him was Sancho, whistle hanging around his neck, either side of them Almogavars forming up into a long line. No one was rushing forward to pursue the enemy.

'There are still hundreds of horsemen out there, Luca,' said Hector firmly. 'They would like nothing more than to be let loose against a mob chasing their foot soldiers.'

Hector released him and grabbed his spear, examining the point, which was smeared with blood.

'Did it get stuck?'

He handed it back.

'No, lord,' said Luca.

'I didn't waste my time, then.'

Sancho pointed at the two unused javelins on Luca's back.

'I wouldn't say that.'

They stayed there for over an hour, waiting for the return of Thomas Doukas, lord of unknown places, and his army. But neither he nor it made an appearance, and as the winter sun began to drop rapidly in the western sky, Sancho gave orders to retrieve the javelins.

Luca's face was permanently screwed up with distaste as he went among the dead and extracted javelin points from bodies, or rather heads and necks. The Almogavars may have been taught to only use short thrusts when fighting with a spear, but they threw their javelins with force. This meant steel blades were embedded deep in skulls and brains, requiring Luca to place the sole of his left foot on a dead man's face and prise the javelin point from the gore. Simply pulling would not suffice, and so he copied Jordi and moved the

87

javelin shaft to and fro before extracting the point, accompanied by a ghastly squelch as he did so.

It was dark by the time he and hundreds of others had finished, huge bonfires on the beach providing illumination as he and they began the process of cleaning the javelin points of blood and gore. The onset of night brought cool temperatures, and Luca welcomed the evening meal of soupy stew of salted meat and legumes, sitting with his friend round a raging fire, one of many that had been lit along the length of the beach. He ate greedily from the wooden bowl, the day's exertions and exhilarations having sapped his strength.

'Would you like some more, Luca?' asked the delightful Carla, soup ladle in hand.

He proffered his bowl. 'Thank you, lady.'

She refilled his bowl from the cauldron hanging over the fire, the stew hot and thick. Carla refilled her son's bowl before sitting next to her husband, who was displaying an almost tender side in the company of his wife. The appearance of Roger de Flor put a scowl back on his face. The knight flopped down beside the Almogavar commander and stared into the flames.

'Today was most unfortunate.'

'That is one way of describing it,' said Sancho.

'Would you like some stew, Roger?' asked Carla.

'Thank you, no. I have no appetite.'

'What troubles you?' probed Sancho.

Roger sighed. 'I fear we will become pawns in the politics of the Roman Empire. It is surely no coincidence Thomas Doukas provoked a fight with us, knowing as he does we go to fight for the emperor in Constantinople.'

'We get to fight the Muslims,' said Sancho. 'Surely the ruler of Epiros would welcome that.'

Roger shook his head. 'This land used to be ruled by the emperor. We help him defeat the Muslims and evict them from his territory, he can then turn his attention to reclaiming other lost lands, including Epiros. I fear this is just a taster of the difficulties we may encounter.'

He looked up and caught sight of Luca feeding his face.

'You survived, Black Sheep.'

Luca wiped his mouth on the sleeve of his tunic. 'Yes, lord.'

'You like fighting?' Roger asked him.

'It is better than swinging from a rope, lord,' replied Luca without thinking.

'Watch your tongue,' snapped Sancho.

Roger looked at the imposing Catalan, his long face framed by the flames. He remembered their conversation in Sicily when he wanted to be rid of the shepherd who had started the battle between the Almogavars and Count Carafa. But the shepherd had shown courage and no army could have enough of that quality.

'We are all exiles, Black Sheep,' reflected Roger. 'It is just as well you like fighting, because it will be many years before you will be able to return to Sicily, if ever.'

'There is nothing for me in Sicily, lord,' Luca told him.

'Home can be overrated,' mused Roger. 'I was born in Brindisi but I have not been back in twenty-seven years. Like you, Black Sheep, there is nothing there for me now. My father died when I was an infant and my mother has also passed away. So, we are both orphans and exiles, and must forge our own destinies. The world does not care about us, so we must not concern ourselves with the world.'

The flames crackled and spat, the wind blew and Luca wondered what fate had in store for him. He had been plucked from the shadow of the gallows, had already fought in two battles and was on the way to Constantinople, which he had been told was the greatest city on earth. That night he dreamed of glory, riches and making a name for himself.

The next day the Catalan Company sailed for Constantinople.

Chapter 5

Treasurer Timothy stood half-naked at the window of his bedroom, looking out over the Golden Horn, the stretch of sea that separated the city of Constantinople from Galata, formerly a suburb of the city but now a Genoese colony, much to the disgust of the city. It also housed a small Jewish community, which further enraged the citizens of Constantinople. The treasurer took a swig of wine and belched, the sound waking the occupant of his over-sized bed, who stirred in the silk sheets. He opened his eyes and smiled at the corpulent Timothy.

The treasurer looked at the boy, no more than fourteen years of age, or at least that had been the number written on the document issued by the slave market official. Young boys were becoming increasingly difficult to get hold of, another consequence of the shrinking of the territory ruled by the emperor. Timothy drained his chalice and smiled back at the boy. One had to take one's pleasures when the opportunity presented itself. There was a knock at the door.

'What?' snapped Timothy.

'The patriarch is here to see you, master,' came the reply from behind the door.

Timothy suddenly felt deflated. After a night of debauchery, he was looking forward to a morning of debauchery. But the arrival of the patriarch put paid to his plans. And unfortunately for him, Patriarch Athanasius was not a man to be dismissed lightly.

'Show him into the reception room,' commanded Timothy. He pointed at the naked boy. 'Stay where you are. I will be back.'

Normally a slave would assist him in dressing, but as time was of the essence he clothed himself, putting on an orange silk *kabbadion* decorated with pearls and rubies and a pair of soft leather slippers.

His mansion resembled a small palace overlooking the Golden Horn: three storeys of brick and stone, with marble floors throughout and walls adorned with murals and mosaics. The large central courtyard and surrounding gardens were filled with fountains of varying sizes, and all the bedrooms, which were located on the third floor, had their own balconies with excellent views over the city and the Golden Horn. Timothy stroked his chin and smiled. One advantage of being a eunuch was not having to shave, or rather not having a slave do it. He descended the ornate staircase to the ground floor where the reception room was located, a spacious, well-appointed chamber with views over the Golden Horn.

He found the patriarch standing beside a wooden chair with velvet upholstery, a young monk behind him. He stifled a laugh. What would be the reply, he wondered, if he asked the head of the Orthodox Church if he liked young boys, too?

'Your eminence,' beamed Timothy, 'you bless this house with your presence. Will you not sit? Bring wine for his eminence.'

Patriarch Athanasius, notwithstanding the intricately embroidered tunic, called a *sakkos*, he wore, was an ascetic. Born in the city of Adrianople, he had been for many years a monk and hermit before being rewarded for his piety by the emperor. He was also fiercely opposed to any union of the Greek and Roman churches.

Athanasius handed his bishop's staff to the young monk and took his seat, Timothy doing likewise. The treasurer clicked his fingers to usher slaves carrying wine, fruit, figs and pancakes into the room. The prelate turned his nose up at the wine.

'It is a little early in the day for wine,' he sniffed.

Timothy raised his full chalice to the patriarch. 'Your health. How may I help you?'

'I wanted to speak to you about these mercenaries you have hired.'

'That the *emperor* has hired,' Timothy corrected him.

The patriarch's high forehead creased into a frown.

'They are on their way?'

'Indeed, your eminence, and you may be interested to know they destroyed the army of Epiros on their journey.'

Athanasius stroked his long white beard.

'They can fight, then?'

'Oh, yes, your eminence, they can fight.'

The patriarch brought his hands together.

'There are some who believe hiring Catholics to fight for the true religion is an abomination, which will prompt God to abandon us.'

Timothy sighed. How he wished he was upstairs enjoying the tender flesh of the young male slave rather than listening to the prattling of this over-promoted hermit.

'Your eminence, the empire is in a precarious position. Most of Anatolia has been overrun and large parts of the Balkans and Greece have also been lost. If we do not take drastic measures, the Muslims will be knocking at the gates of Constantinople itself.'

The patriarch was unimpressed. 'Emperors have always turned to mercenaries as an easy option, which has often proved disastrous. The recent despicable actions of the Alans being but one example, lord treasurer. Emperors have hired Alans, Armenians, Bulgarians, Cumans, Georgians and Hungarians. And the results? We have the infidels breathing down our necks. Why should these Catholics, these Catalans, be any different?'

Timothy emptied his chalice and held it out to be refilled.

'Desperate times call for desperate measures, your eminence. With the defeat of our army at Bapheus, there are no reserves left to halt the Muslims.'

The patriarch closed his eyes.

'That it should come to this. The fate of the Orthodox Church resting in the hands of Catholics.'

Timothy drank some more wine.

'Another way of looking at it, your eminence, is that we are shedding Catholic blood rather than our own.'

Athanasius rolled his tired eyes. 'A small consolation. I suppose these Catalans are charging an exorbitant fee.'

Timothy shrugged. 'They are, but it makes no difference. The royal treasury is empty.'

The prelate leaned forward. 'Then how are you going to pay them?'

Timothy smiled. 'A small amount up front, the rest when they have completed their task, by which time most of them will hopefully be dead.'

'That is a massive leap of faith, lord treasurer.'

'We all need faith in these desperate times, eminence.'

'Does the emperor know of the parlous state of his finances?' enquired the patriarch.

'He leaves the minutiae of royal finances to me, eminence,' smiled Timothy.

'And what if these Catalans are not all killed by the infidels?' asked Athanasius.

'Then the treasury will be asking the church for donations, eminence.'

The patriarch grabbed the solid gold cross hanging around his neck.

'The church has no money, treasurer. Your officials would be wasting their time scouring churches and monasteries for gold. They would be better employed seizing the assets of the Jews and Genoese.'

Timothy wanted to laugh in the prelate's face. He knew, as did everyone else, that the city's churches were filled with gold and silver, notwithstanding the looting of Constantinople by the Latin crusaders a hundred years before. But no one would dare suggest to the emperor that the church should contribute to the upkeep of his crumbling empire. Andronicus believed if one prayed hard enough, money would magically appear. The hard reality was that the crown had to borrow money, from whoever was prepared to lend it, which included Jews and Genoese.

The Genoese were relative newcomers to Constantinople, having been granted their own quarter in the city two hundred and fifty years before. They had settled in Galata, a settlement at the promontory on the north side of the Golden Horn, facing Constantinople. They were allowed to have a trading colony in Galata as a reward for their services to previous emperors.

'Have you been to Galata recently?' asked the patriarch.

'No, eminence.'

'Rosso of Finar is building a wall round the Genoese quarter.'

Rosso of Finar, the physically repugnant leader of what was increasingly becoming a self-governing colony, was the leader of the Genoese. A man prone to violent outbursts, he had a considerable number of soldiers under his command. And the Golden Horn was filled with Genoese trading ships, supplying Constantinople and making the Genoese rich. So rich, in fact, that Timothy had borrowed money from them to finance the passage of the Catalan Company from Sicily to Constantinople. But that was another matter altogether.

'Did you not hear me, lord treasurer?' fumed the patriarch.

According to the terms of the treaty they had signed with the emperor, the Genoese were forbidden from erecting walls around their quarter.

'I suspect it is in response to the ever-increasing Muslim threat,' said Timothy casually. 'Let us pray the Catalans can reverse their advances before their siege engines are battering down the walls of this city.'

'What of the Jews?' pressed Athanasius.

Timothy was growing tired of this austere churchman who regarded self-denial as a virtue. He sighed.

'What of them?'

'They are the enemies of Christ,' said the patriarch loudly.

Timothy shrugged. 'They pay their taxes and cause no trouble.'

He pointed at the churchman's richly decorated *sakkos*.

'Is that silk, your eminence?'

Athanasius' forehead creased into another frown.

'I fail to see what that has to do with anything.'

Timothy sipped at his wine. 'The thing is, much of the silk worn by the worthy of the city is supplied by Jewish merchants. Neither the emperor nor his court, nor I suspect your priests, would wish the supply of silk to dry up. You understand?'

96

The gaunt Athanasius slowly rose and held out his hand so the young tonsured monk could place his stick in it. The old man's brown eyes never left Timothy, whose tongue had been loosened by the wine be had been imbibing.

'It is my duty to care for the souls of this city and the empire, treasurer,' he said, 'including your own. Encouraging usury and mixing with heretics are dangerous practices.'

He turned and walked to the door, the monk opening it for him.

'If we do not halt the Muslims,' Timothy called after him, 'there will be no souls to save, eminence.'

Athanasius did not acknowledge his words. A slave closed the door behind him. Timothy slumped in his chair.

'Just as well I did not tell him I had spent the night abusing a slave boy.'

*****

Luca had enjoyed a calm voyage to Constantinople after the drama in Epiros, the Aegean and Sea of Marmara being remarkably free of ill winds, storms and squalls. The stopping points pre-arranged by Roger allowed the fleet to replenish its food and water supplies, and happily there were no more violent incidents. Roger ensured all supplies were paid for along the way, thus avoiding potential trouble, and Sancho kept his Almogavars under tight control. But for Luca, the further away from Sicily he travelled, the more his spirits sagged. The celebration of Christmas further dampened his morale, the festivities laid on by Roger, paid for out of his own pocket, only highlighting the fact he was alone in the world, with no family and only Jordi as a friend. Sancho's son went out of his way to make him feel a part of the Almogavars, which was relatively easy following his exploits outside Messina, and Hector had taken him under his wing. But the Catalans were hardened soldiers and their camaraderie was one of fighting cocks: brutal and unyielding.

'You need a wife,' said Jordi, standing beside his friend as they approached the shore south of Constantinople, the end of their journey finally in sight.

Luca was surprised. 'A wife? I have no money, no land and few prospects.'

His friend slapped him on the back.

'They say the emperor of Constantinople is rich beyond measure. If we defeat the Muslims, he will shower us with gold. Then you can buy some land and settle down.'

The approaching shoreline looked much the same as they had seen on previous halts – a green strip in the foreground with grey and green mountains further inland.

Jordi slapped him on the back again. 'At the very least, we will no longer have to eat salted meat stew.'

'That is something,' agreed Luca.

George Mouzalon himself greeted the Catalans when they first set foot on Roman soil, the general wearing a suit of glittering scale armour. His horsemen were carrying a host of red banners emblazoned with double-headed yellow eagles – the symbol of Emperor Andronicus. The banners fluttered in the breeze to create an impressive display, but Luca and the rest of the Almogavars barely noticed them, wrapping themselves in their cloaks and pulling their woollen hats down over their ears as a defence against the cold. The wind was bitter and there were flecks of snow in the air, which did nothing to brighten his mood. For some reason, he believed the eastern Mediterranean to be permanently bright and sunny. There was no snow on the ground, which was soft underfoot, indicating recent rainfall.

While the Almogavars and the squires and servants of the Catalan horsemen pitched their tents, George Mouzalon and Roger arranged for the entire company to be paraded in front of the emperor in a display intended to bolster the morale of Constantinople's citizens. After marching through the city, they would be entertained by the emperor himself in the grounds of his palace, prior to their departure. To where no one quite knew, but after the general had departed Roger and Sancho sat in the latter's tent being served hot stew by Jordi and Luca. Both had downcast faces.

'It is a good job the Bastard isn't here,' said Sancho grimly.

Roger frowned. 'You should not call him that. He is the commander of our horsemen and should be treated with respect.'

'The term is one of endearment,' smiled Sancho. 'His parentage will be the least of his problems when he arrives to find his men have no horses.'

Roger stared into the watery stew. 'The emperor's position must have deteriorated since I met with his representatives in Sicily.'

'Surely he has fifteen hundred horses to spare?' said Sancho.

'Not according to his general. They will have to be purchased and that will take time.'

'What do we do in the meanwhile?'

Roger ate a portion of the stew with a spoon, pleasantly surprised by the taste.

'Well, first of all,' said Roger, 'we enjoy the emperor's hospitality. He is laying on a feast at his palace for the whole company.'

He took a piece of bread from the bowl held by Luca.

'Ever met an emperor, Black Sheep?'

'No, lord,' said Luca.

Roger looked at Jordi. 'What about you, son of Sancho?'

'Me neither, lord.'

Sancho glared at the pair, indicating they should retreat into the background. They did so. Roger dipped the bread in his stew.

'The issue of the horses is but a temporary irritant, and besides as the commander of the horsemen has yet to honour us with his presence, a few weeks of preparation will not go amiss.'

Sancho was appalled by his nonchalant attitude.

'Have the Muslims stopped their advances? What if they are besieging Constantinople itself in a few weeks?'

Roger finished his stew and called Luca over. 'Refill this. It does not matter, Sancho, if the Muslims come to us or we go to them. The end result is the same. We will fight them to preserve the emperor and his empire and will be richly rewarded for doing so.'

The Catalan Company made a sorry sight when it gathered at the walls of Constantinople on the morning it was to march through the city to the Blachernae Palace, there to be feasted by Emperor Andronicus in the palace grounds. The horsemen had no horses and trudged along behind their banners, all of which hung limply in the windless, cool morning air. The emperor *had* sent a hundred horses to allow Roger and the captains and knights of the Catalan horsemen to ride into the city, which did nothing to sweeten the humour of those who had to follow on foot.

The Almogavars always moved on foot, of course, but they did so in small groups, and not as large bodies of troops marching in step like the Roman legions of antiquity. This gave them the appearance of a group of refugees who had fled their homes with nothing but the clothes on their backs, and with their wives and children in tow. But unlike refugees, they were heavily armed, spears in hand, javelins and shields on their backs and swords and daggers in scabbards and sheaths at their hips.

The Catalan Company entered Constantinople via the city's main ceremonial entrance – the Golden Gate in the extreme south of the wall that faced west. Luca stared in disbelief at the grandeur and strength of the city fortifications. He had never seen anything like them in his life, even the impressive fortifications of Messina paling into insignificance beside the splendour of Constantinople.

The Golden Gate itself was a combination of show and practicality, being a strongly fortified entrance with a triumphal arch sheathed in marble. But the defences themselves, called the Theodosian Wall after the emperor in whose reign they had been built, comprised three lines. The first was the original wall, which stood forty feet high and had ninety-six towers along its length. In front of it stood a second, lower wall with a hundred and ninety-two towers along its length. And in front of the second wall was a third, lower wall with no towers but with a moat in front of it. Most of the towers were not manned and the city garrison was stretched very thinly along the walls, but Luca did not see an absence of guards; he only saw size and power.

He and the other Almogavars were surprised and delighted when they entered the city where they discovered cheering crowds lining the paved street they walked on. Beautiful young girls tossed laurel leaves at their feet and priests stood beside the street chanting prayers, asking God for his forgiveness for bringing heretics into His city.

Luca fell in love with Constantinople that morning, intoxicated by its spacious, well-paved streets, many fountains and the grand mansions of the wealthy. Plus, the warm welcome extended to him and the rest of the Catalan Company, which appeared genuine and heartfelt. He did not know that the great days of Constantinople were long gone, that many of the splendid buildings of antiquity were either gone or had fallen into disrepair. The Great Palace, the city within a city where Roman emperors had lived, was partly ruined and mostly abandoned. The Forum of Constantine was now the city's main emporium, surrounded by the quarters of artisans. The Forum of Theodosius was now a pig market, with a hay market and slave market just a stone's throw away. Large areas within the city walls were pastoral, given over to grazing cattle. Outside the walls, the quarries that had supplied the city with marble and other luxury stones lay abandoned, builders instead relying on spoil taken from the ruins of old buildings to construct new abodes. But to Luca such things were irrelevant. He was in the greatest city on earth and a guest of its emperor.

That emperor sat on a golden throne surrounded by high priests, nobles and their wives dressed in silks and wearing much gold when the Catalans reached the Blachernae Palace, the impressive Varangian Guard manning its walls and standing guard near Andronicus himself. The emperor smiled and raised his hand when Roger, the mounted Catalan captains and the senior Almogavar commanders passed by, Luca and Jordi trailing close behind. They both gasped in astonishment at the golden armour being worn by

102

Andronicus, which was actually a scale armour cuirass made up of overlapping and highly polished brass plates. The crown he wore on his head *was* gold, as was the pectoral cross around the neck of a frowning Patriarch Athanasius standing next to the emperor.

Treasury Timothy leaned forward to whisper in the ear of the Co-Emperor Michael as the Almogavars filed past the royal party.

'Are we certain we have hired the right mercenaries, highness?' Michael waved at the Almogavars.

'They don't look much, but General Mouzalon assures me they are very good at what they do.'

'They look like a collection of bandits,' said Timothy derisively. 'I hope we do not live to regret bringing these Catholics to Constantinople, highness. They strike the fear of God into me, but I doubt they will have the same effect on the infidels.'

The Catalan Company was entertained in huge pavilions pitched in the sprawling grounds of the Blachernae Palace, the emperor not wanting his home to be invaded by an army of foreign mercenaries and their scruffy camp followers. But, in a scene deliberately reminiscent of the great feasts that took place on the Field of Mars in Rome hundreds of years before, the emperor's hospitality was most generous.

Luca did not know whether to eat the food on offer or wear it, so rich and spectacular was it. The army of cooks in the palace had produced a feast fit for a king, or at least a grand duke, which Roger would become as soon as he married the sixteen-year-old girl waiting in the palace. The leader of the Catalan Company took his leave and accompanied the emperor and his entourage into the palace where Patriarch Athanasius would conduct the ceremony.

Luca did not care about weddings or politics as he sat with Jordi at a long table with his father, the other Almogavar commanders and their wives, around them excited chatter and cheers as dozens of slaves ferried food and drink from the kitchens. And what food!

The first course comprised dishes that were green and gold, a mixture of saffron, egg yolk and green vegetables. Cutlery had been laid on the tables but the Almogavars used their fingers to stuff their faces, much to the amusement of the slaves. The second course of almond milk stews was white, while the third – beef in gravy – was red.

'This city is rich,' smiled Angel, feeding one of his whores a piece of beef with his fingers.

Hector picked up the silver table fork in front of him.

'We should take all these and use them to purchase horses. Far more useful than items decorating tables.'

'We will do no such thing,' said Sancho sternly. 'You must have noticed the disapproving looks on the faces of the high and mighty around the emperor. They already think we are a bunch of unwashed barbarians. We do not want to add thieves to the list.'

Luca's attention was fixed on a beautiful female slave refilling the silver goblets of those around him. She had flawless olive skin, alluring brown eyes and a shapely figure. He could not take his eyes off her. When she stood beside him to charge his goblet, he noticed she was wearing perfume, which only increased her attraction. He closed his eyes and inhaled the sweet aroma of the scent she was wearing. He felt something strike his face.

'The Black Sheep is in love.'

He opened his eyes to see Angel smiling at him and about to throw another piece of bread at him. Luca blushed with embarrassment and stared down at his bowl of meat, aware the others were looking in his direction. Jordi poked him in the ribs.

'He has no time for such things,' growled Sancho, 'not with a war to fight.'

Angel placed an arm around the shoulders of the two whores flanking him.

'There is always time for such things, my friend.'

'Leave the poor boy alone,' said Carla forcefully. 'Try to remember when you were young and infatuated. Ignore them, Luca, they are just resentful they have lost their youth and beauty.'

Hector laughed. 'I doubt Sancho was ever beautiful.'

'Unlike me,' smiled Angel, prompting the whores to kiss him on the cheek.

An Almogavar appeared behind Marc, who turned.

'Yes?'

'Trouble outside, sir.'

The atmosphere changed in an instant. Where before it had been jovial, now it became tense, threatening. Sancho jumped up, picked up the javelins at his feet and yanked free the spear that had been thrust into the earth behind him. It was as if a silent command had been issued and heard by the Almogavars. Like a flock of birds changing shape and direction in mid-air, tables were soon emptying of soldiers, all equipping themselves with spears and javelins and following their commanders from the pavilion.

Once the emperor of Constantinople had a fleet of ships that numbered hundreds of vessels. They transported grain from the colony of Egypt to feed the city and carried soldiers to the far corners

105

of the empire to enforce the emperor's will. That was now a distant memory and most of the ships moored in the Golden Horn were Genoese, the Italian republic having established trading colonies throughout the Mediterranean and made much money from the lucrative slave trade. It was slaves who rowed Genoese galleys, and it was Genoese officials who became princes in the trading colonies, amassing great wealth and surrounding themselves with armed retainers to defend their interests and those of the republic, in that order.

One of those self-made princes now stood in front of a horde of armed men in the grounds of the Blachernae Palace. Such was the power and influence of the Genoese that the guards had meekly stood aside when the armed mob had demanded entry.

Rosso of Finar was an unattractive man. He was a big-boned individual with long, greasy hair, a bulbous nose and a disfigured mouth twisted into a permanent leer. A former galley captain who had shared in a great victory over the Venetian navy at the Battle of Meloria nearly twenty years before, he had cemented Genoese power in the eastern Mediterranean and had amassed a great personal fortune in the process. He had lent money to Treasurer Timothy to ship the Catalan Company to Constantinople.

Rosso was dressed in a fine hauberk and a red surcoat emblazoned with a white cross – the coat of arms of Genoa – but the majority of his followers were dressed in padded jerkins or simple tunics. All had weapons of some sort, ranging from axes and clubs to swords, together with shields bearing the colours of Genoa. Some were drunk. All were up for a fight.

Rosso and Sancho were toe to toe, staring at each other with unblinking eyes. Luca detected the aroma of alcohol in the air.

106

Clearly, many men on both sides had drunk to excess. Though not the two commanders.

'So, you are the saviours of the emperor,' said Rosso dismissively, speaking in his native tongue.

'It is considered bad manners to turn up to a feast uninvited,' replied Sancho.

'I will get straight to the point,' said Rosso, 'I want my money.'

'What money?'

Rosso sighed. 'The money I loaned to the imperial treasury so the emperor could bring you here. Who do you think paid for the ships and their crews that brought your sorry looking arses to this great city?'

'I know nothing about such things,' said Sancho, bored by this loud-mouthed oaf standing before him.

'But you and your mercenaries have been paid four months in advance, have you not?' smiled Rosso.

'Our business is no concern of yours, pirate. Be gone from this place.'

'You think you can intimidate me, you…'

Sancho plunged the knife he had slipped from its sheath into the Italian's throat, holding the blade firmly in place while Rosso thrashed around wildly as his lifeblood showered the leader of the Almogavars. Seconds after he had stabbed the Genoese governor of Galata, hundreds of javelins flew through the air, striking Italian faces and torsos.

Luca knew violence would erupt. He could smell it in the air, which crackled with tension, like the moment before a bowstring was released. Ever since he had provoked the battle outside Messina, Luca realised he relished the experience of battle. His conduct in that encounter had been shaped by pure rage, an uncontrollable fury born of seeing his parents butchered before his eyes. But the battle on the beach had been different. He had experienced a brief moment of hesitation before the training he had received had kicked in, enabling him to perform as an effective part of the Almogavars. But he had felt a surge of elation when he began killing, as though his spirit had been released from captivity and was free to roam at will. It was as if his life as a shepherd had been a disguise, masking his true purpose in life – to excel in battle.

He had never felt so alive, never felt so free of the crushing constrictions that had been his peasant life. He was a man reborn and reinvigorated. Every breath he took seemed to make the blood in his veins flow faster and make his reflexes sharper. As soon as his instincts had detected battle was about to erupt, he had focused on his target: a man in a stained tunic with an enormous pot belly standing a mere ten paces opposite. He held a butcher's cleaver in his hand, a vicious weapon capable of smashing bone and slicing open stomachs, but only if its owner managed to get close to an opponent.

Luca caught the man's eye and winked, which prompted the fat man's face to twist into a livid expression. Luca scratched his right ear, saw Sancho stab the Genoese leader out of the corner of his eye, plucked a javelin from the quiver he had strapped on his back while exiting the pavilion, and hurled it at the target. Normally, he would have aimed it at the man's face, but the belly straining at his tunic was too tempting to ignore. He had already plucked a second javelin from the quiver when the steel head of the first slammed into the blubber of the fat man, disappearing into the abundant flesh on offer.

Luca began laughing as he struck a second man in the front of his neck beside the fat man, around him Almogavars hurling javelins

108

to create large gaps among the Genoese. The Italians had rowed across the Golden Horn looking for a fight but had bitten off more than they could chew.

Luca threw his third javelin, into the groin of a Genoese who had raised his shield as a defence against the missiles flying through the air. He emitted a high-pitched scream and collapsed to the ground, Luca bounding forward gripping his spear with both hands, to plunge the point into his chest.

He moved fast, Jordi on his right side, lunging left and to the front with his spear against targets that presented themselves. His eyes were everywhere: keeping watch for crossbowmen who could drop him with ease, looking for opponents to stab, and guarding his back to ensure no enemy crept up on him from behind. He stepped over the dead fat man, his feet as light as air, pivoting smartly to jab at an opponent with a sword and shield, the Genoese soldier slashing down with his blade in an attempt to splinter the shaft. But Luca was too quick for him, for the haft felt weightless in his hands. Indeed, it seemed to move according to his thoughts, and those thoughts were lightning-fast. Luca threaded the wood back through his hands so the soldier cut only air, then thrust the spear forward, letting it travel forward through his hands at speed, before grasping it firmly and lunging forward. The tip of the point pierced the soldier's right eye, only a tiny amount but enough to send a spasm of pain through his brain. He instinctively closed his eyes, dropping his sword arm, allowing Luca to stab him in his right shoulder, an attack delivered with precision to render his sword arm useless. The soldier, now blind, staggered back. Luca, facing him, ran three paces forward, stabbed the point of his spear into the man's throat, and then retreated smartly to stand beside Jordi once more.

'They are running,' his friend shouted in triumph.

'Almogavars stand.'

Luca heard Sancho's command and cursed his friend's father. He wanted to run after the fleeing Genoese, to get among them to cut down more before they reached their boats. To retain the sensation of supreme satisfaction that gripped him when he was in the pleasing embrace of combat. But the Catalans were professionals and they now formed a long line on either side of their commander, their ranks bristling with bloody spears. He growled in frustration.

'Are you hurt, Luca?' asked a concerned Jordi.

'Just frustrated.'

He nearly lost his footing with a hand slapped him hard on the back.

'Your third battle and not a scratch on you.'

He turned to see Hector behind him.

'Looks like you listened to all that wisdom I imparted during training.'

'We should pursue and finish them,' said Luca.

Hector laughed. 'They are our allies, or should be. This is a strange land and no mistake.'

For the loss of twenty-four men, three thousand Genoese had been killed in the emperor's grounds on the day Roger de Flor married the young niece of Andronicus and the citizens of Constantinople gave thanks to God for the arrival of the Catalan Company, which would deliver them from the infidels.

*****

In the aftermath of the outbreak of violence at the palace, newly created Grand Duke Roger moved the Catalan Company outside Constantinople, having persuaded them not to cross over the Golden

Horn and ransack Galata. The emperor had been appalled and had withdrawn to his private chambers to grieve for the deaths of the Genoese, leaving his son in control.

Michael was now in his mid-twenties, having been co-emperor since his eighteenth birthday. His father had thought the idea of two rulers would both ease his own burden and allow his son to become familiar with the administration of the empire, what was left of it, and for the first few years the arrangement worked well enough. But Michael found his father's prevarications increasingly irksome, especially in the face of the seemingly unstoppable Muslim advance.

'Treasurer Timothy to see you, excellency.'

The portly eunuch swept into the throne room and bowed to Michael.

'Excellency,' smiled Timothy, 'I trust your father is recovering.'

Michael raised an eyebrow. 'He will be assuming his duties in a few days, I have no doubt. What of our Catalan friends?'

'Grand Duke Roger has removed them outside the city, after he had ordered them to remove the Genoese dead from the palace and inter them.'

'So, Rosso is dead.'

Timothy assumed a relieved expression. 'If it is not too seditious to say so, excellency, I believe his demise is most fortuitous for us.'

'How so?'

'The treasury owed a great deal of money to Rosso, excellency, which it would have been unable to pay if it is to subsidise the Catalan Company. The debt to Rosso dies with him, excellency, as it was he rather than the Republic of Genoa which loaned us the money.'

Michael smiled. 'How fortunate. I trust we have money to pay the Catalan Company, since I have no desire to see Constantinople ransacked.'

'Yes, excellency,' said Timothy, 'but it may be prudent to move them to a place where they can do more damage to the enemy than to ourselves.'

'Such as where?'

'The Artake Peninsula, excellency,' replied Timothy.

The peninsula lay on the southern shore of the Sea of Marmara, southwest of Constantinople.

'That would mean they would be cut off from the city,' remarked Michael.

'But Grand Duke Roger has his own ships, excellency, which will allow him and his soldiers to maintain contact with the city, and to place the Catalans on the peninsula would give heart to our beleaguered cities in western Anatolia.'

Michael pondered the suggestion for a minute.

'What does General Mouzalon say about your proposal?'

'The general left the city this morning, excellency, to organise the army for a fresh offensive against the Muslims.'

Michael gave the overweight treasurer a wry look. They both knew that the army was incapable of mounting offensive actions in the wake of the disaster at Bapheus.

'You mean he is gone to keep an eye on our Alan allies who might be tempted to pillage our lands.'

Timothy shifted uncomfortably on his feet.

'I will take your silence as confirmation,' said Michael. 'It might be wise to move the Alans south to Artake as well. To keep all our mercenaries in one place, as it were. And I want them fighting Muslims instead of our own troops.'

'It shall be as you desire, excellency.'

'We stand on the edge of a precipice, lord treasurer,' lamented Michael. 'If we fail to halt the advance of the Muslims, Constantinople will become a Muslim city and a thousand years of history and culture will be lost to the world. Impress that upon our Catalan allies.'

Chapter 6

The Turcomans – Turks – had originally hailed from the vast region between the Caspian Sea and China, a nomadic people that had moved into Anatolia and which would embrace the religion of Islam. These first Turcomans were called Seljuk Turks, and with each victory they expanded their territory at the expense of the Roman emperors of Constantinople. Indeed, they called themselves the Seljuks of Rum – 'Rum' signifying 'Eastern Rome'. But just as the Seljuks had been conquerors, so were they in turn conquered, by the Mongols. Their once-great sultan in Baghdad became a mere vassal of the Mongols, which resulted in the Seljuk areas in Anatolia fracturing into a number of self-governing Muslim emirates.

These kingdoms were called *beyliks*, being controlled by *beys*, meaning 'chieftains'. The absence of any central authority meant individual *beys* often competed with each other, notwithstanding they all followed the Muslim faith. Notions of a holy war against the Christians were all very well, but no *bey* would willingly give up his increasing power to another, especially after they began calling themselves *emir*, meaning 'high king'.

Karesi Bey stood with arms folded staring at the city of Bergama, his new capital captured the year before from the Romans. Bergama was an ancient settlement, the first buildings being built on the steep-sided hill overlooking the rest of the city. These buildings were eventually turned into an acropolis, housing temples to the Goddess Athena, the God Dionysus and the Roman emperor Trajan, a huge library and an impressive palace. The temples had been destroyed long ago but the palace, with its courtyard and many spacious rooms, had been preserved by the Romans. Now the flag of

Karesi Bey – a red banner emblazoned with a golden sword, fluttered from the *emir*'s new residence.

He had always been a warrior, ever since he had accompanied his uncle on campaign when a boy, cleaning armour and being taken on tours of the aftermath of battles where he saw the twisted, mutilated bodies of the dead. This had hardened him to war, which he practised in the years afterwards as his father and uncle fought the Christians and rival Muslim *beys*. His uncle had fallen in battle and his father had died in middle age, leaving him and his brother to fight for the right to rule the so-called Karesi Emirate. In the deciding battle his older brother was on the verge of a crushing victory, but the intervention of a third force tipped the scales in his favour. He won the battle, his brother was slain and Karesi Bey became *emir*.

His deliverance had been at the hands of *ghazis* – 'fighters of the faith' – led by a mystic who had been instructed by the Prophet Muhammad to intervene in the battle to ensure Karesi Bey became *emir*.

'Adviser Arslan to see you, excellency.'

The officer of the guard bowed his head when Karesi turned his gaze away from the city below. He walked from the balcony into the spacious throne room where decorators were painting over the murals depicting victories achieved by previous emperors of Constantinople. He walked to the elaborate throne and sat himself on it.

'Show him in.'

Karesi suddenly felt conspicuous in his red cashmere kaftan and white loose trousers, knowing his adviser and right-hand man frowned upon such ostentatiousness. His adviser did indeed raise an eyebrow when he walked into the chamber, nodding approvingly at

115

the decorators painting over the scenes of apostasy. He stood before the throne and tipped his head in the mere hint of a bow. Compared to the fine attire of the *emir*, he looked like a beggar, and an impoverished one at that.

'I wanted to talk to you about the theatre,' said the beggar.

Karesi was surprised. 'The theatre?'

The ancient Greek theatre at Bergama was a marvel of engineering. Sited against the sheer acropolis hillside, it was the steepest theatre in the world.

'When is it going to be destroyed?'

Karesi sighed. 'I have no plans to destroy it.'

The adviser's brow creased into a glare.

'Entertainments detract from devotion to God and encourage debauchery.'

Karesi wanted to laugh but knew to do so would only incur further wrath from the fierce Izzeddin Arslan. To look at he was insignificant, being slight of build with a gaunt face, straggly hair and beard and threadbare apparel, which looked so out of place in the grand palace that until recently had been the abode of kings and emperors.

'I will forbid performances in the theatre until I have given the matter more consideration,' said Karesi. 'But I have neither the resources nor the inclination to order its destruction.'

Izzeddin mumbled under his breath but did not contradict the *emir*. But he managed a smile when he turned his angry eyes to the murals being painted over.

'It is good you are removing the idolatrous images of the unbelievers, lord.'

Karesi smiled. Izzeddin only called him 'lord' when he was undertaking actions his adviser approved of. Many would have dismissed the wild holy man for his insolence and carping comments, but Izzeddin Arslan was a valuable ally.

A member of the Sufi brand of Islam, like his fellow adherents he abstained from worldly pleasures, embracing a frugal, devout lifestyle. The word 'Sufi' came from the Arabic word *suf*, meaning 'wool', in reference to the traditional rough woollen cloaks Sufis wore. And Karesi was conscious the holy man had saved his life after he and his followers had interceded on his behalf during the battle against his brother's army.

'Will you take refreshment?' asked Karesi, the holy man glaring at the slave who walked forward with a silver tray on which was a beautiful gold chalice filled with wine.

'Such trinkets are a distraction from our true purpose,' remarked Izzeddin, waving the slave away.

'Which is?' probed Karesi, accepting another chalice proffered by a second slave.

'To drive the disbelievers into the sea,' hissed Izzeddin.

Karesi knew what he was alluding to: the Artake Peninsula, the last remaining Christian foothold in his emirate.

'My followers need land to settle on,' remarked the holy man.

Karesi's ears pricked up. The thousands of *ghazi* fighters camped near his new capital made him feel like he was living adjacent to a volatile volcano. He had always considered himself a religious man, but the soldiers of Izzeddin Arslan were fanatics, and fanatics were dangerous. When they and the rest of his army had surrounded Bergama, the intention had been to starve out the Christian defenders. He had no siege engines and knew assaulting defended walls would inevitably incur heavy casualties. But Izzeddin had no such reluctance and hurled his warriors against the walls, equipped only with scaling ladders and their small round shields for protection. Hundreds had died at the hands of archers on the walls, but such was the unrelenting ferocity of the assault that the walls were breached.

Horror ensued.

The *ghazis* spared no one. Infants were ripped from their mothers' arms and hurled against rocks. Women and young girls, usually raped before being enslaved when a city fell, were cut down without mercy. Bergama soon became filled from one end to the other with dead. The paved roads were replaced with carpets of dead as the *ghazis* vented their anger against the unbelievers. When Karesi entered the city, he had to use his own troops to protect those citizens and defenders still alive who wanted to surrender. He was no stranger to the face of battle but he was appalled by what he saw that day, not least because he intended to make Bergama his capital. But what use was a city without citizens?

It took weeks to clear the city of the dead, to wash away blood from walls and streets, and repair the damage wreaked by the *ghazis*. He had insisted the holy warriors withdraw from the city and make camp beyond its walls, placing guards around the acropolis, which had mercifully been untouched by the *ghazis*, who had been distracted by slaughtering the hapless citizens of Bergama rather than seizing the heart of the city.

'They cannot live in tents forever,' said Izzeddin.

'I agree, but the Christians will not surrender Artake lightly. In addition, it will take time to assemble the army, which is scattered throughout the emirate.'

118

'With your permission, lord,' said Izzeddin, 'I would like to attack Artake with the Fighters of the Faith. They succeeded against the walls of this city, and with Allah's blessing they will seize Artake.'

'You will have no horsemen and few missile troops,' cautioned Karesi. 'Even if the Christians are outnumbered, if they attack with their mounted soldiers, your followers will suffer greatly.'

Izzeddin dismissed the warning. 'Allah will be our shield, lord, against which the spears of the enemy will be useless.'

'I do not wish a repeat of the atrocities committed in Bergama, Izzeddin,' said Karesi sternly.

The holy man bristled at the words. 'It is the duty of believers to enforce Allah's will.'

Karesi tossed his empty chalice at a slave, stood and approached the holy man slowly. Izzeddin Arslan was scrawny and of medium height, whereas Karesi was tall and fearsome, especially with his saturnine face. He halted and looked the holy man in the eyes.

'God is also just and merciful and would wish those who are subjected to His authority to be given the chance to convert before they are sent to hell. I ask you this. What use is a land emptied of people? In any case, the farmers who now work the land on the Artake Peninsular will be needed if your warriors are not to starve during the winter.'

The holy man had clearly not considered this and nodded thoughtfully.

'When Allah commanded me to aid you in your fight against your ungodly brother, I initially wondered why He should do so. You were, after all, but one among a number of *emirs* in this land formally ruled by the Seljuks. But your great victory at this city and your

119

foresight regarding the fate of the people of Artake have shown you to be a true visionary. Praise God.'

'Praise God, indeed,' said Karesi, thankful the holy man had not launched into a long and tedious sermon.

Izzeddin bowed his head. 'I will head for Artake immediately, lord.'

'It might be more prudent to wait until I have assembled the army,' cautioned Karesi, suddenly concerned he might lose his adviser and half his army in an ill-considered adventure.

Izzeddin would have none of it. 'With Allah's help I will scatter your enemies and bring the Artake Peninsula under your rule, lord.'

'I have given orders for a mosque to be built on the acropolis,' said Karesi.

Izzeddin was underwhelmed. 'Another building of marble and gold?'

'A place for believers to worship,' the *emir* shot back.

But the holy man ignored him as he took his leave. Karesi found the Sufi liking for the ascetic life amusing but also irritating. Izzeddin had told him that the Sufis believed in approaching Allah during this lifetime, rather than waiting until after death to become closer to God. Part of this dogma was a reaction against what they saw as the materialism of some Islamic practices, such as building grandiose mosques to signify a ruler's devotion. To men such as Izzeddin Arslan, such gestures were meaningless.

*****

As winter gave way to spring, the Catalan Company still found itself near Constantinople, though the emperor's son had moved the mercenaries across the Bosporus to confront an anticipated offensive

120

by Osman Bey, who had established his kingdom in northwest Anatolia four years previously. The victor of the Battle of Bapheus had a large army ready to strike at Constantinople, but his military success had prompted jealousy among the other *beys*, forcing him to split his army into several parts to guard the frontiers of his expanding kingdom. As a result, no attack against Constantinople materialised.

Such things did not concern Luca, who was enjoying the hospitality of the emperor, who sent generous amounts of food across the Bosporus to feed the Catalans. He had never eaten as much or as well in his whole life.

The Catalans feasted on freshly caught fish, mountains of bread and cheese, and an abundance of vegetables, fruit and wine. His body responded to the excellent nutrition and rigorous training the Almogavars undertook each day, becoming stronger, more muscular and possessed of great stamina. Outside Messina he found the incessant long-distant marches tiring. Now he relished them. Whereas before the weapons he was forced to haul on marches had been cumbersome and painful to carry, now they felt part of him. The straps holding the javelin quiver on his back were adjusted so they did not chafe, the scabbard at his hip properly placed so it did not flap around like a fish out of water when on the move, and the small, round shield – around two feet in diameter – was slung on the left side of his back out of the way.

When he had been a shepherd he had lived a life of isolation. Now he was part of a close-knit group of men, and women, whose profession was war. He had given no thought to the revelation that he revelled in the cauldron of battle. But had given thanks to God he had fought well on the three occasions when he had been tested,

121

which had led to him being embraced by the Almogavar brotherhood. Even Sancho Rey was being less hostile to him.

The head of the Almogavar council slammed his fist on the table.

'We have been sitting on our arses for over two months, waiting for the Turks to attack. And now you are telling me they are not going to.'

Grand Duke Roger pointed at Jordi and then his cup, indicating it should be refilled with wine. Sancho's son walked forward and did so. Taking his cue from his friend, Luca also went to top up Sancho's cup, but the Almogavar waved him away.

'I'll have some more,' said Hector.

'Me too,' chimed in Marc.

Sancho pointed at the handsome Corberan of Navarre, knight, crusader and temporary commander of the company's horsemen, which still had no horses.

'What about his horses?'

'Treasurer Timothy has assured me they are on the way from Bulgaria,' explained Roger, 'but craves your patience a little longer.'

'My men are unhappy, lord duke,' said Corberan, immaculate in his red surcoat emblazoned with a shield of gold chains with a green emerald in the centre, representing the breaking of the Muslim slave-soldiers' chains by Spanish horsemen at the Battle of Las Navas de Tolosa, a victory won by King Sancho of Navarre a century before.

'With good reason,' agreed Sancho. 'What use are horsemen without horses?'

'Perhaps we should ask the Genoese for a loan so we can buy our own horses,' suggested Hector.

122

The other Almogavars laughed, but Roger remained stony faced.

'We don't want any more trouble.'

'*We*,' said Sancho, 'have not been corrupted by the court of Constantinople, Roger. Or should I call you lord duke?'

'Of course not,' snapped Roger.

'You want to be careful, Roger,' said Angel. 'You spend too much time at court and they might chop off your balls like they have with the eunuch Timothy.'

'Imagine that,' said Marc, 'a man without any balls as lord treasurer of a great city.'

Luca involuntarily laughed, prompting everyone to look at him. Sancho gave him a wry smile.

'You are right to laugh, Black Sheep, for it is laughable. We are beholden to a man who has no balls.'

'Eunuchs have always held high positions in the empire,' said a stern-faced Roger. 'They are accorded great respect. We are strangers in this land and should respect its laws and customs.'

Angel shuddered. 'How can a man hold his head up high if he has no balls?'

'I wonder when they cut off his balls?' asked Marc.

'When he was a boy,' answered Roger.

'He had done the same to the company,' seethed Sancho. 'For without horses, our effectiveness is greatly diminished.'

'Timothy has agreed to ship the horses directly to Artake,' said Roger. 'I think we should make plans for our departure immediately. The emperor has received an urgent summons from the provincial general there for reinforcements.'

'Is he a eunuch, too?' asked Sancho.

'No,' groaned Roger. 'I think we should move on from eunuchs.'

'Will you be coming with us?' enquired Angel. 'Seeing as you are now a married man with a pretty young wife.'

Roger drank from his cup and held it out for Jordi to top up.

'I will, Angel. I have no desire to stay at the court of the emperor for a day longer than I have to.'

'And your wife?' grinned Hector.

'Is none of your business,' said Roger. 'On a happier note, I can tell you that I have secured the services of a thousand Alan horsemen to bolster our efforts.'

His declaration was met with silence, which surprised him somewhat. Sancho drained his cup and held it out to Luca to be refilled. A brisk breeze that had picked up began to batter the sides of the tent they were seated in. The Almogavars were simple, straightforward individuals who cared little for politics or the machinations of court life. Corberan of Navarre was altogether different, and went out of his way to find out as much as possible about the laws, customs and history of the region he was fighting in. Like many knights, he was fluent in several languages, including Greek, which meant he could converse with the natives of Constantinople. He had also struck up an affinity with the commander of the emperor's army, such as it was, General Mouzalon, who had informed him the Alans had deserted him at Bapheus. Corberan had informed the council of their base actions.

'We have no use for cowards,' said Sancho.

'We should kill the Alans and give their horses to Corberan,' said Hector.

Angel and Marc both laughed but Roger was far from amused.

'It is the emperor's express wish that the Alans accompany us, and I have agreed to his desire. He is our paymaster, after all, and we should respect his wishes.'

'Talking of which,' said Sancho, 'can I reminded your lordship that we have been paid for four months' work, two of which have already expired. I assume we will receive further payment before we depart for our new destination?'

'The treasurer has assured me we will be paid promptly,' Roger assured him.

'You trust this man with no balls?' asked Marc.

'I trust his desire to preserve his great city from the Muslims, Marc,' said Roger irritably.

'Actions speak louder than words,' said Hector.

'An old saying that has much merit,' agreed Corberan.

But, much to the surprise of the Almogavars, two days later hundreds of horses arrived at Constantinople to mount Corberan's men. They were not the destriers that carried Christendom's knights but mares and geldings. Mostly of Hungarian and Thessalian stock, they were in good condition and kitted out with bridles and saddles when they reached Constantinople. Corberan was happy, his men were happy and the Almogavars were pacified, the more so since the Alans had failed to arrive at the city. Sancho, buoyed by the arrival of the horses, gave Jordi and Luca each a pouch of money and acquiesced to their burning desire to explore the great city before they left for Artake.

'Are you armed?' Sancho asked the pair on the morning of their excursion.

They shook their heads.

'No, father,' said Jordi.

125

Sancho offered them a pair of daggers with wicked blades.

'Never go anywhere without a weapon.'

They grinned and reached out to grasp the dagger handles. Sancho held on to the blades.

'Don't get drunk. Don't get robbed. And remember that just because a city has beautiful buildings, it does not mean it is full of virtuous people. Watch your backs.'

Jordi kissed his mother on the cheek and Luca embraced her before the pair sauntered off to the ferry across the Bosporus. She watched them go and gripped her husband's arm.

'I feel helpless,' she said.

'Jordi is a battle-hardened veteran,' Sancho reassured her. 'I think he can handle a stroll through a city.'

'And Luca?'

'The Black Sheep? Hector told me the shepherd is a natural killer and coming from him that is saying something.'

'I hope they stay clear of brothels,' said Carla.

Sancho laughed. 'They are red-blooded young men with pouches of money. What do you think?'

She jabbed him in the ribs. 'Sometimes, you can be so ungodly.'

Constantinople was beautiful that spring morning, the sun shining on a glittering, calm sea, illuminating the great buildings within the metropolis. Each may have harboured salacious thoughts, but as soon as they alighted from the ferry that docked at the harbour on the south side of the city, Luca and Jordi had only one aim: to visit the Church of Saint Sophia. Like thousands of others who had been drawn to the largest Orthodox church in the world like moths to a flame, they were overwhelmed by its scale, beauty and opulence.

126

The church's profile dominated the city skyline, its great dome stunning in size, made more striking by the great buttresses that supported it. The pair could only gawp at the engineering marvel, the like of which they had never seen before. The church was the seat of the Patriarch of Constantinople and the main venue for church councils and imperial ceremonies. But it was also a place of worship, open to all and sundry who wished to pray to the Lord.

In a daze the two friends wandered into the massive church, the interior lit by thousands of candles and giant icons illuminated by lamps hanging in front of them. The church was a treasure trove of coloured marbles and gold and blue mosaics. Semi-domes sheltered the apse and two antechambers at the western entrance, called a narthex, through which Luca and Jordi entered Saint Sophia.

Luca stared up at a mosaic showing a man kneeling at the foot of a man seated on a throne.

'Is that an emperor?'

Jordi shrugged. 'I do not know.'

Both illiterate, they had no idea who they were looking at. The answer was provided by a female voice behind them, who spoke in perfect Italian. They turned and beheld a vision of grace and beauty, a middle-aged woman with flawless fair skin, golden hair, green eyes and a slender figure. That figure was encased in a stunning heavy woven white and red kaftan embroidered with geometric patterns in gold thread. The garment's sleeves were long to ensure none of her flesh above the wrists was exposed, with a tight neckline to preserve modesty. She wore gold earrings, a gold necklace from which hung an emerald-encrusted crucifix, and gold rings on her fingers. The shoes that poked out from beneath her kaftan were red.

She pointed up at the mosaic, her voice soft and soothing.

127

'The man kneeling is Emperor Leo the Sixth, who is performing an act of respect to Christ, who sits on a jewelled throne.'

'That is Christ?' uttered Luca, spellbound.

'He looks just like a man,' said Jordi.

'He *was* a man,' the woman told him, 'a poor carpenter who went among the people to spread the word of God. You see our Lord is holding a book, upon which are the words "Peace be with you. I am the light of the Lord". With his right hand, he is blessing the emperor.'

'Who are the people in the circles either side of Christ?' asked Jordi.

'The woman in the blue dress and headdress is the Virgin Mary,' she answered. 'The other is the Archangel Gabriel.'

They fell into silence, the woman looking at the two young men. They in turn staring in wonder at the beautiful mosaic of Christ, others in the church depicting the Virgin Mary, Christian saints, emperors and empresses.

'You are Italian?' the woman probed.

'From Sicily, lady,' answered Luca.

'We are here to fight for Christ,' said Jordi proudly.

She looked at their curious sheepskin coats and rudimentary footwear and smiled.

'Then may God go with you,' she said before smiling and leaving them.

'Who was she?' asked Jordi.

'A noblewoman, that's for certain,' said Luca, who caught sight of a shifty individual following the woman. He nodded in the man's direction.

'I think she is in trouble.'

128

They followed the swarthy individual out of the church and into the sunshine, around them hundreds of people milling around the streets leading to Saint Sophia.

'Where are her guards?' asked Jordi, curious as to why a woman of obvious wealth was walking around Constantinople alone.

'They are certainly not guards,' said an alarmed Luca, pointing at three more individuals joining the man he had seen in the church, all four dropping in behind her.

They followed the quartet as the wealthy woman sauntered along the paved street, the Mese, the main thoroughfare of the city, leading from the Church of Saint Sophia to the Forum of Constantine. In the centre of the square was a column originally crowned with a statue of the Emperor Constantine but was now topped with a cross. The four rough-looking men in drab clothing kept at a distance behind the woman but they were definitely trailing her, following her into the Forum of Theodosius a short walk from the first forum.

'You have your knife?' Luca asked Jordi.

Jordi nodded but then looked alarmed.

'What if they *are* her bodyguards?'

'What does your instincts tell you?'

'That they are robbers,' said Jordi.

'Mine too.'

The woman, with not a care in the world and unaware she was being trailed by predators, ambled from the forum and walked on to pass the Church of the Holy Apostles, the burial place of the emperors of Constantinople and the patriarchs of the city. It had been ruthlessly plundered by the Latin crusaders a hundred years

129

before but was still an impressive building, being cruciform in shape and surmounted by five domes.

Then the lady left the Mese to head north, towards the emperor's palace, darting into a side street, which was a fatal error. The four shadowing her did likewise, quickening their steps to catch up with her when they realised she had entered a dreary side street that appeared deserted. She was obviously taking a shortcut but had played right into the robbers' hands. They had caught up with her in seconds and surrounded her like a pack of wolves cornering a lone lamb.

Luca and Jordi exchanged no words as they sprinted at the robbers, two of whom had their backs to the pair. Luca felt the same surge of energy and euphoria he had experienced on the beach, which heightened his instincts, made his body feel as light as air and the knife in his hand an integral part of his arm. He thrust the knife into the robber's back, kept it in place and used the victim's body as a shield, shoving it forward towards a second robber who was licking his lips, his eyes wide with relish at the prospect of robbing a rich woman. Perhaps he was thinking of raping her, probably killing her slowly. What he was not thinking about was being a victim himself. But that was what he became when the groaning bulk of his colleague was shoved into him and the silver blur of a knife inflicted a cut to his throat. Not a deep wound but enough to sever his windpipe. He instinctively clutched at his throat as Luca grabbed the woman and forced her behind him.

Everything around him slowed but he moved quickly, shielding the woman, ensuring Jordi, who had similarly stabbed one of the robbers and was tackling another, was safe. Jordi's opponent had seen the pair and had stepped back, drawing his own knife in expectation of a fight. Luca whistled at him to divert his attention, which it did for a split-second. But that was all the time Jordi needed as he sprang at the man, grabbing his knife arm with one hand and plunging his own blade into his belly with the other, shouting in triumph as he stabbed at the man's guts again and again.

He leapt back out of the range of the robber's knife. But the man was bleeding heavily from the stomach and dropped his weapon, doubling over and coughing blood on to the paving stones.

'Are you hurt, lady?' asked Luca, two of the robbers writhing in agony on the ground, the other two already dead.

The saintly woman, stunned by the outbreak of violence that had disturbed her peace, was initially lost for words.

'We must go, Luca,' said Jordi, cleaning his bloody blade on the tunic of one of the dead robbers.

'Where is your home, lady?' asked Luca.

Still mute, the woman pointed in a northerly direction.

'Then that is where we will go.'

Luca linked his arm in hers and urged her forward, away from the scene of carnage, Jordi walking behind to ensure no more miscreants appeared. Blood was oozing on to the street, and now doors were opening and eyes were peering out from opened shutters above them. And soon the screaming started. In the enclosed, claustrophobic street the shrill cries carried far, and soon a small crowd had appeared some way behind the two men with knives in their hands and a solitary woman. A woman in distress!

The cry went up. 'Kidnappers are abducting a woman. To arms.'

Luca and Jordi did not understand the Greek voices but they recognised the intentions of a pack of angry pursuers well enough.

131

They hastened their steps, the woman stumbling as they left the street to enter a wider thoroughfare, at the end of which, rising above the city, was the Blachernae Palace.

Luca and Jordi were in a foreign city but they both recognised the palace where they had been feasted a couple of months before, and the bloodbath they had both taken part in when the Genoese had interrupted their celebrations.

'We must get her to the palace,' said Luca, the woman, ashen faced, nodding frantically.

The crowd pursuing them had grown considerably, several dozen mostly men walking at a brisk pace behind them. Several were armed with knives, others with clubs, and Luca knew they would reach them in a couple of minutes or so. He also knew the woman and Jordi could reach the palace if their pursuers were diverted. He released the woman's arm and turned to face the crowd.

'Get her to the palace,' he said to Jordi.

'Not without you,' his friend shot back.

'I will divert them, Jordi. Otherwise we both die here.'

Jordi was going to remonstrate with his friend but stopped when a trumpet sounded, stopping the crowd in its tracks. Luca smiled when he saw a dozen Varangian Guards marching towards him, axes in hand. The officer at the head of the soldiers barked a command in Greek that scattered the crowd, sending it back from whence it came. Jordi grinned at his friend.

'That was a close call.'

His smiled disappeared when two of the Varangians grabbed his arms and forced him on to his knees, two others doing likewise to Luca. The officer barked another order and two Varangians stepped forward gripping their axes with both hands, ready to lop off the heads of Luca and Jordi. Now the woman found her voice, shouting at the officer, who frowned, pointed at the two Almogavars and shouted at his Varangians, who released them.

The woman, previously in shock and mute, issued a blistering tirade at the officer and his men, all of whom went down on one knee before her. Luca wished he could understand Greek because it was a marvel to witness élite soldiers being reduced to looking like chastised children. She then turned to Luca and Jordi.

'I have just informed this insolent oaf that had it not been for your bravery, I would have certainly been robbed, and perhaps murdered. I am in your debt, as is the emperor.'

She snapped at the Varangians, who as one rose to their feet and fell in behind her as she linked arms with Luca and Jordi and commanded them to tell her all about themselves. They did so as the armed party ambled towards the palace, the guards at the gatehouse snapping to attention as she passed them. A flustered court official in a flowing blue robe, yellow belt and red and gold hat, came from one of the towers, babbling incoherently at the woman. He also bowed his head at her, indicating she was of some importance.

'Speak Italian,' she told the man.

Luca was impressed by the way he effortlessly changed from speaking one language to another, also making him ashamed of his own ignorance when it came to foreign tongues.

'Forgive me, highness,' said the official, 'I had no idea you had left the palace.'

'And why should you? I am not a prisoner, after all.'

'You should not walk around the city unescorted, highness.'

Why was he calling her highness? mused Luca.

'I wish to see my brother immediately.'

133

Her brother turned out to be Emperor Andronicus himself, whom Luca and Jordi met when they accompanied the emperor's sister into the opulent throne room, in the centre of which sat a middle-aged man on a golden throne. Luca stared at the man's extremely long nose before the official who had escorted them from the gates clicked his fingers and glowered at him. Luca bowed his head and kept it bowed. The official walked over to the emperor and whispered in his ear. The room was heavy with the scent of incense, a sweet smell of lily, cinnamon and clove.

'Raise your heads,' commanded the emperor. He stroked his forked beard.

'Has Constantinople become such a lawless place that a woman is no longer free to walk its streets?' asked his sister.

The emperor smiled at Luca and Jordi.

'Allow me to introduce my sister,' he said in flawless Italian. 'Princess Maria is a godly woman, though rather innocent when it comes to the ways of the world.'

'The emperor is quite right,' she retorted. 'Thinking that a woman could walk in his city without being robbed and murdered. And here I was believing it was the responsibility of his Varangian Guards to keep chaos at bay.'

'If you had mentioned to the garrison commander you were leaving the palace,' replied Andronicus irritably, 'he would have arranged an escort.'

'You are embarrassing our guests, brother,' said Maria.

'You are embarrassing *me*,' remarked an exasperated emperor.

'Are you not going to reward them?' asked Maria. 'Seeing as they rescued me from certain doom.'

His gave her a withering look but smiled at the two Almogavars. He waved the official forward and muttered to him, the courtier bowing and hurrying from the throne room. Fierce-looking Varangians stood around the walls and next to the throne, making both Luca and Jordi feel intimidated. That and the grandiose surroundings of gold, marble and ivory. And it was the latter material which drew Luca's eye when the official returned with a slave holding a red velvet cushion, on which rested two ivory handled daggers. They had black blades with strange wavy surface patterns.

'Please accept these gifts by way of our thanks,' said Andronicus. 'The blades are made of Damascus steel. Have you heard of it?'

They shook their heads.

The emperor leaned back in his chair and wagged a finger at the pair.

'The title is really a misnomer. The steel does not come from Damascus, at least not originally. It is over five thousand years old, though I daresay the manufacturing process is different from when the first blades were forged. Today, Damascus blades are produced by hammer-welding strips of steel and iron, followed by repeated heating and forging.'

'How interesting,' said Maria sarcastically.

The emperor ignored her. 'As well as being light, Damascus steel is incredibly strong. May it aid you in your fight against the heretics, young men.'

He gestured at the court official who waved forward a second slave, who also held a velvet cushion. On this were two leather pouches.

135

'Money so you may buy new clothes,' said the emperor to the pair, having noticed their basic attire. 'May God go with you.'

Luca and Jordi accepted the daggers and money and were ushered from the emperor's presence. Princess Maria escorted them both to the private quay adjacent to the palace where a royal barge was waiting. She embraced them both.

'May God protect you both and know that you have my thanks, and my friendship always.'

On the barge they were served food and wine as the boat was rowed down the Golden Horn to the Bosporus. The two friends could not stop smiling as they counted the contents of the two pouches, which had been filled with silver coins. They had no idea how much they were worth and did not care, being more fascinated by their new daggers with strange blades. Had they enquired, they would have learnt each pouch contained enough money to purchase a fine horse, expensive armour, weapons and a squire so they could both fight the enemy from the saddle should they so desire.

Chapter 7

The Catalan Company left Constantinople in high spirits. The rescue of the emperor's sister by Luca and Jordi was viewed as an auspicious omen. Just as they had saved a defenceless woman, so would the company save Constantinople and its empire, such as it was. Feted as heroes, Luca and Jordi basked in the adulation directed at them from every quarter. Even Grand Duke Roger, torn away from the bed of his young bride, took an interest in the two Almogavars who were making a name for themselves. Much to the chagrin of Sancho, he invited them to dine with him on his galley as it sailed across the Sea of Marmara towards the Artake Peninsula. The rest of the Almogavars were following behind in other ships, though the Catalan horsemen and a thousand Alan riders made their way to Artake along the eastern shoreline of the sea.

A large cabin had been constructed at the stern of the vessel to accommodate the grand duke when he was at sea. Containing a sizeable bunk and a rectangular table, it was large enough to accommodate several seated guests without appearing too cramped. Slaves served the four men sitting at the table with fish and shellfish caught that morning and cooked on board, washed down with wine. At one end of the table sat the grand duke and opposite was a man who had visited the city to plead with the emperor to hasten the Catalan Company to Artake. His name was Michael Cosses and he was a Greek from an ancient Roman family. Tall with black hair falling to his shoulders, unusually he kept a clean-shaven face and had blue-green eyes. He listened with interest to the story of how Luca and Jordi had saved the life of Princess Maria, raising his cup to toast the pair. Out of courtesy, he spoke Italian throughout the meal.

137

'We will need all the brave young men we can get our hands on in the coming months,' he said, nibbling on a piece of sea bream.

'General Mouzalon informed me the situation is perilous,' said Roger.

Michael Cosses sipped some wine.

'He does not know the half of it.'

He smiled when he observed Luca and Jordi stuffing their faces with abandon. He found their basic manners and forthright demeanour refreshing. He took another sip.

'My commission from the emperor states that I am the count of the Opsikion Theme, the prestigious military and administrative region close to Constantinople.'

He looked at Luca, whose mouth was full of fish.

'Do you know the size of my region, Black Sheep?'

'No, lord,' said Luca with difficulty.

'Essentially, the Artake Peninsula, which is now very vulnerable.'

Roger was surprised. 'None of the mainland is under the emperor's control?'

'The cities of Magnesia and Philadelphia and the town of Tire are still under the emperor's rule, but they are islands in a Muslim sea. The fact the armies of Islam do not have siege engines is the only reason they have not already fallen.'

'You paint a grim picture, count,' said Roger, who was picking at his food, unlike Luca and Jordi who were attacking the contents of their plates with gusto.

Jordi stopped and looked at the count. 'Have no fear, lord, we will retake the lands lost by the emperor.'

The handsome duke smiled at the younger man.

'There was a time, many years ago now, young Catalan, when the whole of Anatolia was under the emperor's control, divided into themes, which provided soldiers for the imperial army and money for the imperial treasury. But now the enemy is a mere stone's throw away from Constantinople itself. You, my brave warriors, are the empire's last hope.'

'What of your own army?' asked Roger, becoming increasingly alarmed by the count's revelations.

He drained his cup. A slave rushed forward to refill it.

'My *own* army? A thousand foot soldiers and two hundred horsemen, duke. A paltry force, you will agree. The main army has to shield Constantinople from the threat posed by Osman Bey, while Karesi Bey eats away at my domain.'

Luca finished his chunk of bread and began to devour a wedge of cheese.

'Who is Karesi Bey, lord?'

'A great Muslim warlord, Black Sheep, who has a secret weapon to strike fear into his enemies.'

'What weapon?' asked Jordi.

'Izzeddin Arslan, young Almogavar, a fanatic who leads an army of fanatics. Men who do not fear death, for to die in battle is to guarantee a place in paradise, or so they believe. Fighting an enemy that desires death is a daunting prospect.'

Luca grinned at Jordi, who smiled back. Far from being intimidated by the prospect of fighting religious fanatics, they relished the prospect.

The Artake Peninsula was a beautiful place. The fleet docked in the ancient port of Artake on the southwestern side of the peninsula, a walled city surrounded by olive groves, fruit orchards

139

and vineyards. Beyond the cultivated land were expanses of forest containing an abundance of oak, maple, ash, aspen, elm, willow, sycamore and pines. The peninsula was fringed by spectacular white sandy beaches, with villages nestling beside waterfalls and streams. The thousands of small farms on the peninsula produced a huge amount of olives and olive oil for export to Constantinople, as well as timber to the city for shipbuilding. There was also a substantial fishing fleet operating from Artake and the villages along the peninsula's west coast.

The Catalan Company pitched its tents outside Artake, despite Count Cosses offering them lodgings in the city itself, which Luca discovered contained many empty homes and buildings when he was sent into the port to collect provisions for the Almogavars. The market stall holders were beside themselves with joy when they discovered he and they had money to purchase food. But the stay of the Catalan Company outside Artake was short. Two days after setting foot on the peninsula, the Almogavars marched east to take up residence in the ruined city of Cyzicus, which was adjacent to a wall that spanned a narrow isthmus joining the peninsula to the mainland.

Earthquakes had destroyed many of the buildings in the ancient site, which was once a great trading port, and the last inhabitants had left a hundred years before when the Latin crusaders had pillaged the land. Since then, the city's masonry had been plundered by local inhabitants to construct their homes. Stone and marble from Cyzicus could be found throughout the peninsula, as could the squared stones used to construct the wall that spanned the isthmus.

Count Cosses had a thousand foot soldiers, which ordinarily would have been adequate to man the half-mile wall containing a dozen square towers at regular intervals. Built by the ancient Greeks and added to by the Romans, the wall was twenty-feet high, contained two gatehouses and had a wide walkway along its length, from which soldiers could shoot arrows and hurl spears at an attacker. In its heyday, it was a formidable obstacle. Sadly, its glory days were not even a distant memory.

Luca stood with Jordi, Sancho and the count at the western end of the ruins of the wall and its gatehouses and towers.

Sancho was unimpressed. 'Rather than aiding us in our defence, these ruins will impede our mobility and provide assistance to the enemy.'

The count had taken a liking to Luca and Jordi and insisted they accompany him when he visited the Almogavars. The Catalan mercenaries themselves, viewing the pair as lucky mascots, did not object to them receiving favourable treatment, knowing that when the fighting began they would be in the vanguard with Sancho Rey.

The leader of the Almogavar council pointed at the ruins of the wall.

'The length of the wall is around nine hundred paces. There are three large gaps, each one a hundred paces wide, through which the enemy will flood. In addition, the wall is at its full height in only a few places, which means a man can clamber over the rest with ease.'

'We cannot rebuild the wall,' lamented the count, 'but we must defend it because this narrow isthmus is the one place where our paucity of numbers will not work against us.'

Sancho turned to stare at the calm Sea of Marmara.

'Does the enemy have any ships?'

'Fortunately, no,' said the count. 'No yet, anyway.'

Sancho nodded. 'So, the only way they can invade the peninsula is via this isthmus. That is something.'

He pointed to the mainland.

'With your permission, lord, when the enemy arrives I would like to deploy your foot soldiers beyond the wall, to act as bait to lure the enemy to the wall where the company can engage them. I would suggest your horsemen be held back as a reserve, to plug any gaps that may occur. When our horsemen and the Alans arrive, we will take the offensive.'

The count was surprised. 'Karesi Bey has many soldiers.'

'It does not matter, my lord. To remain on the defensive is to endure a slow death.'

Like the other Almogavars, Luca undertook daily training while he and they waited for the enemy to arrive, wondering if their horsemen and Alan allies would reach the peninsula first. The route marches through lush forests and along mountain paths were far from arduous, his body now accustomed to covering long distances on foot carrying weapons, water and food in a knapsack.

The majority of the women and children were billeted outside Artake, though a fair few of the young women hauled weapons with the Almogavar men. Luca lusted after their toned bodies but Jordi warned him off trying anything untoward.

'Those selected to fight alongside us are aware they are outnumbered by many men,' his friend told him. 'They will protect their virtue with their weapons and my father and the other captains will not tolerate them being molested. Best leave them alone.'

'How do they find husbands?' asked Luca.

'They don't. They remain single.'

142

'Like a nun,' said Luca.

'No talking in the ranks,' snapped Sancho.

The weather was getting warmer, the number of daylight hours increasing as mid-spring arrived. The air was heavy with the scent of pine, but the sea breezes blowing over the peninsula made marching pleasant enough. Sweat still coursed down Luca's neck to soak his tunic, but the straps of his quiver no longer chafed and the spear he carried was no longer a burden. He now fitted in among the other Almogavars. Just another individual among the foot soldiers of the Catalan Company.

*****

The approach of summer meant sleeping on the ground with just a blanket for cover was bearable enough. Indeed, for Izzeddin Arslan it was a joy for it brought him closer to Allah. After all, did not the Prophet Muhammad himself prefer to live at the same level as the poorest in society? Only through ordeal could the word of God triumph over the disbelievers.

The great *ghazi* army had meandered its way north through the mountains and valleys of western Anatolia, drawing a host of recruits to its red banners. Some joined out of curiosity, others for the prospect of loot, but all were subject to the harsh discipline of Izzeddin's Sufi lieutenants. They ensured everyone obeyed Salat, the obligatory Muslim prayers, which were performed five times a day: at sunrise, midday, during the latter part of the afternoon, just after sunset, and between sunset and midnight. It was a godly army, determined to erase the blasphemous presence of the apostate Romans from the earth, especially those resident on the Artake Peninsula, notwithstanding Karesi Bey's orders.

143

Izzeddin Arslan marched at the head of the army, a scrawny individual in ragged clothes, sandals on his feet, a stout staff his only weapon. The only musical instruments allowed in the army were drums, which were used to strike fear into the enemy just before battle was joined, and to alert the warriors to dangers during the march. Either side of the column were low mountains, while the dirt track it marched along lanced through a rolling plain dotted with olive groves and abandoned farms. The sound of drums coming from the rear of the column made Izzeddin stop and turn, peering past the thousands of warriors in drab clothes to scour the distance. Those behind him shuffled to a halt, their leaders shouting orders to face the flanks and prepare for battle. Then the drums stopped and everyone began to stare at each other in confusion. Izzeddin's expression hardened when he saw the red flags fluttering in the breeze, and behind them a plethora of red pennants flying from lances and knew the horsemen of Karesi Bey had arrived, led by their charismatic commander, Mahmud of Caesarea.

The *ghazis* began to cheer the armoured horsemen, behind them a long column of horse archers wearing no armour, and packhorses and camels carrying the tents, weapons and supplies of the horsemen. The column of riders presented a colourful spectacle, in stark contrast to the drab hues and threadbare attire of the *ghazis* and the host of hangers-on that had joined the army of the godly. At the head of the horsemen rode an individual in a burnished helmet and a lamellar cuirass, the individual steel scales glinting in the sunlight. A standard bearer carrying a huge red banner emblazoned with a golden sabre rode immediately behind him.

The piercing eyes of Izzeddin Arslan followed the figure of Mahmud as he accepted the acclaim, waving his right arm at the cheering *ghazis*. Izzeddin was not cheering or smiling, his expression not changing when Mahmud pulled up his magnificent black stallion and looked down at the holy man. It was a symbolic moment for Mahmud looked down on Izzeddin in every sense, despising him as a dangerous fanatic who once he had finished slaughtering all the Christians and Jews, would focus on purging the faithful themselves.

'I am here to warn you that a force of Roman horsemen has left Constantinople,' said Mahmud tersely. 'My lord has commanded me to shadow the Romans and loan you some horsemen in case the defenders of Artake have mounted soldiers.'

Izzeddin leaned on his staff. 'I do not want any of your *kafir* horsemen.'

'You mean Lord Karesi's élite corps of horsemen?' smirked Mahmud.

The armoured horsemen he was alluding to cantered past the pair, all resplendent in helmets and lamellar armour cuirasses, their lances flying red pennants, red cloaks billowing in the breeze. But to Izzeddin they were an abomination.

Kafir meant 'unbeliever' and was applied to anyone who did not follow Islam. For individuals such as Izzeddin Arslan, the world was divided into two camps: the faithful and unbelievers. And he had been put on earth to eradicate the latter. But he was continually frustrated in his efforts by individuals such as Mahmud of Caesarea, the aristocrat who indulged in decadent practices and commanded a *kafir* corps.

The corps numbered only five hundred horsemen but each one was superbly armed and equipped. They were the descendants of the cataphracts of ancient Parthia who had smashed Rome's legions at the Battle of Carrhae, and had been copied by the eastern Roman

145

emperors to provide a mailed fist on the battlefield. Each rider wore a short-sleeved padded jacket, a *zoupa*, over his torso, over which was worn a lamellar cuirass, called a *klibanion*. Each *klibanion* comprised overlapping rectangular iron plates arranged in horizontal rows fixed to a leather backing, riveted in place at top and bottom. Arms were protected by upper sleeve guards of lamellar armour, while the forearms were covered with mail. Lamellar greaves were worn on the lower legs and the head was protected by a mail coif and helmet.

The horses of the ancient cataphracts had been fully encased in scale armour, but such was the prohibitive cost of armour protection that the mounts of Mahmud's heavy horsemen wore lamellar armour on their chest, necks and heads only. But like their ancient predecessors, the heavy horsemen were equipped with long lances, though unlike Parthian cataphracts they carried two swords: one single edged and slightly curved called a *paramerion*, and another straight, double-bladed weapon called a *spathion*. But the favourite close-quarter weapons of the heavy horsemen were the *vardoukia* – maces – with either globular or sharp-cornered heads and a combination of iron and wooden shafts. Each rider had two holsters on either side of the pommel to accommodate a number of maces.

Izzeddin may have disliked the heavy horsemen for their brightly coloured cloaks or the heretical designs painted on their teardrop-shaped shields, called *skoutaria* and strapped to their shoulders to allow them to freely use both hands. But what really incensed him was that they were all Christian.

At the height of its power, the emperor in Constantinople ruled over an empire made up of military districts called *themata* – themes – containing farmlands owned by families who provided military service in exchange for the right to live on the land. Over time, wealthy landowners provided the imperial army not only with soldiers, but also resources and money. The imperial treasury in turn paid the estate owners for their time in service. But a succession of inept emperors, combined with powerful external threats, resulted in the relationship being strictly one-way. The imperial army made increasing demands on wealthy landowners in the provinces, but provided little in return, while the imperial treasury's taxes sapped the resources and morale of the wealthy of the *themata*, especially as the money was used to preserve a decadent court. The wealthy of the military districts were ripe for the plucking.

Karesi Bey was an accomplished military leader, but his real talent was diplomacy. During his war of expansion against the *themata*, he won more victories off the battlefield than on it. He saw that the Christian landowners had been abandoned by their emperor, so rather than fight them he offered them peace, a respect for their property rights and religious freedom, in exchange for their services, which he would pay for. They accepted and Karesi Bey doubled the territory he controlled overnight.

'How do you know a Christian force is riding for Artake?' said Izzeddin brusquely.

'I have my spies,' replied Mahmud.

Izzeddin curled at lip at him. 'Christian spies? Only a fool trusts a *kafir.*'

'If you wish to refuse the *emir*'s offer of reinforcements,' said Mahmud, fast losing patience with the fanatic, 'then I will continue on with my journey.'

'I have no wish to ignore the *emir*'s generosity,' sniffed Izzeddin.

'Excellent,' smiled Mahmud, 'I am authorised to allocate two thousand horsemen to your army. The *emir* has ordered me to stress to you that he desires the city of Artake to be taken intact, and the many farms on the peninsula not to be despoiled. After all, is it not written that Allah is the most merciful of the merciful?'

Izzeddin bristled at this. Just as he and his followers had 'cleansed' Bergama so it was fit to be the Islamic capital of the Karesi Emirate, so was he determined to eradicate the last Christian stronghold on the coast of the Sea of Marmara by sending a strong message to the chief *kafir* sitting on his throne in Constantinople. And that message would be written in Christian blood.

'I am merely the instrument of Allah,' said Izzeddin softly. 'But if the Christians submit to His will, then I will extend His mercy to them.'

Mahmud did not believe him but it made no difference. He had instructed the commander of the horsemen he would leave with the holy man that his task was not to support the depredations of his fanatics, but to ensure the city of Artake and the prosperous farms on the peninsula of the same name passed seamlessly to the control of his *emir*.

'Then I will take my leave,' said Mahmud. 'May God go with you.'

He tugged on his reins to turn his horse before Izzeddin had chance to reply, both men glad and relieved to be away from each other's company.

'You dare quote the holy word to me, apostate?' spat the holy man. 'Those who malign Allah will be seized wherever found and slain with a fierce slaughter. So it is written; so let it be done.'

*****

148

It was a beautiful day, the blue sky dotted with white puffy clouds, the sun warming the earth and the sea either side of the isthmus a dazzling sparkling blue. A gentle breeze took the sting out of the rising temperature and also brought the sound of drums to the ears of four thousand Almogavars waiting behind the sections of wall that had once presented a formidable barrier to any hostile force intent on conquering the Artake Peninsula.

How Luca wanted to peer around the end of the stretch of crumbling wall he and the other Almogavars were hidden behind. But Sancho Rey had issued strict instructions that no one was to show their face to the enemy until the trap had been sprung.

Michael Cosses was a competent commander and he had scouts out far and wide to warn him of the assault he knew would come, just as surely as the sun rose each day. Sure enough, they returned with news that a great army was approaching the peninsula, a force comprising thousands of religious warriors armed only with a shield and spear, plus thousands of others, including women and children, who followed behind, hoping to share in the spoils that would come their way when the peninsula and city of Artake fell to the warriors of Allah.

The Catalans and Romans had heard the enemy before they had seen them, the low rumble of hundreds of drums being carried on the wind to the wall and beyond. So often that sound had signalled the defeat of the emperor's army and the remorseless, seemingly unstoppable advance of Islam. Michael Cosses hoped it would be different today.

He sat on his horse a few hundred paces back from the wall, the red and yellow banner of the emperor fluttering behind him, and behind it his two hundred horsemen, all immaculately attired in

149

helmets, mail hauberks and lamellar cuirasses. The points of their lances glinted in the early morning sun and their horses scuffed the ground with their hooves and snorted, restless with anticipation at the approach of the coming fury.

Around a hundred paces from the wall were his foot soldiers, drawn up in three blocks so they could more easily about-face and retreat through the three gaps in the wall they were ostensibly defending. Whether the enemy would fall for the ruse he did not know, but he did know that if the wall itself appeared to be undefended, the horse archers that always accompanied Muslim armies would not shoot volleys at it. His palms were sweaty and his tunic was already soaked with perspiration. He had a lot to worry about, not least being entrusted with the defence of the peninsula. If the Muslims seized it, they would not only deprive Constantinople of wine, olives, olive oil and timber, any ships they based at Artake would be able to threaten the Hellespont, the narrow strait that connected the Aegean with the Sea of Marmara. Much rested on the coming clash.

Luca was not nervous but impatient, eager to get to grips with the enemy.

'Are they going to bang those drums all day?' he said to Jordi, who was equally eager to start killing heathens.

'We should attack them rather than wait behind this wall,' he complained.

'Be quiet, both of you,' commanded his father. 'Obey your orders and stay silent.'

The Almogavar leader was unusually nervous, feeling constrained by the tactics agreed upon before he and his men had moved into position before dawn. The plan had made sense when it

150

had been an abstract notion. Now it was reality he was not so sure. The wall was half a mile in extent, with three substantial gaps along that distance. This created four separate sections of dilapidated wall from coast to coast, behind which waited four groups of Almogavars, each numbering a thousand and led by Angel, Marc, Hector and Sancho, respectively. The latter's force was adjacent to the sea at the western end of the wall, next to the ruins of Cyzicus.

The drumming increased in intensity as the enemy, which none of the Almogavars could see, flooded the plain in front of the isthmus. They carried hundreds of red flags and began chanting as they neared the remains of the wall. Unarmed religious leaders stood in front of the horde and incited their followers to wash the earth with the blood of unbelievers, promising that any who fell this day would be guaranteed a place in paradise, and any who faltered would be damned for all eternity.

The majority of the *ghazi* warriors of Izzeddin Arslan had no armour or headdress, aside from a few white turbans. They carried a small round wooden shield for protection and were armed with a spear. Many were barefoot. The élite *ghazi* soldiers, held back as a reserve, were a different proposition. Well trained and led, every soldier was equipped with a helmet, mail armour and a large oblong wooden shield faced with thick hide. Their primary weapon was a spear, but each soldier was also equipped with a sword and dagger. They also wore stout leather boots for making marching long distances on foot easier. Izzeddin himself stood in front of the phalanx of these troops, coolly observing the infidel army.

His commanders had reported that the wall was essentially a ruin, three large gaps in its length inviting attack. He had been surprised when the enemy had left those gaps to stand in front of the

151

wall in three bodies, each numbering no more than a few hundred. The commander of the *emir*'s horse archers had ridden forward to offer the services of his men to 'soften up' the enemy before the attack was launched. He had declined the offer, having no wish to taint Allah's victory with soldiers who consorted with *kafir* horsemen. So instead of the horse archers forcing the Romans to cower beneath their shields with their volleys, they were reduced to being bystanders in the coming battle.

Whipped into a frenzy by their religious leaders, the armed mob that was the majority of Izzeddin Arslan's army suddenly surged forward, sprinting across the flat, barren ground towards the three Roman formations, which abruptly about-faced, each one heading for a gap in the wall.

The holy warriors raised a great cry as they beheld the infidels melting away before their eyes, spurred on by the exhortations of their holy men. They had been promised an easy victory and it had come about before their very eyes. The enemy had run away from them without even the semblance of a fight. They would soon be feasting in Artake and living on the lush, fertile peninsula, with a host of *kafir* slaves to do their bidding.

They poured past the Almogavars, oblivious to the hundreds of Catalans waiting patiently with javelins clutched in their hands. The warriors only saw the Roman foot soldiers ahead of them, who had stopped and turned to form three tightly packed formations once more, between them horsemen with lances levelled.

'Now!' screamed Sancho.

They had practised for days, performing the drill over and over so when the whistles sounded they would react instinctively, ignoring the prospect of hundreds of *ghazis* flooding through the gaps in the wall to instead focus on what they did best.

Luca and Jordi were smiling as they hurled their javelins at the torrent of enemy warriors rushing past them. Even if they had been blindfolded they could not miss. One, two, three javelins left Luca's hand, each one striking a target, just a trio of missiles among hundreds thrown at the Muslim horde, scything down *ghazis* and felling dozens more as the living tripped over the dead.

Luca felt a thrill such as he had never experienced before as he beheld a seething mass of enemy soldiers within spitting distance, all now slowed by the blizzard of javelins directed at them, those following also moving slowly as they were funnelled through the gaps in the wall.

'Into them,' screamed Sancho, racing forward with spear gripped in both hands. His son and Luca were a split-second behind, stabbing the points of their own spears into enemy bodies.

It was easy at first – jab, pull back, jab, pull back.

Ghazis, surprised to be attacked from the flanks by javelins, were even more startled when fierce spearmen attacked them, Sancho's men from the left, Hector's from the right, to seal the gap nearest to the ruins of Cyzicus.

Luca stabbed a bare-headed warrior in the side of the face, the sharp spear point shattering his jawbone, causing him to crumble in a heap. He stepped over a dead body impaled on a javelin to attack a spearman who had halted and turned to face him, only to be knocked over by another warrior barging forward, who Luca ran through the belly with his spear. He and Jordi worked as a team, one stabbing before pulling back, the other thrusting his spear forward, and vice-versa. They and Sancho were at the tip of the spear and that spear

153

had one purpose – drive forward to seal the gap. On the other side of the gap Hector and his men would be doing the same, as would the Almogavars of the other captains trying to seal the other gaps.

Luca did not know if Hector and his men were triumphing, but he had faith that just as he was grinding forward against the wall of enemy flesh in front of him, so would his mentor and his men be being doing the same.

A *ghazi* swung left to battle him, but too slow, exposing his torso to Luca who thrust his spear into his belly. He yanked it back but the *ghazi* had gripped the shaft with his left hand, having dropped his shield. He looked Luca directly in the eye, his own eyes wild with fury, not pain. Luca screamed and drove the shaft forward with all his might, pushing it deeper into the warrior's body. But the *ghazi* remained standing, thrusting his own spear forward to cut Luca's left arm. Jordi on his friend's right side finished off a *ghazi*, pivoted left and drove his spear point straight through the neck of Luca's opponent, who collapsed to the ground.

Luca stepped over him and the Almogavars forged on, step by step, the hundred paces that made up the gap suddenly turning into the widest chasm on God's earth. He felt no pain in his left arm, just energy pumping through his body to keep his reflexes sharp.

The *ghazi* flood had abated now, the Almogavars having staunched the flow like tourniquets applied to a gaping wound. But there were still hundreds, if not thousands, of enemy warriors on the landward side of the wall, pressing forward to follow their comrades into the gaps. Like human saws, Luca and Jordi worked their spears in unison, jabbing the points at targets lightning-fast, one striking a shield, the other going over or under the obstacle to find flesh. Either side of them Sancho and other Almogavars were doing likewise, the

154

ghazis having no answer to the speed and accuracy of the spear thrusts. And then Luca shouted in triumph as a *ghazi* went down and the black eyes of Hector were staring back at him.

'Seal the gap, seal the gap,' pleaded Sancho, wheeling right to block the flow of enemy warriors trying to infiltrate through the wall. Luca and Jordi did likewise, more and more Almogavars filling in behind them to thicken the Catalan barrier of human flesh that was slowly plugging the gap.

'Good to see you,' said Hector, stabbing his spear at an olive-skinned face, the point glancing off the warrior's cheek.

'And you,' smiled Luca.

'Duck,' shouted someone behind them.

They did so. Luca saw a sequence of brown blurs and saw javelins slam into enemy warriors only feet from him. A second and third volley reaped a cruel harvest erecting a wall of dead and dying in front of him and the others.

'Ground spears, ground spears.'

The order was relayed up and down the line. Luca placed the end of his spear shaft against his withdrawn right foot, his left leg forward, his spear facing the enemy at an angle of forty-five degrees. The men in the second rank behind stood holding their spears horizontally, Almogavars trying to find their footing among the enemy dead that littered the ground around them. Behind the second rank were two other ranks ready to hurl javelins at the enemy should they try to breach the wall of spears that now filled the gap.

That now filled all three gaps in the wall.

The first phase of the battle was over.

Only disciplined troops could have achieved what the Almogavars did that day: half attacking the flanks of the enemy flooding through the gaps to sever the Islamic torrent, then sealing the gaps, and the other half forming a line facing away from the rear of the wall.

'Now is the time, count,' said Grand Duke Roger as a great mass of *ghazis*, now disorganised, leaderless and uncertain what to do, faced Michael Cosses' foot soldiers and horsemen.

The count spun in the saddle and gave the order, a pair of trumpeters sounding their instruments to signal the charge. Two hundred horsemen levelled their lances and the Roman foot soldiers suddenly broke formation and spread into lines, levelling their spears preparatory to charging into the enemy mass.

The dreadful realisation they were surrounded soon began to dawn on the *ghazis* trapped behind the wall, whose resistance suddenly collapsed. Well-trained soldiers could perhaps have retraced their steps to force a way through the gaps they had attacked through, especially as thousands of their kinsmen remained on the other side of the wall. All that separated them from salvation were two thin lines of Almogavars. But all the *ghazis* saw were well-armed horsemen and foot soldiers about to cut them down, while behind them was an unbroken wall of spears. Their faith suddenly deserted them and they began to throw down their meagre weapons and submit to the mercy of the Romans.

The Count of Opsikion held up a hand. Roger beside him pulled up his horse and the lancers likewise reined in their mounts as trumpeters sounded recall. The count's foot soldiers also shuffled to a halt and silence descended on the battlefield.

'I don't hear anything,' said Jordi, tapping an ear to ensure his hearing had not failed.

'Me neither,' agreed Luca, focusing on the stationary mass of *ghazi* warriors to their front, who appeared to be doing nothing aside from standing and waiting. But for what?

The frenzied stabbing and thrusting of only minutes before had given way to an unnerving calm and quiet, interrupted only by the pitiful groans of wounded men unable to move, their lifeblood seeping into the earth, others calling out for their mothers before they lapsed into unconsciousness and death took them. For the first time in the battle, Luca was nervous.

'Why don't they attack?' he uttered to no one in particular.

'Easy,' said Hector beside him. 'They will use their horse archers to soften us up before launching another attack. Don't forget to use your shield for cover when it starts raining arrows.'

Like the others, Luca's shield was strapped to his back. But it suddenly seemed very small to hide beneath. Hector's words did nothing to soothe his trepidation.

*****

'Holy one, now is the time to shower them with arrows.'

Izzeddin Arslan did not look up at the commander of horse archers in his blue felt robe and white turban, instead focusing on the lines of bristling spears now filling the gaps in the ancient wall, the gaps he had sent thousands through to their deaths. Allah was obviously displeased with him. He had allowed his army to be polluted by the *kafir* riders that accompanied Mahmud of Caesarea, or perhaps it was not yet time for the peninsula to fall to the righteous.

'Holy one,' pressed the horse archer.

'Be silent!' hissed Izzeddin.

157

He turned his gaze away from infidel spears to catch the eye of the commander of his bodyguard, waving him forward. The mail-clad officer left his phalanx of élite foot soldiers to stride across to Izzeddin, snapping to attention before the holy man.

'Give the order to withdraw,' said Izzeddin. 'We will march back to Bergama.'

The officer saluted, turned on his heels and paced back to his men, issuing orders to his subordinates who left the ranks to convey the holy man's desire to the hundreds of élite *ghazis* who waited under the afternoon sun.

The commander of horse archers was incredulous.

'You are conceding the field to the infidels, holy one?'

Izzeddin took one last look at the Almogavars defending the wall, sighed and began pacing away from the Artake Peninsula.

'All is as God wills it.'

Chapter 8

The aftermath of battle is never a pretty sight, and the clash at the wall of Cyzicus was no different. The few Almogavar wounded were taken to Artake to receive treatment; the Muslim injured were killed, either strangled or had their throats slit depending on the predilection of those ordered to put them out of their misery.

Grand Duke Roger and Count Cosses were delighted, though for different reasons. For the commander of the Catalan Company, the capture of five thousand prisoners meant a tidy profit when they were shipped to Constantinople to be sold in the slave market. For the Count of Opsikion, it was the first taste of victory against the Turks in a long time, and one to savour. For years he had been steadily pushed back towards the sea and had expected the battle for the Artake Peninsula to be his last, after which his bones would lie in a forgotten grave and Karesi Bey would complete his conquest of his theme. But in the space of a morning everything had changed. Now he could dare to envisage reclaiming the emperor's territories, with the assistance of the strange, fierce Almogavars.

'Make sure they are all disarmed,' Sancho called to his son and Luca, who were among the guards detailed to keep a close eye on the captives as they dumped their weapons in carts, which would take the spears, swords and daggers to Artake.

Translators had been found among Michael Cosses' men to instruct the captives to pick up their spears and other weapons and form orderly queues to deposit them in the carts. It was now late afternoon and Luca felt tired, hungry and thirsty as he watched a sullen line of captives shuffle with heads down towards one of the carts. Count Michael had sent riders to the city to fetch wagons, together with food and wine to celebrate the great victory. Luca uncorked his water bottle and took a sip of the tepid liquid, his eyes wandering over the bedraggled prisoners, soon to be slaves.

'Keep your eyes peeled,' said Sancho behind him, marching up and down the line to stress to his men they should remain vigilant.

'They look beaten,' said Luca.

'Oh, they are beaten. But they are Muslims and they would jump at the chance to kill a Christian.'

'Even if it meant their own death?'

'*Especially* if it meant their own death. They seek a courageous death as a way to enter paradise. They are dangerous fanatics. You did well today.'

He felt his chest swell with pride and any fatigue suddenly left him. He turned to face the broad-shouldered Catalan.

'Thank you, lord.'

The hard visage of the Almogavar showed no emotion.

'We might make an Almogavar of you yet. Eyes front.'

Sancho strode away, leaving Luca to observe the captives. They certainly did not look like fanatics in their shoddy attire, unkempt beards and hair and grimy faces. He wondered if they would be washed and issued with new clothes before being paraded in the slave market.

He went to take another swig from his water bottle but stopped, aware of a pair of dark brown eyes on him. Eyes belonging to an alluring beauty who held out a hand in a pleading fashion. She was dirty, dressed in baggy leggings and tunic and carried a spear. Her thick black hair tumbled to her shoulders and her face was smeared with dirt. She may have looked like a poor wretch but there was still a sensual attraction about her. Luca blushed. She held his eyes and he offered her his water bottle.

She held his gaze as she stopped and raised the water bottle to her full lips, taking gentle sips. Another captive went to grab the container but Luca whipped out the sword at his hip and held the point to the man's throat. Jordi rushed forward to push the man back, likewise pulling his sword and looking menacingly at the man, who slunk away.

The woman handed him back the water bottle.

'Tesekkür ederim,' she said.

Luca had no idea what she was saying but he beamed at her anyway, her eyes meeting his for a final time before she shuffled away. Jordi nudged him in the ribs.

'She should fetch a good sum in the slave market.'

A wave of sadness washed over Luca at the prospect of such a beauty being reduced to a slave, though his spirits were lifted when food and wine began to arrive from Artake. Count Cosses ensured the Almogavars were feasted well that night, fish caught that morning being cooked over campfires and washed down by wine from casks arranged in a long line, along with carts filled with bread and cheese. Luca and Jordi basked in the aftermath of victory, making ridiculous toasts that appeared profound and unbreakable as an excess of wine took hold. Luca gave no thought to the thousands of captives who were tethered together to ensure none escaped, though Grand Duke Roger ensured they were issued with food and water to ensure none expired before they were loaded on his ships in Artake harbour, which would take them to Constantinople.

Having fallen into slumber after a bout of eating and drinking, Luca was in a subdued mood in the morning, as were the other Almogavars. Count Michael had sent mounted patrols beyond the wall to warn of the return of the Turkish army. But they had returned

161

with news that the enemy had seemingly vanished into thin air. He had posted guards on the ruins of the wall as a precaution, allowing the Almogavars to celebrate their victory.

Luca woke with a headache, Sancho kicking his side.

'Get up. Roll call in five minutes.'

He washed his face and retrieved his spear from a nearby stand of weapons, a bleary-eyed Jordi doing likewise.

'My guts feel like they are about to drop from my arse,' he complained.

Luca laughed, the pair of them walking slowly to where the Almogavars were forming up.

'Move!' shouted Sancho, prompting everyone to pick up the pace and fall into line. Within minutes a hollow square of Almogavars had been formed. Facing inwards, each of the four captains — Sancho, Hector, Marc and Angel — stood in front of each side of the square. Grand Duke Roger strode into the square to address the company.

'Yesterday, we won a great victory over Islam.'

The Almogavars rapped the end of their spear shafts on the ground in recognition. The grand duke raised a hand. He looked remarkably fresh and clean, his clothes immaculate, his hair and beard well groomed. No doubt, his feast the evening before with Count Michael and sundry priests and dignitaries had been a more organised and sober affair compared to the Almogavar festivities.

'When our horsemen arrive,' continued the grand duke, 'we will leave Artake to take the fight to the enemy. Just as we achieved victory in Sicily, so shall we triumph in Anatolia against the enemies of God.'

The Almogavars raised their spears and cheered long and hard. They had tasted nothing but victory since their great victory over the French during the Sicilian war, and every one of them, including Luca, believed they could do the same in the service of Constantinople's emperor. Indeed, in Sicily they had been fighting Christians. How easier would their victory be against inferior infidels?

After being told the day was theirs to enjoy and being dismissed, Luca wandered over to where the prisoners were being organised for the short walk to Artake where they would be loaded on ships to take them to Constantinople. The overseers were Count Michael's foot soldiers who had taken no part in the battle the day before, aside from beating a hasty retreat to the wall to entice the enemy to launch an attack. Hundreds were pushing and shoving the hapless prisoners, using their spear shafts to beat individuals for no apparent reason. Lines of despondent captives, wrists bound, were already trudging away from the wall, heading for the city of Artake.

One figure suddenly ran from one of the lines, darting between two guards and heading straight for him. He remembered Sancho's words, plucked a javelin from the quiver on his back and took aim. And lowered the weapon when he realised it was the black-haired beauty he had given his water bottle to the day before. She threw herself at his feet and began babbling incoherently.

'Kurta beni, usta.'

She repeated the phrase over and over again, Luca not understanding what she was saying but immensely pleased she had run to him. Moments later the two guards she had darted between arrived, both looking like they were about to commit murder. Luca moved quickly to place himself between the young woman and them. They were well armed with spears and swords, and protected by shields, helmets and mail armour. One pointed at the woman and spoke something in Greek. Which Luca did not understand. He repeated the words, this time more loudly and forcefully.

'Kurta beni, usta.'

He heard the words behind him and gripped his javelin, ready to throw it at the throat of the soldier gesticulating and now shouting. He reckoned he could kill him and injure the second at least before they could respond.

'What's going on here?'

He heard Hector's voice and smiled at the soldiers.

'Why are you aiding an escaped slave, Luca?'

His smile disappeared. One of the soldiers pointed his spear at Hector, which was foolhardy at best. The Almogavar stood beside Luca, the woman continuing to utter the same words.

'Can't you shut her up?' said Hector, pointing at the soldiers. 'You two, bugger off.'

The commotion had not gone unnoticed, and within minutes a mounted officer had arrived to investigate, as had Grand Duke Roger and Sancho Rey. The latter spoke to Hector to ward off any violence.

'These are our allies, Hector.'

The mounted officer spoke to Roger in Greek, who conveyed his wishes.

'The woman is under Count Michael's jurisdiction.'

Luca gave him a blank look, not knowing what the word meant.

'It means she is his property, at least until she and the others are sold in Constantinople.'

'She is his property, lord?' asked Luca, wondering when a captive actually became a slave.

164

'Yes, now kindly release her to these men.'

'Do as the grand duke commands,' snapped Sancho.

Luca glanced at the sultry beauty, now clutching his ankles and still repeating the three-word phrase. A thought flashed through his mind.

'I would like to buy her, lord?'

Roger frowned at him but Sancho roared with laughter.

'What with?'

But they had forgotten that the emperor himself had rewarded Luca and Jordi for saving his sister. He unfastened the pouch attached to his belt and opened it.

'I have money, lord.'

The grand duke said a few words to the officer, who barked a command to the two soldiers, who returned to their duties with the other slaves. Grand Duke Roger jumped down from his horse and took Jordi's pouch of money, his eyes widening with surprise.

'A princely sum for the life of a princess. God smiles on you, Black Sheep.'

He pulled a couple of coins from the pouch and handed them to the officer, who raised a hand in salute and wheeled his horse to the right before cantering back to the lines of slaves.

Roger looked at Luca. 'Do you know how much money is in this pouch, Black Sheep?'

'No, lord.'

'Enough to buy a hundred slaves,' said Roger, who took a couple for himself. 'As the slaves were going to be sold on my behalf, I am just cutting out the middleman. You understand?'

Luca did not. 'Yes, lord.'

'Well, she is yours now, Black Sheep.'

165

With that he walked over to his horse and regained his saddle, riding away from Luca, a bemused Hector and a frowning Sancho. Hector slapped Luca on the back.

'The spoils of war. I assume you will now rape her until she begs for mercy.'

Luca was shocked. 'No, not at all, I would never.'

'Then what are you going to do with her?'

'She will have to be fed out of your rations,' said Sancho coolly. 'What is she babbling?'

Luca lifted the woman up and pulled his sword from its sheath. She squealed and dropped to her knees, obviously begging him not to kill her.

'Ha, she thinks you are going to kill her,' laughed Hector.

Luca slipped the sword back in its sheath and tried to calm the woman. Sancho groaned and stormed off, washing his hands of the affair. As he departed, however, the officer on horseback returned, pointing at the woman Luca had just purchased.

'She was saying "save me, master",' he told Luca, 'which you appear to have done.'

'Can you ask her what her name is, sir?' requested Luca.

The man spoke to the woman, who was now more composed, having worked out she was not going to be killed, at least not immediately.

'Her name is Ayna,' the officer informed him.

'One more thing, sir,' said Luca, 'can you tell her I am going to draw my sword to cut the cord around her wrist.'

The officer did so. Ayna held out her arms, Luca unsheathed his sword and cut the cord.

The officer pointed to beyond the wall.

'If I could offer some advice, young warrior. Her people are just a short distance away and you have a pouch full of money. If I were you, I would watch her closely, lest she slits your throat and takes herself off with your money.'

'Sound advice,' agreed Hector.

But Luca would have none of it and Ayna showed nothing but gratitude for having been saved from being shipped to Constantinople, even if she was a still a slave in Artake. But life as a slave did not initially appear that onerous. The Almogavar women and children lived in and around the city of Artake, their lodgings provided for free by a grateful Count Michael and the city authorities, who knew the Catalan Company would soon be leaving the peninsula to wage war against the Muslims. Until that day arrived, Luca and the others swapped their tents for stone billets. He had been given a small crofter's hovel in the hills above Artake, a simple one-room stone building with a dilapidated tile roof.

As the days grew warmer life became more idyllic. Luca spent his days tramping through the hills of the peninsula, practising weapon drills and Almogavar tactics, and enjoying the hospitality of a grateful population. Ayna was left to her own devices during the day, and Luca fully expected her to abscond at the first opportunity. But she did not, instead attending to their hovel to make it more liveable. They both fixed the roof and cleared the brambles from around the building, Jordi, who much to his disgust was lodged with his parents in Artake itself, lending a hand whenever he could. Because Sancho Rey was the head of the Almogavar council, he and his family were given a large house fronting the harbour to live in.

Luca and Jordi were a rarity among the Almogavars as they alone had money to spend, the wages of the Almogavars being used up at an alarming rate to purchase food and supplies so as not to alienate the citizens of Artake. Grand Duke Roger, resident in a mansion in the city with his young wife, eagerly waited for the profits of the sale of the slaves that had been shipped to Constantinople. His concern turned into alarm when fifteen hundred Almogavar horsemen and a thousand Alan riders rode into the Artake Peninsula.

Corberan's horsemen only had a small pool of remounts, having been supplied with horseflesh by a parsimonious royal treasury in Constantinople, but each Alan horseman had up to five remounts to ensure he was always riding a fresh horse. Led by a tall, slender individual named Arabates, the Alans wore a variety of different coloured felt robes over their long-sleeved linen shirts. Their baggy leggings, leather boots and tall, broad-brimmed hats gave them an exotic appearance, that and their unruly behaviour. Their main armament was a composite bow, identical to the bows used hundreds of years before by the horsemen of the steppes. Each rider also carried a sabre and some were equipped with a spear and small round shield. The arrival of the horsemen placed an intolerable strain on the finances of the Catalan Company, resulting in a flurry of letters from Grand Duke Roger to the imperial court.

*****

Co-Emperor Michael descended the steps leading to the marble quay decorated with lions, Varangian Guards standing like statues at regular intervals, immaculate in burnished helmets and scarlet cloaks. At the bottom of the steps stood the portly figure of Treasurer Timothy, who bowed his head at the emperor's son. Moored to wooden posts topped with gold leaf was the royal barge, its oarsmen ready at their stations and the captain standing beside the gangplank. Since the attempt on Princess Maria's life, Michael had taken to using the barge if he ventured out of the Blachernae Palace into the city. Besides, being rowed to Saint Sophia or other destinations was far more preferable to enduring the close proximity of the common folk, even if they pressed round his entourage to cheer and wave. They also held up their infants to him, which he found abhorrent, the babies invariably bawling their heads off and emitting ear-splitting wails. No, travel by imperial barge was far more enjoyable.

'A fine day, lord treasurer,' he said to Timothy, stepping on the gangplank. 'Will you join me on the voyage to Saint Sophia's?'

Timothy followed Michael on to the vessel and into the coach at the rear of the barge, treading on a soft red carpet inlaid with yellow crosses and the royal cypher. The eighteen rowers, all attired in red and gold imperial livery, stood to attention as the pair entered the coach and seated themselves on plush couches, slaves waiting to serve them refreshments. Varangians stepped on to the barge and took up position at the entrance to the coach.

The captain, a rosy cheeked individual with a thick beard, removed his hat and bowed his head.

'All is ready, highness.'

Michael took the silver cup on the tray offered to him by a slave, another filling it with wine. He nodded at the captain who walked to the rear of the coach, exited the door, closed it and took up position at the stern of the vessel, which was raised to give him a clear view of the bow of the vessel and the route the barge would be taking. He barked an order and the oarsmen took up position, two of the crew using long poles to push the barge away from the quay.

Michael took a sip of wine. 'The sale of the slaves has been completed?'

Timothy took a large gulp of wine. 'Yes, highness. I will send the profits to Grand Duke Roger immediately.'

'You will do no such thing,' said Michael tartly. 'All monies raised will be channelled to the emperor's army across the Bosporus, which faces the massed ranks of Osman Bey's army.'

Timothy drank more wine. 'Grand Duke Roger might take offence, highness, seeing it was his soldiers that captured the slaves.'

Michael waved a dismissive hand at him.

'Grand Duke Roger is a mercenary, apostate and low-ranking son of a German. My father, in his naïve innocence, saw fit to give him a high rank. But the Catalan Company has been hired to liberate the cities of Philadelphia and Magnesia and the town of Tire. Once it begins its campaign, it will be able to live off the land to provide it with supplies.'

'Forgive me, highness, but if the Catalan Company liberates the aforementioned cities and surrounding areas, but then plunders them, will it not impoverish the local populations beyond repair, thus making them more disposed to Muslim rule?'

Michael froze him with a hateful stare, causing the eunuch to squirm with discomfort.

'I am not here to elicit your views on the grand strategy of the empire. You will do as instructed. The slaves were taken on imperial territory and the imperial army will benefit.'

Timothy's double chin wobbled with trepidation. He had no desire to be thrown from the barge, which was now being rowed down the Golden Horn, especially as he could not swim.

'Yes, highness.'

Chapter 9

Having sailed to Artake, four thousand Almogavars stood ready to take ship back to Constantinople to save the city from a grave threat. Osman Bey was leading a huge army against the city and the emperor needed all the soldiers he could muster to save a thousand years of civilisation. Corberan of Navarre and the Alan commander Arabates rode north back to Constantinople with all haste to join with the forces of General George Mouzalon to give battle to the Turks on the eastern side of the Bosporus.

Each day Luca and the other Almogavars reported to the harbour where Grand Duke Roger's ships waited to ship them to Constantinople, and each day he returned to his home in the hills overlooking the city of Artake with Ayna in tow. Much to his frustration, nothing happened. Via Jordi he heard that Grand Duke Roger and his father received conflicting reports from Constantinople. Osman Bey had retreated. Osman Bey had never been leading an army towards Constantinople. Osman Bey was advancing south, intent on dealing with the Almogavars himself, which prompted the Catalan Company deploying to the wall once more. Osman Bey had fallen from his horse, had broken his leg and had died of an infection caused by the injury. A week, two weeks, a month passed and only one thing became certain: Osman Bey, wherever he was, was not marching on Constantinople, or indeed marching anywhere.

Summer came and went and the horsemen did not return. The emperor's general, having received twenty-five hundred mounted reinforcements, was eager for them to remain, and in truth Grand Duke Roger did not press for their return as autumn arrived. He knew that the campaigning season was drawing to a close and had no

171

wish to billet hundreds of horsemen and thousands of horses on the peninsula, where they would have to be fed and housed.

And then the rains arrived.

Ordinarily, the weather in Anatolia in autumn is pleasant, with mild temperatures and bright spells. Of course, the days became shorter and the land could be subjected to cloud bursts, but Luca's first autumn in the Roman Empire was extremely wet. Most days were overcast with a constant drizzle that found a way of infiltrating his cloak and clothing and soaking his woollen hat. On the daily route marches and weapons practise this was bearable enough, but he and the other Almogavars were forced to carry out the bane of soldiers everywhere: sentry duty.

The wind blew the rain in his face as he and Jordi walked up and down a section of the ruined wall they had defended in what seemed like a lifetime ago. Sharpened wooden stakes had been placed in the gaps in the wall to deter enemy horsemen infiltrating the stone ruins. Not that any enemy had shown their faces. The isthmus was slowly becoming waterlogged as the heavens opened on a daily basis, great pools of water forming on both sides of the wall, around them the dry earth turning into a glutinous mud that impeded all movement. The Almogavars responded by installing a labyrinth-like system of wooden walk boards behind the wall.

'My father wants me to marry,' said a disconsolate Jordi.

'Who to?' asked Luca, glancing at the mainland-side of the wall as they paced side-by-side along the dilapidated walkway.

'The Count of Opsikion's daughter,' he said.

'I did not know you had met her.'

172

Jordi shook his head. 'I haven't. She lives in Constantinople, in a great house the count has in the city. I do not wish to marry someone I have never set eyes on.'

It was dull and rainy, which suited Jordi's mood perfectly. Luca tried to cheer up his friend.

'Perhaps she does not want to marry *you*.'

'I pointed that out to my father, who told me the desires of those betrothed to each other is of secondary importance.'

'To what?'

'A marriage that will tie the Catalan Company more closely to the Roman Empire,' sighed Jordi. 'My father believes that we must look to put down roots in this region. He sees no future in being mercenaries forever.'

The rain increased in intensity, lashing the wall and the Almogavars patrolling it. The sea either side of the isthmus had become a brooding expanse of dark grey, the mainland shrouded in low cloud.

'At least you have Ayna to warm your bed,' said Jordi matter-of-factly.

Luca blushed but Jordi, his head down, did not see his friend's embarrassment. In the days after he had purchased Ayna, Hector had been bending his ear about the importance of putting slaves in their place, which meant raping female slaves to make them more 'pliant'. He did nothing of the sort, and the initial jubilation he had experienced when he had bought Ayna quickly gave way to embarrassment and shame. Shame that he had purchased another human being. This made him go out of his way to make her feel as comfortable as possible, in so far as it was possible bearing in mind she had become a human chattel.

173

At first, she slept on the floor at the bottom of his bed. Not that he slept much at all during the first few days of their stay in the crofter's hut, not least because when it rained the leaky roof meant they both got wet. But the disrepair proved something of a blessing because it meant they could both focus on something else rather than their enforced proximity. And to his relief, Ayna quickly realised she was not going to be raped or abused by her new master, who was of a similar age.

Luca came to appreciate two things about Ayna: her beauty and her intelligence. The former had been apparent on the day he had first encountered her, but her sharp mind manifested itself soon after. Realising that language between the two would be a problem, Luca was delighted to discover that she was a quick learner when it came to picking up Italian, which was just as well because he was both illiterate and only understood the rudiments of Spanish, despite living among Catalans. His understanding of Turkish was non-existent. But Ayna was soon conversing with him in pigeon Italian, facilitated by the visits of Carla, who was concerned for Luca's welfare, as well as his Muslim 'guest'. She disapproved of slavery, even for Saracens as she quaintly called all non-Christians, but was pleased to discover that Ayna was not being physically abused.

Carla was amiable and friendly, in sharp contrast to her husband, which is one reason they got on so well, and she and Ayna struck up a kind of friendship, spending much time together in between the chores that dominated women's lives. This resulted in Ayna becoming familiar with Catalan as well as Italian, her enquiring mind absorbing knowledge like a sponge. As the autumn faded, she was able to converse with Luca more fully, which they both found agreeable. But it was not Ayna's language ability that was uppermost

174

in Luca's mind. He requested an urgent meeting with the Almogavar Council to discuss the weather.

'The weather?'

Angel gave him a bemused look as he poured himself more wine. After the heroics at the wall, the mayor of Artake had given the Almogavar Council its own room in the grandiose city hall in which to hold meetings. The count, city authorities and population in general looked upon the Catalans favourably, not least because they were punctilious when it came to paying for food and supplies, notwithstanding the money from the purchase of the slaves had yet to arrive.

'It is going to be a very harsh winter, lord.'

'We are not your lords, Black Sheep,' said Marc, helping himself to a cake from the pastries piled high on the plate on the table he and the others sat round.

'Sir will do,' said Sancho sternly. 'And sit down, for pity's sake. You look like a hangman about to escort one of us to the scaffold.'

Luca smiled and pulled up a chair. Hector poured him some wine.

'Well, tell us about the coming winter.'

'I was a shepherd for many years,' began Luca, 'and I was taught to look for the signs that nature revealed so we could prepare. Now we should prepare.'

'For what?' asked a sceptical Marc.

Luca sipped at the wine. 'The geese and ducks have all left the land early to fly to warmer places. There is thick hair on the nape of the cows' necks, there were heavy fogs in the summer, and mice have been flocking into my home.'

175

'You should get your slave to kill them,' suggested Angel. 'How is she, by the way? Accommodating, I trust?'

Luca felt his cheeks burn with embarrassment, made worse when the others guffawed.

'She is well, thank you.'

'The mice were not alone,' continued Luca. 'We are loused out with spiders whose webs are larger than usual. Pigs are gathering sticks, bees are seeking sanctuary in their hives to prepare for the coming test, and squirrels are gathering nuts early as they too prepare. And I have seen frequent rings around the moon.

'Any one of these things would be a warning, but to see them all is an omen of an approaching great freeze.'

'What do you want us to do about it?' asked Sancho.

'Get the priests to say more prayers?' offered Marc.

'God helps those who help themselves,' said Hector.

'Grand Duke Roger should be told, sir,' Luca told Sancho, 'so his ships can be used to fetch more food. And Count Opsikion should also be warned so his people can prepare.'

'That is very presumptuous of you,' growled Sancho. 'I am sure the count has his own weather forecasters to warn him of approaching calamities.'

'You mean witches?' smiled Hector. 'We burn them.'

Marc raised a finger. 'Perhaps if we burnt a few witches, God would save us from a harsh winter.'

'I do not approve of the burning of young women,' said Angel solemnly.

'Only old and ugly ones,' retorted Hector, prompting belly laughs.

Luca was not laughing. 'As God is my judge, sirs, this is no laughing matter.'

Sancho pointed at him. 'Very well, Black Sheep, we will take your impudent advice, though on your head be it if your prophecy of doom fails to materialise.'

Winter arrived but there was nothing untoward about the temperature. The days became shorter, darker and people could see their breath when they exhaled. But it was no different from the previous winters as far as anyone in Artake could remember. Deprived of their horsemen, the Almogavars continued to train, patrol the wall and watch for any signs of an enemy that had seemingly vanished from the face of the earth. And still no money came from Constantinople.

Grand Duke Roger, a superstitious individual who looked for divine signs everywhere, took Luca's warning at face value and despatched his ships to Egypt to purchase grain. That land, once the granary for the Roman Empire, was now under the control of a fierce people called Mamelukes: Muslim slave warriors who overthrew their masters to rule in their stead. But as long as one had gold, they were quite prepared to trade with Christians. Roger convinced Count Michael and the city fathers of Artake to invest in his expedition to purchase food, the good faith he and the Catalan Company had built up working in his favour. The ships returned with holds filled with grain, which was stored in the city granaries. Christmas came and went, and in early January the city square was filled with citizens, soldiers and Almogavars to celebrate the Feast of Epiphany.

Luca knew she was an unbeliever, but he brought Ayna along nevertheless, the Muslim woman fascinated by the rich robes of the bishop and priests who officiated at the ceremony that celebrated the

177

Catholic rite celebrating Jesus being the Son of God. It focused on this revelation to the Three Wise Men, and happily it coincided with the Orthodox rite of Theophany, which was essentially the same celebration but focused primarily on the manifestation of Jesus' divinity at his baptism in the River Jordan. He noticed Ayna was shivering despite the thick, fur-lined cloak he had wrapped her in, and became aware his ears were numb. He thought nothing of it, until the next morning.

During the night, the temperature had plummeted and over the subsequent days continued to drop. A keen easterly wind brought snow, light flurries at first but then an unending stream of large white flakes falling day and night that lasted for days. And when the snow stopped falling a merciless iron frost gripped the land. All training and weapons drills ceased. The wall was abandoned and Grand Duke Roger issued just one order to the Catalan Company and its dependents: stay alive.

Wrapped in furs, Luca and Ayna had already stockpiled firewood and insulated their hut by packing straw bales around the outside. A fire was kept burning at all times, which required access to the woodshed a short distance from the hut's entrance. So, every day any snowfall between the hut and the shed was cleared and firewood used up during the evening replaced. Even so, as the great freeze continued, the interior of the hut was never warm.

The whole land was enveloped by silence. Game lay down in the fields and died and small birds quickly succumbed to the weather. Fish froze in the rivers and even at the edge of the sea, which also froze. All tracks and roads became impassable on account of being blocked by snow and ice, which meant it was impossible to transport food to villages on the peninsula. Fruit, nut and olive trees died, the

178

winter wheat crop was destroyed, and when the churches tried to raise the spirits of the despondent and freezing citizens of Artake by ringing church bells, they fractured due to the extreme cold.

'I'm cold.'

When she had first arrived, Ayna had slept on the mud floor, but that did not last for long. After a while she slept in the single bed. Luca slept on the floor, on the wooden boards he had placed to cover the frozen dirt, with straw beneath the boards for insulation.

'I'm cold as well,' he complained, the interior of the hut cast in a yellow light from the flickering flames of the fire.

'Then come here for warmth.'

His teeth had been chattering and his fingers had gone numb, but her invitation was like a fire being ignited in his belly. He needed no second prompting, joining her under the thick blanket and each wrapping their arms around the other. They eagerly sought each other's mouths, their tongues becoming one like two snakes performing a mating ritual. Their hands worked like skilled tailors, deftly removing the other's garments until they were both naked. The outside world may have been dying a slow, freezing death, but their bed was like a hot cauldron of desire. Luca found her breasts, his manhood aching as it became a pillar of stone. She moaned with delight when his fingers found her inner thigh, slipping into her body with ease so aroused was she. She groaned with pleasure when she opened her legs to allow him to enter her, gasping as he experienced a sensation he had never tasted before.

Their lovemaking was both tender and raw, both of them young and energetic, eager to taste the delights of the other's body. They did not notice the passing of the hours as they locked their bodies together and writhed on top of the bed. For Luca, her olive-skinned body was a marvel to behold and he could not fulfil his appetite to caress and taste every inch of it. She likewise did things to his manhood that took his breath away, moaning loudly when she took him to a place of utter fulfilment. It was just as well they were not in close proximity to other huts as her moans and cries became louder and more piercing as the night wore on. They only interrupted their insatiable desire for each other to throw more tinder on the fire to ensure it did not go out, thereafter resuming their carnal appetites.

That winter, harsh as it was, was for Luca the most enjoyable he had ever experienced. Each day, he reported for duty in Artake, forming a party with Sancho, Jordi and two other Almogavars, which along with others, assisted the authorities in clearing paths of snow and ice and collecting frozen bodies. The ground resembled concrete so burying them was out of the question. So, they were stacked outside cemeteries until they could be interred.

'This cold is the worst I have ever experienced,' complained Jordi, grabbing the stiff legs of the corpse, Luca the shoulders.

'It will be worse in spring.'

They removed the body from the handcart and manhandled it to the stack of frozen dead piled against the cemetery wall. A priest wrapped in an enormous bearskin cloak was saying prayers as the stack grew higher.

'How so?' asked a shivering Jordi, his skin pinched by the cold.

'When the snows melt there will be floods, which will kill any seeds in the ground, which will result in a food shortage. Many who escape being frozen to death will die from starvation.'

'But not us,' grinned Jordi, 'not with the grain that the grand duke purchased in Egypt. How is Ayna?'

180

Luca gave him a mischievous grin. 'There are no words, my friend, no words at all.'

'You lucky bastard.'

They walked back to the cart and hoisted another corpse to the wall, this one very slight and fragile. It was an old lady, her expression one of peace and calm. Luca wondered where her family was; if she had one. Perhaps they too were dead. Ordinarily, such a thought would have depressed him. But such was his perpetual state of ecstasy he felt nothing. He had duties and he would carry them out. Jordi, on the other hand, was morose, made worse by the extreme weather conditions.

'I envy you, my friend. You have found a woman who makes you happy.'

They laid the old lady on the pile, stood back and bowed their heads. They did not know her but thought it was fitting a person who had lived to old age should be shown some respect.

'My father is determined to marry me to Count Michael's daughter,' complained Jordi.

'But not until after our campaign against the Muslims,' Luca reminded him, 'so you don't have to worry for a few months yet.'

'You mean take comfort like a condemned man who had been given a temporary reprieve?'

Luca said nothing.

'He is still executed in the end.'

Luca slapped him on the back. 'Perhaps the count's daughter is beautiful.'

Jordi sighed. 'And perhaps she is fat and ugly. Not like Ayna.'

He had already convinced himself that the count's daughter was a bad match, and because he had no idea what she looked like, the more he pondered the coming marriage, the more grotesque she became in his mind.

He suddenly turned to Luca. 'Ayna is Muslim. How does that affect things?'

Luca considered his question. He had given their religious differences little thought, and in truth questions of faith had not got in the way of him enjoying carnal delights with her. He believed in God and tried to live a good life, but he had never understood the Latin prayers of his local priest in Rometta and could not forget that the same priest had sanctioned his execution when he had been unjustly accused. Ayna might be a Muslim but she had a gorgeous body and they loved each other. That was enough for him.

'It doesn't,' he answered.

'Get back to work,' roared Sancho.

The very young and the very old died in droves, along with those outside the city in the more isolated parts of the peninsula who had failed to heed the warnings of a great freeze. The citizens of the city of Artake fared better, Count Michael convincing the rich to donate food from their personal granaries to alleviate the plight of the poor, an unpopular order that was supported by Artake's bishop, who realised the count and his soldiers were the only things that stood between the poor taking what they wanted for themselves. Luca was oblivious to the suffering of the population as he was supplied with food from the Almogavars' own warehouses in the city, had enough firewood to see out the freeze, and was only concerned with sharing a bed with Ayna in the evenings. Life was good and could only get better.

And then it got slightly warmer, the snows melted and the land flooded.

Because Luca's hut was in the hills immediately above Artake, it was immune from the violent torrents of water flowing downhill. Despite the thaw, the ground was still frozen, which meant melting snow or rain could not seep into the earth but rather ran off the surface into lakes, streams and rivers. Small streams, previously ice bound, became impassable torrents. Normally livestock would be at risk from floodwaters, but as they had already died of exposure during the great freeze, it was one less thing for farmers to worry about. The isthmus became a waterlogged marsh, cutting off the mainland from the peninsula, which meant no enemy raiders would be able to cross it.

The sea around the peninsula was no longer frozen, which meant Grand Duke Roger's ships and those of Count Michael could once again set sail for Egypt to purchase grain to feed the Almogavars and the population of Artake. And fishing boats once again dotted the sea around the peninsula. Ships arrived from Constantinople to report the city had also been snowbound, though had escaped relatively unscathed.

Luca grinned at Ayna and rubbed his hands. The pair of sea bass cooking on a grill over the fire looked mouth-watering. Caught that morning, it was the first fish they had eaten since before Christmas.

'Luca, Luca, are you there?'

He heard Jordi's voice and left his love to walk outside, to find his friend in an agitated state. Utter relief was etched on Jordi's face. He grabbed Luca's arms.

'She's dead, praise be.'

'Who?'

183

'The count's daughter. She succumbed to the cold in Constantinople a month ago.'

Jordi hugged his friend. 'I am saved.'

Luca laughed. 'Come inside and share our meal. We must celebrate your stroke of luck.'

Jordi slapped him on the back and entered the hut. Luca wondered if the count had more than one daughter.

Chapter 10

'What are you going to do about Ayna?'

Carla's question surprised him. Her face was still attractive but it needed filling out. Wholesome food would do that, but the hard winter and the subsequent food shortages had obviously taken their toll on her body. And not only hers. All the Almogavars had grown leaner, even more gaunt, during the winter, but at least the majority had survived. Now it was April, the sun was shining, the land was no longer flooded and life was at last returning to Anatolia.

He had finished his training for the day and had visited the Almogavar bakery to pick up his issue of bread, freshly baked that morning. He was well known in the city now, not only for the fame resulting in saving Princess Maria's life, but also for his part in convincing Grand Duke Roger and Count Michael to purchase Egyptian grain, or so the rumour had it. Whatever the truth, the Black Sheep was a welcome sight for many citizens of Artake, who stopped and thanked him when he passed them by. He had paid a courtesy visit to Carla on account of not having seen her in an age. She, her husband and son lived in a spacious two-storey house near the mansion of Count Michael, who had allocated soldiers to stand sentry outside the building. The property, owned by the church, was lavishly furnished with tapestries, religious icons and sumptuous furnishings. Carla looked totally out of place amid such grandeur.

Luca, loaf tucked under his arm, accepted her offer of wine served to him in a silver chalice. He raised it to the wife of his commander.

'Your health, lady.'

'And Ayna?' she probed. 'Is she still your slave?'

He looked horrified. 'No, lady.'

'As I suspected. Your lover, then?'

He suppressed a smile and looked away from her, embarrassed.

'Then you must marry her.'

He nearly choked on his wine. 'Marry her?'

'Is Ayna a whore, then?' she scolded him. 'Someone to be used and abused like Angel's harem of whores?'

'I would never hurt her,' he insisted.

'Then you must marry her, Luca, for others will see only a Saracen slave or whore, and soon you and the other men will be leaving Artake.'

He failed to see how that had any relevance to him or Ayna. She rolled her eyes.

'Oh, Luca, how innocent you are. Do you think a young Saracen woman living alone in a hut will not attract unwanted attention?'

'I do not understand, lady.'

She told him to sit, doing the same and sipping at her wine.

'At the moment, the Black Sheep is held in high regard among the people of Artake. But how long will it be before some blame a Saracen witch for the harsh winter and the deaths of their loved ones?'

'That is ridiculous,' he said dismissively.

'How quickly you forget your own experience, Luca. Your own people, who you had grown up among, did not raise any objections when you were sentenced to hang. How easier it would be for a mob to burn a foreign witch they blamed for their misfortunes.'

He was speechless and his ebullience evaporated.

186

'Fortunately, unlike you I think with my head and not my loins. Ayna will come to live with me while the company is away. As the count insists on stationing guards around my home, the likelihood of Ayna being seized will be remote.'

Luca nodded like a slavering dog.

'For appearances sake, she will be living here as the betrothed of Luca Baldi, who was called away before the marriage ceremony could be arranged. This will convince any who may show an interest that Ayna has converted to the true religion, since it is inconceivable that a Christian would convert to the Saracen faith.'

He was still nodding, though cared little for religious conversion or indeed marriage. He knew Ayna would be safe and that was all that mattered. It would allow him to concentrate fully on killing the enemy.

'You are very kind, lady,' he beamed.

'Kindness has nothing to do with it, Luca. And when you return, you will marry Ayna. Let us hope there no unwelcome arrivals before then.'

'I would not worry about the enemy, lady,' he assured her. 'After their battering at the wall they will be reluctant to venture near to Artake again, and we will be taking the fight to them once our horsemen arrive.'

She rolled her eyes again. 'I was not referring to that kind of arrival but something altogether smaller.'

He gave her a quizzical look.

'I thank God for the extreme cold, which would have inhibited your body's ability to function fully.'

He laughed, thinking about how he and Ayna had made love for hours at a time during the winter evenings, still blissfully unaware

187

she was referring to Ayna becoming pregnant rather than his sexual athleticism. She regarded him coolly.

'Still thinking with your loins, Luca?'

'No, lady,' he insisted.

He thought Ayna might have been resistant to leaving their home, which he had come to regard with affection during the preceding weeks. But she was all too ready to leave the bare, stone hut and exchange it for a comfortable room in a well-appointed house in the city. He would have found living in such grandeur awkward, but she took to it like a duck to water. She and Carla had formed something of a close bond, which made the transition easier, that and the fact Sancho and Jordi would be soon leaving with the Catalan Company. But when Ayna moved into the house, Luca realised he knew absolutely nothing about her family or background. She had never discussed her past life and their lust for each other had made family histories irrelevant. He naively reasoned that if a couple loved each other, nothing else mattered. Nevertheless, his curiosity had been aroused, only to be extinguished when the Catalan horsemen and their Alan allies arrived at the wall.

Arabates was like a bear with a sore head, eager to unleash his horsemen against the enemy and be away from the restraints of law and order. The Alans and the horsemen of Corberan of Navarre had been fed and maintained by the imperial granaries and warehouses in Constantinople, which meant they had survived the harsh winter. But General Mouzalon had kept the Alans on a tight leash and had placed guards around their encampment to ensure they did not loot and plunder the emperor's territory on the eastern side of the Bosporus, such as it was. Being placed under armed guard offended the gruff Alans greatly, which amused the Almogavar Council immensely.

188

The handsome Corberan finished his report to the council and looked around the dining room of Sancho's grandiose house, appreciating the fine fresco on the wall behind him depicting the ascension of Christ into heaven. Luca and Jordi stood beside the seated Sancho, ready to serve those around the table with wine. Luca found such duties tedious, but Sancho thought such menial tasks appropriate to remind his son and the Black Sheep they were still low-ranking Almogavars, despite their fame and also fortune.

'I don't trust these Alans,' grumbled Hector. 'They deserted the Romans and there is no guarantee they won't do the same to us.'

'That's true,' agreed Marc.

Corberan pointed at Luca and Jordi.

'If they do, we will send these two to hunt them down and kill them. Princess Maria asked me to convey her eternal gratitude and love to both of you, by the way.'

The Almogavars banged their fists on the table, Sancho shaking his head in despair. The door opened and Grand Duke Roger swept in, sitting himself at the table opposite Sancho.

'We march in two days,' he told them. 'I have just come from Count Michael's mansion. I left him unhappy.'

Jordi placed a cup before Roger and Luca filled it with wine. The grand duke smiled at them.

'Unhappy, why?' asked Sancho.

'I told him his foot soldiers must remain here. They would only slow us down, and in the forthcoming campaign speed will be our greatest ally.'

'Not the Alans?' asked Angel sarcastically.

189

Roger ignored him. 'Our aim will be to relieve the besieged cities of Philadelphia and Magnesia and the town of Tire, which all lie a hundred miles south of Artake and deep in hostile territory.'

'How do we know they did not fall to the enemy during the winter?' asked Sancho.

'We don't,' conceded Roger. 'But from what Count Michael has told me, I believe they are still under imperial control.'

'What did he tell you?' said Hector.

Roger took a swig of wine. 'That they all have strong walls, the Muslims have no siege engines, and no army could have maintained a siege during the winter just passed.'

Marc was troubled. 'Once we have relieved those places, and destroyed whatever the enemy places in our path, what happens then? Does the emperor expect us to garrison them as well?'

'We are mercenaries, not night watchmen,' growled Hector.

'Count Michael will decide what happens after we have concluded our mission,' said Roger. 'But whatever he decides, we will be undertaking no further service for the emperor after the campaign until we are paid.'

He looked at Corberan.

'The fact you returned from Constantinople with no gold from the sale of the slaves we took last year, indicates to me that the money has been retained by the eunuch treasurer, on the orders of the emperor, since no man who has lost his balls would have the courage to treat the Catalan Company so basely on his own volition.'

'Perhaps we should march on Constantinople,' suggested Hector.

'No,' said Roger firmly. 'We have entered into a contract with the emperor and will honour it. The time for settling grievances will be after the campaign has been concluded. Besides, we are leaving our women and children in the care of Count Michael's soldiers here in Artake. We must not take any action that places them in danger.'

Roger's ability to weigh up arguments and see all sides of a problem was why he was the leader of the Catalans, that and his skill at diplomacy, a profession the Almogavars had to time for.

'We still need to eat,' said Sancho.

Roger nodded. 'We will live off the land during the campaign. We will, after all, be moving through enemy territory. The emperor will have no objection to us taking food from the mouths of Muslims.'

Luca said goodbye to Ayna outside Sancho's house, the Almogavar commander embracing his wife and Jordi standing in full war gear beside him, having already bid his mother farewell. He held his beloved tenderly, staring into her brown eyes.

'When I return, we are to be married,' he told her.

'Make sure you do return,' she said softly, her eyes moist with tears.

Her Italian had come on leaps and bounds, though he could not speak a word of her language, much to his regret. Then again, the fact she was mastering his language meant he had no need to master hers.

'You never told me about your family,' he said.

'You did not ask.'

'Time to go, soldier,' barked Sancho.

Luca kissed her on the lips one last time, embraced Carla and followed Sancho and Jordi to the great muster at the wall.

Nearly seven thousand soldiers gathered at the site of the battle the previous year, only two hundred of whom – all horsemen –

were imperial soldiers. Superbly attired in mail and lamellar armour and helmets, they made the Catalan horseman look poor and inadequate. But all of Corberan's horsemen were kitted out in mail hauberks and helmets and were equipped with lances and swords. Only a tiny proportion of his riders were knights, but all were veterans of the war in Sicily where they had enjoyed an unbroken run of victories. In contrast, the count's horsemen had tasted nothing but defeat at the hands of the Muslims.

Count Michael's standard was a huge yellow banner emblazoned with a red double-headed eagle – the symbol of the Palaiologos dynasty, to which Emperor Andronicus belonged – selected because it proclaimed the dynasty bestrode both Europe and Asia, even though most of the emperor's Asian territories had been lost to Islam. Among his horsemen there were also a number of banners showing a red cross on a white background and a yellow cross on a red background. Among the Catalan horsemen were a profusion of banners showing red horizontal stripes on a golden background – the sacred *Senyera*.

*****

The Christian murals and frescoes had all been painted over now, though the intricate mosaics on the floor of the palace had been retained, much to the disgust of Izzeddin Arslan. Many had thought the Sufi zealot had perished during the harsh winter, the holy man having left Bergama after marching what was left of his army back to the *bey*'s capital in the aftermath of the crushing defeat at the wall of Artake. The remnants of his army had been housed in the city, which saved them from certain death when the great freeze began. Karesi Bey was still determined to keep the *ghazis* at arm's length, not least because they were impossible to control. But the holy man's élite

192

guard were a different proposition. Well-armed, equipped and subject to rigorous discipline, they would be a valuable addition to his army. Or at least would have been had not Izzeddin Arslan returned from the dead. Not only that, but with reinforcements – more *ghazi* warriors.

A gentle wind ruffled the white silk drapes at the entrance to the suite to the rear of the throne room. Karesi Bey and Mahmud of Caesarea stretched out on plush couches as Izzeddin Arslan paced the terrace. Below was the lush valley extending east towards the town of Soma, and west towards the glittering Aegean Sea, the hills on either side filled with olive orchards and vineyards, which had suffered so cruelly during the winter. Bergama was usually blessed with mild winters and warm summers, which made olive and grape growing so easy, and lucrative.

'We thought you had perished in the severe cold,' said Karesi, extending an arm to a third couch to indicate the holy man should take the weight off his dirty feet.

'I was praying,' sniffed Izzeddin, raising an eyebrow when slaves appeared with golden goblets and jugs of wine. Others brought water and fruit juice for the holy man, Izzeddin selecting the former.

He frowned when Karesi and Mahmud were served wine and toasted each other. The Prophet himself declared alcohol to be *haraam* – unlawful – though many wealthy, powerful Muslims did imbibe to show their moneyed, cultured status. They also believed that their consumption of alcohol was a decision reached between themselves and Allah, and was nothing to do with low-born holy men.

Izzeddin smiled. 'During my time of prayer, it was revealed to me why the faithful failed at the broken wall.'

193

'Poor tactics and even poorer soldiers?' offered Mahmud offishly.

Izzeddin glared at him. 'The *kafir* Count Opsikion and his infidel allies will succumb to the true faith, of that I have no doubt. But the great loss of life at the wall, added to the cleansing of this city when it fell to my *ghazis*, was all part of Allah's great scheme.'

'Which was?' enquired Karesi.

'To ensure your rule continued uninterrupted, lord *emir*. For did not you have enough room in this city to accommodate all your soldiers and my *ghazis*, and have food to feed them during the great trial?'

'We still had to purchase grain,' the *emir* reminded him.

'But Allah provided you with a gold mine to make such purchases painless, lord,' retorted Izzeddin, referring to the gold mine in the hills near to the city.

There was also a copper mine on the other side of the valley, both being closely guarded and worked by a small army of slaves. The mined gold allowed Karesi to maintain a large, formidable army, which included Mahmud's Christian horsemen, as well as a small fleet of merchant ships operating out of the port of Dikili immediately to the west.

'Please seat yourself,' Karesi implored the holy man, 'you are making me nervous with your pacing.'

He clapped his hands as Izzeddin did so, perching himself on the edge of the couch like a bird on a rock ledge. More slaves arrived with trays heaped with figs, *basbousa* sweet cake, crunchy and creamy *kanafeh* dessert, sweet *baklava* pastry, and a delightful Egyptian pastry called *feteer* made up of many thin layers of dough and ghee with sweet fillings. They were delicacies fit for kings and princes, which is what Karesi and Mahmud were. But while they consumed the fare with gusto, Izzeddin waved away the slaves, his weathered brow creasing with disapproval at the decadence on show. Karesi swallowed his pastry.

'My agents in Alexandria inform me that the Count of Opsikion also purchased grain, which was shipped to Artake in vessels belonging to a mercenary called Roger de Flor, who leads a band named the Catalan Company. It was he and they who defeated your *ghazis* last year.'

'Another *kafir*?' scoffed Izzeddin. 'He will fail just like all the Emperor of Constantinople's generals.'

'I have heard this Catalan Company is formidable,' said Mahmud. 'We should not underestimate it.'

'Nor will we,' promised Karesi. 'To which end, I have decided to avoid any battle with this Roger de Flor and his mercenaries until we have the measure of them.'

Izzeddin sprang from the couch. 'God is on our side, lord, and with such an ally we cannot fail.'

'God *is* on our side,' agreed Karesi, 'but He would want us to be both cautious and pragmatic to ensure our great task comes to fruition.'

He rose from the couch and walked to the balcony's marble balustrade and rested his hands on the cool stone. Below was the sprawling city of Bergama nestled in the fertile valley between the Bakircay and Kestel rivers.

'Our rivals to the north and south are preoccupied with their own difficulties. Osman Bey in the north faces the main Christian army. To the south, our rivals are fully engaged in the sieges of the city of Philadelphia and the town of Tire.

'Only we are free from distractions, which allows us to focus on our immediate priorities.'

'Which are, lord?' asked Mahmud, still devouring the tasty pastries.

'To profit from our enemies and rivals fighting each other, and hopefully weakening each other fatally so we may profit from their subsequent frailties.'

'You have forgotten one thing, lord,' said Izzeddin. 'To get to grips with your rivals, the enemy will have to pass through your territory. Surely you will not allow infidels to pollute the soil of your emirate?'

'Have you considered, Izzeddin, that it is Allah's will that they should do so?' asked Karesi.

'He has you there,' joked Mahmud.

The holy man turned his piercing eyes on the dashing commander of the *emir*'s horsemen, barely being able to contain his wrath.

'Your *kafir* horsemen insult Allah,' he shouted, veins bulging in his neck. 'They should be banished at least, though execution would be preferable.'

'Enough!' commanded Karesi. 'It is for me to decide our strategy, and I will hear no talk of atrocities against our Christian allies.'

Izzeddin's eyes appeared to be on the verge of bulging from their sockets, but the *emir* matched his stare with an iron glower.

'For hundreds of years, this was a Christian land, and I have no intention of turning it into a wasteland for the sake of religious fanaticism. I have assured the Christians still resident in my emirate that their property and religious rights will be respected. I have also assured Mahmud's armoured horsemen that they are a valued and integral part of the army, which they are.'

Mahmud looked very smug as he waited for another outburst from the Sufi zealot. But instead the holy man bowed his head to the *emir*.

'As ever, lord, your wisdom calms the waters of conflict, which is why Allah chose you for the great task in hand. And now, if you will forgive me, I have religious matters to attend to.'

He walked from the terrace, stopping when the *emir* spoke to him.

'I meant what I said about respecting the Christians, Izzeddin. Any atrocities committed by the *ghazis* in my lands will be severely punished.'

The holy man turned, smiled and bowed once more.

'It shall be as you command, lord.'

Mahmud sighed and took a large gulp of wine.

'His followers are a liability, lord, a dangerous rabble who are under the control of a madman.'

'You should not goad him, Mahmud,' said Karesi, not disagreeing that Izzeddin was unhinged. 'Besides, were it not for him and his followers, we would not be sitting in this great city.'

'I remember that day, lord, and not with affection. It was shameful the way the *ghazis* acted against the civilian population and contrary to what I was brought up to believe about the teaching of Islam.'

Karesi nodded solemnly. 'You are not wrong in what you say. But we are where we are and must use our privileged position to ensure the like does not happen again.'

197

Mahmud grinned. 'You will really allow the Christian army to march through your territory unmolested?'

Karesi nibbled on a pastry. 'I will. Why should I do the work of other *emirs* who have shown no inclination to support me? Time is on our side, Mahmud. If the Christian emperor has been reduced to hiring mercenaries to save his throne rather than trusting his own army, then truly his power is on the wane.'

'This Catalan Company is very good, lord,' reported Mahmud. 'My commander of horse archers informed me they cut the *ghazis* to pieces at Artake.'

Karesi pondered his subordinate's words.

'I wonder how they will fare against real soldiers?'

Chapter 11

The Catalan Company and Count Michael's horsemen left Artake on a warm May morning. The bishop and his priests had come from the city with crosses and icons to bless the soldiers and fortify their spirits, though Luca found their incessant chanting annoying, swinging incense burners hilarious and the bishop's rich attire ridiculous. He knew he was an Orthodox bishop, which he had been told was radically different from an equivalent position in the Catholic Church, but he had little interest in religious doctrine and, after his experience at Rometta, even less in the witterings of priests. He was torn between wanting to stay with Ayna and thirsting for more battle against the enemy.

He felt like a mule, with his javelin quiver on his back, the shafts protruding over his right shoulder for ease of plucking. His shield, or buckler to be more accurate, was strapped over his left shoulder. Used to parry or block blows, it was light enough and the metal boss could be used as a weapon in its own right. At his left hip was his short sword, while on his right side was a large textile bag carried by a strap going over his left shoulder, which contained small pies, bread and biscuits. He also carried a water bottle and his Damascus dagger attached to his belt.

The Almogavars had no baggage train to slow them down, and Corberan's horsemen used mules to transport their tents, spare weapons and other supplies. Luca and the thousands of other Almogavars would sleep out in the open, the winter now long passed and the nights pleasant enough. Besides, there would be plenty of firewood to be had because western Anatolia was covered in pine, juniper, oak and fig trees, as well as large expanses of vineyards around towns and cities. Anatolia had a central massif, from which flowed an abundance of water to fill streams and rivers to quench the thirsts of men and beasts alike.

The Catalan Company set a cruel pace, initially striking east rather than south, following the Roman road that had been laid two hundred years before the birth of Christ. The Imperial Highways Department had long ceased to exist as the power of subsequent emperors of Constantinople had waned, but the roads that had been constructed throughout Anatolia were still extant. Their main objective had been to link cities often hundreds of miles apart to facilitate trade, but they were also excellent for the rapid movement of armies. The road network had been a huge engineering undertaking that was beyond the resources of the current Roman emperor, or indeed the Muslim settlers who were now threatening to conquer what was left of his Asian territories.

As Luca fast-paced over the large polygonal stone slabs, he would not have realised the immense effort required to construct the road that was as straight as an arrow. The curb stones had been laid first, after which a ditch between them – a *fossa* – was dug, which became the width of the road. This depression was filled with a large amount of rubble, earth and stone, which was covered with gravel and tampered down, a process the Romans called *pavimentare*. Then came a layer of flat stones set in cement, on top of which was laid a layer of coarse concrete. Finally, the road was topped by polygonal paving stones, the gaps between them filled with concrete to give a smooth, even surface. As the miles passed by, Luca might have noticed the road was slightly cambered for drainage purposes. Resistant to floods and frosts and requiring little maintenance, the road network was still one of the jewels in the Anatolian landscape.

The Alans were a law unto themselves, leaving the main column to ride far and wide, ostensibly to scout but in reality to plunder farms and villages. They found little to fill their saddlebags as many had perished during the winter or had taken themselves off to the towns and cities to beg for relief. Farmlands were abandoned, vineyards and orchards were overgrown and barren, and the land had an empty feel about it, notwithstanding its lush greenery.

The plan was to reach Philadelphia as quickly as possible. Count Michael had assured Grand Duke Roger that the city was large and would have adequate supplies to feed his soldiers, notwithstanding it was under siege. Having no siege engines and scant knowledge of siege warfare, the Turks had only loosely invested the city, or so his spies had reported. That was before the dreadful winter, of course, so the Catalan Company might be marching to its doom if the city had already fallen. But such was the high spirits of the mercenaries, especially the Almogavars after their crushing victory at the wall, that no one considered defeat or even withdrawal.

Notwithstanding their coarse appearance and apparent indiscipline, the Almogavars adhered to a strict routine. One day was given over to a long march that covered around thirty miles. But on each second day the morning was given over to foraging for food, a multitude of small parties being sent out in all directions to collect greens – mainly hardal, kenker and turpotu – as well as berries such as elderberries, gooseberries, mulberries and wolfberries. The latter was regarded as a mythical food capable of prolonging life if ingested in large quantities. After a morning searching for food, the Catalan Company covered an average of only ten miles on the afternoon to allow stamina reserves to be replenished.

201

Luca sat with his back against a pine tree chewing on some fresh roots plucked from the ground that very morning, Jordi doing the same. The Almogavars had left the road to make camp in a forest of pine the road cut through, sentries having been placed around the perimeter to warn of any enemy approach. There were grumblings in camp concerning the absence of Arabates and his Alans, with many voicing the opinion he and they had deserted to the enemy. Luca was unconcerned. The days were warm, he tingled with the prospect of fighting the Muslims once more, and he had a beautiful woman to return to when the campaign was over. The company was a few miles north of the Turkish-held town of Soma, which Grand Duke Roger intended to bypass to strike directly for Philadelphia.

'Who will you marry now?' he asked his friend.

'No one I have not seen before the marriage ceremony, that is for sure,' said Jordi.

'You had a lucky escape with the count's daughter,' agreed Luca.

'Not so lucky for her, though.'

'We will find you a good Muslim woman for you, Jordi, like Ayna.'

Jordi's eyes lit up. 'You struck gold there, my friend. You will marry her?'

Luca spat out a piece of dirt he had been unwittingly chewing.

'Your mother insists that I should, and in truth she makes me happy.'

'What about her religion?'

Luca shrugged. 'What about it? She worships Allah and I pray to God. It has not got in the way so far.'

Jordi looked serious. 'Ayna will have to convert to Christianity before you can marry her.'

Luca nodded. 'I doubt she will object. I care little for the church and I suspect she is of the same opinion.'

They stopped talking when Sancho Rey appeared, the big man pointing at them both.

'Guard duty for you two, and no talking when you are keeping watch.'

They both jumped to their feet, grabbing their spears and shields and slinging their javelin quivers on their backs. There was a full moon so visibility was not a problem as the sun dropped and night enveloped the land. There was no wind so any sound carried great distances, the laughter and revelry coming from where Count Michael was entertaining Corberan and his small number of knights travelling through the trees to make Luca smile. So much for keeping quiet.

He nodded to Jordi to his right and Roc, the large Almogavar who was a friend of Sancho, on his left, both standing behind trees to make themselves invisible to any approaching the camp but allowing them to peer round the trunk into the blackness of the forest. Luca focused on his hearing but heard no sounds. It would be a long two hours.

'Allahu Akbar!'

He may have heard the Muslim battle cry at the wall, though if he had he would have certainly ignored it. But now the same cry cut through the night air, immediately followed by wild cheering as the enemy attacked.

'Fall back,' called Roc, already taking to his heels.

Luca momentarily thought of fighting where he stood, intoxicated by the surge of energy rushing through his body like a mighty torrent. But then he remembered his training, hearing Hector's words in his head.

'One man alone is weak and vulnerable. But one thousand standing shoulder-to-shoulder is an unbreakable wall.'

He ran back towards the campfires, already horns and whistles being sounded to call the Almogavars to arms. And behind him, a mass of wraith-like figures came running, stumbling and cursing from the blackness of the forest.

'Rally, rally.'

Schhwaff. Schhwaff.

Arrows flew through the night air, too close to him for Luca's liking. He saw Jordi out of the corner of his eye and then a thick line of Almogavars to his front, spears levelled and shields tucked tight to their bodies.

'Let them through.'

He heard Sancho's gruff voice and saw a gap opening in the wall of Catalans, the Almogavars framed against the dull red glow of the campfires behind them. There was no great clearing where they had camped, only trees irregularly spaced and broken branches, moss and bushes on the forest floor, which had been cleared for firewood and tinder.

The professional soldiers surrounding Karesi Bey regarded Izzeddin Arslan and his *ghazis* with indifference, mild contempt or open hostility, believing them and him to be dangerous zealots who were of dubious military value, and an outright threat to the day-to-day affairs of the emirate. His warriors had captured Bergama for the *emir*, it was true, though the price had been dreadful, but now the

204

wealthy and powerful of the emirate wanted him and his fanatics gone.

Izzeddin knew he was both despised and feared, and also knew his *ghazis* were of little value against professional soldiers. But he also knew that faith could overcome many deficiencies, such as lack of military training, if the opposition could be weakened before battle was joined. And what better way to reduce the effectiveness of trained soldiers than to make them fight in a forest, in the dark? Like Karesi Bey, he had been following the progress of the Catalan Company closely. But unlike his *emir*, he was determined to wipe out the infidel mercenaries rather than allowing them to march through Muslim lands. For just as Allah had cleared Arabia, Egypt and the Holy Land of infidels, so had He promised Anatolia to the faithful.

Luca stumbled to the rear of the now dense line of Almogavars and embraced his friend.

'So much for a quiet night,' said Jordi.

Arrows, shot inaccurately and high, thudded into tree trunks around them, at the same time that a mighty roar came from in front of the Almogavars to signal the *ghazis* were about to engage them in hand-to-hand combat. The Almogavar front rank stood with left leg extended, the end of each spear wedged against the right foot and the shaft held at an angle of forty-five degrees to the front. The men in the second rank held their spears upright and made ready to unleash their javelins against the oncoming enemy, sergeants blowing whistles to unleash the flurry of missiles.

Luca experienced a new sensation during battle: alarm. Disorientated by the limited visibility and shouts and cries bombarding his ears, he was unsure what to do. Jordi shook him.

'Javelin, Luca. Form up in the rear of the line.'

205

Shrill whistle blasts rent the air, followed by screams and groans as javelins found their targets. But the *ghazis* did not press their attack, retreating back into the darkness of the forest to regroup. Fighting at night demands great discipline and organisation, two attributes alien to the religious warriors. But their Sufi leaders rallied them with chants of 'Allahu Akbar' and reformed them in the darkness, out of sight of the Almogavars.

Sancho was walking rapidly up and down the line, issuing orders, while behind him and the Almogavars, Corberan's horsemen and Count Michael's soldiers were extinguishing the fires to plunge the forest into pitch-black darkness to deny the enemy archers any sight of targets. Silence descended on the scene, Luca straining his eyes trying to make out shapes behind him and on the flanks. As far as he could discern, the Almogavars were drawn up in a line four ranks deep, he and Jordi being in the fourth line. He hoped the Catalan horsemen were guarding their rear.

He felt a hand on his shoulder.

'Kneel,' whispered Sancho. 'Keep your shield up as a defence against arrows.'

He did as commanded, as did hundreds of others around him. Jordi was on his right, though he could hardly make him out. It was so very dark and so quiet.

'Allahu Akbar!'

He tightened the grip on his spear shaft and a few arrows flew through the air, but no attack was launched against the Almogavars. Then there was silence once more, which did nothing to calm Luca's nerves.

'Allahu Akbar! Allahu Akbar!'

The forest was suddenly filled with the Muslim war cry, which seemed to be coming from every direction, the night playing tricks on the hearing. Then there was a series of sharp cracks from the Catalan ranks as the crossbowmen shot their bolts into the darkness, in the general direction of the Turks. There were only around two hundred Almogavar crossbowmen and so even if all their bolts found a target, it would make little impact on the thousands of *ghazis* lurking in the forest. But at least it cheered the Almogavars.

Luca and hundreds of others sat in stony silence as the forest reverberated with the Muslim war cry, the din rising in intensity as the *ghazis* whipped themselves up into a frenzy. It was a testament to the discipline of the Almogavars that they remained stoic in the face of such intimidation, each man alone with his thoughts as he considered what the dawn, just a short time away, might bring. Luca knew the enemy would launch their attack just as dawn was breaking, when their archers would be able to identify the Catalans and lend their support to the *ghazi* assault. All that was left was to wait. Wait for the dawn, and the inevitable spilling of blood.

Luca shivered. Not because he was afraid, the nervousness having left him, to be replaced by a calm determination, but because the temperature had dropped. The dawn was about to break. Because of the thick canopy blocking out the sun, light was slow to return to the forest. But agonisingly slowly, he began to identify shapes around him: the kneeling figure of Jordi, the white teeth of his friend when he gave him a reassuring smile, the forest of spear shafts being held vertically to the left and right and in front of him, and the imposing figure of Sancho Rey standing with his back to the enemy.

'Almogavars, forward!'

His voice sounded louder than normal when it broke the silence, immediately followed by dozens of whistles being blown as the order to attack was relayed to four thousand Almogavars. And then the Catalans were on their feet and walking forward, breaking into a quick pace to cover the space between them and the enemy ahead. An enemy that responded in kind, holy men shouting their encouragement and then the whole *ghazi* force screaming 'Allahu Akbar' as it surged forward. Sancho's quick thinking had negated the enemy's advantage in archers. But the Turks still had a substantial numerical advantage.

In the half-light the two sides closed on each other, the Almogavars maintaining their steady pace, parting to pass trees in their path before closing ranks again. The first rank gripped its spears with both hands, the second and third holding javelins ready to throw. The fourth, having no sightline to the enemy, formed a de facto reserve. The *ghazis* swept forward like a tidal wave, bereft of discipline and cohesion but infused with religious fervour. They carried an assortment of clubs, spears, axes and a few swords, most carrying a round wooden shield, all without head protection.

For twenty years the Almogavars had plied their deadly trade in Sicily, fighting commoners and nobles alike, defeating richly clad aristocrats on warhorses and slaughtering well-armed and equipped foot soldiers. They did not have better weapons than those they encountered, and always had a paucity of crossbowmen compared to the foe. But they were quicker than the enemy when it came to assaults, feints and retreats, handled their weapons with a dexterity far greater than opponents, and possessed a discipline unknown among the retinues of the Christian lords they had fought.

That discipline came into play now as a screaming horde rushed towards the Almogavars, the *ghazis* hollering their blood-curdling war cries, their only desire to impale themselves on the spears of the infidels to gain their entry into paradise. They *were* impaled, but on the steel tips of hundreds of javelins thrown by the second and third ranks of the Catalans, which cut down hundreds of Turks. A second and third volley cut down more and then the Almogavars were among the *ghazis*, thrusting their spears into olive-skinned faces, the second rank also bringing their spears to bear to turn the Catalan line into a giant saw that began to chew the *ghazis* to pieces. It was another easy victory and Jordi grinned at Luca in triumph. The dawn had broken to herald another glorious chapter in the history of the Catalan Company, and Luca had not even dipped his weapons in enemy blood.

'They're behind us! Have a care!'

Seconds after hearing the warning, Luca instinctively turned. To be confronted by a wild-haired demon with bulging bloodshot eyes screaming as he swung an axe at his head. He thrust his spear forward into the man's face, the demon emitting a high-pitched squeal as the metal point entered his left eye socket. The axe tumbled from his hand to land at Luca's feet.

'Luca, on your right.'

Luca heard Jordi's call, let go of the spear and just as Hector had taught him, pulled his sword from its scabbard, swung his shield to the right and manged to catch the spear point aimed at his chest on the metal boss of his buckler. Roc on his right rammed his own spear through the naked torso of the holy warrior, whose face contorted into a vision of agony as Roc buried the metal point in his flesh.

'Leave it,' ordered Roc as Luca went to retrieve his spear, still lodged in the eye socket of the now prostrate and dead *ghazi*. 'Close ranks.'

The *ghazis* were now in front, behind and on the flanks of the Almogavars, hacking and stabbing at the infidels. Any commander worth his salt would have withdrawn the holy warriors and let his archers pepper the Catalans with arrows. Izzeddin Arslan was many things but he was no military mastermind. He existed to enforce the will of Allah and if that meant that a thousand, a hundred thousand should die, then so be it. His warriors had taken a circuitous route from the town of Soma to descend on the infidels from the hills, nightfall masking their approach, and now they had the unbelievers surrounded. He was not entirely devoid of common sense, though, having been instrumental in luring away the Catalan horsemen.

'Where are our horsemen?' called Luca in frustration, ducking low to allow the man behind him to hurl his javelin over his head into the fat belly of a *ghazi*.

'Dead, most likely,' grunted Roc, fencing with a pair of Turks armed with clubs who were intent on reducing his large head to a pulp.

The Almogavars were now in a rough hollow rectangle among the trees, all sides two ranks deep, the *ghazis* swarming around it like angry hornets.

'Keep formation. Keep formation.'

Sancho Rey was bellowing at the top of his voice to his men. He had no need to urge them to keep the enemy at bay because they were more than holding their own. The risk was over-confidence: the urge to race forward after winning a single duel and in doing so shatter the formation that the enemy had failed to break.

210

The *ghazis* were tiring now, their attacks no longer the frenzied affairs of early morning. Luca was sweating and panting, accrediting it to the stress of battle. But a neutral observer would have informed him he had been fighting for over three hours, during which time the sun had risen and was warming the earth from a cloudless sky. The forest floor was littered with dead, the maimed and wounded having crawled away to either die in another place or be helped back to Soma when the battle was over. But the battle went on.

It had descended into a desultory affair: tired, exhausted men standing a few paces apart eyeing each other, trying to summon up the energy and courage to once more face death in the face. One or two *ghazis* would suddenly dash forward against the unbroken Catalans, swinging axes and swords or jabbing spears. To be stopped in their tracks by an unbroken row of spears and bucklers. The *ghazis*, wary of Catalans adept in the use of spears, javelins and swords, became increasingly unwilling to press their attacks. And their dead comrades forming an unbroken carpet round the Almogavars created a further disincentive to attack.

Luca glanced at Jordi, both of them soaked in sweat but as yet unhurt. His friend gave him a wan smile but said nothing. They were both thinking the same thing: the Catalan horsemen must have been overrun and slaughtered in the first *ghazi* assault. Their thoughts were interrupted by a small group of enemy warriors shuffling towards them with leaden steps, shields tucked tight to their bodies and spears levelled. Luca slipped the sword back into its scabbard and reached behind with his right hand, feeling the number of javelins in his quiver. One. Two. Three. He not yet used one.

His arms, legs and back ached. In battle his limbs became as light as feathers; but when the fury of combat abated they cried out for rest.

He was not alone. Even the best soldiers tire in battle, and if the Almogavars were approaching the end of their endurance, the *ghazis* were in a far worse condition. They had failed to rout the Catalans in the first attack, and subsequently had made little impression of the hedgehog-like rectangle that had formed in response to their assaults. Tired, thirsty, their limbs bleeding and their bodies drained of energy as a result of hours of futile attacks, they became listless, leaden. Until the trumpets sounded.

Luca saw them before he heard them, pointing them out to Jordi as they came from the road a short distance away to enter the forest, the sun glinting off spear points, swords and helmets before they rode under the canopy of vegetation. The horsemen moved swiftly among the trees, cutting down many *ghazis* before the religious warriors realised what was happening.

Corberan and Count Michael kept their men under tight control. They had already been engaged in a fierce battle and many of their soldiers were riding blown horses. But their appearance had a dramatic effect on the *ghazis*, who fled before them, passing the Almogavars who began to whistle and jeer at them as they fled back towards the hills. But the Catalans did not pursue. They too were tired and thirsty, many falling to their knees in prayer to give thanks for their deliverance. For surely God had intervened to save the Catalan Company, which was on a crusade to save the believers from the infidels.

*****

212

Izzeddin Arslan calmly walked back to where his élite *ghazi* soldiers stood at the edge of the forest in a great phalanx, their commander saluting him smartly.

'The infidel horsemen have arrived to save the *kafirs*.'

'My men stand ready, lord.'

Izzeddin flicked a bony hand at him. 'We have been betrayed, that much is certain. The governor of Soma has failed Allah, so I will not waste the lives of His warriors after such treachery.'

Already *ghazis* were flooding from the trees to take shelter behind the hundreds of mail-clad soldiers standing to attention in the meadow at the base of the hills they had made their initial approach from.

'The Christians might launch an attack against us, lord.'

Izzeddin shook his head. 'No, their foot soldiers are exhausted like my brave *ghazis* and their horsemen will wish to stop and boast of their so-called achievement. We will withdraw through the hills and pray for those who are now in paradise.'

Yakub I Alisir, the Governor of Soma, was one of Karesi Bey's most loyal and effective administrators. Like many high-ranking Muslims, he drank alcohol and had acquired a taste for the trappings of wealth. He tolerated Christians and Jews in his town and viewed the zealotry of the *ghazis* with disdain. But he was also proud and ambitious, and when Izzeddin approached him with a plan to destroy the invading Christian mercenaries, he jumped at the chance. A two-pronged attack against the infidels was an ambitious plan, but Izzeddin assured him that his *ghazis* would do the majority of the fighting, aware Karesi Bey had forbidden his governor to engage the invaders. All the governor had to do was lead his horsemen and foot soldiers north from the town in the early morning to provide the coup de grâce against the infidels. It was easy to convince a man who had been jealous of the holy man's success at Bergama to disobey his lord, to dangle the prospect of military glory before his eyes.

Unfortunately for Yakub I Alisir, his actions were too tardy to catch the Catalan Company by surprise. His column of horse and foot was spotted by Corberan's scouts, and knowing that his Almogavars were difficult to kill, Grand Duke Roger persuaded Count Michael to join him with his horsemen to attack the column. The Muslims fought well, and for a while the outcome was in the balance. But the sudden attack against the column meant the governor could not utilise his horse archers to full effect, and the Christian horsemen were able to get among the foot soldiers, resulting in great disorder and loss.

Yakub I Alisir stayed until the end, attempting to rally his men as the tide of battle turned against him. He did not lack for courage, but courage alone rarely wins battles. His horse killed under him, he refused a remount, electing instead to remain with what remained of his foot soldiers. The Governor of Soma died on the Roman road two miles to the north of his town, a loss Karesi Bey would have regarded as a futile waste. But for Izzeddin Arslan, it was indicative of the ungodly men the *emir* was surrounding himself, which was losing him Allah's support. And a ruler without the help of God was lost in every way.

Chapter 12

Luca and the rest of the Catalan Company spent a day marching following the battle, followed by two days resting and recuperating. Grand Duke Roger, on the advice of Count Michael, moved the company off the road and into the hills in a westerly direction, away from Soma and also Bergama, the capital of the Karesi Emirate. This was to both guard against any retaliation launched against the Catalans and to reach Philadelphia as quickly as possible. The shortest route to the city was directly south, but that would risk leaving hostile forces to the north, as well as having to fight at least another battle against the forces of the so-called Germiyanid Emirate, which was laying siege to Philadelphia.

Luca, stripped naked, plunged into the lake where hundreds of others were bathing in the cool waters. It was a hot day in the hills of Anatolia, but the water was ice-cold, initially taking his breath away. But after a few moments his body adapted and he let his tired limbs be massaged by the intoxicating water. It was the first time he had had a bath in months, though Ayna had insisted they both have strip-washes even during the coldest months, which had inevitably led to long periods of lovemaking afterwards. He smiled at the memory.

'Count Michael has sent his horsemen to scour the land for game,' said Jordi, shaking his head after immersing it in the water. 'I pray God they come back with some meat.'

Meat did not constitute a large part of the Almogavar diet, but in the aftermath of battle they had consumed most of the meagre rations in their bags to replenish their energy reserves. And there had been no enemy camp to plunder in the aftermath of their victory. As a result, hunger began to stalk the Catalan Company. The horses could be grazed on the lush meadows dotted among the hills, as well as the grass on the slopes themselves. But for soldiers on the march, the countryside provided scant food aside from roots, berries and fruit. It was made worse by the winter that had killed a lot of the wildlife. At least Sancho Rey had ordered that the lake be fished, which so far had produced no tangible results.

'Where are the Alans?' asked Luca, a question on everyone's lips.

The wild mercenary horsemen had been conspicuous by their absence, which aroused the anger of many among the Almogavars. Everyone knew how they had deserted the Romans in battle, and now they had more or less done the same to the Catalans. It did not bode well for the future.

'It is Luca, is it not?'

He looked towards the bank to see a priest standing beside the water, dressed in a long black woollen gown, a wooden crucifix suspended by a simple cord around his neck. Luca had seen Father Ramon on numerous occasions. He was among the small number of priests accompanying the Almogavars, all being Catalans like the soldiers they preached to. Since his unhappy experience in Rometta, however, his opinion of religion and priests in general had dropped and he had avoided holy men. Luca nodded.

Father Ramon smiled. 'I wonder if I might have a word with you?'

He looked at Jordi who gave a shrug. He waded from the water to stand naked before the priest, who unusually for a Catalan had blue eyes. Those eyes stared unblinkingly at Luca.

'Perhaps you would like to put your clothes on.'

Luca flopped down on the ground on his back.

'I will let the sun dry my skin first, Father Ramon.'

216

His tone was sharp. He was now a veteran of three battles, and while that was no boast among a company that had fought countless battles, long gone were the days when a priest could cower him into submission. Ramon sat on the ground cross-legged beside him, staring at the shimmering waters of the lake.

'You are famous, Black Sheep,' he began. 'Many among the Almogavars believe you to be a lucky mascot, the more so after you and Jordi Rey rescued the Princess Maria in Constantinople.'

'We were in the right place at the right time,' said Luca.

'Or perhaps God placed you both in the right place so you could render invaluable service to the princess,' opined Ramon. 'Do you think about God, Luca?'

'Not really.'

Ramon took a sharp intake of breath. He was used to dealing with blunt, coarse Catalan soldiers. But still.

'He is thinking of you, Luca,' said Ramon, 'especially your immortal soul. You purchased a Muslim woman as a slave last year, I believe.'

Tension seeped through Luca's body. He jumped up and grabbed his leggings, pulling them on, afterwards his shirt and *zamarra*. He glanced at his weapons lying near his feet.

'What of it?'

Ramon calmly stood and faced him. 'You are entitled to take Muslim slaves, of course. It is your right as a Christian warrior. However, I have heard that your slave is in fact your lover, which greatly alarms me.'

Luca picked up his sword belt and strapped it on.

'You think she might try to murder me in my sleep, father?'

217

'My fear is greater. I fear she will entice you into the Muslim heresy, which will damn your soul for all eternity.'

He buckled his belt and picked up his quiver of javelins.

'She has not tried to convert me, father, and nor will she.'

Ramon gave a him a supercilious smile.

'Satan adopts many guises, Luca. The entire Muslim faith is but one of his manifestations, and those who follow that foul religion are nothing more than the Devil's agents on earth.'

'Then you should be pleased I have been killing many of them.'

Ramon pressed a bony finger in his chest. Like all men who subsisted on a pious priest's diet of coarse bread, vegetables and beans, he had a lean almost gaunt frame and sunken cheeks.

'You should desist regarding this woman, this heretic, as a lover and treat her like the slave she is.'

Luca swatted away his hand. 'I will do as I please, Father Ramon, and if I offend God doing so, then he will surely strike me down.'

'You speak blasphemy,' spat Ramon.

Luca secured his quiver of javelins in place.

'Have you heard of a lord named Giovanni Carafa, Father Ramon?'

'I have heard of him, yes.'

'He is a Christian lord who murdered my parents before thousands of witnesses, and yet I saw no priests stepping forward to stop his crime. You yourself were there among the Almogavars, and yet you did nothing. What right do you have to accuse me of blasphemy when you were silent when murder was committed before your very eyes?'

Ramon folded his arms across his scrawny chest.

'I have often wondered why you were given the title Black Sheep, but I see now it is entirely appropriate. Just as a black sheep is a portent of evil, I wonder if we have clasped a viper to our breast, just as our Lord welcomed Judas into his family?'

'I'll make this agreement with you, father. You take measures to bring Count Carafa to account, and I will obey your command regarding my lover.'

Ramon, unused to being talked to in such a manner, bristled in the face of Luca's rebellious tongue. But he resisted the urge to threaten the Italian with ruin and damnation, not least because he sincerely believed he would be impaled on one of the two spears lying on the ground nearby. So, he coolly made the sign of the cross at Luca, turned and walked away without saying a word.

Jordi, who had exited the water and also dressed, stood beside his friend.

'What did he want?'

'To try to convince me to treat Ayna as a slave. He did not like my reply.'

'You should be wary of Father Ramon. He can make great trouble for you if he so desires.'

'What trouble?'

'Nothing on campaign. But when we return to Artake, he could accuse Ayna of witchcraft. And you know what that means.'

'If he did, I will kill him myself.'

Jordi was stunned. 'To kill a priest is to risk eternal damnation, Luca.'

'As I told Father Ramon, if I have offended God, then the Lord has had many opportunities to strike me down by using the weapons of the enemy to cut me to pieces. So far, I have escaped unscathed, which suggests to me the Lord is not unduly upset with me. Come on, let's get something to eat.'

The Alans returned the next day, Arabates and his mounted rascals riding into camp with quantities of plundered grain, wine and cheese, which they offered to share with the Almogavars. Count Michael and Grand Duke Roger would have liked to place the Alan leader under arrest for his dereliction of duty, but thought better of it as they were heading ever deeper into enemy territory.

The company saw no one as it snaked across green hills and bypassed rocky crags, heading first west and then south. The days were getting warmer but a pleasant breeze each day made marching bearable. Less tolerable was the constant hunger pain that gripped Luca as he fast-walked across empty meadows and through pine forests, his food bag almost empty. So bad was the situation that the column was forced to halt for a day so everyone could collect madimak, a type of edible grass native to the Anatolian plateau, which could be turned into a soup.

It took five days to traverse the meadows, forests and hills, each day large parties of horsemen being sent ahead as scouts to reconnoitre the route and scour the land for supplies. They returned in the late afternoon with scant food and reported the uplands to be free of enemy soldiers. Roman watchtowers and outposts lay abandoned, most being in a state of disrepair, relics of a bygone era when the emperors of Constantinople had ruled the land all the way east to the River Euphrates, and south to Syria and Egypt.

On the sixth day the Catalan Company, now resembling ravenous wolves after its soldiers had consumed all their supplies and anything in their path, which in truth was little, arrived in the hills to the north of Philadelphia. The city itself lay in the fertile Cogamus Valley, at the foot of Mount Tmolus. Watered by many streams running off the high ground, the valley was a narrow, hundred-mile strip of abundance. The company made camp in the rolling countryside north of the valley, well out of sight of any Muslim mounted patrols in the valley or on its northern slopes.

Luca was called to Grand Duke Roger's tent as the sun began its slow descent in the western sky, casting long shadows as it dropped behind tall peaks in the distance. There were no pleasing aromas of food being cooked as he made his way through the rows of horses, stands of weapons and circular tents of the horsemen of Count Michael. The tent of Grand Duke Roger was a rather austere rectangular affair that had seen better days, its walls showing several patches covering rips and holes. The Almogavar guards standing sentry outside nodded to Luca when he stopped at the entrance to the tent, one darting inside to announce his arrival.

'Get yourself in here,' came Sancho's brusque order.

The Almogavar leader had black rings around his eyes, his hair and beard were long and unkempt, and his temper was short. Like the others, he sat on a stool for there was no table or other ornaments. Only things that could be carried on the backs of mules and packhorses had been brought on this campaign. Arabates raised a thin eyebrow when Luca stood to attention before the commanders. One of his Alan soldiers stood next to him to translate the Italian and Spanish words spoken by the others, for the illiterate Arabates had no knowledge of either language.

Count Michael, who had no stubble on his chin and whose hair was well groomed, also had tired eyes and a drawn expression. Only Grand Duke Roger seemed of good cheer.

221

'You are well, Black Sheep?'

'Well, lord, thank you.'

'Father Ramon has been tormenting my ears about your Muslim lover, Black Sheep.'

Luca's expression hardened but Roger took the sting out of any rising anger.

'I did not summon you here to discuss the rights and wrongs of carnal relations with Muslims, but I am interested in their prayer rituals. Tell me, your woman...'

'Ayna is her name, lord.'

Sancho glared at him but Roger merely smiled.

'Can you tell me the precise times Ayna prays to her god?' asked Roger.

Luca saw the Alan babbling into Arabates' ear as he recounted Ayna's prayer times.

'At dawn, midday, in the late part of the afternoon, just after sunset, and between sunset and midnight, lord.'

'I am surprised she has time for anything else,' joked Roger.

A wry smile creased Luca's lips as he thought of the long winter nights they had spent wrapped around each other. The sharp-nosed Arabates was talking to his translator, who then spoke to Luca.

'My lord wants to know what you will do if you produce a bastard by this Muslim woman. What will you call such a mongrel child?'

Arabates gave Luca a superior leer.

'An Alan,' replied Luca. 'For what are they but landless half-breeds?'

Grand Duke Roger and Sancho roared with laughter and Count Michael winced. But Arabates growled with anger, jumped to

222

his feet and drew his sword at the insult. Luca also unsheathed his weapon.

'Halt,' shouted Sancho, also rising to his feet. 'Put that sword away and get out, Luca.'

He placed himself between Luca and Arabates, Count Michael talking to the Alan leader in his native tongue in an effort to calm him. Grand Duke Roger remained seated and caught Luca's eye, giving him a wink but waving him away. Luca slid the sword back in its scabbard and exited the tent, pleased with himself that he had defended Ayna's honour. He had no idea why he had been summoned to the meeting to impart the timing of his lover's prayers.

He found out later that day when the order was given to quit camp and move south through the trees that blanketed the slopes of the northern ridge of the Cogamus Valley. The Almogavars moved fast, eager to traverse the forest before the light faded and made movement among the trees treacherous. Luca had nothing in his food bag and felt very hungry. Around him dozens of other Catalans were grumbling about the lack of food.

'Silence,' hissed Sancho, who in the half-light of the forest appeared even more gaunt than earlier. 'Enemy scouts can hear as well as see.'

Jordi, also hungry, had sunk into a sullen silence, his mood prickly. Men slipped or tripped on branches and cursed under their breaths as the Catalans descended the slope leading to the valley below, the forest eerily silent as thousands of men and hundreds of horses moved through the trees. The Alans and Count Michael's horsemen led their mounts on foot, and it was testament to the skill with which they did so that Luca did not hear a single whinny or

223

squeal from a horse. But the rumblings in his stomach threatened to echo through the trees so loud were they.

The light faded fast and the last part of the journey was conducted in darkness. It was agonisingly slow and Luca had difficulty making out shapes around him. By this time, the Almogavars had been deployed into a line, in preparation for the morning attack, which would be launched just before dawn to hopefully surprise the enemy while they were conducting prayers.

'Halt.'

Sancho's quiet order was conveyed along the line and Luca crouched down beside a tree, Jordi on the other side of trunk. The Almogavars and their allies were near the edge of the forest and Luca could make out flickers of yellow ahead through the trees – the enemy camp. As he sat in silence with hundreds of others, faint voices reached his ears, accompanied by occasional laughter. He was glad, the sounds of merriment would have hopefully masked any sounds coming from the tree-covered hill.

Luca sat alone with his thoughts, which revolved around where his next meal was coming from. That and the cold that seeped into his limbs as he sat on the ground, waiting. Waiting for Sancho Rey to give the command to launch the Almogavar attack. Alarm shot through him and he reached for his belt, smiling with relief when he felt the leather pouch attached to it, the same pouch gifted him by Princess Maria in what seemed an age away. He moved his hand along the belt to caress the hilt of the dagger that had also been a gift from the princess. A weapon with a strange blade that cut through anything, though as yet no enemy flesh.

That enemy became upper-most in his mind when he heard thousands of voices chanting 'Allahu Akbar' – *God is the Greatest* –

'Subhana rabbiyal adheem' – *Glory be to my Lord Almighty* – and 'Sam'i Allahu liman hamidah, Rabbana wa lakal hamd'– *God hears those who call upon Him; Our Lord, praise be to You* – all part of the prayer sequence he had seen Ayna perform may times. He found her prostrating herself on the ground, bowing and raising her hands up all rather odd, but no odder than Christian priests reciting in Latin, a language he did not understand. The forest was filled with half-light once more and he saw Sancho, his eyes large black holes in the dimness, turn and gesture to those nearby to follow him. He glanced at Jordi who gave him a thin smile. He rose to his feet and followed the Almogavar leader.

The army of Sasa Bey, the *emir* of the Germiyanid Emirate, had arrayed itself in a great crescent before the walls of Philadelphia, the city backed by volcanic cliffs and perched on a large plateau. They had erected rows of wooden stakes in front of the city and a deep ditch in front of them. All the *emir*'s soldiers were well out of range of any arrows or crossbow bolts shot from the city walls, and those walls were tall and strong, making the city almost impregnable. Especially so since the *emir* had no siege engines with which to batter down Philadelphia's walls. But he had a greater weapon than a mangonel or trebuchet: hunger.

The city had an unlimited supply of water, an abundance of springs ensuring its citizens would not die of thirst. But when the city granaries emptied, there would be a choice between surrender or starvation. The fertile valley was occupied by the *emir*, the nearest Roman army was at Artake, over a hundred miles to the north, and the Germiyanids knew that no help was coming. All they had to do was sit and wait for the city to yield.

Luca, minutes before tired and hungry, moved quickly to leave the treeline and race across the open ground between the forest and the enemy camp, a huge sprawl of round tents of various sizes. The Almogavars, as was their custom, did not scream or holler war cries, focusing instead on reaching their target as quickly as possible.

But not quickly enough.

Trumpets and drums sounded the alarm as sentries who had not been saying prayers, having been given special dispensation, spotted the hundreds of soldiers exiting the trees. And they also heard the whooping and shouts of the Alans, rushing from the trees on their steeds with recurve bows in their hands. The mercenary horsemen reached the Turkish camp first, riding between tents and shooting down anything in their path. Count Michael and his two hundred horsemen plus Corberan's fifteen hundred Spanish riders kept tight to the Almogavars to lend their support when the inevitable counterattack came.

The Almogavars also moved through the camp, which stood between them and the thousands of Muslim soldiers that had been praying behind the rows of stakes in a mass show of piety. And to intimidate the besieged citizens of Philadelphia. Now those soldiers were rushing away from the city to deal with the soldiers that had, like ghosts, appeared from the forest. The two forces clashed in the sprawl of the Germiyanid camp. Trained to fight in small units, the Almogavars had the advantage from the beginning as the blocks of tents divided the two forces into many separate parts.

The world suddenly became much smaller for Luca as the camp acted like a giant sieve to reduce the number of soldiers moving between rows of tents. The foot soldiers of Count Michael, trained to fight shoulder-to-shoulder like their Roman forefathers, would have become hopelessly disorganised in the maze of tents, but not so the Almogavars.

Spear in his left hand, right hand holding a javelin, senses heightened, Luca rounded a tent and saw a man with bow nocked. The two spotted each other at the same time and the next two seconds would decide their fate. Luca threw the javelin as the Turk raised his bow to take aim, the steel point of Luca's missile striking the man in the chest, causing him to spin to the left and shoot his arrow harmlessly into the sky. He, Sancho and Jordi raced forward to attack other archers coming into view between a row of tents, Sancho and his son plunging their spears into unprotected bellies before they were shot by arrows, Luca doing likewise to a bowman about to put an arrow in his friend

Using the skewered archers as shields, Almogavars behind them, the trio held the writhing Turks in place as Catalans behind them hurled javelins at the remaining archers, one or two managing to hit Almogavars with their arrows before recoiling as they were struck. The rest fled. Luca yanked the spear point out of the Turk, leaped over his body and carried on, racing into a clearing where food in cauldrons was being cooked over campfires.

Suddenly, from the front, left and right, came screaming soldiers wearing red turbans, armed with spears, axes and clubs, and protected by round wooden shields, slightly larger than the Almogavar buckler.

'All-round defence,' screamed Sancho.

Now the Almogavars fought shoulder-to-shoulder, forming a circle as the enemy closed in on them like wolves.

'Duck,' came a gruff voice behind Luca.

He did as commanded, crouching low with spear in his right hand, buckler in his left, fending off a Turk with an axe. A Turk who wore a surprised expression as the javelin point went straight through his neck. Luca shouted in triumph, sprang to his feet and plunged his spear point into the right shoulder of the Turk immediately behind, sending him reeling backwards. Luca's elation was brief. Out of the corner of his eye he saw a big brute swinging a club over his head. He just had time to raise his buckler to defeat the blow, the club splintering the wood of his shield and causing him to stumble. The brute swung the cudgel up again but let out a low groan when Jordi stabbed him in the belly with his spear. The big man went down on one knee, dropped his club and died when Luca pushed his spear point through his right eye socket. Which was promptly lopped off by a screeching Turk wielding a two-handed axe.

Luca killed him with the last of his javelins, other Almogavars throwing missiles from the circle like a cobra spitting poison. He drew his sword and prepared to fight fresh attackers. His weapon had a straight blade nearly two feet in length, a grooved wooden handle for grip, and a round pommel at the end of the handle for balance. Its point and cutting edge on both sides made it ideal for close-quarters combat, as opposed to the heavier and longer swords used by other European soldiers, or scimitars favoured by the Muslims. These weapons were ideal for slashing but the Almogavar short sword was designed for jabbing and stabbing at close quarters.

He heard Hector's voice.

'You don't need to lop off an enemy's head or run him through, just put three inches of the point into him and he'll go down.'

228

It was so now as he used his battered buckler to parry spear points and sword thrusts, and then struck like the sting of a scorpion to wound opponents.

The enemy were now few in numbers and became fewer still when whistle blasts announced the arrival of more Almogavars at the scene, weapons smeared with enemy blood. The camp was slowly being cleared, Corberan's horsemen forming a perimeter around it to cut down any Turks seeking to escape what was becoming a rout.

Sancho, Angel, Marc and Hector kept their men under tight control as they swept the camp after Turkish resistance had collapsed, many of the *emir*'s men throwing down their weapons, falling to their knees and begging for mercy. Mostly, they were granted it as the Almogavars turned their attention from killing to eating.

An individual suddenly ran from one of the tents and threw himself at Luca's feet, babbling incomprehensibly. He was short and portly and appeared to be unarmed. Luca pressed the point of his sword under his chin and forced him to his feet. Jordi, fit to drop, was using his spear as a support.

'Shut up,' said an equally exhausted Luca, withdrawing his sword when the man began to sob. It was pathetic. He began pointing to a nearby pot hanging over a fire and making gestures mimicking eating.

'Perhaps he's a cook,' mused Jordi.

Luca's eyes lit up. He pointed at the pot and then at the man with the double chin and thinning hair, who began nodding and smiling. Luca rubbed his belly and also mimicked eating.

'Hungry.'

The portly man nodded with excitement and walked over to the cooking pot, then pointed at the group of Almogavars standing round it.

'He *is* a cook,' said a delighted Luca.

They cleared the area of bodies, dumping them a short distance away between two rows of tents, and eagerly awaited the fare being prepared by the cook. No one considered he might be a poisoner who was preparing their last meal. They were all too hungry.

He did not poison the Catalans but rather gave Luca and the others wooden bowls, into which he heaped a delicious stew made from eggplant, onions and tomatoes, stiffened by herbs and spices. It was accompanied by bread made just the day before, which Luca and the others devoured with relish. The cook also brought cheese and olive oil from other tents, which the Almogavars also wolfed down.

The camp was bursting with food, and the field kitchens that had been left unmolested were soon being used to bake fresh bread from the abundance of flour on site. The Almogavar commanders and Count Michael soon had the camp secured and the prisoners corralled into a small section and placed under guard. It was soon discovered that the Turks used slaves to undertake menial duties, such as digging latrines, cleaning and tending to their senior officers. Luca's cook had been one such captive, hence his eagerness to ingratiate himself with his 'liberators'.

Luca, his belly full and the air warm, closed his eyes and let the sun warm his face. The stench of death had yet to permeate the camp, the slain all around but as yet not bloated and filled with noxious gases. The other Almogavars were also taking the opportunity to sleep on a full stomach, a rarity over the past few days. The cook was still fussing around them, taking away empty bowls and refilling wooden cups with water. Despite obviously being a foreigner and presumably Muslim, no one interrupted him. But they did open their eyes when he began babbling in an animated fashion.

Luca sighed and opened his eyes. To see four Alan horsemen nearby, one of them pointing at the cook. Luca recognised him. He was the translator who had stood beside Arabates when he had been summoned to the meeting of the commanders by Sancho. He rose to his feet, those around him doing likewise.

'What do you want?' he said to the translator, who was dressed in a blue felt robe and yellow baggy leggings.

The translator looked at him, his expression one of disdain as he recognised him as the low-born individual who had insulted his lord.

'All slaves are to be collected and interned in the space allocated to them.' He pointed at the cook. 'He is not an Almogavar.'

'You have the eyes of an eagle,' said Luca, mockingly.

The translator spoke to the Turk in his native tongue but the cook clearly did not wish to depart with the horsemen. One of the Alans nudged his horse forward, levelling his spear to point it at the cook. Luca stood between the rider and the Turk.

'He stays here. We have need of a good cook.'

The translator curled his lip. 'Did you not hear what I said, Catalan? All slaves are to be taken to the internment area.'

He spoke to the rider with the levelled spear, who leaned forward and placed the tip of his spear point against Luca's neck.

'I do not wish to spill more blood, but…'

The rider stiffened in the saddle, dropped his spear at Luca's feet and slid from the saddle, a javelin embedded in his chest. Luca

231

turned to see Jordi with a satisfied smile on his face. Luca nodded in thanks.

Another Alan nocked an arrow in his bowstring but was dead before he could draw it back, an Almogavar having thrown a javelin at him with such force that the steel point went straight through his heart and out of his back.

'Leave now,' Luca told the translator.

The Alan looked around at the row of determined faces staring back at him, and the javelins in their hands. He had seen the deadly efficiency with which the Catalans handled their missiles and knew he would follow his two men to the grave if he provoked further violence. He shrugged. Who wanted to die for a Muslim slave? He turned his horse and trotted away, the other Alan following. The cook fell to his knees, clutching his hands together and thanking Luca for his intervention, or that is how the former shepherd interpreted the show of deference. Luca grabbed his shoulders and raised him up, the other Almogavars resuming their slumbers, the outbreak of violence just an inconvenient interruption.

Sancho let his men loot and rest for the remainder of the morning before holding a roll call, at which it was revealed the Almogavars has lost a mere hundred men, Count Michael a dozen, and the Alans around a hundred and fifty, several of whom had been killed squabbling over loot after the Turks had been defeated. The enemy had lost several thousand dead and several thousand more captured, who were given to the Governor of Philadelphia as a gift. The governor himself extended an invitation to the leaders of the relief force to attend a banquet to celebrate the great victory outside the walls of his city. A detachment of horsemen attired in mail armour, helmets and shields decorated with yellow crosses on a red

232

background rode out of the city in the afternoon to escort the captives into the city.

Luca and Jordi spent the afternoon trying to converse, after a fashion, with the cook. They discovered his name was Ertan and that he liked to call both of them 'efendi', which they believed was a term of endearment. Beyond that was incomprehension.

Sancho issued orders for parties to be sent back into the forest to cut down trees for firewood to burn the bodies of the enemy slain, the Christian dead to be interred in a mass grave according to religious doctrine. Together with the stakes that had pointed at the city, a series of huge funeral pyres was turning the Turkish dead into ash. Ertan clawed at his breast and wept uncontrollably at the sight, which Luca could not fathom.

After they had finished stacking wood, Sancho Rey appeared to congratulate his son, and Luca, on their bravery during the battle, Roc and the other Almogavars slapping the pair on the back. Sancho pulled the two aside.

'Word reached me that two Alans were killed in a dispute with you two.'

'It's true, father,' admitted Jordi.

'They tried to take our cook,' added Luca.

Sancho frowned. 'Your cook?'

Jordi pointed at the still-weeping Ertan.

'We have adopted him, father.'

'He's a good cook,' said Luca.

Sancho held out his hand.

'Captives count as spoils of war, all of which are to be given to the Governor of Philadelphia. Since you have deprived him of a slave, I will take his value in coin and give it to the city treasurer. Open your pouches.'

They both reluctantly gave Sancho some of the coins given to them by the emperor. They still had a substantial amount left but felt cheated.

'Where are the Alan bodies?' asked Sancho.

Jordi jerked a thumb behind him.

'We cremated them with the Muslims.'

'Poor Muslims,' said Luca.

Sancho suppressed a smile. 'Oh, by the way. Count Michael has told me that the governor is an old admirer of Princess Maria and would be interested to meet the pair who saved her life. So, you will be accompanying us into the city. Try not to kill anyone when you get inside. And don't get drunk.'

Chapter 13

Philadelphia was a beautiful city, which was called 'Little Athens' on account of the magnificence of the temples and public buildings that filled it. Its ancient Greek roots were reflected in the city's layout, its main thoroughfares intersecting at right angles to produce a symmetrical grid system. The streets were clean and litter free, the main streets being colonnaded with white marble pillars. The city was filled with many churches with domed roofs supported by heavy piers, marble walls, vaults and coloured glass mosaics. The mosaics and frescoes decorating the vaults and domes took advantage of their curved surfaces to bring the religious stories they were depicting to life.

The city was filled with fountains, cool spring water providing citizens with clean drinking water and also used to water the municipal gardens dotted throughout Philadelphia. And also allowed the streets to be washed each day. Most cities stank as a result of rubbish dumped in the streets and open cess pits located outside the city walls. But Philadelphia was different. Its air was fresh and healthy, breezes blowing away nauseous odours. Even the citizens, though the city was far from a teeming metropolis, looked hale and well attired.

Luca, Jordi and Sancho walked behind the mounted figures of Grand Duke Roger, Arabates, Corberan and Count Michael, with their respective standard bearers holding the banners of Catalonia, the flag of the Emperor of Constantinople, and a strange blue banner depicting a golden lion rampant wearing a crown, which was the personal motif of Arabates. The Alan leader kept glancing behind him to give Luca hateful stares.

'Looks like you have made another friend, Black Sheep,' mused Sancho.

Luca had discovered that when the Almogavar leader was displeased with him, he referred to him by his nickname, whereas when he was in his favour, he called him by his first name.

'Yes, lord,' he replied, unconcerned about the boorish Alan.

He was far more interested in the magnificent walls that guarded Philadelphia. As befitting the important and wealthy trade centre the city had been, and perhaps would be once again, those walls were at least thirty feet in height and ten feet thick. They consisted of a core of mortar and rubble faced with well-dressed stone blocks. Stairways had been built into the walls at regular intervals to allow members of the garrison to ascend to parapets constructed of brick. In addition, semi-circular towers protruding outwards from the walls, spaced at one-hundred-yard intervals, allowed archers and crossbowmen to direct volleys of missiles against the flanks of any enemy assaulting the walls.

The gates into the city were also impressive, the one Luca and the others walked through comprising two arches supported by six stone pillars. Waiting for the group was a colour party of fully armoured horsemen called cataphracts, each rider wearing a mail hauberk, coif, chausses and a helmet, and sitting on a horse protected by scale armour on its body, neck and head. Beneath their mail they wore red tunics fringed with gold, with red and yellow plumes on their helmets. They numbered a score, with an additional six mounted trumpeters who blew a fanfare that startled the horse Arabates was riding, nearly throwing the Alan leader. Luca smiled but Sancho jabbed him in the ribs.

'Remember what I said. You will be on your best behaviour.'

236

The city sat above the valley, but above the city stood the citadel, the ancient Greek acropolis where pagan shrines and statues had been replaced by Christian churches, barracks, stables and the governor's palace. Surrounding the whole were walls with rectangular towers spaced at regular intervals.

The governor, Ioannes Komnenos, and his family were waiting for their saviours in the spacious courtyard in the citadel, Luca feeling like the peasant he was when he stood in a line with the others to accept the applause of the governor and his family. The Komnenos dynasty had once ruled the Roman Empire, though that had been two hundred years before, but it was still a powerful and wealthy family. That wealth was displayed in the rich attire worn by the governor, his wife and their three children, all adults. They all wore silk *kabbadions* with gold embroideries on the collars, sleeves and hems, the women's garments also decorated with pearls. The governor wore no sword and neither did his son, as was the custom of the court in Constantinople.

Luca estimated the governor, tall and lean with a weathered, clean-shaven face and kind blue eyes, to be in his fifties or late forties, his beautiful olive-skinned wife with raven-black hair to be slightly younger. After the obligatory fanfare of trumpets, he stepped forward to speak to the new arrivals in turn. Luca glanced at Jordi who was ogling the governor's daughters, both in their twenties and both having inherited their mother's good looks. They politely stared into space as the governor spoke first to his friend, Count Michael, and then to Grand Duke Roger. Luca was mortified when Arabates next to him broke wind loudly, hoping no one would think he was responsible. The Alan grinned but Luca was disgusted.

Governor Ioannes spoke to Sancho in Italian, having conversed with Count Michael in Greek, which he also spoke to the boorish Arabates. He laid a hand on Luca's shoulder when he faced the young Italian.

'Count Michael has informed me of your bravery in saving the life of Princess Maria,' his voice was slightly hoarse. 'As one of her oldest friends, I thank you from the bottom of my heart.'

'Thank you, lord.'

He noticed the Damascus daggers on his and Jordi's right sides.

'Being a mercenary must be very profitable these days to afford such expensive weapons.'

'They were a gift from the emperor, lord,' Luca told him.

'After we saved the princess,' added Jordi.

The governor smiled at Sancho's son. 'Then they were a measly gift for the life of such a great lady.'

The governor had a few words with Jordi before walking back to his family and inviting the visitors into his palace, the chief eunuch requesting they follow him to their allotted quarters. Arabates grabbed Luca's tunic.

'Do not think I have forgotten the murder of two of my men.'

So, he did speak Italian.

Luca yanked his sleeve free.

'Your men need to learn more manners.'

The interior of the palace was exquisite. Doors were decorated with sheaths of gold and silver leaf. Corridors were painted with murals of past glories, beautiful enamelled pottery stood on mahogany cabinets, and miniatures of members of the Komnenos family decorated the walls. These things were pleasant to look at, but

238

for Luca and Jordi the true jewel in the governor's palace was his private bathhouse.

Fed by mountain spring water, it had three rooms – warm, hot and cold – where guests could refresh themselves. It was a far cry from jumping into a lake or a river, slaves taking their clothes in the changing room before they were shown naked into the warm room. The walls and floor were heated to make the body sweat, after which they were shown into the next room where they immersed themselves in an invigorating hot bath. Now sweating profusely, they were shown into another room where slaves were waiting to massage their bodies with oils, after which the dirt and sweat were scraped off their bodies using a curved instrument called a *strigil*. Their hair was also trimmed and their beards removed, for they had not shaved since they had left Artake. The final part of the bathing process involved them jumping into cold baths, which caused them to gasp but banished any drowsiness they may have felt. War seemed a thousand miles away, but was uppermost in the thoughts of the governor the next day when he laid bare the woeful position he and his city were in.

He spoke in Greek but had provided a translator so Sancho would understand what he said. Luca and Jordi stood behind the seated Almogavar leader in the spacious meeting room, the walls of which were decorated with murals depicting the recapture of Philadelphia by the Emperor Alexios from the Turks two hundred years before. Slaves served wine to those seated at a table with heavy, carved legs, Ioannes staring at his silver, jewelled chalice.

'There was a time when the *doux* of the Thrakesion Theme was able to supply ten thousand soldiers to the imperial army, along with great quantities of wine, olives, wheat, barley, corn, biscuit, flour and beasts of burden to keep those soldiers in the field.'

The governor looked up and remembered that neither Sancho nor Arabates were familiar with the organisation of the empire, so explained that a theme was a province of the empire, administered by a governor called a *doux*, and a military commander called a *stratopedarches*. He undertook both roles, seeing as little of the once-great Thrakesion Theme remained under the emperor's control.

'With the shrinkage of the theme's territory came a reduction in the number of soldiers it could muster,' continued Ioannes, 'since the theme's soldiers are recruited from its landowners.'

'How many men can you raise, lord?' asked Sancho.

'A thousand at most,' came the blunt answer.

Roger raised an eyebrow.

'Of those, half must remain in the city to guard against a surprise attack,' said Ioannes.

'Five hundred men,' lamented Roger, 'is not a large number to add to our own forces. The emperor has tasked us with relieving Magnesia and Tire as well as this great city.'

Ioannes took a sip of wine, observing the standing Luca and Jordi.

'As far as I know and bearing in mind I have not heard anything from its governor in over a month, Magnesia still holds out, though for how much longer I do not know. As for Tire, it is in a similar perilous condition.'

'Time is of the essence,' said Count Michael.

'We will march first to Magnesia,' declared Sancho, prompting smiles from the pair behind him. Ioannes pointed at them.

240

'With wolves like these under your command, I have no doubt Mehmed Bey will be running for the hills.'

Roger wore a blank expression. 'Who is that, my lord?'

'The ruler of the Aydin Emirate, duke,' the governor told him. 'Just one of the Muslim warlords who now infest this once-great land.'

'Thank God they do not have siege engines,' said Roger.

'Even if they did, they would only use them as a last resort,' Ioannes told him. 'They do not wish to destroy the towns and cities in this land but desire to possess them, just as they have done to countless farms, villages and towns throughout Anatolia.'

'After first killing the inhabitants,' said Arabates.

Ioannes shook his head. 'They are not like the Mongols.'

'Who are the Mongols?' asked Sancho.

Ioannes laughed. 'What would I give to be able to ask that question? The Mongols are a godless people from the east who slaughter everyone who does not immediately yield to them. The Turks, in contrast, offer to preserve the lives of Christians in the lands they conquer, and even respect their religion, up to a point. But they build mosques to replace churches, levy additional taxes on Christians in their domains, and bar non-Muslims from holding positions of power.'

'They are soft,' mocked Arabates.

'They are *clever*,' Ioannes corrected him, 'for they know that in time the Christians under their control will either convert to Islam or depart their lands, never to return.'

'Never to return?' said Roger.

241

Ioannes emptied his chalice. 'I will be frank with you, grand duke, seeing as your great service to me and this city deserves honesty. Two hundred and thirty years ago, the empire suffered a great defeat at the hands of the Turks at a place called Manzikert. Prior to that battle, Anatolia was the nursery of the empire's armies. After it, the empire suffered perpetual shrinkage and decline at the hands of the Turks.'

'There have been many defeats since that clash,' said Count Michael, 'though Manzikert was a hammer blow, second only to the treachery of the Latin crusaders a hundred years ago.'

'When the Pope's soldiers sacked Constantinople,' mused Roger, 'that was a black day for Christendom. And yet, my lords, all is not lost. We have won three great victories against the Turks, and God willing, we shall win many more before this campaign is done.'

'How far away is Magnesia?' asked Sancho, bored by tales of Roman history.

'Forty miles to the west,' Ioannes informed him, 'near the port of Izmir, Mehmed Bey's capital.

'This Mehmed Bey must now be in a weakened position,' said Roger, 'seeing as we have just destroyed his army.'

Ioannes gave him a kindly smile. 'Alas, grand duke, you have just destroyed the Germiyanid army of Sasa Bey, who is another *emir*.'

'We will need replacement spears and javelins before we can march to relieve Magnesia,' said Sancho. 'This *emir*, this Mehmed Bey, he has a large army?'

A slave refilled the governor's chalice. 'He can field around ten thousand men.'

'Then it is better if we strike first as opposed to waiting for him to march through the valley to attack us,' stated Sancho.

242

The Almogavars, Catalan horsemen and Alans emptied the Turkish camp of all food before they marched west on the second morning after their arrival before the city. The tents were left standing as the Catalan Company would be returning to Philadelphia after relieving Magnesia, afterwards striking south to relieve the town of Tire. Their food bags full to bursting and equipped with replacement spears and javelins from Philadelphia's armouries, the Almogavars were in high spirits as they marched through the lush valley. It was dotted with farms and villages, all of which they skirted and did not molest, Corberan's horsemen ensuring the Alans, who had already claimed the hundreds of captured horses for their own, did not plunder the countryside. Count Komnenos had joined the expedition with a hundred of his magnificent cataphracts, two hundred more lightly armed horsemen, and a similar number of squires and servants to attend him and his armoured riders. They were all mounted, but they and the rest of the relief column were preceded by the aged Archbishop of Philadelphia, behind him three of his priests holding icons of Jesus, the Virgin Mary and Emperor Basil. The arrival of the Catalan Company before the walls of Philadelphia was interpreted as a miracle by the archbishop. His request that he and a coterie of his priests be allowed to join the expedition with holy icons was gladly welcomed by the pious governor. The presence of the icons stiffened the resolve of the emperor's soldiers but slowed the column to a crawl.

It should have taken two days to reach Magnesia, but when the company and its Alan allies made camp among the trees on a hill above the valley at the end of the first day, the column had advanced a mere ten miles. It would take a further three at least to reach Magnesia, by which time any scouts or spies of the enemy would

243

have alerted the besiegers of the approach of the company, thereby wrecking any hope of surprise, especially so since the Turkish-held town of Salihli guarded the approach to Magnesia from the east. The Turks were known to have developed a signalling system of beacons and flags in the valley to warn of any threat to the port of Izmir. The town, nestled on the southern slopes of the valley, was small but would have to be invested to prevent the garrison commander sending out parties to attack the relief column.

Sancho Rey, never the most patient of men, wanted to strike fast and quickly to utilise the Almogavars to maximum effect. He had no interest in trailing behind priests swinging incense burners and holding icons aloft. He therefor devised a scheme to rid him and his men of the priests, the fractious Alans and Count Komnenos and his horsemen that required a small army of servants to maintain them and attend to their every need.

'We are going over the hills to bypass the town and strike directly for Magnesia,' he told his son as Jordi, Luca and Roc sat round a campfire eating bread cooked that morning in Philadelphia. 'We will leave just after dawn tomorrow. This is Romanus, a native of these parts, who will show us the way. Make him feel at home, Luca. Like you he was a shepherd in a former life.'

Romanus looked like a beggar in his dirty tunic and leggings, though he was wearing a pair of stout leather shoes. Roc passed him a leather flask filled with wine and offered him a place beside the fire, which he accepted.

Luca pointed at himself. 'Shepherd, like you.'

'Shep-herd,' said Romanus slowly. Italian was obviously a foreign language to him.

244

Jordi repeated the sentence in Catalan, which elicited a similar confused look from the shaggy haired Roman.

'Count Komnenos informed me Romanus is familiar with the Cogamus Valley, having worked in these hills all his life,' said Sancho.

Luca looked at the sombre Roman. They were probably the same age, both being lean and sinewy on account of the hard life of a shepherd – an over-weight shepherd did not exist. He and Jordi did their best to make the newcomer welcome but the inability to converse with him was an insurmountable barrier, and so he and they merely sat and watched the flames of the fire before falling asleep. Luca was woken to stand guard during the night and before the first rays of the sun had lanced through the forest canopy, he and the others were being led through the trees by Romanus, Sancho by his side and nearly four thousand Almogavars following. The horsemen were left behind to make a loud show of noise and colour before the walls of Salihli, to divert the enemy's attention away from the real relief force that was snaking its way over the hills to arrive at the camp of Mehmed Bey before the walls of Magnesia. The Almogavars, rested and rejuvenated, maintained a cruel pace in their eagerness to achieve maximum surprise, descending the mountainside to the immediate south of the city, which was surrounded on three sides by a plain through which the River Gediz meandered.

To find no enemy army anywhere in sight.

But the sight of hundreds of Almogavars descending the range of hills behind the city was enough to scatter the people working in the fields and in the vineyards and orchards surrounding Magnesia. They abandoned their tools, wagons and animals to flee back to the city, Luca bemused by their reaction at the appearance of their saviours.

245

'This is most odd,' growled Sancho, holding up a hand to halt the long column behind him.

Romanus turned, grinned at him and pointed at Sancho.

'Magnesia.'

Sancho ignored him but pointed at Luca and Jordi.

'Fetch Marc, Angel and Hector.'

They did as they were told, running back up the slope to search for the other council members and division commanders. The Almogavars sat down to drink from their water bottles in preparation. For what? There was no enemy army before the walls of the city and no sign that a siege had ever taken place.

'The Turks may have packed up and left,' suggested Marc.

'Perhaps the governor destroyed them just as we did at Philadelphia,' opined Angel.

Sancho discounted the notions, making a sweep with his arm.

'This valley has not been touched by war in a long time. I see no ditches, traces of an encampment or large areas of dug-up earth to indicate mass graves.'

'Perhaps the Turks captured it before winter,' said Hector, 'and *we* are the ones who will be besieging it.'

Sancho looked at the impressive city of white stone and the high walls that surrounded it, stout round towers at regular intervals along their length and four huge gatehouses giving entry into Magnesia. Count Michael had told him that the city had been founded by veterans of the Trojan War two thousand years before and had subsequently become an important Greek and then Roman trading centre. And when the Latin crusaders had taken Constantinople in the last century, Magnesia was for a brief time the capital of the Roman Empire, housing the imperial mint and imperial

246

treasury. He could see soldiers on the walls and in the towers, the sun reflecting off their helmets and spear points. He could also identify flags fluttering in the morning breeze, small squares of red and yellow.

'No, this city is not yet under Muslim control. But perhaps they think *we* are Turks. The men will stay here until I have spoken to the governor.'

'Do you speak Greek?' asked Marc. 'I doubt the governor can speak our language.'

'I'm sure there is someone in that fine city who can act as a translator,' replied Sancho.

'What about our guide?' suggested Luca.

They all looked at him.

'He can't understand what *we* are saying. Idiot,' scoffed Marc.

'That may be, but he's the best we've got,' said Sancho. 'If I get shot, you will command, Hector.'

He pointed at Jordi and Luca. 'You two are with me.'

Luca felt distinctly nervous as he descended the grassy slope above the city, Sancho diverting to the right to avoid the towers where archers were nocking arrows in their bowstrings. There were no clouds in the sky and only a soft breeze, which meant any archer worth his salt would be able to shoot at the four individuals with ease should they come within range, especially as none wore any body armour.

The tension rose as the group neared the eastern gatehouse, halting a safe distance from the battlements where many soldiers peered down at the Almogavars. Luca glanced back at the mass of Almogavars on the hillside and wished he was with them. The more so when a single arrow left the battlements, arched into the air and slammed into the ground a few feet in front of Sancho.

'We are friends,' called the Almogavar leader.

Another arrow was shot at them, this one thudding into the earth closer to his feet. He turned and ordered the scout to plead the Catalan's cause. He may have been a poor shepherd, but Luca was proud of him as he walked past Sancho towards the closed gates, shouting something in Greek. It must have resonated with those on the walls as no more arrows were shot at Sancho and those with him. The guide continued to shout up at the walls, no response coming from the battlements for what seemed like an age. But then, as Luca scuffed at the ground in boredom, a shrill voice was heard from the gatehouse.

'Who comes with an army to the city of Magnesia?'

The words were Catalan, a language Luca was familiar with and could now speak if not fluently, then certainly adequately. Sancho handed his spear to his son and walked forward, slapping the guide on the back in thanks.

'I am Sancho Rey, leader of the Almogavars, part of the Catalan Company sent by Emperor Andronicus to aid you in your fight against the Turks.'

'We have not heard of you,' came the blunt reply.

'I am the vanguard of a great army led by Count Ioannes Komnenos, Count Michael Cosses and Grand Duke Roger de Flor, who is married to the emperor's niece.'

There was a long silence and Luca thought Sancho's words had had no effect. But then one of the heavy wooden gates beneath the battlements creaked open.

'You and your three companions may enter the city, Sancho Rey,' came the reply. 'You must surrender your weapons to the guards when you do so.'

Sancho turned and beckoned Romanus, Luca and Jordi follow him, before striding towards the open gate. Once inside, they were disarmed by soldiers in pure white, knee-length tunics, white leggings, mail corselets, helmets and teardrop-shaped shields bearing a gold lion on a red background. Their spear points looked like mirrors so burnished were they. Luca and Jordi were very impressed, though Sancho viewed them with mild contempt. The officer in turn screwed up his face at the drab clothes worn by the Almogavars.

Like Philadelphia, Magnesia was clean and tidy, with well-maintained streets, splendid buildings and impressive churches. Curious citizens stared at the Almogavars being escorted from the gatehouse to the palace located in the centre of the city. Neither they nor Magnesia gave the impression of having suffered the trial of a siege.

The palace was a place of beauty surrounded by gardens and fountains. Large bronze doors gave access to the main entrance, leading to a corridor containing statues of former Roman emperors, generals and philosophers. Luca walked on a mosaic floor depicting the recapture of Magnesia from the Muslims by the Emperor Alexios two hundred years before. He and the others gasped when they were led into the Golden Hall, which was decorated with gold leaf, had half a dozen vaulted niches, a score of windows to allow light to flood in, and a massive domed ceiling. It looked like something out of a Greek myth. The white-uniformed guards standing by each niche appeared almost transparent in the dazzling light. And there, at the far end of the hall, sat the governor, dressed in a gold-trimmed blue

249

kabbadion decorated with brocaded lions in silver thread, sitting on the golden throne once used by the emperors of Constantinople when they had been in exile.

A court official in a white *kabbadion* marched to stand beside the throne and nodded to the officer escorting Luca and the others, who ushered them forward. All subdued chatter ceased as courtiers and officials looked at the Almogavars and their guide as they walked towards the governor, stopping when the officer held out his left arm to halt their progress. The voice of the white-dressed court official filled the hall, speaking in Catalan.

'You are in the presence of Count Arcadius Drogon, General of the Emperor, Governor of Magnesia and Scourge of the Godless.'

Perhaps in his early thirties, Arcadius Drogon was an exceptionally handsome man erring to feminine beauty, with a mass of blonde curls and ringlets that resembled liquid gold in the bright light of the hall. He toyed with one of those ringlets as he indicated the Almogavars should approach him. Luca noticed he had a gold ring on every finger, and also noticed that though he was talking to Sancho, his hazel eyes were examining him and Jordi closely, making him feel very uncomfortable.

The court official, who was obviously an expert in languages, listened to Arcadius and then spoke to Sancho in fluent Catalan.

'My lord wishes to know how many men are loitering in the hills above his city.'

'Nearly four thousand.'

'And how many more are marching with counts Komnenos and Cosses?'

'Three thousand horsemen,' answered Sancho.

'It would have been courteous to have sent word that you intended to march to my city, Sancho Rey. Your sudden appearance has frightened the populace.'

'We heard the city was under siege, like Philadelphia, so speed was essential,' said Sancho.

Arcadius licked his lips as he studied Luca.

'As you can see, Magnesia is not under siege.'

'What of this Muslim leader, this Mehmed Bey?'

Arcadius' blemish-free brow creased. 'What of him? He resides in his palace in Izmir and I reside in mine.'

Sancho, his instincts honed by years of soldiering, smelled a rat. He could see for himself the opulence of the governor's palace and his non-martial bearing. He doubted if Arcadius Drogon had ever wielded a sword in anger, though he believed he was well capable of thrusting a dagger into someone's back, be they friend or enemy. He wondered why, if the Turks had posed no threat to his own city, he had not lifted a finger to assist Philadelphia? But he was also astute enough to know not to pose these questions to the preening peacock seated in front of him.

'The rest of our army might be held up at the town of Salihli, lord,' said Sancho.

'Salihli is under the control of Saruhan Bey, who wishes to establish his own emirate, just as Sasa Bey and Mehmed Bey have done. Perhaps he will succeed.'

'He will with men like you opposing him,' thought Sancho.

Arcadius waved a hand at the Almogavars.

'Now you may leave us,' he commanded, 'and please remove your soldiers from the hills above my city. They are upsetting the common folk.'

251

Arcadius nodded at the officer who had escorted Sancho and the others from the city gates, who saluted, turned and indicated to the Almogavars they should leave.

'Wait,' said Arcadius, pointing at Luca and Jordi. 'They may stay if they so desire.'

For the first time in a long time, Luca felt real fear. He had grown increasingly uncomfortable during the interview when the governor had been speaking to Sancho but had been ogling him and Jordi. He had no desire to spend any more time in Arcadius Drogon's company, and by the concerned look on Jordi's face, neither did his friend.

'They are soldiers,' replied a testy Sancho, 'and cannot be spared.'

The Almogavars left the hills to enter the valley and march back east, towards the town of Salihli to link up with the rest of the army. After an hour of marching, they ran into a mounted patrol of Catalans, which informed Sancho the garrison of Salihli had surrendered after thousands of horsemen had been arrayed before the town walls. The meagre and half-starving garrison, ravaged by the harsh winter, had gladly surrendered their weapons to hobble north with their lives and the rags on their backs. For Count Cosses and Count Komnenos, it was another victory after the great defeat of the Germiyanids outside Philadelphia. The counts were delighted to hear the news the city of Magnesia was not in peril, which left only the besieged town of Tire to be relieved to bring the campaign to a successful end. Grand Duke Roger was also delighted, for different reasons.

Count Komnenos sent soldiers into Salihli to secure it for the emperor, and sent a courier to Magnesia to invite Count Drogon to join him and the others in the march to Tire. Grand Duke Roger assembled his officers in his tent to discuss other matters.

Luca and Jordi performed their duties as servers of wine as Roger sat huddled with the others in a small circle, perched on stools and resembling thieves in the night, their features made harsh by the half-light cast by a pair of flickering candles that provided the only illumination.

'Sancho has informed me of the situation at Magnesia,' began Roger, 'which confirms what I have believed for some time now.'

'Which is what?' asked Marc, holding out his cup for Luca to fill.

'That Emperor Andronicus is ruling over a rotting empire. Were it not for us, Artake would have already fallen and it would have been only a matter of time before Philadelphia would have suffered the same fate.'

'That is why the emperor hired us,' said Angel.

'It is accepted custom that mercenaries are paid for their services,' said Roger, 'but we are now in many weeks' arrears, and I fear the imperial treasury will renege on its promises made to us.'

'Then we will leave him to his many enemies,' shrugged Hector.

'Roger has another idea,' said Sancho, 'one we should seriously consider.'

'What I am about to say must not be spoken of to anyone outside this tent,' said Roger sternly, 'and that includes you Jordi and Black Sheep.'

Luca looked at Jordi and nodded to the grand duke.

'Yes, lord.'

'On pain of death,' emphasised Roger.

253

'I know the Almogavars do not accept the absolute ruler of a single lord,' said Roger, 'preferring to come to important decisions by common consensus. Therefore, I ask you, their captains, to consider my proposal, which is to remain in Anatolia and make it our home.'

'Home?' said Angel. 'Our home is Catalonia.'

'Is it, Angel?' replied Roger. 'Can you even remember what Anatolia looks like? The harsh truth is your king does not want you back, and neither will any king look kindly on a ruthless band of mercenaries that has spent the last twenty years fighting.'

'That is what we do,' said Hector.

'We are good at it,' added Marc.

'Which is why I am suggesting putting down roots here, in Anatolia,' said Roger, 'to establish our own kingdom, which we will defend against the Turks.'

'And the Romans?' asked Sancho. 'For they will be reluctant to swap one invader for another.'

'From what I have seen, the Romans have neither the means nor the will to reclaim their lost lands,' opined Roger. 'But we have both the means and the will, should your men so desire.'

Angel looked at Marc, who appeared thoughtful. Hector, relishing the idea of fighting all and sundry, whatever the location, was nodding at Sancho.

'We will certainly consider it, Roger,' said the Almogavar leader. He looked at the silent Corberan. 'What of you, my lord?'

'I am a lord without lands and a castle,' smiled the noble. 'I crave a place to call home as much as you do, Sancho Rey.'

Roger rubbed his hands together. 'Excellent, but we must be discreet when around our Roman allies.'

The hoarse voice of Count Komnenos outside the tent interrupted their plotting.

'Out of my way, I need to see the grand duke.'

The occupants of the tent all stood and Roger went outside, reappearing seconds later with a concerned Governor of Philadelphia.

Jordi offered him a cup of wine but he waved him away.

'A courier has just arrived from Philadelphia. The town of Tire is on the verge of being captured by the Turks. The governor sent an urgent message to the city, thinking I was in residence. The garrison is most depleted so he informs me.'

'We will leave in the morning, lord,' Roger assured him.

By the look on the count's weather-beaten face, he clearly believed the town would fall before any relief arrived.

'We must march east back to Philadelphia, skirt the hills and then head west to Tire. It will take at least three days.'

'Why don't we just go directly south, over the hills?' said Hector.

'It would take just as long for thousands of horses going through the hills using a handful of narrow, rocky tracks as it would riding around them,' replied a dejected Ioannes.

'Not for a small party on foot,' said Sancho.

'What are you thinking?' asked Roger.

'We send our crossbowmen and an equal number of our most agile foot soldiers to stiffen the garrison until the main force arrives. That guide who led us to Magnesia could show us the way through the hills and on to Tire.'

'Us?' said Roger.

'Never ask someone to do something you would not do yourself,' came the reply.

Jordi looked at Luca.

'I would go with you, father.'

'And me,' added Luca.

'We leave within the hour,' Sancho told them.

He took only the fastest and youngest, reasoning that a night journey through the hills, followed by a dash through the enemy's siege lines and then a battle manning the walls for those who made it would be a taxing affair. He was a weak link in the chain and so were the crossbowmen, who like him were in their early forties. When the Almogavars had first arrived in Sicily, they had comprised half spearmen-cum-javelineers and half crossbowmen, the former being assigned to guard the latter on the battlefield. But the Almogavars were themselves missile soldiers, albeit armed with javelins and not crossbows. Moreover, they could defend themselves against horsemen and fight at close quarters against enemy foot soldiers, something crossbowmen could not do. And so, as the Catalan crossbowmen were either killed, deserted to join other armies or retired, they were not replaced. Those remaining were the last veterans of a dying unit but were still greatly respected for their service and skill with a crossbow.

God had blessed the venture with a full moon and Sancho would have liked to set a hard pace. But the reality was the column moved at a walking pace through the hills. Marching through trees meant tramping through the undergrowth in pitch black, and the higher the Almogavars climbed to leave the trees behind, the more the ground turned into a mass of scree and stones. It took all of Luca's attention to avoid the outcrops and stop himself from slipping

256

on the loose rubble beneath his feet. Beside him was Jordi, ahead of him Sancho and in the vanguard the guide Romanus who had led the Almogavars to Magnesia.

Remote and a man of few words, just as Luca had spent his youth in the hills around Rometta, so had he tended to his sheep in the highlands between Philadelphia and Magnesia. His simple, harsh life had been interrupted by the incursions of Sasa Bey's soldiers. They had burnt his hovel in the hills, killed his flock of sheep and turned him into a penniless refugee. A priest might have told him he had been fortunate not to have lost a family as well, but Romanus had no time for small mercies. Only revenge. Luca liked him, his story a sad reflection of his own.

'Silence!' hissed Sancho, Luca having cursed after stubbing his foot on a large stone.

The night march was like wading through thick mud, not that Luca had ever attempted that. It was actually more frustrating, the hills bathed in an otherworldly silver light to seemingly provide an easy passage through them. But the track was narrow and treacherous, and a misplaced step could result in a twisted or broken ankle.

The night seemed to last forever, the Almogavars inching through the silent, ghostly hills, the air still to allow sounds to travel a great distance. Aware of this, the Almogavars slowed their pace further as they gingerly took small steps to avoid disturbing any loose stones, much to the frustration of Sancho. His food bag filled with crossbow bolts gifted by Philadelphia's armouries like the other Almogavars, Luca felt the same tingle of excitement and anticipation he had experienced on the eve of previous battles, relishing the opportunity to get to grips with the enemy. He never thought about

257

being killed or injured. Why should he? He had been saved from the gallows at the eleventh hour, had along with Jordi saved the life of Princess Maria, which had allowed him to free Ayna, and he had never suffered even a scratch in the battles he had fought in. He had no time for priests, but surely God had spared him and continued to spare him for some great purpose, which as yet had not revealed itself.

The Almogavars began their descent into the black mass that was a forest on the southern slopes of the hills they had journeyed through, the air becoming tinged with the scent of pine as they entered the trees. The dawn was now breaking, moonlight suddenly vanishing and the eastern sky changing from black to purple and then blue hues. Then came small shards of yellow to announce the birth of a new day, the temperature plummeting to make men shiver as they paced through the forest. They halted at the edge of the treeline, giving them a panoramic view of the valley and the town of Tire some three miles distant.

The sun was rising in a clear sky to herald a hot summer's day, and to highlight the town of Tire nestled at the foot of the Bozdaglar Mountains directly opposite to where the Almogavars waited in the trees. Between them and the small walled town stood a forest of tents and a besieging army. The ominous sound of war drums echoed across the valley, indicating the Aydinids were already attacking the town.

The battle to save Tire was about to begin.

Chapter 14

The tactics were simple: the Almogavars would form a hollow
column once they exited the trees, with the crossbowmen inside the
formation, ready to shoot at any enemy soldiers trying to break the
column or stand in its way. Luca licked his lips as he strained at the
leash, wanting to sprint across the valley to get to beleaguered Tire as
quickly as possible. But, like his night-time trek through the hills, the
reality would be different. Luca could cover the three miles in fifteen
minutes, even carrying a full equipment load, and so could most of
the others kneeling at the treeline, waiting for Sancho's order. But
retaining formation would add at least five minutes to that time, more
if they had they had to fight their way through to the gates.

Romanus opted to stay with the Almogavars, despite Sancho's
efforts to get rid of him, forcibly pointing in the direction from
whence they had come. But Romanus stood his ground. Sancho
threw up his arms.

'Very well, this is as good a place to die as anywhere.'

He walked out into the sunlight and four hundred others
followed, Sancho Rey setting a rapid pace as he put himself at the tip
of the column, Luca and Jordi flanking him and behind them two
files forming each side of the column – an outer file of Almogavars;
an inner one of crossbowmen. And one native guide armed only with
a knife.

Everyone instinctively crouched low as they paced across the
lush grass, a vivid green in the early morning sun. Sancho knew Tire
had three entry gates – north, west and east – and so aimed for the
eastern gate, which would take him and his column around the great
camp planted directly in front of the town. Unlike the one before
Philadelphia, this one was entrenched, being surrounded by a small

ditch and rampart, with soldiers pacing up and down the latter. Those guards soon spotted the drab brown column snaking across the valley towards the town. Luca noticed the guards leaving the ramparts, to no doubt alert their officers to the presence of the relief column. He and the others subconsciously increased their pace, breaking into a run to reach Tire as quickly as possible. He felt his heart pounding in his chest, knowing it was inevitable Turkish horsemen would be appearing to either charge the Almogavars or, worse, stand off and shoot volleys of arrows at them. It was a race against time and Sancho was determined to win it.

The Almogavars moved past the camp and saw the town ringed by enemy soldiers, among them a multitude of maroon banners with a black circle in the centre. The eastern gate was already under attack, as were the walls either side of it, archers shooting up at figures on the battlements and others ascending scaling ladders. He smiled. If the archers were directing their arrows against the defenders, it meant their horses were safely corralled in camp. But they could still turn around and shoot their missiles at the Almogavars. But with the whole Aydinid army committed against Tire along the entire extent of its walls, it would take time to re-orientate it towards the Almogavars.

A frantic banging of kettledrums and blowing of trumpets recalled the troops on the scaling ladders and stopped the volleys of arrows being shot at the defenders. A thickening mass of Turkish soldiers began to deploy immediately to the front of the Almogavars, around a hundred paces away.

'Into them,' hollered Sancho, plucking a javelin from his quiver.

Luca also pulled a javelin from behind him and waited until Sancho threw his before launching his own. He saw the closed gates behind the Aydinid soldiers, who were now closely packed with spears levelled to form an unbroken wall of shields and spear points.

It takes skill to determine the right moment to throw a javelin while running at an enemy.

Each Almogavar could hit a small target – a face, for example – at a range of twenty-five yards, though Sancho threw his javelin at around forty yards from the enemy, the steel head smashing into the head of an enemy soldier immediately in front of him. Luca threw his own javelin a second afterwards, the metal point striking an Aydinid soldier in the left shoulder, just above his small round shield. He pulled a second and hurled it directly at the face of dark-skinned man a mere ten or so paces from him, screaming in triumph as the steel point went straight through his right eye socket.

The Aydinid line buckled when the Almogavars smashed into it, the arrowhead formation flattening to allow more than a handful of Catalans to hit the stationary enemy, stabbing with their spears against a foe stunned by the ferocity of the assault they were subjected to. Perhaps they did not expect the Christian soldiers to close on them, thinking a row of levelled spears was a sufficient deterrent. But at the point of impact those spears had disappeared, their owners felled by a brutal javelin volley. And before those behind them could step forward to seal the gap, the Almogavars were among them.

Luca thrust his spear into the belly of the man behind the one he had killed with a javelin, more javelins thrown by those immediately behind him adding to the chaos and carnage. The Aydinid had been frozen with fear, his shield hanging loosely by his

261

side and useless. He doubled over after Luca extracted the point from his guts, jabbing it forward into the face of a third Aydinid, causing him to shriek in pain and recoil away. He stepped over the two dead men and stabbed the third trying to flee from him in the back, the point easily penetrating his tunic. Around him there was pandemonium as the Aydinids crumbled and attempted to get out of the way of the Almogavars stabbing at them with their spears and short swords, crossbowmen adding to the confusion with aimed shots that cut down more Turks.

Romanus was shouting up at the walls as Sancho, Jordi and Luca broke through the crumbling enemy line to reach the gates. Arrows were being shot from above the gates, by the garrison, adding to the enemy's desire to be as far away from the Almogavars as possible. And then the gates began to creak open, just a few inches at first.

'Come on,' shouted Luca, 'open the gates.'

Jordi added his voice to the appeal, echoed by dozens of others as the Almogavars began to crowd around the gatehouse. Sancho grabbed one of the gates and pushed it, Luca, Jordi and others doing likewise to assist the garrison. As they did so Almogavars flooded past them into the town.

Thud, thud, thud.

Arrows slammed into the timbers of the gates, shot by enemy archers. When the Almogavars had been battling the enemy at close quarters, they had been too close and intermingled with Aydinids to give the Muslim archers clear shots. But now the Islamic soldiers were scattering out of the Catalans' way, allowing the archers to shoot at the Almogavars. But now the gates were fully open and the Catalans were flooding into the town, in no time running out of harm's way. Luca ducked behind the gate as two arrows hissed past him, Sancho also ducking low and scrambling behind the other gate. He and his son helped the soldiers of the garrison close it, Luca doing likewise with the other gate, to the sound of arrows thudding into the thick wooden beams. When the gates had been closed, Sancho turned and raised his spear in the air, prompting cheers from the Almogavars. Luca gave Jordi a grin.

A grim-faced man in a dazzling scale-armour cuirass, a shining helmet and a long-sleeved blue tunic edged with red and gold marched up to Sancho and removed his helmet.

'I am Nikephoros Bryennios, governor of Tire. I welcome you to my town and invite you and your men to assist me and my own soldiers to defend it against the host assaulting it.'

Curt and to the point, and spoken in perfect Spanish, he bowed his head, put his helmet back on his head and returned to the battlements to supervise the defence.

'You heard the governor,' Sancho called to his men huddled round him. 'Pair up with a crossbowman. Move!'

The relief column's appearance had temporarily interrupted the Aydinid assault. But now the Catalans were inside the town and the gates had been shut, the Muslims once again focused their attention on taking Tire. Drummers recommenced their incessant noise and once more the battlements became the focus of the struggle.

Luca and his crossbowman companion, a gaunt man with sunken cheeks and lank black hair, hurried up the stone steps leading to the battlemented walkway, which was wide enough to allow two men to pass each other with ease. The battlements were around five feet in height, the gaps in the wall between them some three feet in

263

width to allow an archer or crossbowman to shoot down at attackers. And there were many attackers.

A host of scaling ladders had been placed against the wall, some of which had been pushed away by the defenders, sending their occupants crashing to the ground. But the garrison was spread thinly along the walls, and where there were gaps the enemy was about to scale the walls and reach the battlements. But the Almogavars tipped the balance in the defenders' favour.

Luca and his companion headed for a section of the battlements that was empty, soldiers with teardrop-shaped shields either side stabbing with their spears down at attackers, and archers in towers shooting at Aydinids on ladders. The crossbowman stopped, brought the stubby stock of his weapon to his shoulder and pulled the trigger, the bolt shooting through the air to hit a soldier scrambling over the battlements. The bolt struck him and swept him off the wall like a brush sweeping leaves.

'The next one's yours, Black Sheep,' said the crossbowman, placing his foot in the arming stirrup of the crossbow to begin the process of reloading his weapon.

Luca rushed to the gap in battlements against which the top of the ladder had been placed and saw two hands and a helmet appear in front of him. He waited a few seconds before stabbing the soldier in the chest, toppling him from the ladder. He stepped forward to take a look below and recoiled when a pair of arrows hissed by him, one deflecting off his helmet.

'Watch yourself,' warned the crossbowman. 'Their archers are just as good as we are. Get your shield up to cover me.'

The small shield seemed totally inadequate in the face of the arrow storm being directed at the walls, but Luca held his in the gap to allow the crossbowman to shoot down at those on the ladder. It took around fifteen seconds to reload his weapon, but each bolt knocked an enemy soldier from the ladder, which he and Luca then shoved away from the wall to send it and its remaining occupants crashing to the ground.

'Behind you,' shouted the crossbowman in alarm.

They may have dealt with one ladder, but there were many planted against Tire's battlements and there were too few defenders to guard every section of wall.

Luca spun, shield in his left hand, spear in his right, and jabbed the point into the enemy's left thigh. The Aydinid was wearing mail armour and carrying a shield, both of which protected his left side when he jumped down from the rampart. But his legs were vulnerable and the injury to his thigh was enough to make him sprawl on to the walkway. Face down, he was out of the fight, at least temporarily, giving Luca time to jump forward, twist and thrust his spear point into the groin of the Aydinid following. His face contorted in agony, he collapsed backwards, tumbling down the ladder, one of his feet getting stuck in a rung and preventing anyone else reaching the battlements, at least from that particular ladder.

The Almogavars and garrison were spread thinly, and soon more and more Turks were clambering on to the ramparts, to be killed by Catalan spears or swords. The crossbowmen were shooting at men on the walls now, Almogavar shields and weapons covering them when they reloaded or the enemy got too close. Luca saw a yellow and red flag fall from one of the towers, to be replaced by a maroon standard with a black circle in the centre.

Another Turk came over the battlements. The crossbowman shot him. But then another, a spearman, sprang on to the walkway.

265

Luca jabbed his spear point at his face but the Turk stepped back out of range, Luca stepped forward but was forced to stop when the crossbowman shot a bolt right past him. He spun and saw a Turk staggering on the walkway before collapsing, another armed with an axe behind him. He dropped his spear, turned back to face the front, plucked his one remaining javelin from the quiver, hurled it at the spearman's face, picked up his spear, spun, ducked low and impaled the axe man on the end of it as he ran forward.

Highly trained professional that he was, the crossbowman went about his work in a methodical manner, relying on Luca to keep the enemy away as he reloaded his weapon, shot it and placed his foot in its stirrup to begin the process all over again. The bolts in Luca's bag were nearing their end, however, and so was the garrison of Tire and its Catalan allies as more and more Turks reached the battlements. The walkway was choked with dead and injured, which impeded the enemy's progress, but did not halt it.

'I have no more bolts.'

Luca glanced at the crossbowman with his now useless weapon and knew their lifespan was shortening by the second. Either side of them lay dead enemy soldiers, but more were readying themselves for a final attack, which would sweep them aside. Above the din of drums, shouts and cries came a new sound – multiple trumpet blasts coming from beyond the town. The Turks on the walls suddenly became uninterested in the defenders and began to clamber back down the scaling ladders. Luca and the crossbowman, amazed and surprised, just looked at them as they did so, energy suddenly draining from their limbs as the realisation they would not die that day dawned on them.

When the last Turk had left the battlements, Luca rushed to the wall.

'Don't be a fool,' the crossbowman warned him. 'They still have a small army of archers on the ground.'

Luca kept low and peeked over the stone rampart. To see a most wondrous sight.

He jumped up and could not help but smile at the splendid view the walls gave him of the sprawling Turkish camp immediately to the front, and the Christian horsemen charging at it from the east, the sun at their backs and banners fluttering among their ranks. In the vanguard were the magnificent cataphracts of Count Ioannes, behind them the other horsemen of Philadelphia and Count Michael. On the left wing were Corberan's horsemen, and on the right flank of the relief force a mass of whooping and hollering Alans.

The Aydinid army had been fully committed to the assault against Tire, thousands of soldiers ascending scaling ladders or shooting arrows at the defenders on the walls. The mounted relief force was now riding into the gap between the town and the enemy camp, to kill as many Turks as possible before they could seek sanctuary inside their fortified camp. It was a race against time, a race the Turks lost.

Luca and others on the walls stood and cheered when nearly three thousand horsemen charged into the great mass of enemy soldiers trying to withdraw to their camp, the Alans for once proving their worth as they shot their recurve bows with abandon at the throng, the cataphracts and Catalans going about their work with lances, swords and maces, cutting down everything in their path. Luca had never seen anything like it, his jaw dropping in admiration and awe at the terrible spectacle unfolding in front of his eyes.

267

An intact formation of foot soldiers cannot be broken by horsemen, for a horse will not gallop straight at a wall, be it of stone, brick or human flesh. Horse archers can ride around the formation and attempt to shoot it to pieces, but if foot soldiers keep their nerve and stand in their ranks, they become like a stronghold. But if horsemen get among foot soldiers, they can do murder. It was so now, as thousands of Turks were cut down, shot or skewered. So many were killed that the Almogavar foot soldiers following closely on the heels of the horsemen enjoyed only meagre pickings when they reached the scene of the slaughter.

The Catalan Company had been hired to save the cities of Philadelphia and Magnesia, plus the town of Tire. In the space of three months they had routed three Turkish armies, relieved the town and both cities, though for some strange reason Magnesia and its suspicious governor were not threatened by the Muslims, and re-established Roman rule in western Anatolia.

Luca felt an immense sense of pride in the achievements of the Almogavars, of which he was a member, together with feeling privileged at being allowed to join such a formidable organisation. In that moment, when the Turks were being put to the sword, he gave thanks to God for setting him on the path he was now treading alongside Jordi, Sancho Rey, Hector and the thousands of other Almogavars who were reversing the decline of an ancient empire.

Chapter 15

Thousands of Turks lay dead before the walls of Tire, their scaling ladders still propped up against its defences, thousands of horses still corralled in their camp. A camp now being thoroughly looted by the Alans, Arabates' horsemen dismounting to search tents and wagons for anything of value. Their chief had placed guards around the camp to ensure no Almogavar or Roman gained entry, counts Michael and Komnenos and their men riding into the town to greet the governor and attend a church service to give thanks to God for the great victory they had won. Grand Duke Roger joined them, partly to celebrate the triumph but also to pray for soul of Corberan of Navarre, who had been killed in the initial charge, an arrow severing his windpipe. His distraught horsemen had been sent to scour the countryside for stragglers, to either kill them or bring them back as captives, to be sold as slaves.

Sancho Rey, however, was in no mood for piety. He led his Almogavars back out of the town to link up with the captains who had accompanied the horsemen.

Hector offered him his hand. 'Still alive, then?'

'Still alive. Have you taken a roll call?'

'No need,' said Angel. 'We arrived too late to do any fighting.'

'How many men did *you* lose?' asked Marc.

The Romans would have been appalled to have witnessed a subordinate talk to his lord in such a way. But the Almogavars elected their leaders, which meant they were all equal and free to say what they wanted, a notion that would also have appalled the Romans.

'Fifty dead,' snapped Sancho, 'another score wounded.'

Marc looked around at the corpse-filled ground around them.

'The enemy lost more.'

269

'Throw a cordon around the camp,' commanded Sancho. 'Hector, you are with me.'

The lean Hector gave Luca a slap on the arm. 'Good to see you, Luca, and you, Jordi. How did you like defending a town?'

'I felt as though the whole Turkish army was shooting at me,' replied Jordi.

Luca nodded. 'I prefer to take the fight to the enemy.'

'Well, you are in luck,' smiled Hector, 'because it looks like Sancho wants to do some more fighting.'

Parts of the camp were on fire now, three divisions of Almogavars surrounding it and the fourth infiltrating the tents, Sancho and Hector at its head. Luca and Jordi were also in the vanguard as Sancho Rey went in search of Arabates. Whooping and raucous Alans raised their weapons to the Almogavars in salute as the Catalans passed them, many throwing coins in the air to show off their plunder. Sancho ignored them, heading for that part of the camp where the enemy's horses were corralled, thousands of them in a vast enclosure, which was guarded by Alans.

It was a warm July day, but the temperature dropped rapidly when Sancho and his men faced Arabates and around a hundred of his Alans, the two leaders squaring up to each other in the midday heat. As the Alan leader pretended he could understand neither Catalan nor Italian, he summoned his interpreter. The atmosphere continued to get frostier as the two sides stared at each other while they waited. Eventually, the interpreter arrived, bowing to his lord and frowning at Sancho. Arabates scratched his sharp nose in a disinterested manner.

'Tell your master these horses are not all his,' said Sancho. 'We demand half of them.'

Arabates laughed when he was informed of the Catalan's words.

'We claim all the plunder in this camp, as is our right,' said the Alan leader. 'Besides, what do foot soldiers want with horses?'

'It is no business of the Alans what the Catalan Company does,' snapped Sancho, 'but seeing as I am in a good mood.'

Hector guffawed.

Sancho ignored him. 'Horses can be sold to raise money for supplies, weapons, armour and clothing. And since we, or you for that matter, have not been paid these past six months, we need to look to our own means to ensure we do not starve.'

Arabates sighed. 'I do not care if you live or die. These horses are ours, according to the rules of war. Furthermore Catalan…'

He stopped speaking when Hector thrust his spear into the interpreter, everyone staring with incredulity at the violent act. Within seconds, Alans were pulling arrows from their quivers, but not before a host of javelins had been plucked from quivers and thrown at the archers. Alans went down in droves, Almogavars stabbing with their spears and throwing javelins at Alans within range. It was carnage, and all the while Sancho Rey stared unblinking at Arabates, untouched amid the outbreak of bloodshed but utterly alone.

Luca and Jordi, having no javelins, did not participate in the fighting, though were at its epicentre. They stood guarding Jordi's father while Hector ran amok with his men, relishing the opportunity to kill. Roman, Alan, Turk. It made no difference to a man who was born to fight and kill. He and the Almogavars fought savagely, but not blindly. When the short bout of bloodletting was over, not one Alan horse had been even wounded, though dozens of their owners lay dead on the ground.

Then there was silence.

Sancho looked down at the dead interpreter beside an Arabates quaking with fury, but not without reason. He knew he would be cut down if he made a move against the Almogavar leader. So, he calmly walked over to the nearest horse, placed a foot in a stirrup and hoisted himself into the saddle. He took hold of the reins and gently nudged the animal forward, passing Sancho, Jordi and Luca without looking at any of them. The Almogavars had taken possession of the captured Turkish horses, three hundred Alans had been killed in the fight, and Arabates led his surviving horsemen away from Tire, and out of the emperor's service. When the two counts and Grand Duke Roger emerged from the service of thanksgiving, they discovered they had just lost a third of their horsemen. Roger was unconcerned. The Catalan Company had fulfilled its promise to Emperor Andronicus, though for his part the emperor had defaulted on the terms of the agreement between him and the Catalans.

The company returned to Philadelphia in a leisurely fashion, taking the thousands of captured horses with it. The two dukes and their horsemen accompanied the Almogavars, though Ioannes Komnenos left half of his men at Tire to stiffen the depleted garrison. Having seen his imperilled theme saved, he was in an ebullient mood, leading his horse as he walked alongside Sancho Rey. Luca and Jordi tramped behind, both in high spirits after emerging from another battle victorious and unscathed. Grand Duke Roger and the Catalan horsemen had ridden ahead with the captured mounts so they could be auctioned as quickly as possible, so that the Catalan Company could pay for the food, replacement weapons and other supplies it now desperately needed.

'When we reach Philadelphia, I intend to order the archbishop to hold a celebratory mass to thank the Catalan Company for its great service to the empire,' enthused Ioannes.

'You are most generous, lord,' said Sancho flatly. 'But church services will not fill the bellies of my men. We have received no pay for six months and our pouches are empty.'

Jordi and Luca exchanged knowing glances. They both still had coin in their pouches, courtesy of Princess Maria.

'The sale of the captured horses will help your finances,' Count Ioannes assured him.

'And the slaves,' added Sancho.

The count was confused. 'The slaves are to be sent to Constantinople, Sancho, to serve in the houses of the wealthy and carry out duties in the palace.'

Sancho's eyes narrowed. 'No, my lord. They were taken by the Catalan Company and will be used for its benefit.'

'The Catalan Company is in the service of the emperor,' said the count testily, 'and this land is this emperor's where his law prevails above anything else.'

Sancho laughed. 'I am new to this land, lord, but even I can see that the emperor's law rules over small islands in what is a Muslim sea.'

'God sent the Catalan Company to us,' replied the count, 'and He will ensure that the Muslim sea, as you call it, will drain away, of that I am certain.'

Sancho had enough experience of dealing with nobles and churchmen to know it was useless to argue when they brought the Almighty into the argument.

'The churches in Constantinople use slaves, my lord?'

273

'Naturally,' replied the count.

'Perhaps you can clarify something for me, lord,' said Sancho. 'I am of the Catholic faith and have little knowledge of the Orthodox religion. According to Catholic beliefs, all humans are equal before God whatever their social status.'

'As they are in the Orthodox Church,' affirmed the count.

'And yet, your empire has a great many slaves. Is there not a contradiction there?'

The count's bushy eyebrows closed in a frown.

'I do not question church doctrine, but I do know that the majority of slaves are Muslims and are therefore not visible in the eyes of God. That said, I also know that Christian slaves are allowed to receive the basic sacraments of baptism, the Eucharist and funeral rights. Slaves are also allowed to marry.'

'To produce future slaves,' quipped Sancho.

'The masters of great households often grant slaves their freedom in recognition of long years of faithful service,' said the count. 'I myself have granted freedom to those who have served me and my family well.'

'I need weapons, food and clothing for over six thousand soldiers and many of the horses need re-shoeing, new bridles and saddles, my lord,' emphasised Sancho, 'and the sad truth is we have yet to receive our pay from the emperor.'

'I am not in charge of imperial finances,' snapped the count. 'But the emperor will want to know why I did not send him the slaves captured outside my city after God's great victory.'

Sancho fell into a sullen silence and after a few moments the count made his excuses, mounted his horse and rode off to seek the company of Count Michael, who was with the vanguard to ensure the army was not attacked by any roving bands of Aydinids.

The Almogavars were in high spirits when they reached the former Turkish camp outside Philadelphia, soldiers of the garrison having kept watch over the captives during their absence. A few had escaped but the majority had accepted their fate and had spent their time praying, cooking for their captors and being assigned to work gangs for duties inside the city. They were not maltreated because no one wanted to purchase ill or infirm slaves.

Luca and Jordi returned to the tent Ertan had launched himself from when the Almogavars had stormed the Turkish camp. To find their own slave cooking a meal to welcome them back. The portly man smiled, clasped his hands together and muttered 'effendi, effendi' when they appeared, bringing a pair of stools from the tent for them to sit on. He then served them a delicious vegetable stew, stiffened with spices that made their noses run but which was mouth-watering, nevertheless.

Ertan refilled their bowls as they sat on the stools, babbling something incomprehensible and periodically bringing his hands together in a submissive gesture. They both ignored him as they gorged on his delicious recipe, beaming with delight when he brought them fresh bread on a wooden platter. Clearly, the Turkish field kitchens were still working. After they had finished, Ertan relieved them of their bowls. Luca stretched out his legs.

'I like Muslim food.'

'Has not Ayna cooked you any of her native recipes?' asked Jordi.

'You remember the winter? We had to get by on what was available.'

'You must miss her.'

'I do,' sighed Luca.

'Apologies for the interruption.'

Their conversation was interrupted by the appearance of a tall, striking man with olive skin, black hair falling to his shoulders and a well-trimmed moustache. He wore leather riding boots, baggy tan leggings and a loose, open blue coat. He tipped his head at Luca and Jordi, both of whom sprang to their feet and drew their swords.

'There is no need for that, masters,' the stranger said in Italian. 'I wish you no harm.'

A clearly agitated Ertan spoke something to the tall individual, who brushed aside the cook's concern.

'What do you want?' demanded Jordi.

The stranger placed a hand on Ertan's shoulder.

'My friend here told me that you two are men of importance in this mercenary band.'

Luca laughed.

'I'm just a poor shepherd.'

The stranger looked at the knives at their waists.

'Then shepherds must be paid a great deal in your homeland for you to be able to purchase a Damascus blade.'

'They were gifts,' said Jordi.

'As I said, you both must be men of importance to be given such expensive gifts. Perhaps we might talk without blades being held to my chest?'

By his bearing and manner, Luca surmised the stranger was a soldier, or former soldier, and he doubted if he was a friend of Ertan. Still, he was intriguing. He slipped his sword back in its scabbard. Jordi did likewise. Luca pointed at his friend.

276

'He is important, being the son of the Almogavar commander.'

The stranger's brow creased. 'Almogavar?'

'The foot soldiers of the mercenary band, as you describe us,' explained Jordi. 'Who are you?'

'Melek Kose at your service. In your language, Melek means "Angel", but alas for my parents, I turned out to be more devil.'

He looked at Luca. 'And your name?'

'Luca Baldi, from Sicily.'

'A beautiful island,' enthused Melek, 'I have been there a number of times during my service with the Venetians, which is when I learned your language.'

'You were a soldier?' asked Jordi.

Melek laughed. 'A mercenary, like you. And though I am currently a slave, I would like to make myself more useful to fellow mercenaries.'

He may have been an infidel, but Melek had a silver tongue and was soon having Luca and Jordi eating out of his hand, using flattery to ingratiate himself to them. He asked about their recent victory at Tire and complimented the Almogavars on their even greater victory outside the walls of Philadelphia. And when he casually asked whether it would be possible to meet with Sancho Rey, Jordi was more than willing to facilitate his request.

The Almogavar leader was irritated that his son and his friend should bother him with the request of a slave, but he was in a generous mood after the spate of victories and agreed to see the former Muslim soldier. The whole company would soon be on the move, back to Artake to be united with its dependents and thereafter to find a new home in Anatolia.

277

'Thank you for seeing me, lord,' smiled Melek as he stood before Sancho in the latter's tent, which had been the residence of a senior Turkish officer but a few days before.

Like the others in camp, the tent was circular and made in two layers: an outer layer of heavy, waterproof material that was a rusty copper colour, and a brightly coloured inner layer, red being the preferred hue. At night the tents were illuminated by candles inside and lanterns hung around the exterior.

Sancho poured himself some wine and offered his guest a cup.

'Thank you, but no,' said Melek. 'I do not drink alcohol.'

'My son and his friend, naïve as they are,' said Sancho, 'seem to think you have something of value to offer me. What is it?'

'Straight and to the point, like your way of conducting war. I would like to offer my services to your company, me and three hundred like me.'

Sancho drank some wine. 'A few days ago, you were preparing to slit Christian throats in Philadelphia. Now you are offering to fight for a Christian company. Why should you wish to fight for those who are not of your faith?'

'For money,' replied Melek bluntly. 'I am a mercenary like you who fights for pay, regardless of the religion of those hiring me.'

'We have enough horsemen,' said Sancho.

'You have no horse archers,' replied Melek, 'for I have seen no Alans return with your company and the Romans.'

Sancho was surprised by his knowledge and cast an accusing glance at his son. He and Luca had obviously been too free with their tongues.

Melek pressed the argument.

278

'When the Alans fight, they do so as a separate body, one that lacks discipline and control. I am proposing something different, lord.'

Sancho's ears pricked up. 'Oh? What?'

Melek looked at the spare stool.

'May I take a seat?'

Sancho nodded. Melek smiled and sat on the stool, leaning in towards the Almogavar leader.

'Horse archers trained to fight alongside your own horsemen would make them more formidable on the battlefield, for even the most noble knight in the most expensive armour can be killed by a single arrow.'

Sancho was no fool and knew the Turk was speaking sense, for he had seen with his own eyes how effective horse archers could be, as long as they were used properly. There was still the subject of trust, however.

'For the sake of argument, let us say we give you back your horses and weapons,' said Sancho. 'What is to stop you and your men riding away after slitting our throats.'

'Nothing,' replied Melek candidly. 'But why should we wish to ride away, lord? I am a simple mercenary and am offering you my services, a contract if you will. As for slitting your throats, we are but few and you are many.'

'I do not command the Catalan Company,' said Sancho, 'and cannot answer for it. But I promise to bring your proposal before the rest of the leadership. In the meantime, you will be escorted back to your living quarters by my son and his friend.'

Melek stood, placed a hand on his chest and bowed to Sancho, turning and walking from the tent flanked by Luca and Jordi. Sancho

279

was intrigued by the proposal but had other, more pressing, matters to attend to. First and foremost was the issue of pay, or lack of it. The money given to the company by the emperor in Constantinople had been left with the company's dependents in Artake, which would at least ensure they were clothed, fed and housed until the company returned to them. But the soldiers of the company itself were in effect living off the land. The lavishly stocked Turkish camp outside Philadelphia had been a boon, but the captured food supplies were steadily decreasing to feed thousands of men on a daily basis, to say nothing about the slaves that the Governor of Philadelphia and Count Cosses had yet to transport to Constantinople. To make matters worse, the city merchants and workshops were refusing to sell goods or undertake repairs to weapons, armour and saddlery unless they were paid in cash. The situation became critical when two hundred horsemen and a thousand Almogavars marched into camp, led by Bernat de Rocafort, nicknamed 'The Bastard'.

Grand Duke Roger was nothing if not pragmatic. As soon as the war against the French in Sicily had ended, he had despatched Bernat with twelve hundred men to the Italian mainland to seize land from Charles, King of Naples, their former foe in the War of the Sicilian Vespers. Charles might have been the son of the formidable Charles of Anjou of France, but he was a weak, vacillating individual, whose defeat in the war against King Frederick made his lands ripe for the plucking. Roger's grand scheme was to establish a Catalan enclave on the Italian mainland, from where the company could offer its services throughout the Mediterranean. Alas for Bernat de Rocafort, his arrival on the mainland with a division of Almogavars provoked horror among the Italian kingdoms, which soon rallied behind the Pope to demand their expulsion. Despite Bernat travelling

280

to Rome itself to plead his case, he received short shrift from the Papacy, though Pope Benedict did pay for the ships to take the Catalans to Constantinople, from where they were shipped south to the ruins of Ephesus on the Aegean coast. It was a mere two day's march to the recently liberated town of Tire to the west, from where Bernat and his men made their way to Philadelphia.

He may have had two hundred horsemen but the majority marched on foot with the Almogavars, Bernat having no money to purchase enough horses. He made sure he himself was mounted, on a magnificent black stallion, and his standard bearer behind him was also riding a horse. That standard showed the arms of his native Catalonia: four red vertical bands on a gold background, the same device worn on his surcoat.

The son of Ricardo de Rocafort, the infant was born some ten months after his father's death in battle, leading to rumours that Bernat was in fact a bastard sired by a French knight who was the lover of Lady Rocafort. So strong were the rumours that both his mother and his relatives were eager for him to depart Catalonia, to save his own and his family's honour. It was fortunate that the War of the Sicilian Vespers was raging, in which 'The Bastard' proved himself an accomplished knight, rising to command the Catalan's Company horsemen and earning the respect of his peers for his battlefield prowess. But the rumours of his parentage followed him to Sicily, resulting in him becoming extremely defensive when it came to any slights, both real and imaginary, against his honour.

'It would appear our world is getting smaller and smaller,' reflected Roger, he and the other commanders sat round the table in his plush Turkish tent, which had crimson carpets on the floor.

Luca was again a servant, pouring wine into cups along with Jordi.

'We are destitute,' stated Sancho bluntly.

Bernat was amazed. 'I thought the Roman emperor had promised to pay the company for the duration of the campaign.'

'The emperor is proving tardy when it comes to paying those hired to serve him,' complained Roger. 'We would have been forced to plunder the land to survive had it not been for this well-stocked camp we captured.'

'We left what monies we had with our dependents in Artake,' Sancho told Bernat, 'to ensure they would be safe until we returned.'

'But when we return,' said Roger, 'both we and they will be in a perilous position. We are owed half a year's wages and I do not believe we will get them.'

Bernat looked at Roger, who was related to the imperial family. But the downcast look on his face spoke volumes.

'Then what is to be done?' asked Bernat.

Bernat looked at Luca and pointed to his cup, the former shepherd coming forward to refill it. The Catalan noble noticed the beautiful dagger attached to Luca's belt and pointed at it.

'A fine dagger. How is it a poor Almogavar has such a valuable weapon? May I take a peek at your blade, Almogavar?'

Luca put down the wine jug and drew the dagger from its ornate sheath, holding out the handle to Bernat. The noble was impressed.

'A Damascus blade, no less. I think you are deceiving us, Sancho, by letting us believe that you and the Almogavars are paupers.'

Sancho chuckled. 'This is Luca Baldi, nicknamed the Black Sheep on account of an unfortunate incident in Sicily. He and my son rescued Princess Maria in Constantinople and were richly rewarded by the emperor.'

Bernat handed the dagger back to Luca and looked at Jordi, noticing a similar weapon attached to his belt.

'Perhaps we should send them back to Constantinople to beg the emperor for more money,' suggested Bernat, 'seeing as they are so high in his favour.'

Sancho glanced at Luca and Jordi before smiling.

'It is good to have you back, Bernat. You have given me an idea.'

Chapter 16

Two groups of mercenaries left the liberated city of Philadelphia, their aim to alleviate the dire state of the Catalan Company's finances. Immediately prior to their departure, Melek's request was approved, if for the only reason that Bernat was intrigued by the idea of horse archers fighting alongside his own horsemen, who used lances in the charge and swords in the mêlée. After fighting fellow Catholics for years in Sicily, he had no qualms about fighting alongside Muslims, as long as their prayer times did not interrupt his battle plans. Melek and his three hundred volunteers were separated from the other slaves, along with those who had been 'adopted' by the Almogavars, such as Ertan due to his culinary skills. The rest were herded west on Sancho's orders and with Grand Duke Roger's blessing, beginning their journey on a bright August day, a contingent of Bernat's horsemen providing an escort. Herding tethered slaves was far beneath his dignity, but he was prepared to temporarily 'debase' himself for the sake of the company.

The second group was spearheaded by Romanus who once again led the Almogavars through the hills, the second journey being less fraught than the first, being carried out in daylight. The Almogavars, now numbering nearly five thousand men, were in high spirits. They had won a string of victories for little loss, excepting Corberan, and they were no longer half-starving, having feasted on Turkish hospitality. What's more, soon they would be travelling back to Artake to be reunited with their families. Luca wore a permanent smile as he anticipated wrapping himself around the lithe body of Ayna once more.

The march was more like an afternoon stroll, men chatting to each other in a nonchalant fashion with spears rested on their shoulders, though scouts on the flanks and in the vanguard kept a watchful eye on the hills and rocky outcrops the Almogavars were tramping through. The pace was deliberately slow because the slaves being marshalled by Bernat de Rocafort would take at least two days to reach the city of Magnesia.

The summer nights were cooler in the hills, a brisk wind making men wrap cloaks around themselves, especially as Sancho had forbidden the lighting of any campfires. But the Almogavars had plenty of freshly baked bread and cheese to feast on, along with apples and apricots plucked that very morning.

Luca paced up and down on guard duty, stopping at regular intervals to stare at the black ridges that were the hills framed against the slightly lighter night sky, the moon once again obliging the Almogavars in their mission. He did not know what that mission was but did not care. He loved being a member of the Catalan Company and found it difficult to believe he was once a poor shepherd in far-off Sicily. And yet, an Almogavar was not so far removed from those armed only with crooks who guarded and watched over flocks of sheep the world over. They lived an austere life, covered great distances on their feet and subsisted on a simple diet. Sometimes no diet at all! His *zamarra*, his sheepskin coat, was an item of clothing worn by Spanish shepherds, as was his footwear. He gripped his eight-foot spear and smiled. But these shepherds were lethal and fought not wild dogs and wolves, but noble knights on horseback and heavily armed foot soldiers. He was now a wolf and the enemy were his prey.

The next day the march continued, Romanus leading the Almogavars into the trees that covered the hills behind the glittering white walls of Magnesia. Then they halted to await the arrival of Bernat and his mob of slaves.

'What did you notice about the ruler of Magnesia?' Sancho asked him as they both peered out from the trees to study the valley below.

The sun was again shining to give an uninterrupted view of the area around Magnesia, a patchwork of fields, orchards and vineyards filling the lush valley.

'He has an unnatural interest in young men,' said Luca.

Sancho laughed. 'Yes, he does, but I was thinking more of the clothes he was wearing when he granted me an audience.'

'They looked expensive,' offered Luca, being no expert on the apparel of lords and ladies.

'They did indeed, because they *were* expensive. Two things struck me about our friend Arcadius Drogon, Luca. When you have been a soldier for as long as I have, you can sense when there is fear in the air. The first thing I noticed about the governor and his court was the carefree atmosphere around him. He did not have a care in the world, which is odd seeing as his city is supposed to be ringed by enemies.'

'We defeated those enemies,' said Luca with pride.

Sancho nodded. 'We did, but he did not know that, and frankly, given his attitude, he did not care one way or another. This suggests to me he has come to some sort of agreement with the *emirs* who rule the lands around him.'

'The emperor will have his head for such treachery,' said Luca.

'The emperor? A man who can barely control the city he lives in? Who has to hire mercenaries to save what's left of his empire in Anatolia? No, Luca, the emperor is a broken reed who has no real power. He and his eunuch treasurer have not paid the company, which is why we are here, and which brings me to my second point.'

'I do not understand lord.'

Sancho tipped his head at the city nestled at the foot of the mountain.

'Counts Ioannes and Michael are honest men, in as much as nobles can be truthful. They are also worried men. Worried about the long-term prospects of their themes, and worried what is left of the cities they still rule will be captured and sacked by the Turks. They have no money, but Magnesia has money, which is why we are here.'

Luca was totally confused.

'The emperor and his servants think the Almogavars are coarse, illiterate peasants. Mostly, they are right, Luca. But some of us use our eyes and ears. For example, did you know that a hundred years ago Latin crusaders captured Constantinople?'

'Latins, lord?'

'Catholics who were journeying to the Holy Land but decided Constantinople would be easier to take than Jerusalem,' said Sancho. 'Anyway, the Romans who were not slaughtered in Constantinople fled the city and established two new empires. One, the Despotate of Epiros, we have already encountered. The second was called the Empire of Nicaea. And do you know where the imperial treasury of Nicaea was based?'

'No, lord.'

Sancho pointed at the city. 'Magnesia. Now, some forty years ago the Latins were ejected from Constantinople and the Romans moved back in. But they obviously left a lot of gold behind in Magnesia in their rush to reclaim their city. Gold that I believe

287

Arcadius Drogon is using to bribe the *emirs* to leave his city alone. And gold that he won't mind sharing with the Catalan Company.'

'He might object to parting with any of his wealth, lord.'

Sancho chuckled. 'I'm sure he will. But five thousand Almogavars will beg to differ.'

Sancho slapped him on the shoulder.

'You have done well, Luca, notwithstanding your inauspicious beginning. You must be looking forward to seeing the Muslim woman you purchased.'

'Ayna. Yes, lord.'

'Carla told me that she is no longer a slave.'

'No, lord.'

'What is she, then?'

Luca pondered the question. He was unsure of the answer. He loved Ayna but he had given her status no thought.

'Probably best if you marry her. Father Ramon has been bending my ear about the inadvisability of the Almogavars keeping Muslim whores.'

Luca felt anger flow throw his body.

'Ayna is not a whore, and I will have words with any who say she is, even priests.'

'Easy, Black Sheep, save your fury for the enemy, whether they follow God or Allah.'

Bernat and around two hundred of his horsemen arrived just after midday, herding the slaves towards the city's eastern entrance. Bernat himself and half a dozen of his horsemen rode into Magnesia, the huge red and gold banner fluttering behind them. Watching from the trees above the city, Sancho gave the order for the Almogavars to prepare to move. There was open ground between the city and the forest of pine and aspen on the hill behind Magnesia, perhaps half a mile in length. Sentries manning the walls would spot the Almogavars emerging from the treeline and would be able to alert those manning the gates to close all entrances to the city. But only if those entrances were clear of obstructions.

The slaves shuffled towards the eastern gates, horsemen from the city riding out to meet with those escorting the Catalan Company's great gift to Arcadius Drogon. Once he had sifted out those young, attractive males from among the captives, the rest would either be sold to rich households in the city, or sold to the city of Izmir, where no doubt they would be freed and enlisted in the army of Mehmed Bey.

Arcadius Drogon was an attractive, powerful man, but he was also vain. And so, when an over-dressed officer of his palace guard informed him that a Spanish knight was at the eastern gates with a great gift from the Catalan Company, and that gift was hundreds of slaves, he could not resist the temptation to see the sight for himself. It was only fitting that the Catalan Company should recompense him for the inconvenience of dealing with its Almogavars, a rude, brutish group of commoners who sullied his beautiful palace with their presence. But how gratifying it was to now see his social inferiors grovel at his feet.

The governor, riding a white horse to match his brilliant white gold-edged coat, white leggings and white cloak, road out of the city to view the large group of slaves, behind him his immaculately attired and equipped bodyguard. Bernat rode out with him, the Catalan horsemen slowly leaving their positions as guards of the slaves to circle the governor and his entourage. And all the while, Bernat de Rocafort flattered and humoured Arcadius Drogon.

'Now!' shouted Sancho, bounding from the trees and down the grassy, rock-littered slope.

Luca and Jordi followed closely on his heels, and either side of them hundreds of Almogavars flooded from the forest. The sentries on the walls would have spotted them at once and even though the Almogavars could cover the half mile in around five minutes, the gates would have been slammed shut before then. But not with the governor outside the walls, a governor who was swiftly apprehended and his bodyguard disarmed. More of Bernat's riders galloped into the city to secure the gatehouse, cutting down anyone who got in their way.

Sancho was remarkably agile for a man in his forties, bounding down the hill, spear and shield in hand. Arrows came flying through the air from the battlements, but the Almogavar leader swerved right to lead his men away from the walls, increasing his pace without losing his footing and tumbling down the hillside. Luca, Jordi and those following moved silently, thousands of feet pounding the earth producing a sound resembling a herd of stampeding cattle.

The slaves, now unguarded, instinctively began to move away from the horde of Almogavars flooding down the hillside into the valley and towards the open gates.

All the gates into the city were reached by way of wooden drawbridges over a moat fed by the nearby river, the gates themselves being flanked by towers and bastions.

Sancho led the charge on to the drawbridge, arrows shot from the towers and walls thudding into the planks. Almogavar crossbowmen flanked the drawbridge and began shooting up at the walls to keep the enemy archers' heads down. Luca, his shield held above his head, followed Sancho under the gatehouse and into the city. Some of Bernat's horsemen had dismounted and were guarding the entrance, though keeping out of sight of archers on the walls inside the city.

Five divisions of Almogavars swept into the city, the one leading under Sancho heading for the palace in the centre of the city. Hector's division would secure the eastern gates when it had traversed the drawbridge, the other three would follow Sancho's formation into the city to seize the palace.

Alarm bells were being sounded throughout Magnesia and citizens were scattering like rats when they spotted the Almogavars, leaving their shops, market stalls and conversations as they sought sanctuary in the many churches in the city. The mercenaries fast-paced along well-maintained paved streets towards the centre of Magnesia, Sancho remembering the route he had taken when he had recently visited the city.

Luca also remembered the white stone buildings, fountains and colonnades and hoped there would be no violence that would spill blood on the neat and tidy streets of Magnesia. The Almogavars slowed as they neared the palace, which was surrounded by ornate marble churches with statues of Christ and the saints before them. Centuries before they had been pagan temples dedicated to Zeus, Artemis and Athena, but after being destroyed by an earthquake and rebuilt by the Romans, they had been re-dedicated to the Christian god.

The walls of the palace were high, thick and slightly sloped, made up of well-dressed stone blocks, at the top of which were battlements where archers and spearmen waited for the Almogavar attack. Small round towers giving archers a bird's eye view of the area around the palace were evenly spaced along the extent of the walls, though Sancho had no intention of giving those archers an easy kill.

'What now, father?' asked Jordi.

'Now we wait for Bernat to bring the governor here.'

Keeping out of range of the archers, the Almogavars rapidly surrounded the palace in a show of force intended to intimidate the defenders. The Catalans had no way of crossing the water-filled moat surrounding the palace, much less scaling the walls in the face of arrows, spears and rocks hurled at them from the defenders. Not that Sancho intended to assault the palace.

Angel and Marc reported to their commander.

'All the entrances into the palace are secure, as are the surrounding streets,' said Marc.

The sound of hymns being sung reached their ears and everyone turned to stare at the nearest church, a great rectangular structure with a red-tiled roof surrounded by thick columns.

'Place guards on all the churches near the palace,' Sancho instructed Angel. 'Make sure no one leaves, but do not interfere with the congregations.'

Angel and Marc departed for their commands, the mournful sound of the hymns adding to the ominous atmosphere that was building. Almogavars stood in their ranks in silence, staring at the palace walls, the garrison staring back at them. Luca felt a trickle of sweat run down his neck. He suddenly realised it was very warm in the city, the sun roasting the buildings of Magnesia and anyone still roaming its streets. The tension was palpable.

Beyond the temples were the mansions of the wealthy, all guarded by their own walls and surrounded by gardens. Luca turned when he heard the sound of iron-shod hooves clattering on the paved road, catching sight of Bernat de Rocafort riding beside a man with a mass of lazy blonde curls and ringlets that appeared molten gold in the sunlight. Arcadius Drogon looked even more magnificently attired than the last time Luca had seen him, though now his face wore a scowl rather than a smile. Behind the pair were around a score of Catalan horsemen, looking rough and unsophisticated compared to the *Kephale* of Magnesia.

'Good morning, governor,' said Sancho tersely.

'What is the meaning of this outrage?' Drogon demanded to know.

Sancho debated whether to wrench the boy-lover from his saddle but decided against it. He wanted to be away as quickly as possible.

'Money, governor, or rather lack of it. Your emperor hired the Catalan Company to lift the sieges of Philadelphia, Tire and Magnesia, which it has achieved. I will concede we did not have to battle for your beautiful city, which I am sure your emperor would wish to know more about.

'It is now August and we have received no pay for eight months. So, I am here to receive payment from your treasury.'

Drogon's face became contorted with indignation.

'Is this how you treat allies? Is this how you repay an emperor who has placed faith in fellow Christians?'

'The emperor has not paid us at all this year,' said Sancho.

'We are mercenaries, governor,' smiled Bernat beside him. 'We fight for pay, which we have not received.'

'We are allies only as long as we are paid,' added Sancho.

'I have no authority to enter into financial arrangements on behalf of the emperor,' remarked Drogon dismissively.

'Well, be that as it may,' said Sancho casually, 'if you do not order your treasury to pay us, I will order my men to burn this fine city, to kill every one of its citizens, and plunder those fine houses nearby that have caught my eye.

'We will strip this city of every item of gold and silver, including crosses and icons in churches, requisition horses and other livestock, empty Magnesia of all food, lay waste to the fields, orchards and vineyards around it, and finally, pour molten gold down your throat while the garrison of your palace watches.'

Drogon swayed in the saddle. The last threat emphasised these base barbarians in their rags and ugly faces would indeed destroy his city and, more importantly, put him to death.

'Or, we can be paid what we are owed, nothing more, nothing less,' said Sancho, 'and we will be on our way.'

'The emperor will hear of this outrage,' threatened Arcadius, an ethereal light around his head as the sun reflected off his golden locks.

'I hope so,' said Sancho, 'because he can then understand the ramifications of hiring a mercenary company and failing to pay it. Oh, and perhaps you could remind him that despite not being paid, the Catalan Company has smashed three Muslim armies since it marched from Artake, a feat beyond his own armies.

'But we are wandering from the point. Do you agree to my terms, or will you see this fine city burn?'

'I want the slaves,' sniffed Arcadius.

Bernat laughed. 'The slaves?'

'You brought them here as a present for me,' snapped Arcadius. 'Or are you going to default on your promise of a gift to me?'

294

Sancho was bemused. 'The slaves were a ruse to lure you out of the city, governor. The rest you know.'

Arcadius curled a lip at the brutish Almogavar.

'Nevertheless, they are here. I will agree to your terms if you leave the slaves here.'

Bernat looked at Sancho, who shrugged.

'Very well, you may have the slaves. Now, where is your treasury?'

'In the palace,' replied Arcadius, his face a mask of smugness.

The governor's eyes settled on Luca and Jordi standing next to Sancho.

'If I paid you an additional amount, would you leave those two with me?'

Luca was enraged. 'What? Get off your horse and face me, man to man.'

The Almogavars within earshot raised their spears and cheered, urging Luca to fight the preening Roman peacock, chanting 'Black Sheep, Black Sheep' in encouragement. Jordi pointed his spear point at the governor.

'You may die today.'

'Silence!' hollered Sancho, his patience rapidly wearing thin.

The cheering petered out and an icy glare from his father convinced Jordi to lower his spear. Arcadius Drogon was leering at Luca and his friend, delighted to have caused a slight ruckus among the Almogavars. His arrogance was breath-taking and for a moment Sancho considered plundering Magnesia and burning it afterwards.

'You will ride to the palace gates, order them to be thrown open and command your treasurer to open his coffers,' he said to Arcadius.

'*My* coffers,' the governor corrected him.

'Do it,' shouted Sancho.

He was surrounded by hundreds of enemy soldiers who had taken control of his city, but Arcadius Drogon was smiling when he nudged his splendid stallion forward towards the gates of his palace, to the accompaniment of hymns coming from every church surrounding it.

Sancho worked out as precisely as he could with the city treasurer, a shrewish man with a wispy beard and meticulous manner, the amount owed to the Catalan Company.

Luca had never seen so much wealth when he, Sancho, Jordi and two score other Almogavars were finally allowed into the palace to oversee the loading of small chests filled with coins onto carts, under the watchful eye of palace guards and archers and recorded by treasury officials. One frowned when Angel open one of the chests and sifted through the coins inside it with his hands. They looked gold but were in fact made from electrum, an alloy of gold and silver. The coins, *hyperpyrons*, had entered circulation two hundred years before and were in wide use throughout the eastern Mediterranean, as well as being the standard coinage of the empire.

'As rich as Croesus,' he purred.

'Lord?' said Luca.

Angel closed the lid.

'Hundreds of years ago, this city was part of a kingdom called Lydia,' explained Angel. 'Its ruler, King Croesus, was rich, very rich. He possessed gold mines and his servants sifted for gold in the rivers. My guess is that our friend, Arcadius Drogon, has discovered one of his gold mines and uses its riches to bribe the Turks to stay away from his city.'

296

'He is not my friend,' hissed Luca.

Angel put an arm round his shoulders.

'Don't be so hasty, Black Sheep. You could swap the hard, sometimes brief life of an Almogavar for the comfort of a long life, silk sheets and the lavish gifts of the Governor of Magnesia. Some might say a sore arse is a small price to pay for such an easy life.'

'I have always lived a hard life and prefer to keep it that way.'

Sancho left the slaves behind in Magnesia. As they had to be fed it was a blessing they could be left behind to the tender mercies of Arcadius Drogon, who would probably sell them on to authorities in Izmir for a tidy profit. The carts heaving with coins also represented a tidy sum, though one that would diminish by the day once the company had returned to Philadelphia. Weapons, specifically javelins, needed replacing and others needed mending. Links in mail armour needed replacing, spears purchased, saddlery repaired and horses re-shoeing. To say nothing of the great quantities of food required to feed upwards of seven thousand soldiers and the new servants and horse archers acquired by the company.

Ioannes Komnenos was furious with Grand Duke Roger when he learned of the extortion of money from Magnesia, though his citizens were relieved when the Catalans paid in full for the goods they purchased in their city, rather than plundering Philadelphia and the surrounding countryside. But his anger was tempered by the knowledge that the Catalan Company had saved his city, as well as the town of Tire. Roger's mercenaries had achieved more in six months than the imperial army had done in six years. Nevertheless, he was glad to see the red and gold banner disappearing to the north when the Catalans quit their camp and headed back to Artake in the third week of August.

297

Chapter 17

'We are all powerless and feeble, and yet Allah has provided us with a remedy for the predicament we find ourselves in.'

Izzeddin Arslan, dressed in rags, his hair and beard straggly and matted, walked around the open courtyard where the dignitaries sat in opulent chairs arranged in a circle. The surrounding palace still had walls decorated with Christian images and mosaics depicting past emperors of Constantinople. The new ruler, Mehmed Bey, had instructed his architects to make the palace more fitting for the resident of a Muslim *emir*, but his immediate priority was to be polite to the religious fanatic whose army was camped outside his city.

That city was Anaia, a prosperous settlement positioned between the Aegean coast and the edge of a fertile plain of the Büyuk Menderes River. For generations, the farms on the plain had produced wheat in abundance, which in the days when the Romans had controlled the area had been exported to foreign lands. Now the Aydin Emirate controlled Anaia and the surrounding area.

Mehmed Bey, a middle-aged man with a sharp nose and beard, was a canny individual. A man who used a combination of veiled threats and charm to achieve his goals, he had watched with immense satisfaction as Christian mercenaries had recently savaged the armies of his rivals, the Karesi Emirate, the Germiyanid Emirate and the upstart Saruhan Bey, who fancied himself as a ruler in his own right, though bandit would be a more accurate description of him and his followers. He viewed the arrival of the deranged Izzeddin Arslan and his fanatics with horror, though went out of his way to accommodate the Sufi fanatic and his ten thousand *ghazi* warriors. The memory of Bergama had instilled fear not only in Christian but also in Muslim hearts.

'These mercenaries the Romans have hired are not to be underestimated,' cautioned Karesi Bey, still smarting from the loss of his governor of Soma, for which he blamed Izzeddin Arslan.

After the battle, the Sufi had taken himself and his army east, and Karesi Bey had hoped that was the last he would see of him and them. But three months later he was back, appearing at Anaia with a large army and requesting the presence of himself and other *emirs* for the final offensive that would establish the 'caliphate'. He had to admit he was tempted by the offer, because to be made a 'caliph', which meant 'successor' to the Prophet Muhammad himself, meant becoming a religious and political leader of immense power and prestige in the Muslim world.

The Sufi rounded on him.

'The mercenaries are nothing but instruments of Allah's displeasure.'

The holy man walked slowly around the courtyard of bubbling fountains, statues of Roman emperors in niches and ornamental flower beds. He stopped and pointed at Karesi Bey.

'You still employ infidel horsemen in your army?'

'I do,' replied the *emir*, 'and may I remind you under Sharia law I am entitled to do so, as all my Christian horsemen pay the *jizya*.'

Christians living in lands conquered by Muslims were exempted from automatic execution as long as they did not resist their new government. Indeed, they were permitted to live as long as they acknowledged their subjugation and paid a special tax call the *jizya*.

'It would be a foolish warlord who got rid of his best troops,' grunted Sasa Bey, the leader of the Germiyanid Emirate, a huge brute with a large head and enormous beard.

Izzeddin Arslan regarded him with barely concealed contempt.

'You can have the best soldiers in the world and it will avail you nothing, Sasa Bey, not if you do not follow the laws laid down by the Prophet.'

'What laws do you speak of?' demanded Sasa.

'When you laid siege to Philadelphia,' said Izzeddin, 'did you destroy the crops in the fields and poison the city's water supply?'

Sasa threw back his head and roared with laughter.

'Are you mad? I wanted to take the city and the valley around it, not create a wasteland. What is the point of taking a dead city?'

Izzeddin pointed a bony finger at him.

'Did not Muhammad say that when you are in the land of the *kuffar*, all crops should be destroyed and the water poisoned? By turning a blind eye to the *al salaf al salih*, you diminish your chances of victory.'

The *al salaf al salih* were Islam's 'pious forefathers', which were the Prophet himself and his earliest adherents. They were the models for all Muslim behaviour and to deviate from their teachings was to walk down a road that led to apostasy.

'If we unite our forces, then we can defeat the Romans and their allies.'

All eyes switched to Saruhan Bey, the youngest present who had the most in common with Izzeddin Arslan, in that he and his thousand followers had no land to speak of and relied on the charity of others to subsist. Though unlike the Sufi and his *ghazis*, none of the other *emirs* viewed him as much of a threat.

'Exactly,' said Izzeddin with relish. 'We must wage offensive *jihad* to forcibly remove the infidels from the few lands that remain to them in Anatolia.'

He observed Mehmed Bey coolly.

'And we must not enter into agreements with infidels.'

The ruler of the Aydin Emirate frowned at the holy man dressed in rags, in stark contrast to the expensive brocaded garment covering his own body.

'I am fully acquainted with Sharia law and was quite within my rights to sign a peace treaty with the governor of Magnesia.'

Izzeddin allowed a wry smile to crease his lips.

'The Koran also states the devout must not rest or they will fall into a state of sin. Those who persist in supporting non-Muslim governments, after being duly warned and educated about their sins, are considered apostates. I am warning you, Mehmed Bey, against tolerating the presence of Romans and their *kafir* ways.'

Mehmed Bey jumped from his chair. As the ruler of a large swathe of land in western Anatolia, he was unused to being talked to in such a manner.

'Watch your mouth, Arslan.'

'Or what, you will cut off my head?' sneered Izzeddin.

Karesi Bey also rose from his chair.

'If we argue among ourselves, the laughter of the Romans will be our only reward. We came here to listen to your proposals, Izzeddin. What are they?'

The holy man was still holding the angry stare of Mehmed Bey but turned away to address the man he had installed as ruler of his own emirate.

'We unite under a single banner, as suggested by Saruhan Bey, after which we capture Tire, Magnesia and Philadelphia, before marching north to link up with the army of Osman Bey for the final assault on Constantinople itself.'

Karesi Bey nodded and spoke a few quiet words with Mehmed Bey to persuade the Aydin *emir* to retake his seat.

'That is an ambitious plan, Izzeddin,' said Sasa, 'though not impossible if we unite. But what happens after we have conquered Constantinople? Who then becomes caliph?'

The Romans were on their last legs, even the most feeble-minded could see that. And when their last outposts in Anatolia had been conquered, a caliphate would be established to unite all the emirates under a single leader. But which leader? Of all those present, the dishevelled Izzeddin Arslan had the strongest claim to be caliph. This was because true caliphs had to be descended from the tribe of the Prophet – the Quraysh. He dressed in rags, had no horse, no land and no wealth, but Izzeddin Arslan possessed something more precious that elevated him above the great majority in the Muslim world: he was of Quraysh descent. That was why he commanded such respect and wielded so much power in Anatolia. It was why thousands flocked to his banner, that and the fact he promised free food, clothing and weapons for all who joined his *ghazis*. Charity was one of the central planks of Islam, to offer food and housing to impoverished strangers. The Prophet himself stated: 'You will not believe until you love for your brother what you love for yourself.' Of course, the sudden appearance of a horde of *ghazis* persuaded local rulers to gladly provide food, clothes, tents and anything else the fanatics required to hurry them on their way.

'Until we have removed the infidels from the whole of Anatolia,' said Izzeddin, 'everything else is just speculation, which will promote vanity, which encourages sin.'

The others looked at Karesi Bey with envious eyes, for he was, or had been, Izzeddin's protégé, the *emir* earmarked for great things.

But their falling out after the disaster at Soma may have damaged the brooding Karesi's prospects. In any case, he was not of Quraysh descent and so could not be a true caliph. Neither could they, or Osman Bey in the north for that matter. One thing they could all agree on, though they would never state it openly. No one wanted the fanatic Izzeddin Arslan to be caliph.

'Send word to your commanders,' said the holy man, 'to bring all their men here, to Anaia, from where we will march to finally rid all Anatolia of the *kafir*.'

Resigned nods greeted the 'suggestion'. Only Saruhan Bey was enthusiastic. Unlike the others, he had nothing to lose and everything to gain.

*****

The Catalan Company maintained a leisurely pace returning to Artake. Count Michael Cosses, though grateful it had lifted the sieges of Philadelphia and Tire, smashing two enemy armies in the process, was aggrieved the Almogavars had plundered the imperial treasury at Magnesia. In addition, and perhaps much worse, they had humiliated Arcadius Drogon, friend of the emperor's son who had been appointed by Andronicus himself. He had no doubt an angry letter was already making its way to Constantinople.

None of this concerned Luca, who had a spring in his step after tasting nothing but victory with the Almogavars. Now he was making his way back to Artake and his beloved Ayna. The days were hot and dry, the hills and valleys verdant and teeming with wildlife, mostly brown bear, wolves, lynx and wild cats. Most of the forests were pine, though there was also a sprinkling of oak, hazel, alder, maple and hornbeam.

Romanus had elected to stay with the Almogavars, and so Luca and Jordi began teaching him the rudiments of using a spear and throwing a javelin. He was an eager recruit, albeit one handicapped by the language barrier. Nevertheless, each day he learned a little Italian and Catalan as he practised with the weapons of the Almogavars.

Count Michael sent his scouts out every day to reconnoitre the route, preferring to ride with Grand Duke Roger and Bernat de Rocafort rather than mix with the Almogavars. Not that it bothered Sancho and his captains. They and their men had full bellies, coin in their pouches and had acquired both servants, horses and tents courtesy of the enemy. The servants, individuals such as Ertan, had in reality swapped one set of masters for another, though the Almogavars were fairly lenient owners, having few material possessions or desire to achieve high social status. They insisted on keeping to their low-born status as shepherds and forest dwellers, believing an adherence to a simple creed made them more effective, more ruthless soldiers.

Luca and Jordi had purchased Ertan and were determined to free him, just as Luca had done with Ayna. But Sancho pointed out that if they did then the Turk would be free to leave camp and go where he wanted, meaning they would no longer have anyone to cook the delicious meals they had been feasting on. They therefore agreed between them to free Ertan when they reached Artake. Despite the Almogavars maintaining a leisurely pace, Ertan soon found walking too taxing, and so the overweight cook was allowed to ride the packhorse carrying his cooking utensils and spices. He had begun to learn the language of the Catalans, as indeed had Luca, though conversation between the two was reduced to one-word

305

sentences and much pointing and gestures. It was with the help of Melek and his gift for languages that the story of Ertan could be told.

He was in fact not a Turk but a Syrian, being a renowned cook in the house of a wealthy citizen in the city of Aleppo. But Ertan was a notorious gambler as well as a skilled cook, and when his wages had all been wasted on bets, he stole from his master. Under Islamic Sharia law, the punishment for theft was to lose a hand, but his master, charitable individual that he was, decided the world should not lose a talented cook, and so had Ertan reduced to a slave and sold him to a Turkish lord who was visiting the city and who had been staying in his mansion. Ertan had begged to be allowed to stay in the house of his master, to no avail. For once trust has been abused, it can never be regained.

'Ertan's master was killed when the brave Almogavars stormed the camp of those besieging Philadelphia,' reported Melek, walking on foot beside Luca and leading his horse by the reins.

'He liked his master?' asked Luca.

Melek spoke a few words to Ertan on the packhorse, who promptly spat on the ground and spat out a stream of invective.

Melek shook his head. 'His master was a cruel man who beat him often.'

'Then why was he crying like a baby when we cremated his master's body?' asked Jordi.

'It is a great sin in Islam to cremate the dead,' Melek answered for the cook. 'When a Muslim dies, his body should be washed, wrapped in a white cloth and prayers said over it before it is interred. What you did outside Philadelphia was a great desecration.'

Sancho ahead of Luca and Jordi turned his head to speak to Melek.

'We had neither the time nor the inclination to dig a mass grave and seeing as there was a forest of stakes available, it made sense to light a great pyre.'

'I hope Allah will forgive you, lord,' said Melek, 'and all the Almogavars.'

'Will he forgive *you* for fighting beside infidels, Melek?' asked Sancho.

Melek flashed a smile. 'There is no god but Allah, but he is generous and forgiving, lord. Besides, are we not leaving Anatolia now you have fulfilled your contract with the Roman emperor? Allah will be delighted if I am in foreign lands killing Christians. You yourself have killed Christians, lord?'

'I have lost count of the number,' said Sancho.

'And your god will forgive you for doing so?'

'I am like every soldier,' replied Sancho, smiling. 'I have God on my side.'

Their conversation was interrupted by a group of riders galloping past them, all wearing mail armour, helmets and lances, a great red banner emblazoned with a yellow cross billowing in their midst. They ignored the Almogavars to gallop to where Grand Duke Roger was riding with Count Michael, their respective banners fluttering behind them. Sancho thought nothing of it, presuming it was a letter written by Count Ioannes addressed to the emperor complaining of the behaviour of the Catalan Company. Grand Duke Roger, who was after all now related to the imperial family, could deal with all matters pertaining to diplomacy and politics.

But a few minutes later, Bernat was beside Sancho requesting the Almogavar leader attend Roger and Count Michael.

'Tell them to come here,' snapped Sancho. 'They have horses; I do not. What is so urgent, anyway?'

'A huge Muslim army is gathering to the south of Philadelphia,' said Bernat, glancing at Melek. 'Count Komnenos requests we turn around and join him in the defence of his city.'

Luca nodded at Jordi and jabbed him in the stomach. His friend grinned. They were both thinking of new victories and more glory. Sancho poured cold water on their dreams.

'We have fulfilled our contractual obligations, Bernat, and now we are going home.'

'We have no home,' said Bernat pathetically. 'We are wanderers in this land and our dependents live in Artake at the behest of Count Michael. Roger has told me about your plans to stay in Anatolia…'

'That has yet to be put to the men,' interrupted Sancho. 'And is a topic for another day.'

Sancho turned to Jordi and Luca.

'Make use of your legs and inform the captains I request their presence.'

Grand Duke Roger commanded the Catalan Company but he knew that without the Almogavars he ruled over only Bernat and his horsemen. He also knew that the Almogavars would not take any action without the consent of their elected council. Count Michael had never heard of such a thing, but then he had never seen a group of poor shepherds from northern Spain destroy the empire's foes so quickly.

The Almogavars halted and made camp, Luca and Jordi joining other details in digging a ditch around the tents being erected in the valley through which ran a fast-flowing stream filled with ice-cold water. Other groups were sent into the trees on the hillsides to collect firewood, and soon the smell of wood smoke was drifting through the early evening air. Horsemen were removing saddles from their mounts, rubbing down the beasts and checking for lameness and nails missing from shoes. Crossbowmen were posted around the ditch along with spearmen, for as well as game the trees could easily hide an enemy raiding party.

As they had begun the campaign with no tents, the Catalan Company had requisitioned large numbers of captured Turkish tents, which were infinitely more comfortable and practical than the meagre structures they had lived in during the Sicilian campaign. Even the reserved, austere Sancho Rey had to admit that his own rigid, domed wooden frame, over which was placed a heavy waterproof felt exterior with a red linen or silk inner layer, with rugs and cushions on the floors, was far better.

When the Almogavar captains reported to Sancho's tent, they were served a delicious hot stew called *chorba* by Ertan, a simple dish made from onions, garlic, pepper, crushed wheat, tomatoes, parsley, coriander and mint leaves. But one requiring a skilled cook to achieve the correct blend of ingredients to maximise taste. Once again, Luca and Jordi waited on the captains with wine.

Marc nodded at the Syrian. 'He may be a godless heathen but he can cook.'

'He's the slave of Jordi and the Black Sheep,' said Angel, spooning the stew into his mouth.

'He takes a Muslim woman to his bed,' Hector grinned at Luca, 'has a Muslim cook and is a friend of that infidel horseman who has recently joined us. Father Ramon thinks all these things are

309

signs of the Black Sheep's heresy, and you know the punishment for heresy.'

'Father Ramon should stick to religion and keep his nose out of Almogavar business,' growled Sancho.

Luca smiled.

'So, the governor of Philadelphia wants us to save his arse for a second time,' said Marc.

'Is he going to pay us for doing so?' asked Hector, finishing his stew and handing his bowl to a loitering Ertan. 'More.'

'Effendi,' smiled Ertan, taking the bowl.

'Let the Romans fend for themselves,' said Angel, 'they defaulted on their payment to us once; they will do so again.'

'He has a point,' agreed Hector, licking his bowl.

'What if Count Komnenos guarantees to pay us, and I confirm he has the gold to honour his pledge?' said Sancho.

Angel shrugged. 'The men will take your word as guarantee of payment, Sancho.'

'Make sure we get a substantial bonus, though,' said Hector.

'Otherwise we will go back to Magnesia and hang its deviant governor after first emptying his treasury,' threatened Marc.

Sancho nodded. 'It is agreed, then. I will inform Roger of our decision.'

Chapter 18

Anatolia in August is hot and sweat was coursing off Luca's face as
he and thousands of others fast-paced back to Philadelphia, retracing
the route they had taken after leaving the city. Sancho had put the
Almogavar proposal to Grand Duke Roger, who had in turn relayed
it to Count Michael. The Roman aristocrat had bitten his tongue and
agreed to stand surety himself for the amount the Catalan Company
wished to charge for their services. Better that than waiting for days
until the demand was received by Count Ioannes and he sent a reply.
The ways of the Catalans were strange to him, as was the way they
conducted warfare. But he had seen with his own eyes how effective
they were, and at the current juncture they were the best hope of
saving what was left of the emperor's possessions in Anatolia. No,
they were the *only* hope.

Ertan had never a ridden a horse until his capture by the
Almogavars and he clearly did not enjoy the experience of having to
stay in the saddle as the packhorse cantered along the uneven track.
But as he was too overweight to keep up with Luca and Jordi on foot,
riding was his only alternative, as it was for the other servants with
the company. It had been Grand Duke Roger's intention to sell the
horses captured at Philadelphia. But the need for remounts,
packhorses to carry the captured Turkish tents, other supplies and
servants, plus the requirement to mount those horsemen that arrived
with Bernat de Rocafort, meant the plan fell through.

'The Bastard' had taken a keen interest in Melek and his horse
archers, seizing every opportunity to conduct joint training exercises
involving his own riders and the Muslim volunteers. Father Ramon
and his priests raged at the presence of disbelievers in the company,
but after being denounced as heretics, devil worshippers and

311

blasphemers by their French enemies during the Sicilian war, the company and the Almogavars in particular took a more pragmatic approach to the recruitment of Muslim horsemen. Most viewed them as a welcome addition to the company, albeit as yet untested in battle.

Ertan was complaining under his breath, giving the appearance he was about to topple from the saddle any second.

'Keep your feet in the stirrups,' Luca said to him, watching the track for any large stones he might trip over.

'He does not understand your words,' said Jordi beside him.

'He falls from the saddle, we leave him,' Sancho ahead of them called, as usual out in front of all the Almogavars.

But the portly Turk did not fall off his horse and by the end of the day, the sun gently dipping on the western horizon to turn the white walls and buildings of Philadelphia molten gold, the Catalan Company arrived before the city once more. It had covered nearly thirty miles to try once again to save Emperor Andronicus' fast-shrinking empire.

The next day, Grand Duke Roger, Count Michael and Bernat rode into the city, their banner men behind them. Sancho, who commanded the largest contingent of the Catalan Company, walked into Philadelphia, taking Luca and Jordi with him. He had invited the other captains to accompany him, but they had told him in no uncertain terms they had no time for court politics. Sancho took long strides as he paced towards the palace, magnificently equipped guards wearing yellow cloaks patrolling the streets, eyeing the trio with disdain as they passed. This did nothing to sweeten Sancho's humour.

He jerked a thumb at a pair of garrison soldiers they had just passed on the main road leading from the northern gatehouse to the palace.

'I wonder how many of them will be joining us on the battlefield?'

'We do not need them, father,' said Jordi.

'Just as well,' sneered Sancho.

They all stopped when they turned a corner to enter a small square, in the centre of which were two white stone columns close together, at the top of which was a stunning sculpture of an angry lion on the back of a bull. It was as if the two beasts had been turned to stone during their life-or-death battle by some divine power, to preserve their titanic struggle for all eternity. It was a magnificent work of art and its silent power stood in stark contrast to the noise and bustle in the square, which had shops around its sides and was filled with citizens going about their everyday business.

Sancho pointed up at the sculpture.

'That is the only lion left in Philadelphia.'

Luca thought the judgement harsh, and when he and Jordi stood against the wall of the meeting room in which he council of war took place in the palace, the blue eyes of Ioannes Komnenos were burning with enthusiasm. He may have had grey hair and a weather-beaten face, but his hoarse voice spoke with determination and authority. He pounded the table around which Sancho, Bernat, Count Michael, Roger and himself stood.

'The Turks are massing here, at Anaia.'

He was pointing to a point on a hastily made sketch map of the area around Philadelphia. To the west was Magnesia, to the south Tire and southwest of that place, Anaia, which appeared to be a short distance inland from the coast. Sancho saw another place marked on the map and pointed to it.

'What is this city?'

The fire in Count Ioannes' eyes burned low.

'Nearly thirty years ago, the emperor led a great army through Anatolia, during which he visited the ruins of the ancient city of Tralles, which he ordered should be rebuilt and its defences strengthened. It was subsequently renamed Andronikopolis.'

'What is the size of its garrison?' asked Roger.

The count's head dropped.

'Alas, it is now a ruin once again following its sacking by the Turks twenty years ago. It was never rebuilt.'

Bernat shifted uncomfortably on his feet and Count Michael stared into space. The fire returned to the governor's eyes.

'If we do not destroy this Turkish horde gathering at Anaia, the same fate will befall Philadelphia, Tire and Magnesia. But if we prevail, it will set back the Muslim advance for years.'

The room fell silent. No one said it, but they were all thinking the same thing: the advance may be slowed but it could not be reversed. Luca looked around the frescoed walls and felt sad. For such beauty and elegance to vanish from the world would be a tragedy. He gripped the ornate handle of his Damascus dagger and his heart hardened. Just as it had been his destiny to join the Almogavars, so was it the destiny of the Catalan Company to save a great empire.

'Well,' said Roger to break the air of gloom that hung over them all, 'let us take the fight to the enemy forthwith.'

The quickest route to Anaia was directly south through the hills, though Count Ioannes wanted to take his horsemen and those of Count Michael southeast along the old Roman road until it reached the Maeander Valley. Sancho wanted to take his Almogavars directly south, but Count Ioannes persuaded him it would be folly to

314

divide their forces. The Germiyanids, through whose territory they would be marching, would have scouts watching all the roads and valleys, thus it made no sense to give the enemy the opportunity to engage an army that had been separated into two separate and widely spaced parts.

Once again, only horsemen would ride with the two counts, the garrison of Philadelphia being left in the city to protect its citizens, though if the Catalan Company and its allies were defeated then it would fall to the enemy anyway. The threat of a renewal of a siege meant the company's servants would also be lodged in the city until the company returned. If it returned.

Luca tried to explain to Ertan what was happening, failing completely until the swaggering Melek arrive to enlighten the cook. Ertan was unhappy.

'He says he should accompany you and Jordi, to make sure you eat well.'

'Tell him he will be safer here, in the city.'

Melek translated Luca's words, prompting a resigned shrug from the cook. Ertan then began babbling to the Turk and pointing at the white walls of Philadelphia.

'He says the Romans do not like Turks, and he fears they may kill him while you are away.'

Without waiting for a reply, Melek replied to Ertan, his words appearing the soothe the agitated cook.

'What did you tell him?' asked Luca.

'I told him the Romans were very particular when it came to respecting the property of others, and since he is your slave, they would not dare harm him.'

Ertan smiled and nodded at Luca, who smiled back.

'I do not hold with slavery,' he told Melek. 'As soon as we reach Artake, I am going to free him.'

Melek laughed. 'A freed Muslim slave roaming in a Christian land? He will be in greater peril than if you left him alone in this camp outside the city.'

Once more Turkish tents were pitched outside Philadelphia, though they were now occupied by the Catalan Company. They would be left standing empty while the company was away.

Despite the threat hanging over the city, there was no shortage of food to fill Almogavar bellies. The largest concentration of arable land lay northwest of the city, on both sides of the River Cogamus. The estates in the area were criss-crossed with a system of canals and irrigation ditches to increase crop yields. Some had been abandoned when the Turks had approached the city, though the Germiyanids had been careful not to damage any of the economic infrastructure they themselves desired to possess.

As well as crops, animals reared for food and hides included swine, cattle, buffaloes and sheep, large flocks of the latter still present in the valley. Philadelphia had once supplied the empire's mounted soldiers with woollen horse cloths for their animals, though those days were long past. Nevertheless, the city was still a centre for dyers, wool washers, linen workers, fullers, felt makers and carpet weavers. But the most famous product of Philadelphia and the surrounding region was honey. Every Almogavar was issued with a flask of the pale-yellow sticky fluid to provide energy for their journey.

That journey began on the second day after their arrival back at the city, Luca and five thousand others following the pace set by Sancho Rey at the head of the column of foot soldiers. Ahead of

316

them rode Grand Duke Roger and Bernat de Rocafort with the Catalan horsemen, accompanying them the two counts and in the vanguard Roman horsemen, which also brought up the rearguard. The counts had brought their servants and squires, which were all mounted, but there were no wagons carrying grand pavilions, musical instruments to entertain the Roman nobles at night, and no camp followers to entertain the troops with their bodies for hire. Melek and his horsemen rode on the flanks of the Almogavars, bows at the ready to see off any enemy raiders that might chance their luck against them. In total, seven thousand six hundred horse and foot marched from Philadelphia to engage the great Muslim army assembling at the city of Anaia.

As before, the Almogavars set a cruel stride to keep up with the horsemen, Sancho having instructed Bernat to set the pace, and also keep the Romans from treating the expedition as a grand tour of the theme they no longer ruled. There were no drums, trumpets or other musical instruments to accompany the sounds of horses' hooves and feet pounding the sun-hardened ground, only a steely determination to reach Anaia as quickly as possible. At the end of the first day, the army reached the eastern end of the Maeander Valley, through which the river of the same name flowed.

Then the soldiers disappeared into the trees.

The valley itself is a luscious green in summer, sprinkled with pale-pink almond trees in blossom in the spring. Count Ioannes may have lost most of his theme, but he knew the geography of the land well enough and now used it to his advantage. The valley appears as flat as a table but is in fact slightly tilted, which means when the winter floods came and the river broke its banks, the deluge was far worse on the south side of the valley. Conversely, the northern part of the valley drained much earlier in springtime and in some winters did not flood at all.

As the valley floor was essentially a floodplain, it was ideally suited to agriculture but unsuitable for human habitation. In contrast, the lower slopes of both sides of the valley were unsuitable for arable cultivation but still suitable for vines, olives and fruit trees, as well as being ideal for permanent settlements. The lower slopes on the northern side of the valley were blanketed with groves of orange, apple and fig trees, now sadly untended and overgrown, nearby settlements abandoned and derelict after the great slaughter at Tralles twenty years before.

There were signs of decay everywhere, not only in the untended orchards but also the settlements the Almogavars came upon. The villages they passed through varied in size between five to fifteen households, each one of stone with a tile roof. But two decades of being vacant had resulted in their roofs caving in and the stonework being covered in mould. It was the same with the manor houses, the former homes of the landed nobility who had administered what had been a prosperous valley. All the buildings – the small churches, the domed cruciform dining halls, bedrooms and outbuildings – had been gutted of anything of value, to be left empty, decaying husks. The stench of decline hung over the valley as the army threaded its way west through the trees. The rate of advance was markedly slower than it had been, both because of the terrain the troops were moving through, and the need to stay hidden for as long as possible from the enemy.

It was hot and humid in the trees, made worse by each Almogavar carrying his food bag, water bottle, spear, javelins, shield and sword. But at least the atmosphere was more relaxed, Sancho

318

walking ahead in the company of his captains and Grand Duke Roger and the two counts leading their horses on foot. Even the fearsome cataphracts were walking, though not in their mail armour, their squires leading their own and their masters' horses to save the nobles the effort of pulling their own reins! The fine young aristocrats were unused to sleeping in small tents among foreign mercenaries, who they were shocked to discover were originally shepherds and foresters. In what was left of the Roman Empire, shepherds were regarded as coming from the most primitive and uncivilised layer of society, inferior even to bandits. It was made worse by the realisation that these base shepherds were the emperor's only hope of salvation.

'Count Ioannes' scouts' have returned with reports of many tents pitched outside Anaia,' said Sancho. 'They have identified the banners of a number of *emirs*, leading me to believe they have formed an alliance.'

'How many troops in total?' asked Hector.

'Over twenty thousand at least,' answered Sancho.

'Odds of three-to-one,' mused Marc. 'I'll take that.'

'Our inferior numbers will encourage the Turks to seek battle,' said Angel. 'They will think we are out of our minds to seek an engagement with so few troops.'

'That is what I am banking on,' said Sancho. 'An over-confident enemy works to our advantage.'

'What of your Muslim mercenaries? Will they fight or desert to the enemy on the eve of battle?' asked Hector.

'They are not *my* Muslims,' Sancho corrected him, 'more Luca's recruits.'

The all turned to look at him, causing him to blush.

'Well, Black Sheep,' said Marc, 'can we rely on these infidels?'

319

'Yes, lord,' replied Luca.

'How can you be certain?' probed Angel.

'Melek has given me his word,' said Luca, rather naively.

Hector and Sancho guffawed.

'Then I will hold you personally accountable for their actions during the impending battle,' threatened Sancho.

'You are not thinking of becoming one, are you, Black Sheep? A Muslim, I mean?' asked Marc.

'No, lord.'

'What about that woman of yours?' asked Angel. 'She is a Muslim, is she not?'

'Yes, lord.'

'Father Ramon wants her to convert to our religion, or burn her,' said Marc.

Luca was enraged. 'He touches her, I will kill him myself.'

'That's the spirit, Luca,' smiled Hector. 'Model yourself on Sancho, here. He likes killing priests.'

'I would like to remind you I did it to save my only son,' grunted Sancho.

'For which I am most grateful, father,' said Jordi.

Tralles was a ghost city, its gates smashed in and the gatehouses burnt-out as a result of the Turkish siege that had emptied the city of its inhabitants. But the walls were still in a good condition and inside the perimeter many of the buildings were in an adequate state of repair. All the domed churches had been looted and destroyed by fire, as had the monasteries. The paved streets were still extant, though curiously two marble-paved streets near the centre of the city had been stripped of their flagstones.

Only the two counts, Roger and Sancho entered the city, along with a small escort, which included Luca and Jordi. Ionnes Komnenos was distraught at the violation that had been wrought on the city, which he had helped liberate as a young man. Tralles occupied a strong position, being built on a plateau with a steep acropolis. But like all Roman cities surrounded by enemies, unless constantly relieved and supplied, it was terribly vulnerable. A gentle breeze was blowing through the empty city, which was filled with a dread silence, its grand, despoiled buildings standing in mute testimony to the horror that had taken place a generation before.

They were standing in the middle of the forum in the centre of the city, a paved circular space with a large stone column in the centre, which had been surmounted by a cross before the Turks came. Around the perimeter had been shops, porticoes, churches and offices, all now empty and gutted of anything of worth. Ahead, looming over the city, was the fortified acropolis that appeared impregnable, with deep gorges on either side.

'How did such a strong city fall?' said Luca absently.

Sancho turned on him. 'Speak only when you are spoken to.'

But Count Ioannes was in a reflective mood.

'How? I will tell you, young Luca, for the tale of Tralles deserves to be heard. As your young eyes have noted, the city has strong defences, but what are strong defences without food and water? Nothing.'

His head dropped. 'The city had no wells from which to draw water, relying solely on the river below. When the Turks laid siege to Tralles, it was only a matter of time before it fell. There were thirty-five thousand people living here once. Fifteen thousand were

321

butchered when the gates were opened to the Turks. The rest were sold into slavery.'

'Where was your army?' asked Luca naively.

Roger laughed but Sancho was fuming. The governor of Philadelphia laid a hand on Luca's shoulder.

'What is left of the emperor's army is in the north, on the eastern side of the Bosporus, defending Constantinople from the army of another Turk called Osman Bey. Indeed, Luca, it was a defeat at the hands of Osman Bey that brought you and the rest of the Catalan Company here.'

'For which we thank God,' said Count Michael.

'For which we thank God,' echoed Count Ioannes.

'And with God's help we will destroy the Turkish army at Anaia,' added Roger.

'God helps those who help themselves,' growled Sancho.

The ruins of Tralles were some thirty miles east of Anaia, which the Catalan Company and its Roman allies took a further day to cover, staying among the trees on the northern side of the valley. The valley itself was largely deserted, fields laying empty and overgrown, though enemy scouting parties were operating from Anaia itself. And it was one such group that spotted soldiers moving through the trees on the lower slopes on the north side of the valley. Melek led some of his horse archers out of the trees and they shot a few arrows at the riders who were dressed and equipped in an identical fashion. The scouts wheeled about and galloped back to Anaia with news that infidel soldiers were advancing on the city.

*****

'Thank you for accepting my invitation.'

Mehmed Bey smiled, extending an arm to his guest, invited him to relax on one of the couches in the office. Though grand viewing chamber would be a more apt description. It gave panoramic views of the countryside around Anaia, extending to the blue waters of the Aegean some ten miles to the west.

Karesi Bey accepted the proposal and took the weight off his feet, accepting the offer of warm water in a silver bowl in which he washed his hands, drying them on a towel offered by another Christian slave, one of several in the room.

Mehmed Bey, dressed in a white silk shirt and blue silk kaftan, also seated himself, more slaves coming forward with a fresh bowl of water and clean towel. All were under the watchful eyes of guards standing around the walls, for Mehmed Bey was not a trusting individual. He clapped his hands to signal he and his guest should be served wine.

'I trust you still imbibe?' he asked his fellow *emir*.

'I do, though only in moderation.'

'If your Sufi had his way, we would all be living like hermits, scraping the earth for a living.'

Karesi Bey sipped at the wine served in a silver chalice, its previous owner being the Roman governor of the city. It was most excellent.

'He and his followers are bleeding my granaries dry,' complained Mehmed Bey, 'though fortunately their dislike of alcohol means at least my wine cellar is safe. For the moment.'

Karesi Bey looked around the room, the walls of which were still decorated with Christian frescoes denoting Christ being served by kneeling Roman emperors. His host noticed his stares.

'Quaint, are they not? I really should remove them but I have to confess I quite like them.'

'You have retained many Christian images?' asked Karesi.

'I have found it is easier and far less distasteful to tax Christians and their churches, rather than kill them and destroy their places of worship. This is not Bergama.'

Karesi Bey shuddered. 'That atrocity was not of my making.'

'Destruction and slaughter are bad for trade,' said Mehmed. 'And fanaticism can be a double-edged sword.'

'In what way?'

'Once Izzeddin Arslan has finished killing all the Christians and Jews in this land, he will begin a purge of those he considers apostates. We might all find ourselves at the mercy of him and his *ghazis*.'

He clapped his hands. 'Let us eat.'

More slaves brought dishes served on silver platters, too much for two individuals to consume, but were a display of Mehmed Bey's power and hospitality. They barely touched the *dolma* made from aubergines, courgettes, onions, peppers and tomatoes stuffed with minced meat and rice. It was a similar tale with the mountain of *fattoush* that was brought from the kitchens: a salad of chopped cucumbers, radishes, tomatoes and pita bread. Though both enjoyed the endless number of kebabs of chicken roasted on skewers, Mehmed Bey instructing that the leftovers be given to the poor. By the time *musakhan* was being served, consisting of whole chickens baked with onion, saffron and fried pine nuts, the two *emirs* were only picking at their food.

Karesi Bey's dark and gloomy face was briefly lightened by a smile.

324

'Izzeddin Arslan would say such opulence and easy living are signs of a dissolute life.'

'If that was so,' said Mehmed Bey, 'then why does Allah allow us to live in the cities and palaces of the enemy? If we are so corrupt, why have our armies been so successful against the Romans?'

'Perhaps you should point out to him the contradiction in his argument,' suggested Karesi Bey.

'And have ten thousand enraged *ghazis* vent their fury on this fine city? I think not. Anyway, are you not the chosen one as far as the fanatic is concerned?'

Karesi Bey nodded to a waiting slave with a fresh bowl of water, the man walking forward with head bowed to allow the *emir* to wash his hands a second time.

'Alas, I am out of favour due to allowing the enemy to march through my lands uninterrupted, that and berating him in public for convincing one of my governors to join him in a reckless military adventure.'

'The clash outside Soma,' nodded Mehmed Bey, 'I heard about it. These Catalans are not to be tangled with lightly.'

'Fortunately, they are marching back to Artake, so the reports say.'

Mehmed Bey accepted the offer of a slice of orange, one of several arranged in a circle on a small silver dish.

'These Catalans have been like a whirlwind charging through Anatolia. But the thing about whirlwinds is that they are only temporary. When they have departed, we will still be here.'

He put the orange slice into his mouth.

'But there is another problem which is less temporary and needs to be dealt with speedily if it is not to sweep us all away.'

Karesi Bey accepted the offer of a slice of orange.

'What problem?'

'Izzeddin Arslan and his fanatical following. The cave dweller is right in insisting we pool our resources to regain the losses suffered at the hands of the Catalan infidels, I will concede that. But once we have done so and forced Philadelphia to surrender, what then?'

'Then we will conquer Artake, the last great Roman province left in Anatolia,' said Karesi Bey.

'But that still does not solve the problem of Izzeddin Arslan, who draws the rabble of humanity to his banner, which then becomes his own private army.'

'He is a descendent of the Quraysh, my lord. Only a Muslim with a death wish would raise his sword against him.'

Mehmed Bey took a fig from a plate offered him.

'So, you accept he and his followers are a problem?'

Another smile creased Karesi Bey's face. 'I am a soldier, my lord, not a politician.'

Mehmed Bey nodded sagely. 'A politician's answer, my congratulations. But when the Catalans return to the abyss from which they came from, Izzeddin Arslan and thousands of his followers will still be roaming this land like a plague of locusts, stripping the land bare whenever they appear.'

'Perhaps when the Romans have all been conquered, they and their leader will disappear.'

Mehmed Bey nibbled on a second fig.

'I have used a combination of flattery, bribery, threats and a limited amount of force to create the domain I now rule. But I learned very quickly that fanatics can rarely be reasoned with. You either submit to them or eradicate them. There is no middle course.'

'Allah will reveal his plans, my lord.'

They fell into silence, the *Emir* of Aydin chewing on his fig, Karesi Bey running a finger around the lip of his silver cup. Both stopped their activities when an officer of the palace guard in red leggings, a short-sleeved red tunic and thigh-length mail armour appeared, snapping to attention before Mehmed Bey and handing him a note. The hairs on the back of Karesi Bey's neck stood up. He did not know the contents of the letter but his sixth sense honed on the battlefield told him something was amiss. His gut did not lie because Mehmed Bey's eyes opened wide with alarm while reading the note. He sighed and looked up at the officer.

'Assemble the army.'

Karesi Bey sprang up from the couch, staring at the other *emir* in anticipation.

'It would appear the reports you read concerning the Catalans returning to Artake were wrong, my lord,' said Mehmed Bey, slowly rising from the couch. 'They have been identified, along with their Roman paymasters, a mere ten miles from this very palace.'

Karesi Bey smiled. 'They are the ones with the death wish, my lord, for they have unwittingly stumbled upon a great host that will surely annihilate them, God willing.'

'Fetch my armour,' called Mehmed Bey without enthusiasm.

Allah had indeed revealed a plan, though it was not to the *Emir* of Aydin's liking. The ferocious reputation of the Catalans had spread far and wide in a very short time, and he had no desire to witness their battlefield prowess at close quarters.

Chapter 19

The Maeander Valley runs from east to west, the river of the same name flowing across the plain in a winding fashion as it heads toward the Aegean. But around fifteen miles from the coast the valley curves in a southwestern direction to reach the sea. Anaia was positioned on the northern side of the valley, at roughly the mid-point of the 'curve', steep hills behind it, the valley floor extending east from the city to the river. The river itself follows the course of the valley, flowing through its centre. It is deep but not very broad – around twenty yards – but presents a formidable obstacle for foot soldiers and horsemen without boats or bridging equipment.

The distance from the city's eastern gates to the river is around three miles, a similar length from the river eastwards to the hills on the other side of the valley. Because of the geography of the whole length of the valley, the land south of the river often experiences severe flooding, resulting in an absence of trees and sandy earth sprinkled with tufts of rushes. The soil itself is covered with a thin layer of heather and is brackish in colour. Horses' hooves will sink into it without a sound, which makes it unsuitable for large-scale military operations involving sizeable numbers of horsemen and foot soldiers.

The space between the city and the river was where the Turkish army – over twenty thousand strong – formed its battle line against the Romans and their Catalan allies. The *emirs* were aware their forces outnumbered the enemy but had no experience of battlefield cooperation. And they also knew that Izzeddin Arslan and his *ghazis* were almost impossible to control in battle. They thus adopted a strategy they hoped would maximise their advantages while minimising their deficiencies. It was Karesi Bey who thought of the plan, the Turk who had been fighting in the saddle since he had been a boy.

In his scale armour and oversized helmet, Mehmed Bey looked ridiculous, though his foot soldiers clustered near the city gates were a magnificent spectacle. Disciplined, well equipped in helmets and leather corselets worn over scale body armour, they used the teardrop-shaped shields of the Romans and were armed with spears and swords. Unfortunately, they numbered only a thousand and their *emir* had issued strict instructions they were to stick to the city like glue. They thus formed the left wing of the Turkish army.

'I hope I do not live to regret this, my lord,' whined Mehmed Bey. 'I would have preferred to close the gates of Anaia and let the enemy waste their time and lives on a futile siege, rather than sit on an uncomfortable horse in this heat.'

'Allah has presented us with a chance to destroy these Catalans,' said Karesi Bey, 'and we should take it. Once they have been defeated, the remaining Roman garrisons in Anatolia will quickly surrender.'

A mighty cheer went up from the great horde of *ghazis* deployed on the right of the Aydin foot soldiers, though 'deployed' hinted at a military formation rather than the mob of ten thousand *ghazis* clustered around the emaciated figure of Izzeddin Arslan. In the midst of the unruly host stood the holy man's élite soldiers, immaculate in their mail armour and rigid in their disciplined ranks. The reason for the rising noise was the unfurling of the sacred banner of the Prophet. It was a huge green flag made from silk, on the end of its pole a gold clenched fist holding a Koran. Any Christian whose eyes looked on the banner was to be put to immediate death, though no one dared touch Karesi Bey's Christian heavy horsemen deployed to the rear of the *ghazis*.

They along with the rest of Karesi Bey's horsemen – two thousand horse archers and fifteen hundred mounted lancers – stood ready to charge through the gap between the *ghazis* and the river. In addition to Karesi Bey's horsemen, there were the riders of Mehmed Bey – three thousand horse archers – and the five hundred horse archers and five hundred mounted spearmen led by Saruhan Bey. The final mounted element of the Turkish army were the three thousand horse archers of Sasa Bey, the unstable, brutish leader of the Germiyanid Emirate. The horsemen were a blaze of colour. The horses wore thick saddle blankets – called *içlik* – in red, purple, green and blue. There were many red banners sporting a sword, the emblem of Karesi Bey. Others were maroon with a black circle in the centre, the standard of Mehmed Bey, while the plain black flags carried by other horsemen designated those loyal to Sasa Bey, and Saruhan Bey's horsemen carried purple flags.

Karesi Bey knew his horsemen were head and shoulders above the other Turkish riders when it came to battlefield tactics, being fully trained in close cooperation between horse archers and lancers. But he also knew that the Catalan mercenaries would immediately attack once they came within range of the Turkish army. He gambled that the thousands of *ghazis* would be the main focus of the Christian attack, and while the Catalans were busy slaughtering Izzeddin Arslan's followers, he would lead thousands of horsemen through the gap to envelop the Catalans and their Roman allies. Caught between the *ghazis* to their front and thousands of horse archers raining missiles down on them in the rear, the Christians would either be slaughtered or they would throw down their weapons and beg for mercy.

There was a reason he had suggested the Turkish foot soldiers should form the left flank and centre, because there were olive groves near the city, which would disrupt the Catalan attack. The excellent foot soldiers of Mehmed Bey would hopefully be able to use the trees to their advantage when battling the enemy. Beyond the olive groves extending eastwards was pastureland, which was largely flat and sparsely populated with trees. It was where the *ghazis* stood and where they would bear the full brunt of the Christian attack. Izzeddin Arslan was no fool and knew his followers were being used as bait for the Christians. But such was his blind faith that he did not care. *Ghazis* killed in battle would enter paradise and so he relished the opportunity to give his followers a chance to reach heaven. Tactics were irrelevant. Allah would decide the outcome of the battle.

Five divisions of Almogavars were running towards the mass of enemy soldiers mustered to the right of the gleaming city of Anaia, their whoops and cheers reaching Luca's ears as he paced forward beside Jordi Rey. He was in the first rank made up of two hundred and fifty in total, behind him three other ranks of equal number. Each man occupied around three feet of space, which meant the Almogavar battle line covered a distance of three-quarters of a mile.

Luca felt the same emotions as he had during other battles: intense exhilaration coupled with a thirst to get to grips with the enemy as soon as possible. His legs felt as light as feathers, as did the spear he held in his left hand. His javelins were tucked in the quiver strapped to his back and his shield hung by a strap on the left side of his back. He and the thousands of others made no sound as they

331

raced across the grass, on their left hundreds of horsemen cantering forward towards the inviting gap on the Turkish right flank.

The tactics were simple enough: close with the enemy as quickly as possible to negate their greatest asset – their horse archers. Foot soldiers, regardless if they are disciplined or not, are extremely vulnerable to arrows and crossbow bolts, the more so if missiles are shot at them from mobile horsemen who can withdraw, reform and charge to get behind any units of foot soldiers. But once the Almogavars were in a close-quarters mêlée with the enemy, the foe's horse archers would be immediately rendered ineffective.

The endless training and route marches had produced soldiers who were both physically strong and knew drills off by heart. They were striding across the ground but did not break formation, every man constantly glancing left and right to ensure the ranks were maintained. Enemy horsemen could appear at any minute; indeed, many were wondering where were the Turkish riders? And if they did it would be imperative to maintain formation. Horsemen could not break a discipline formation of foot soldiers, and if the Almogavars were surrounded it would fall to Bernat de Rocafort and his riders to chase away any horse archers.

But there were no horse archers today.

Luca could see individual faces among the enemy throng now. He also saw a smattering of white turbans among the mostly unprotected heads, and out of the corner of his eye a huge green flag fluttering in the breeze. Then he heard a great cheer and the enemy surged forward. Unencumbered as they were by helmets and armour, and equipped only with round wooden shield and spears, the enemy sprinted forward at great speed. Sancho Rey blew the whistle in his mouth, a signal that was echoed up and down the line, and hundreds of javelins flew through the air in response.

Luca plucked one from his quiver and threw it at the torso of a wild-haired man armed only with a spear whose face was twisted with hate. The man was closing fast but the javelin was travelling faster and he collapsed to the ground when the steel head slammed into his body. The air was thick with missiles as the Almogavar front rank emptied their quivers, Luca and Jordi throwing their second and third javelins in quick succession. Each one found a target but the enemy fanatics kept on coming.

Javelins from the ranks behind lanced through the air to ensure the enemy warriors would run into a rain of deadly rain of steel-tipped missiles before they reached the front ranks of the Almogavars. This had the result of culling hundreds of warriors and taking the sting out of their wild charge.

But still they kept coming.

Luca took the shield off his back and gripped its central handgrip, his spear now in his right hand. A screaming Turk running at him tripped over a dead comrade impaled on a javelin, and tried to clamber to his feet, only to be killed when Luca thrust his spear into his heart. Luca stepped over him to fight a more-wary spearman who had his own shield tucked tightly to his body. But he was barefoot and a lightning-fast lunge and jab to his toes made him lose his balance. His spear arm faltered, Luca lunged forward again and stabbed him in his belly. Not a deep wound but enough to make him drop his spear and shield.

The Almogavars pushed on against successive waves of enemy warriors, which broke against Catalan spears. But the Catalan advance slowed to a crawl. Sancho gave two sharp blasts on his whistle to indicate the front rank should turn about and withdraw to the rear. Luca, Jordi, Romanus and the others were bundled to the back of the formation to allow the second rank to take over the close-quarters killing. Luca did not like to be wrenched away from what for him had become an exhilarating activity, but it had been drilled into him that orders came before private pleasure.

He and his friend grinned like imbeciles at each other. They were drenched in sweat but there was not a scratch on them. He slapped Romanus on the back. It was his first battle and so far, despite two of his javelins missing their targets, he had not faltered and was unhurt. Others had not been so lucky and there were a few gaps in the now rear rank of the formation, but only a few. And the Almogavars continued to move forward, stepping over dead Turks killed in the earlier javelin storm.

The Turks were now a dense mass in front of the Almogavars, which meant the advance was slow and grim, akin to hacking through thick foliage with an axe. It required skill and reserves of stamina against a foe possessed of religious fervour.

*****

Karesi Bey's battle plan was falling to pieces. He had deliberately left a gap where the Turkish right flank should have been to allow his and the other horsemen to flood through it when the Christians directed their attack against the *ghazis*. Instead, the Roman riders and their mounted Catalan allies headed straight for the gap, forsaking their own foot soldiers. He saw the enemy riders approach, red and yellow banners among them, the mighty cataphracts in the vanguard. Only his own heavy horsemen and lancers could hope to stop the Christian riders. He turned to Mahmud.

'Sound the charge.'

334

But before he could do so, the horse archers of Sasa Bey, Saruhan Bey and Mehmed Bey cantered forward, breaking into a gallop as they headed straight for the Christian horsemen.

'Idiots,' hissed Karesi Bey in helpless rage.

Hundreds of horse archers wearing no armour and only soft headdresses charged headlong at the Christian riders, all of whom had levelled their lances in expectation of close-quarter combat. The horse archers began shooting arrows at the enemy, the thin black missiles arching into the sky before falling among the Catalans and Romans. Those striking the armour of the cataphracts and their mounts bounced off. But others struck unarmoured horses, sending beast and rider crashing to the ground. But then the Romans and Catalans were among the Turks.

The horse archers, or rather their commanders, had made a fatal mistake. In their eagerness to attack the Christian riders, they had sent their men into a limited space in which they would find it impossible to manoeuvre. The river prevented them wheeling to the right, and the great contest between the Almogavars and *ghazis* was occupying the ground on their left. This meant they charged into a narrow space, which prevented many escaping when the enemy horsemen reached them. Dozens were skewered on lances as they attempted to wheel around and flee, many stabbed in the back by pursuing Christian horsemen. Then the Romans and Catalans went about their deadly work with swords and maces. Soon, dozens of horse archers and horses with empty saddles were streaming past a livid and helpless Karesi Bey, Mahmud sitting in the saddle beside him shaking his head as they witnessed the routing of six thousand Turkish horse archers.

Bernat's Catalan horsemen, like their Roman counterparts, highly trained and disciplined, reformed on the corpse-littered ground. The initial arrow volleys had emptied a number of saddles but they had inflicted many more casualties on the hapless horse archers they had cornered. Now all that remained was to wheel right to envelop what was left of the Turkish centre.

*****

Luca could see the large green banner now as he and Jordi moved forward to relieve those in front, taking up position in the second rank of the Almogavars. He had no idea what was happening to the other divisions, or indeed the Catalan and Roman horsemen. But he did know that he and those around him had killed many Turks because he had been stepping over their pierced and bloody bodies for what seemed like an age. Then he experienced something different – men in the first rank stopped and then began to fall back, others falling to the ground, clutching wounded bellies or lacerated faces. The man directly in front of him groaned and crumpled, to reveal a line of large oblong shields and a row of spears pointing menacingly at the Almogavars. They had swept aside the *ghazis* but now came face-to-face with Izzeddin Arslan's élite foot soldiers.

As well as their religious fervour, they were former professional soldiers in the finest war gear. Crucially, they were highly disciplined and remained in their ranks as they stepped forward to halt the Almogavars.

Luca had never faced a seemingly impenetrable wall of shields and spears before, black eyes staring back at him above the top rim of shields and below helmet rims. He searched for suitable targets for his spear but had to react with his own shield when a spear point was jabbed at him. Unlike the Turkish soldiers, he was wearing no armour

336

and his shield suddenly seemed tiny and wholly inadequate compared to the large oblong ones he faced. But his instincts were still fast and he brushed the spear point aside, thrusting his right arm forward at the face of the man who had just tried to stab him. Who brought up his own shield to block the blow. Sensing an opportunity, Luca whipped back his spear and tried to stab the soldier in his shins. But his opponent also had fast reactions and dropped his shield to stop the point.

An endless rasping sound filled the air as men on both sides stabbed and jabbed with spears, striking shields as they search for an opening. The first two ranks of the Turks began working in unison, the front rank crouching to allow the one behind to thrust their spears forward. Almogavars parried the first strike but were caught by the second spear point. Men began to fall, to be roughly dragged back by those behind before they were trampled on or finished off by a spear thrust.

Luca, Jordi and a wide-eyed Romanus were now fully occupied with fending off multiple spear attacks. Then Romanus beside Luca went down with a shoulder wound. He was pulled back out of the fray. The Turk who had stabbed him stepped forward, Luca pivoted low and delivered a jab to his momentarily exposed left thigh, the point of his spear piercing flesh. The Turk faltered but Luca's attention was drawn back to his front and he had no choice but to step back to avoid the wicked metal points being directed at his face and torso. He and Jordi continued to step back as the Almogavars went through an unusual experience – retreating.

Their discipline and formation were still holding, but the Catalan foot soldiers were steadily and surely being pushed back. Out of javelins, many of their spear shafts broken, they had no answer to the unbroken wall of shields and spears that was retaking the ground they had won earlier.

'Allahu Akbar! Allahu Akbar!'

The religious chant drowned out all other sounds as the Turks sensed victory. Luca saw the green banner fluttering defiantly out of the corner of his eye, though only fleetingly as he used his now damaged shield to block spears thrust at him.

'Forgive me, Hector,' he said to himself, bringing up his spear to shoulder height and hurling it at the black-eyed demon who had been tormenting him for what seemed like an age.

He shouted in triumph as the metal point went straight though the Turk's left eye socket and into his brain. The hideous spectacle of a dead man with an eight-foot spear lodged in his head remained in place for a few seconds before he and the shaft fell to the ground. Luca drew his sword, leaped forward and stabbed a Turk in the neck, blood sheeting over his arm. He whipped the blade back and slashed it across another Turk's neck to his right, causing the man to drop his spear and collapse into the spearman on his left. Then he speedily withdrew before the Turks used him as a pin cushion. It was a small victory in a battle that was being lost. And now he had no spear with which to fend off the enemy assaults. Before he could do anything, he was grabbed and yanked back by a gruff Almogavar behind.

'You're no use in the front rank now, boy.'

A shrill whistle blast signalled the front rank should retire to the rear. Tired and bleeding men gladly obeyed the order, but those behind were equally fatigued, whereas the Turks were relatively fresh.

It was only a matter of time before the Almogavars would be forced to break off contact to try and save themselves from being overrun.

*****

The majority of the Turkish horsemen had fled. Sasa Bey was dead. Saruhan Bey had been wounded and had limped from the battlefield with what was left of his horsemen. Mehmed Bey, not a scratch on him, had been the first to turn and run, ordering his horse archers to accompany him to safety. He and a host of maroon banners were last seen galloping towards the coast. They had all gone. All save one.

Karesi Bey drew his sword, turned and nodded to his subordinate. Mahmud gave the order to the signallers behind the pair and a loud blast of trumpets prompted over two thousand horsemen to nudge their mounts forward. In the vanguard were the magnificently attired and armed cataphracts – all Christian – armed with lances, swords and maces, the chests, necks and heads of their horses protected by armour. Accompanying them were their 'spear companion' squires, ready to fight and die beside their masters. Behind the cataphracts were fifteen hundred lancers, not as heavily armed or armoured but still formidable horsemen.

Most of Karesi Bey's horse archers had either fled with the others or lay dead on the battlefield, but he and his two thousand horsemen could still scatter the Christian riders to their front, who had already been involved in a mêlée.

The Turkish horsemen broke into a canter and then a gallop, lowering their lances in unison as they thundered across the grass towards the enemy. The Catalans and their Roman allies also broke into a gallop, for to meet a charge of heavy horsemen while stationary was to invite certain disaster. The thunder of hooves was replaced by a frenzied clattering sound when the two sides clashed, men and horses going down as lance points were driven into human or horse flesh. Then came a more sustained sound, that of sword blades

339

clashing as a furious mêlée erupted. Both sides were professional soldiers and at first the struggle was one of equals, men using their shields and swords and manoeuvring their horses in an attempt to give them the edge against a skilled opponent.

Count Ioannes Komnenos, Governor of Philadelphia and commander of the Thrakesion Theme, was in his element. For years, he had seen the empire's strength and prestige diminish at an alarming rate. The imperial army had become a pale shadow of the force of his youth, and every year Turkish power increased. Their minarets filled the towns and cities that used to resonate with Christian hymns, and their ships brought more Muslims to the shores of what had been the great bastion of Christianity when the world had descended into pagan darkness. When he had first clapped his eyes on the Almogavars he had thought them godless barbarians, and he still believed they were rough-hewn individuals devoted to violence. But their arrival in the empire had breathed fresh life into the emperor's cause. They had achieved more in six months than the imperial army in six years, and had given him the chance to once again lead men into battle rather than hide behind city walls and wait for the inevitable Turkish siege and subsequent humiliating surrender. But now, thanks to the Catholic barbarians, he could meet the enemy face-to-face with a sword in his hand.

His sword cut down many Turkish horsemen that day and for a brief while the banner of the *Stratopedarches* soared like a Roman eagle above the fray. But Karesi Bey's cataphracts were many and gradually they closed in on the great Christian banner, hacking left and right with their maces and swords, first isolating and then bludgeoning the armour and helmets of their enemies – two bodies

340

of cataphracts doing battle in a scene reminiscent of battles fought over a thousand years before.

In one of the tragic ironies of the times in which he had lived, the *Doux* of Philadelphia died at the hands of a Christian cataphract in the service of Karesi Bey, his cataphract bodyguard dying around him. The people of Philadelphia would have wept at seeing their lord fall, but for Ioannes Komnenos it was a better death than he could have previously hoped for.

Karesi Bey sensed victory, and with a battlefield triumph would come the prestige of leading the Muslim cause against the Romans. What legitimacy would those *beys* who had fled the battlefield have against one who had stayed and snapped victory from the jaws of defeat? The enemy horsemen were surrounded and being whittled down in a merciless struggle, but his instincts told him the red banner emblazoned with a sword was about to triumph. And when it did he would seal his victory by slaughtering the Catalan foot soldiers who were being forced back by the *ghazi* élite and the soldiers of Mehmed Bey battling bravely among the olive groves. Praise Allah.

Arrows!

To the maelstrom of battling horsemen was added a new element – the missiles of Melek's horse archers. He had been carefully observing the course of the battle and from his vantage point behind the Almogavars was able to time his intervention precisely. He saw the Almogavars cut the *ghazis* to pieces, only to be stopped and pushed back by the élite soldiers of Izzeddin Arslan. On the right, he saw one division of Almogavars enter the olive groves where Mehmed Bey's foot soldiers fought them among the trees. The *ghazi* élite had struck Sancho Rey's men hard, but they were outnumbered by the Almogavars and so the latter began to assault

341

the Turks on their flanks as the Almogavar line became concave in shape. Melek realised his men could have a pivotal impact on the engagement by intervening on the left where horsemen were doing battle.

Three hundred horse archers galloped over to the left flank where they circled the great mêlée, riding forward to take aimed shots against the horsemen with red saddlecloths, before withdrawing and reforming. Any Turkish horsemen who spotted the horse archers and gave chase were immediately surrounded and shot. The tactics were akin to nibbling the edge of a round piece of bread. It was a slow, methodical process, but the arrows of Melek's soldiers shot many Turks from their saddles and in consequence, Mahmud gave the order to break contact and withdraw.

Karesi Bey, sweating, angry and frustrated, rode over to where his commander of horsemen was issuing his orders, already parties of riders disengaging from the battle to withdraw south.

'Explain yourself.'

'We are losing too many to arrows, lord. The battle is lost. The horsemen of the other *emirs* have already deserted. My first duty is to you and your horsemen. Let the Romans enjoy this day. We are many, they are few. Allah's cause will triumph in the end. But it is now only vanity that keeps us here today.'

The words stung the *emir* but Karesi Bey knew his subordinate was right. He cried out in frustration but then turned his horse, following others obeying the signallers blasting instructions for a general withdrawal.

The Romans and Catalan did not follow. Many among them had been killed, many more had been wounded. Tired men on blown horses were glad to be alive and drank tepid liquid from their water bottles. Bernat de Rocafort, his mail hauberk missing many links and his shield splintered from repeated mace blows, rode over to Melek when the Turks had left the field. The Catalan removed his battered helmet and beamed at him.

'Never have I been so glad to see Muslim horsemen. You and your men have cemented their place in the Catalan Company this day.'

Melek placed a hand on his heart and bowed his head.

'We are your loyal servants, lord.'

Grand Duke Roger, the huge Catalan banner flying behind him, rode over in the company of Count Michael, whose blue-green eyes were full of sorrow.

'Count Komnenos is dead,' he lamented.

'I will pray for his soul, lord,' said Melek earnestly.

'Prayers will have to wait,' said Roger. 'We have to aid Sancho in his fight.'

*****

Jordi was bleeding heavily from a head wound. His helmet had been knocked off and a sword had inflicted a nasty skull injury. He sat on the ground, disorientated, Luca frantically applying a bandage round his crown. Like many head wounds, it looked worse than it was and as far as Luca could tell, the blade had mercifully glanced off his friend's skull rather than bite into it. But there was still much blood.

'No more fighting for you,' he said to his friend.

There were many others lying or sitting on the ground in the rear of the division, which was no longer being pushed back. Unknown to Luca, the *ghazi* élite were now fighting Almogavars on both flanks as well as in front, and the pressure on them was beginning to tell. It was fortuitous, because Sancho Rey's division had

343

been sorely pressed and its soldiers roughly handled in a bloody, bruising contest. Sancho himself, looking tired, his arm gashed and bleeding, knelt down beside his son, examining Luca's handiwork. He slapped his son on the arm.

'You'll live.'

Luca was very pleased with himself, until Sancho stood and looked at the sword in his hand.

'Your spear broke?'

'No, lord, I threw it straight through a Turk's head,' he replied without thinking.

Sancho grabbed his son's spear and handed it to Luca.

'Are you injured?'

'No, lord.'

'Then back in the line for you. The tide is turning against the Turks.'

Luca laid a comforting hand on Jordi's shoulder and retook his position in the rear rank of the division. He was not at the back for long, whistles blasts announcing the withdrawal of the front rank to the rear and the advance of the ranks behind. Because fatigue was sapping the strength of the Almogavars, the time the front rank spent fighting the enemy decreased as the battle wore on. In what seemed like no time at all, Luca was once again facing the enemy.

The enemy was also tired, their wall of shields and spears no longer tight but broken in places. The battle between the two formations had degenerated into a desultory affair, in which both sides probed for weaknesses, aware that if they broke formation their foes might surge forward, prompting a general collapse and slaughter. The ferocity of the initial combat had disappeared as men summoned up their last reserves of strength.

344

'Allahu Akbar! Allahu Akbar!'

Even the enemy's war cries were not as forceful as they were.

Luca scanned the shields in front of him, searching for an opening. But even if a Turk suddenly revealed a vulnerable spot, he would have to traverse the dead bodies between him and the enemy – the result of the final Turkish attempt to break the Almogavars. He jabbed his spear forward over the carpet of dead, directed at the face of the Turk opposite, but immediately withdraw his blade and stepped back when the Turk attempted the same. To the right and left came the sound of battle: weapons clashing, men hollering war cries and their high-pitched screams when weapons found flesh and bone.

Then the Turks began to edge back and the Almogavars sensed victory. Ostensibly, nothing had changed, but alarm began to show in the enemy's faces as they stepped back, still retaining their formation. Like everyone else, Luca sensed the change. He could almost taste it. His tired, heavy limbs were suddenly reinvigorated by the palpable presence of victory in the air. There were whistle blasts and he and the others in the front rank stepped forward, having a care to place their feet on earth and not dead flesh.

The Turks continued to edge back, increasing in speed as some tripped and fell backwards. The sounds on the flanks were getting louder and he knew the Turkish wings were collapsing.

Then the enemy showed their backs to the Almogavars. The withdrawal was turning into a rout.

'Into them!'

He did not know who gave the command but he and those around him needed no second prompting. His legs once again felt like feathers as he sprang forward, reaching a Turk who attempted to turn around to face him, but too late and was skewered in the underarm by Luca's spear. He saw Turks shedding their shields and running, desperate to escape the Almogavars. But the Catalans were on them like ravenous wolves, ramming their spears into thighs, faces and necks. There was little point in trying to drive spear points through mail armour, which all the Turks wore.

And then Luca stopped in his tracks. In front of him, clutching a flagstaff attached to which was a huge green banner, was a deranged, wild-haired man with rage-filled eyes, daring him to harm him. Without hesitation Luca drove his spear into his belly with all his energy, yanked back the point and stabbed him again, and again and again. The fanatic's filthy clothes became stained with blood and gore and he collapsed to the ground, still clutching the shaft. Luca placed a foot on the dead man's chest, bent down and picked up the banner, rolling the green silk around the shaft to make it easier to carry.

And so it was that Luca Baldi captured the sacred banner of the Prophet. And the Catalan Company won a resounding victory outside the walls of Anaia in what was the greatest Christian triumph over Islam in two hundred years.

Chapter 20

Luca presented the captured banner to Sancho Rey after the last remnants of the Turkish army had been slaughtered. There were thousands of bodies strewn across the valley floor, the olive groves close to the city also choked with dead and dying. The gates of the city had been slammed shut in the faces of the victors, parties of which ignored Anaia and trudged over to the river to slake their thirsts. The victorious commanders held an impromptu council of war in the middle of the dead.

'A gift for you, Roger,' said Sancho, holding out the captured green banner to the leader of the Catalan Company.

Roger slid off his horse and stretched his back. Bernat did likewise, taking off his helmet and breathing a huge sigh of relief.

'That was too close for my liking.'

Roger took the banner.

'Well done, Sancho.'

The Almogavar pointed at Luca.

'He captured it.'

'The Black Sheep covers himself in glory once more,' smiled Roger. 'You should reward him, Sancho.'

'I promise I will,' said the Almogavar.

The next day Sancho organised work parties to dig graves for those who had fallen during the battle, which also included the Muslim dead. Aware that it had been Melek and his horse archers that had proved decisive, Roger had insisted the enemy dead be interred in the ground and, in a gesture designed to win over the city authorities, sent a message to Anaia that Muslim priests could say their prayers over the dead. But first, graves had to be dug.

Luca hacked at the earth, cursing under his breath so Sancho standing nearby would not hear. Around him, dozens of others with spades were also digging. Sancho saw Luca shaking his head.

'I promised Grand Duke Roger I would reward you and so I am. This is your reward for throwing away your spear during the battle.'

Luca and thousands of others had slept in the open the night before, waking with aching joints, dry mouths and rumbling bellies, having emptied their food bags. Count Michael and Bernat had sent mounted parties to plunder the valley of food, but the Catalan Company needed the city's granaries. Otherwise, it and its allies would have to retrace their steps back to Philadelphia. Sancho strode off to meet with the other captains, leaving Luca and the others to dig the mass grave. Jordi, his head now heavily bandaged, brought a pair of water bottles to quench his friend's thirst, Luca taking the opportunity to take a break from the back-breaking work.

'My father says yesterday was the greatest victory in the history of the Almogavars,' said Jordi.

The thought cheered Luca. 'I wish Ertan was here. I'm starving.'

'Me, too.'

'How is Romanus?'

'He'll live,' said Jordi, 'though he will not be doing any fighting for a few weeks.'

It was not Ertan but another Muslim who arrived, Melek jumping down from his saddle to greet the pair of Almogavars.

'It gladdens me to see you both alive,' he grinned. 'Allah smiles on you.'

348

'Not on me,' complained Luca. 'I am reduced to a gravedigger.'

'Allah will smile on you more for caring for His dead, Luca,' said Melek. 'For an enemy to care for the remains of his foe will surely be blessed.'

He did not feel blessed, but it cheered him that Melek thought he was. He liked the Turk, who had an easy-going manner that endeared him even to those he had been trying to kill just a few weeks before. And it was Melek who acted as a negotiator on behalf of Grand Duke Roger and the city authorities that afternoon, the Turk conveying the Catalan Company's terms for the surrender of Anaia. Of course, the city authorities could choose to defy the Catalans in the hope of relief. But what relief would come? The thousands of bodies being prepared for burial were mute evidence of the absence of any army of note that could march to Anaia's relief. More likely, the *emirs* who had been worsted before the city walls would flee back to their own capitals and leave the city to its fate. On the other hand, Roger offered safe passage to any Muslim wishing to leave the city to seek sanctuary elsewhere, and would even provide Muslim horsemen as an escort to guarantee their safety. Moreover, any Muslim wishing to remain in Anaia would not be reduced to slavery, would not have his or her property molested, and would be allowed to practise his or her religion. They were generous terms. But then, the exhausted Catalan Company had neither the means nor inclination to mount a siege that might last for months.

The city authorities agreed to Grand Duke Roger's terms, subject to the Muslim dead being given proper and respectful burials. Every Almogavar was therefore assigned to grave-digging duties so the thousands of dead could be interred as speedily as possible, Jordi

349

joining Luca in the grave pits. After two days, the city having provided white sheets for every Muslim corpse and priests – *imams* – having conducted the funeral rights, what remained of the garrison of Anaia, plus a few thousand of the city's most important and wealthiest citizens, marched out of the city gates where Melek and his men met them and escorted them from the Maeander Valley.

The Catalan Company had won a resounding victory and now it had its own city.

Grand Duke Roger assumed the duties of city governor, moving into the grand residence of the holder of that position. His Turkish predecessor had had no time to remove the frescoes on the walls or indeed crosses surmounting the palace entrance and roof, so the commander of the Catalan Company found his new quarters most agreeable. Almogavars assumed the duties of the garrison, most being housed in the city's barracks, gate houses and palace barracks. Others found accommodation in houses abandoned by their Turkish owners and requisitioned by the new arrivals. Those who had fled, taking their belongings with them, were for the most part the affluent and religiously devout. Those who had business interests in and around the city remained in the hope their new masters would wish to see commerce continue. The population was a mixture of Roman and Turks, and the latter hoped that just as the Muslim authorities had allowed the Christians to live and work in Anaia, subject to paying the *jizya*, so the Catalans would allow them to go about their business in peace. For a price. Grand Duke Roger was more than happy to oblige.

Sancho was lodged in a fine two-storey mansion near the palace, which was enclosed by a wall encompassing the residence itself, stables, storerooms and gardens. Melek was given a similar-sized residence nearby, as a reward for his intervention in the battle outside the city. Roger also wanted him close to advise him on matters pertaining to Islam and Muslim ways in general.

Like most cities in Anatolia, Anaia had been turned into a 'machine for defence', being surrounded by thick, high defensive walls to thwart the Turkish invaders, and like countless other towns, now long lost to the enemy, its population had diminished compared to when it had been a glittering urban centre to rival nearby Philadelphia. And as the population shrunk, the fortifications were reduced in length but also substantially strengthened, not only because of the drop in the number of citizens, but also because they could be defended more effectively by a smaller garrison. Its occupation by over six thousand soldiers of the Catalan Company turned it into the most heavily defended city in the entire Roman Empire, Constantinople included. The fortifications towered over the city's buildings, a deliberate policy designed to give the inhabitants a sense of security, though they also reminded the population they were under constant threat.

August was gone and September had now arrived. The weather was still warm, the valley no longer a furnace but cooled by pleasing winds from the east. To Luca on the walls staring south, the river looked like a giant blue snake slithering its way through the Maeander on its way to the sea. Two large brown patches were the only things interrupting the endless green belt stretching east and west – the mass graves where the dead had been interred after the battle. The body of Count Komnenos had been taken back to Philadelphia for burial, escorted by his own horsemen and those of Count Michael. Bernat de Rocafort had also ridden back to

Philadelphia to escort the servants the Catalans had collected back to Anaia.

'I wonder what Ayna is doing at this moment?' said Luca wistfully, staring to the west and the sea.

'You must miss her greatly,' offered Jordi, his head still heavily bandaged.

'Now we are not fighting and my mind is not concentrating on staying alive, yes.'

Luca looked around at the stout walls and the city within them.

'I like these Roman cities. They are clean and the air inside them is fresh.'

'And they have baths,' smiled his friend.

'I wonder if we will be returning to Artake before autumn arrives?' pondered Luca. 'Now there is no one left to fight.'

'My father is always telling me there is always someone to fight, which is just as well seeing as we are mercenaries.'

'How's the head?'

'The headaches have stopped,' said Jordi, 'though I will have a scar for life.'

'It is a curious thing,' reflected Luca, 'if it had not been for Melek and his horsemen, the Turks would most likely have won the battle.'

'And if it had not been for our coming across Ertan when we stormed the Turkish camp outside Philadelphia, we would not have met Melek and he would not have joined the company.'

'Life is strange,' agreed Luca.

'Why did you keep it?' said Jordi.

'Keep what?'

'The black sheep that caused you so many problems, when you were a shepherd in Sicily, I mean?'

Luca thought for a minute.

'The life of a shepherd is one of hardship and loneliness, my friend. If the weather and starvation do not ravage a flock, then wolves or bandits might. Every lamb born to a flock is precious and has to fight for its existence from the moment it takes its first breath. One is born with a black coat and I am expected to kill it just for that?'

'Because the church commands it,' said Jordi solemnly.

'Where was the church when my parents were murdered? I will tell you. Standing right beside those responsible. I have no time for the church or its priests.'

Jordi was shocked. 'You risk eternal damnation for saying such things.'

'I had heard that to battle and slay Muslims would redeem me in the eyes of the church. I must have killed many Turks during our campaign, so I believe I am safe from the pit of hell.'

He laughed but Jordi was shaking his head.

'You should not mock the church, Luca. It has great power. It burns people it believes to be heretics.'

'I would like to burn Father Ramon and his priests,' hissed Luca, 'just to see the look on their faces as their skin was peeled from them in strips.'

'I think you are the one who has received a blow to the head, not I.'

But Luca was not really listening.

'I wonder what Father Ramon thinks of our new Turkish allies?'

353

'He believes it is a sin they have been recruited, or at least that is what he told my father.'

Luca scoffed at the idea.

'If it is such a sin, how is it that Melek and his men were such a great help during the recent battle? Surely if God was angry with the company for recruiting infidels, He would have made sure we were defeated?'

Jordi wore a perplexed expression.

'Proves my point.'

'What point?'

'That Father Ramon talks out of his arse,' said Luca.

'I cannot see Melek and his horsemen remaining with the company when we return to Artake,' mused Jordi.

Returning to Artake was the reason the Almogavars were called to the city's open-air theatre the next day. Built hundreds of years before and named after the Greek word for viewing – *theatron* – audiences sat on stone seats arranged in ascending curved tiers, so that the people in the tiers above could see the stage below without their vision being obscured.

Almogavars filed into the theatre, which was cut into the hill on which the original Greek acropolis had been built. Now a walled citadel, sentries patrolling its walls could look down on the audience and the performers on the marble-paved stage. The seats slowly began to fill with Almogavars carrying their spears, shield and swords, though not their javelins. And they wore soft hats instead of helmets. Bernat's horsemen had assumed temporary sentry duty of the city walls and citadel in their absence, for there was no democracy among the company's mounted troops.

Hector, Marc, Angel and Biel, the latter a brooding individual whose face had probably never worn a smile who commanded the division that had arrived with Bernat de Rocafort, sat at the front as befitting their rank. Hector spotted Luca and Jordi and insisted they sit with the senior captains, a few feet from the stage.

'Well, Black Sheep,' said Angel, 'you will have a great story to tell your Muslim woman when she arrives.'

Luca's eyes lit up. 'When she arrives?'

Angel put a finger to his lips. 'All will be revealed.'

When nearly five thousand Almogavars had taken their seats, the afternoon sun glinting off their spear points, Sancho Rey appeared from the *skene*, the stone building behind the stage where the actors changed costumes and made their entrances. The ends of hundreds of spear shafts were rapped on stone in salute. Sancho held up his arms to call for silence. The rapping ceased.

'My brothers,' he began, 'after our great victory outside the walls of this city...'

He waited for the ensuing rapping to die down.

'After our great victory, Grand Duke Roger proposes that the company stays here in Anaia for the winter rather than return to Artake. If you are in agreement, and following a vote, his ships will bring our families and loved ones here from Artake.

'Our contract with the emperor has now been fulfilled. We have taken Anaia from the Turks and that makes it a Catalan city by right of conquest, for surely the Romans have not the means to wrest their lost lands from the enemy.'

He stopped to let what he was saying sink in, stern-faced Almogavars nodding and mumbling to each other. Sancho held up his hands again.

'Grand Duke Roger, who is related through marriage to the Roman emperor, believes Andronicus will allow us to remain here permanently to make Anaia our home. To become a bulwark against the Turks whom we have so easily defeated these past few months.'

There was a great rapping of shafts on stone and hard visages cracked smiles as the Almogavars remembered their recent triumphs. Sancho allowed them their celebration, folding his arms to become a statue like the stone ones in the niches behind him in the *skene*'s façade. Then there was silence as five thousand pairs of eyes studied the broad-shouldered Almogavar leader.

'My brothers,' his deep voiced echoed around the theatre. 'It is now time to vote. All those in favour of remaining here and bringing our families to Anaia on the grand duke's ships, raise your hands.'

Luca, thoughts of Ayna uppermost in his mind and totally unconcerned with what the emperor might or might not want, instantly raised his hand. Around him thousands of others did likewise, including the captains sitting with him and his friend beside him. Sancho's thin lips creased into a smile.

'Any against?'

Not one arm was raised.

'Very well,' said Sancho. 'We stay in Anaia and Grand Duke Roger will use his ships to bring our families here as quickly as possible.'

In the days following, Melek became the most important member of the Catalan Company, riding west to the port of Ephesus Neopolis, which was just over twenty miles from Anaia. The crushing victory the Catalans had inflicted on the Turkish alliance meant the company controlled not only the entire Maeander Valley, but also the Aegean coast where the valley met the sea, which included Ephesus

Neopolis. It had been stripped of its garrison by Mehmed Bey, who had then proceeded to flee back to his capital Izmir, sixty miles to the north where he locked himself in his palace and awaited Catalan retaliation. This meant Ephesus Neopolis was defenceless and at the mercy of Grand Duke Roger, who sent a message to its Turkish governor assuring him he and his town would be safe, on condition he allow the port to be used for the company's benefit. The governor readily agreed.

It took a month to organise the shipping of the company's families from Artake to Ephesus Neopolis, not least because the money left at Artake to feed its dependents and the sailors who crewed Grand Duke Roger's ships had run out. This produced a near mutiny among the crews, who had heard from the returning Count Michael of the great fortune extorted from the governor of Magnesia. They demanded prompt payment before they would sail, messages travelling between Anaia and Artake trying to thrash out an agreement. Eventually, after Roger promised to pay them their outstanding wages and a bonus, the crews put to sea. The small fleet made good progress in the mild waters of the eastern Aegean, hugging the coast and putting into shore each night on one of the many islands in the region.

Using a Turkish-held port for disembarkation obviously involved risks, not least the possibility the garrison, albeit greatly depleted, might seize the ships and their precious cargoes when they docked. If this happened, the families would either be slaughtered or ransomed, neither of which would the Catalans tolerate. It was Melek who found a solution to the problem, suggesting the governor, his few soldiers and any Turkish inhabitants of the town who wished to do so withdraw into the citadel on 'bird island'. The Romans had

357

built a castle on the island to protect the mouth of the harbour, which the Turks had taken over and built a mole from the mainland to the island. It was a strong position and would require a joint naval-ground attack to take the citadel. To further encourage the governor to agree to the proposal, Grand Duke Roger offered an exchange of hostages to soothe any fears the Turks might have regarding treachery.

Luca was far from amused.

'Why do I have to be one of the hostages?'

'Your fame has gone before you, Luca,' Sancho told him. 'Melek has impressed the Turkish governor with tales of the Black Sheep of the Almogavars.'

Luca warmed to the idea.

'Really?'

'Yes, indeed. And Father Ramon was most eager you should be one of the hostages.'

Luca smelled a rat. 'Why, lord?'

'He is of the opinion that should the agreement go wrong, it is only fitting you should be the first to die, seeing as you are responsible for infecting, as he termed it, the Catalan Company with infidels and their abominable religion.'

Luca turned to Jordi. 'If I die, I would ask a favour of you.'

'Anything, my friend,' he replied.

'Cut Father Ramon's throat.'

'Admirable words,' said Sancho, 'but Jordi will also be one of the hostages. The offer of the son of the commander of the Almogavars, plus the Black sheep and a score of others, was enough to convince the governor of our sincerity and good faith.'

He saw the disconsolate looks in front of him.

'There is no need for such long faces. Melek has assured me the governor has no wish to see his town burn, which will happen if you are killed.'

'I have to confess that gives me little comfort father,' complained Jordi.

The pair felt like sacrificial lambs when they joined three thousand other Almogavars and a thousand Catalan horsemen for the short journey to Ephesus Neopolis, the heat of summer having departed the land, to be replaced by mild weather ideal for marching. Melek and his men rode ahead to announce the approach of the Catalans to give the governor and his citizens time to evacuate to Bird Island. Those chosen to be Turkish hostages would wait on the mole where they would be exchanged for Luca, Jordi and the other Christian hostages.

Before it fell to the Turks, the port's defences had been significantly strengthened, the walls and dry moat surrounding it being formidable obstacles to a landward assault. Unfortunately, the lack of an imperial army to provide a relief force, coupled with Mehmed Bey's fleet of galleys, rendered those defences useless. Like many towns throughout Anatolia, Ephesus Neopolis had fallen without a fight, the small Roman garrison being given the option of quietly leaving the town unmolested to seek sanctuary elsewhere before they faced certain death. Just like grapes dying on the vine, the emperor's outposts had fallen one by one.

It took a morning to reach the port, the Aegean sparkling under an autumn sun, the turquoise waters at the foot of a magnificent backdrop of green hillside forests and grey, snow-capped mountains beyond. Many Catalan banners flew among the horsemen to emphasise to the Turks who was approaching their port. But when

359

Bernat de Rocafort led a vanguard of a hundred lancers to the gates of the town, he found them open and the walls either side abandoned. Cautiously venturing into the town, he found the streets deserted and silent. The entire population had fled to Bird Island.

Luca thought Ephesus Neopolis much the same as Anaia, albeit much smaller and filled with a sea breeze. But its streets were paved and clean, shops fronted the main streets and there was the ubiquitous bathhouse just off what had once been the Roman forum. Sancho ordered the walls to be patrolled and the town searched, ordering the gates to be closed when the last of the Almogavars had entered. Then he and Bernat made their way to the mole on the southern side of the harbour, Luca, Jordi and the other hostages joining him. Luca was slightly comforted when he saw the dashing Melek chatting to a group of individuals wearing turbans on the mole that led to Bird Island. All conversation ceased when they spotted the mail-clad Bernat and the Almogavars. Melek flashed a smile to one of the Turks and walked towards Sancho and Bernat.

'It is all arranged,' he smiled. 'The governor's son and a great sea captain will be included in the Turkish hostages to match your own generosity.'

'Let's get it over with, then,' said Sancho, nodding to Luca and Jordi. 'Off you go. Surrender your weapons first. The rest of you also leave your weapons here.'

Luca felt naked without his weapons as he and the others trudged towards the island, passing the Turkish hostages as they did so, each side barely giving the other a sideways glance. His heart began beating faster when he saw the gates of the impressive castle, the walls of which encompassed the perimeter of the whole island, opening to allow the hostages to enter. He wondered if he would ever see Ayna again.

Chapter 21

'Eat, eat. The food will not devour itself.'

Luca wondered if his host intended to kill the hostages with kindness during the time they were in his custody. Bayezid Islam was the most generous man he had ever met. As soon as he and the other hostages had entered the imposing castle on Bird Island, he had gone out of his way to be accommodating. Luca had expected to be lodged in quarters resembling a cell and fed on a meagre diet. Instead, he and the others were treated like honoured guests, the town governor insisting the hostages were quartered in large, well-appointed rooms and fed from dawn till dusk.

He was a small, portly man with a round face who gestured with his hands in an effusive manner. He looked more like a tradesman than a governor, though no merchant he had ever met wore such distinctive headgear. Called a *horasani*, it comprised a long, tubular piece of white felt, half of which was folded back and hung to the rear. Luca was informed it was a badge of high rank among the Turks.

'Do not stand on ceremony,' beamed Bayezid, 'satisfy your appetites.'

Luca and Jordi were sitting on couches in the castle's dining hall, which overlooked the empty harbour and the town. Evening was encroaching and the hall was lit with candles to illuminate the interior. Luca hoped the Turkish hostages were being treated as well as he and the others were. Around him was a dazzling display of dishes, some of which he was enjoying for the first time. He had never heard of melon *dolma* before, which at first sight appeared strange and unappetising. It comprised a hollowed-out melon filled with lamb, spices, rice, almonds, pistachios and currants and cooked in an oven. The result was wholly delicious.

Luca and the others gorged themselves on that and *mutancana* – a stew of lamb, apricot, shallots, red grapes, honey and almonds – and bird soup, which was made by boiling thrushes in a pan and afterwards roasting them in another pan with oil and onions. Finally, they were marinated with flour and served with cinnamon and black pepper. There was also rye bread stuffed with beef and a mouth-watering chicken stew called *mahmudiye*.

Luca had been surprised to discover the castle was not crowded with civilians, the governor having ordered their evacuation to nearby islands until the Catalan ships had arrived and unloaded their human cargoes. Hence the absence of ships in the harbour. The soldiers of the garrison were well-armed with bows and spears, though took no interest in the hostages after they had first been searched for hidden weapons. Guards were placed outside their sleeping quarters to ensure none wandered around the castle during the hours of darkness. But otherwise they were not interfered with in any way.

'More wine for our guests.'

Bayezid clicked his fingers to prompt slaves to refill the hostages' silver cups.

'Tell me again why you are called the Black Sheep,' Bayezid said to Luca.

A slightly inebriated Luca retold his story. Of how he had become friends with Jordi, how his flock possessing a black sheep had provoked an altercation with Fabrizio Carafa, how he and Jordi were sentenced to die and were subsequently rescued by Sancho Rey, and how his parents were murdered before his eyes on the orders of

363

Giovanni Carafa. The action prompted his attempt to kill the Italian count, which earned him his nickname among the Almogavars. Bayezid smiled and nodded, shovelling stuffed rye bread into his mouth. He pointed at Luca and Jordi.

'Do you know why violence and war follow you both like loyal dogs?'

They shook their heads. Bayezid belched.

'It is because you have no meat on your bones. When I first saw you both and the other hostages, I thought you would expire on the spot. I have seen beggars with more meat on them.'

He picked up an apricot from one of the many bowls in front of him and handed it to a slave to be cut into slices. The guards behind the governor watched the slave closely to ensure he tried nothing untoward with the blade. Luca thought it amusing because the slave was also fat and had clearly benefited from his master's seemingly limitless food supplies.

'Skinny individuals are invariably mean-spirited and restless,' opined Bayezid, 'whereas corpulence leads to contentment and an easy-going manner.'

The slave finished his work and proffered a plate on which the apricot slices were arranged in a neat circle. Bayezid took a slice.

'You will stay in Anaia permanently?'

His question was directed at Jordi, though Sancho's son had no insight into the long-term strategy of the Catalan Company.

'For the winter, lord, certainly,' he answered. 'After that, perhaps.'

'You know there is no future for the Romans in Anatolia,' said Bayezid. 'Their empire is like a diseased tree. Rotten to the core. This land and all who live in it belong to Allah.'

364

Luca was emboldened by the wine.

'We defeated every Turkish army we encountered, lord.'

Bayezid ate another slice of apricot.

'You are like a pack of ravenous wolves, devouring everything in its path. But when the pack moves on the land returns to normal. And when you have departed, how long do you think the city of Philadelphia will be able to hold out?'

'The Roman emperor has an army,' said Jordi, his cheeks flushed by too much wine.

Bayezid smiled. 'It will not leave its position to the east of Constantinople, not while Osman Bey stands like a lion ready to pounce against the Roman emperor's capital.'

'Perhaps we will march north in the spring and crush this Osman Bey's army,' boasted Luca.

Bayezid looked thoughtful. 'Perhaps you will, and perhaps you will be as successful next year as you have been this year. But mercenaries fight for pay, Black Sheep, and I know that the emperor's coffers are empty. Do you think we do not have spies in the enemy's lands? Next year fresh recruits will arrive from Egypt and Syria, transported by ships that will dock in the harbour below, as well as other ports. They come as fighters and settlers, and not just Muslims.'

Luca was surprised. 'That's right, Black Sheep. We also welcome Christians and Jews, for we do not persecute other faiths as the Romans do. One more reason why we will ultimately triumph.'

He clapped his hands. 'But let us not talk of war and politics. It is so depressing.'

Two women walked forward, both tall and attractive, dressed in figure-hugging robes and smelling of perfume.

365

'A gift for each of you,' beamed Bayezid. 'Two Jewish slaves to warm your beds until your families arrive.'

Luca was embarrassed but Jordi was intoxicated, his eyes opening wide at the beauty in front of him, her eyes cast down.

'I thank you for your generosity, lord,' said Luca, 'but I am promised to another and will not break my vow to her.'

Bayezid adopted a sly expression. 'She will never know, Black Sheep.'

'*I* would know, lord,' replied Luca.

Bayezid sighed and waved the female slave earmarked for him away. But Jordi was bewitched by the vision of feminine grace before him and gladly accepted the governor's offer. He did not care if she was Jewish, was a slave and perhaps had been a whore during her time in Muslim captivity. He was a lustful young man and he wanted her in his bed. As quickly as possible. The woman sat on his couch and he sidled up to her, offering her a grape. She opened her mouth seductively so he could place it on her tongue. Luca went back to stuffing his face and drinking wine, smiling at the good fortune showered on his friend.

Musicians and jugglers entered the chamber to entertain the governor and his guests but Jordi hardly noticed them, his eyes focused on the beauty who was accepting his advances.

'Her name is Chana,' said Bayezid.

In Hebrew her name meant 'grace', though how she found herself a slave in the Aydin Emirate only the pirates who had brought her to Bayezid's port for sale knew. She had been spotted by the governor's chief steward who had purchased her for a tidy sum, the pirate captain assuring him she was still a virgin. The steward doubted that but he had to admit there was something about her. Buxom and

366

beautiful with full lips, she had all the attributes of female attractiveness. But her large hazel eyes suggested intelligence and even cunning.

Jordi was playing with her long, thick black hair that fell in ringlets to the middle of her back. They spoke little to each other as he did not speak Hebrew and she did not understand Italian or Catalan. Bayezid, in contrast, was fluent in both Italian and Greek, as well as his mother tongue, a consequence of years spent dealing with Genoese, Venetians and also Romans. But then, the pair would not require their tongues for what Jordi had in mind when they got to his bedroom, not for talking, anyway. When Jordi made his excuses to Bayezid and took his leave with Chana, Luca wished his friend well and continued drinking, eventually being assisted back to his own bedroom by two guards in a semi-conscious state.

Luca did not see Jordi for two days. While his friend was locked away with his slave, he wandered the battlements and spent hours staring at the turquoise waters of the Aegean. He always looked north, the direction from where the fleet carrying Ayna would come from. Each day he also saw Melek, who acted as a go-between during the strange truce between the Catalan Company and the Turks. Melek assured Bayezid that his son and the other Turkish hostages were being well treated, and in turn the governor stated the Christians in his care were having an agreeable time. It was no lie. Every day Luca was treated to a massage at the hands of a skilled masseuse, before entering the bathhouse to be washed and sweated, afterwards the dirt scraped from his skin by a slave. His hair was cut, his toe and fingernails trimmed, and the cares of the world expunged from his mind. He and the others were treated to archery lessons in the courtyard, falconry demonstrations and an abundance of food and drink from the kitchens. Then, on the fourth day, the alarm bell was sounded and the insouciant atmosphere that had hung over the castle vanished.

Luca dashed to the battlements. He peered to the north and saw a host of two-masted ships with lateen sails – Grand Duke Roger's galleys. The ramparts began to fill with soldiers, though their demeanour was more one of curiosity rather than preparing for battle. Luca felt a surge of excitement course through him, as did the other hostages now on the stone walkway behind the battlements. He searched for Jordi in vain and smiled. Clearly his friend was determined to extract the last moments of pleasure from his liaison with the alluring Chana. The alarm bell ceased ringing and the majority of the soldiers were ordered back to their duties, leaving the normal complement of sentries to patrol the walls. Luca stayed on the ramparts and watched the fleet of ships inch its way towards the port. There was a gentle breeze and the sea was as flat as a tabletop, and when the *dromons* neared the harbour their crews dipped their oars in the water and began rowing. The sails were furled and the ships were rowed into the harbour, berthing at the stone quays that had been built by the Romans several centuries before. Luca could not stop smiling when he saw the decks crowded with people – women, children and infants. He knew one among them was Ayna. Dear, sweet Ayna. A mischievous leer spread across his face. He would be indulging in carnal pleasures before the day was out.

He was to be sadly disappointed.

He had envisaged running across the mole and into the harbour to sweep Ayna into his arms, but technicalities dashed his plans.

There was a flurry of couriers between the town and the castle, with a flustered Melek acting as a coordinator. Now the Catalan ships had docked, Bayezid wanted to know when the company's civilians were leaving his town. Grand Duke Roger replied regretfully it would be another day before the carts for their transport he had ordered to be sent from Anaia would arrive at Ephesus Neopolis. Bayezid said this would mean the company would have to pay for lodging them in his town for a night. Grand Duke Roger agreed. Luca saw the throng of civilians on the quays and on the dockside and searched in vain for Ayna. Dark thoughts she may have died of disease or at the hands of an angry mob filled his mind. He desperately wanted to leave the castle but protocol dictated otherwise. Then he was summoned to the great hall and his sense of foreboding increased.

He found Bayezid sitting on what to all intents and purposes was a throne, guards flanking the ornate wooden chair, maroon banners with black circles in the centre hanging from the walls. Standing beside the seated governor was a thin man wearing a white turban with a stooping posture. In front of him stood Jordi and Chana.

'Ah, Black Sheep, welcome,' enthused Bayezid. 'Your friend has returned from his self-imposed exile in his bedroom.'

Luca strode over to stand beside Jordi, who looked totally exhausted, dark rings around his eyes from lack of sleep. The alluring Chana, who looked remarkably fresh, gave him a smile.

'Your friend wishes to steal some of my property,' said Bayezid sternly. · ˙

'My lord,' protested Jordi, to be stopped by a raised hand from the governor.

'Your friend wishes to take the delightful Chana with him when he leaves my castle,' Bayezid said to Luca. 'Some might say he is taking advantage of my generosity. What do you say, Black Sheep?'

'I am sure Jordi meant no offence, lord,' replied Luca.

Bayezid nodded earnestly.

'That may be, but she,' he pointed at Chana, 'is my property. I did not gift her to him, I only loaned her out for a short period.'

Bayezid's words may have been severe but the glint in his eye suggested to Luca he was in a mischievous mood. He looked at the stooping figure beside him.

'This is Alton, one of my scholars who is fluent in many languages, including Hebrew, Chana's tongue. Even though she is a slave, I want to hear what she has to say on leaving Ephesus Neopolis. I have spent a considerable amount of money on her clothes and general wellbeing, which I intend to recoup.'

'I will purchase her from you, lord,' said Jordi.

Bayezid laughed. 'Forgive me. You may be a great warrior, but it is common knowledge the Catalan Company has little money, aside from what it steals. With what would you purchase such a valuable slave?'

'The princess' reward, you still have your share?' Luca whispered to Jordi.

His friend's weary expression was broken by a smile. He plucked the pouch from his belt. He had carried it for so long he had forgotten it contained a king's ransom.

'I have money, lord.'

He walked forward to hand the governor the pouch but was intercepted by a burly guard who blocked his way. Bayezid waved the soldier away and held out his hand. Jordi gave him the pouch, Bayezid opened it and his eyes lit up.

'I underestimated you, young Catalan. There is enough here to secure the purchase of Chana.'

Jordi beamed with delight.

'However,' cautioned Bayezid, 'I wish to know if she desires to leave me, who has been like a father to her in her time of distress. Alton, ask her if she desires to leave the comfort and security of Ephesus Neopolis and become the courtesan of this young Catalan warrior.'

Alton translated the governor's words into Hebrew. Chana, her eyes full of sorrow, looked directly at Bayezid when she replied. Alton spoke her answer to the governor as she did so.

'My lord, you have been both kind and generous since you rescued me from the pirates who snatched me away from my home and family. At Ephesus Neopolis I have found peace and affection and I know you have taken a keen interest in my welfare.'

This was music to Bayezid's ears, who clasped his hands together, his eyes misting with emotion as she spoke with a quivering voice.

'You are a kind and generous lord, but I beg you allow me to leave Ephesus Neopolis as I believe I can find happiness with Jordi, son of Sancho Rey. And it is because you are both magnanimous and pious that I know you will receive my request with a generous heart.'

Chana wiped a tear from her cheek, her large brown eyes full of pleading. She was a seductress and just as she had used her body to besot Jordi, so she now used what was obviously her keen intellect to seduce the governor with her words and emotion. He too succumbed to her charms.

'There comes a time when a father must let his children fly the nest,' he said, caressing the pouch of money. 'I therefore give you to Jordi Rey. Go with my love and my blessings.'

When Chana heard his translated words, she rushed forward to fall at Bayezid's feet, clutching his ankles and babbling incoherently. Bayezid smiled and lifted her up, standing to embrace her.

'I know it must be difficult to leave me. But go with God, and my blessings.'

A tearful Chana returned to a euphoric Jordi's arms and the pair, plus Luca, bowed their heads and walked from the hall. As they passed by the doors Chana's expression changed from being a helpless, distraught slave to a determined woman wearing a smug expression. Whatever Chana was, she was far from helpless.

As well as the money Jordi had paid him, Bayezid Islam received a substantial payment from Grand Duke Roger for the privilege of allowing his ships to dock in the harbour, for the temporary Catalan occupation of Ephesus Neopolis, and for the lodging of its dependents in the town for a single night.

The next morning, after an agonising wait, Luca and the others, plus the redoubtable Chana, left the castle to walk along the mole, passing the Turkish hostages along the way. There had been a meticulous count before the exchange, and Bayezid had insisted his people be interviewed to ascertain they had been treated fairly. They had, though not plied with the large amounts of food and drink enjoyed by Luca and his fellow hostages.

Though it was now autumn, the day was pleasant enough, with a gentle breeze blowing off the sea and the sun ducking in and out of white clouds sprinkling the sky above. Luca ambled along the narrow mole, a group at the shore end waiting for him and the others. Jordi was more interested in the woman beside him, placing an arm around her shoulders and running his other hand through her lustrous black hair. Luca and the others quickened their steps when they recognised their loved ones waiting for them. He saw Sancho and Carla standing together and beside them the woman who owned his heart. She gave him a beautiful smile as he bounded towards her, she rushing to him and the pair locking themselves in an embrace.

'I love you,' he said, tears running down his cheeks.

'I prayed for your safety and thanked Allah when I was told you were safe and unhurt.'

He buried his face in her hair, never wanting to leave her embrace. Around them others were embracing, laughing and exchanging declarations of love. It was a happy moment, one that Luca wanted to go on forever.

'It is good to see you again, Luca.'

He reluctantly pulled away from Ayna when he heard Carla's voice, embracing her warmly and thanking her for taking care of his beloved.

'You will find her Italian has improved remarkably,' she told him, her arm still around her son's shoulders.

'Who's this?'

The gruff voice of Sancho Rey shattered the happiness. His severe face was examining the busty, black-haired woman standing behind his son, Chana's hazel eyes narrowing when she heard the suspicion in the big Almogavar's voice.

Jordi grabbed Chana's arm and pulled her forward.

'This is Chana, the woman I am going to marry.'

The long line of wagons carrying the women and children and flanked by three thousand Almogavars wound its way across the valley towards Anaia. Bernat and his horsemen provided outer flank, rearguard and vanguard protection, for neither Grand Duke Roger nor Sancho were taking any chances when it came to the security of the column. Melek and his horse archers stayed close to the wagons to provide missile support should the Turks attempt to raid the column. But it was not the threat of attack that had darkened Sancho's mood as the carts trundle through the lush valley. He marched beside the lead wagon, which contained a driver, Carla, Ayna and Chana, the Almogavar leader continually frowning and shaking his head at Jordi who walked behind him, holding the hand of his new-found love. Luca walked on the other side of the vehicle, smiling at Ayna staring down at him lovingly.

'Try to remember we are in enemy territory,' snapped Sancho. 'This is not a pleasure trip.'

But it was for his son and Luca, very much so.

'You were supposed to marry into Roman royalty,' grumbled Sancho, 'and now you bring a Muslim slave before me and declare you are going to marry her.'

Jordi sprang to Chana's defence. 'She is not a Muslim. She is Jewish.'

'Please remember Ayna is Muslim and has been welcomed into the Almogavar family,' Carla scolded her husband.

'A Muslim, a Jew, an Italian and a Catalan,' scoffed Sancho. 'It sounds like some alehouse ballad, one that will have an unhappy ending.'

'I am free to marry whom I wish,' insisted Jordi.

'Perhaps you should give the matter more thought,' suggested Carla.

'No!' snapped Jordi. 'My mind is made up.'

374

Ayna poured more oil on the fire.

'Perhaps we could hear Chana's opinion on the matter.'

Luca was impressed. Her Italian had indeed come on leaps and bounds.

'She cannot speak any Italian or Catalan, at least not yet,' said Jordi.

'I will teach her,' offered Ayna, 'then we will both be able to speak for ourselves.'

'A chilling thought,' grumbled Sancho.

But nothing could dampen the spirits of the soldiers of the Catalan Company, now reunited with their loved ones and in possession of a fine city sited in a fertile valley. Grand Duke Roger, Sancho Rey and Bernat de Rocafort made up the newly formed city council and all were determined to ensure the economic life of Anaia continued uninterrupted, and no enemy would breach its walls. The Almogavars resumed their training routine, Luca, Jordi, a healed Romanus and thousands of others tramping across the hills on either side of the valley, practising battle drills and undertaking joint exercises with Bernat's riders and Melek's horse archers. The autumn was mild, the land was green and pleasant and the Catalan Company stood at the pinnacle of its power.

While Luca and Jordi fulfilled their military obligations, Ayna taught Chana Italian and Catalan, as well as assisting Carla in domestic chores. Ertan had arrived from Philadelphia along with the other Turkish slaves, and quickly established himself as a master chef among the Almogavars. Sancho, delighted by his exotic dishes, became less angry at the world and settled into the life of an important city dignitary. He did not approve of Jordi and Luca sharing their beds with women they had not married. But as both

Ayna and Chana had been purchased and were in any case infidels, he turned a blind eye. Carla, though, was always pestering her son and Luca on the need for both women to convert to the 'true faith' so both couples could be married. But as neither Ayna nor Chana would renounce their own religions, her pleas fell on deaf ears.

With the power of the Turkish *emirs* severely curtailed, and the fanatic Izzeddin Arslan removed from the world, there was no enthusiasm for a renewal of hostilities against the Romans in Anatolia, much less against the fearsome and seemingly unbeatable Catalan Company. The peace Grand Duke Roger's mercenaries had won had reversed decades of imperial decline, and the Catalan Company waited for an invitation to Constantinople to be awarded a Roman triumph through the city.

Chapter 22

Michael Cosses, Count of Opsikion, victor at Philadelphia and Anaia, now the most senior Roman commander in Anatolia, was surprised he had been summoned to the Blachernae Palace like some low-ranking official. He had expected to be rewarded with a triumph through the streets of Constantinople for the recent successes against the Turks, which had turned the tide of war in favour of the Romans. He had journeyed to the city after reaching Artake to await the emperor's pleasure. But the emperor was not pleased, far from it.

From a distance the Blachernae looked austere, its thick walls and high towers projecting strength rather that grace and beauty. After he had ridden into the huge courtyard and left his horse at the stables, he was escorted to the throne room where Emperor Andronicus waited for him. There was no empress as the ruler's wife Irene was in Greece, estranged from the emperor years ago and now the head of a rival court.

'Welcome, count.'

The shaven-headed eunuch with gold earrings bowed his head at Michael.

'The emperor awaits, lord.'

He turned on his dainty heels and marched into the palace, leading the way down a long corridor resplendent with gold mosaics depicting ancient Roman triumphs against the barbarians, beside him and behind him an escort of *Pelekyphoroi* – axe bearers – élite Varangians who never left the emperor's side. How he would love to command a formation of Varangians on the battlefield, to see their axes cleave a path through the infidels and water the holy soil of the empire with their godless blood.

The palace was like a maze, its harsh exterior housing no less than three hundred rooms and twenty chapels. But at its centre was the throne room, from where the emperor received guests and issued decrees to his subjects. When the party had reached the red leather doors studded with gold, the eunuch knocked on one of them. A Varangian opened it and the eunuch waited for the court chamberlain to appear, a middle-aged man with a huge belly and bulbous head that made him look like a pig standing on its hind legs. Michael smiled at the master of ceremonies, who ordered the Varangian to open the other door before asking the count to wait at the entrance. He then turned and addressed the assembled court in a booming voice.

'Count Michael Cosses, commander of the Opsikion Theme, Governor of Artake and Admiral of the Imperial Fleet, defender of the Orthodox Faith, shield of the Roman Empire, requests an audience, highness.'

'Let him come forward,' commanded the emperor.

The chamberlain walked beside Michael as the count strode confidently into the gilded chamber, courtiers bowing their heads to one of the most senior military commanders of the empire. Perfumed ladies looked admiringly at the handsome count, and young pages near the dais where the emperor sat dreamed of becoming a slayer of Turks like the famed Count of Opsikion. And as the noble made his way towards the emperor, a black-robed priest near the dais reminded him and the whole court who sat on the throne.

'Behold Andronicus, elect of God, crowned by God and defended by God, who sits in the Queen of Cities and rules over the Kingdom of Heaven on earth, who holds the reins of all human affairs, both temporal and spiritual, in his hands.'

Michael had deliberately chosen to wear soft-soled leather boots so that his steps would not make a sound in the throne room, as it was common knowledge the emperor disliked loud noises. The throne room itself projected two distinct concepts. The first was power and wealth. The palace was the epicentre of the Roman Empire, after all, and was expected to reflect the empire's might and longevity. Palace decoration thus propagated imperial ideology symbolically, with displays of military triumphs, religious scenes and huge imperial portraits.

The ceiling of the throne room was decorated with gold leaf, which had been arranged to appear like ethereal dust. The columns in the throne room had also been overlaid with gold and silver to emphasise the wealth and power of the emperor, and thus the empire he ruled over.

The second idea that the palace decoration projected was religious authority, reinforcing the notion that the emperor had indeed been appointed by God. The walls of the throne room thus contained paintings of the four virtues – Prudence, Justice, Fortitude and Temperance – depicted as saintly maidens. There were also images of previous emperors kneeling either side of Christ, promoting the idea that Roman rulers took their orders and advice from the Son of God.

Andronicus, dressed in a dazzling silver kabbadion, sat on a gold throne inlaid with precious stones. Suspended above his head and hanging on a gold chain was a golden crown. Even the scarlet cloaks of the Varangians around the throne were edged with gold. Michael bowed deeply to the emperor.

'Welcome, count,' said Andronicus, studying his commander. 'I trust your family are well.'

'Well, highness, thank you.'

'We were sad to hear of the death of your eldest daughter during the harsh winter just passed. We continue to pray for her soul.'

'You are most generous and devout, highness.'

Polite applause greeted the count's words, the emperor's advisers standing next to the dais nodding in approval. They nodded more enthusiastically when the emperor got to the kernel of why he had summoned the count to the palace.

'We were surprised, count, when word reached us that the Catalans have taken possession of our fair city of Anaia.'

'It is as I feared, great one,' said Patriarch Athanasius. 'We hired the servants of the apostate Bishop of Rome and now they are intent on establishing a Catholic enclave in the heart of the empire.'

There were groans and gasps from the courtiers, which were stilled by Andronicus raising a hand.

'It does seem curious, count, that you returned to Artake without the Catalans. Is there any reason why they should remain in Anaia?'

The count felt every pair of eyes on him as the court waited for his answer.

'In truth, highness, neither myself nor the governor of Philadelphia have the resources to protect our own lands and garrison the city of Anaia.'

'Who is the governor of Philadelphia now that Count Komnenos is dead?' asked Co-Emperor Michael standing near his father.

'His son, majesty,' replied the count, who looked at General Mouzalon beside the detested Timothy the Forest Dweller. 'Perhaps if the imperial army could be moved south...'

'Impossible,' snapped the emperor's son. 'The army defends Constantinople against the might of Osman Bey and his Muslim hordes.'

'It is as my son says,' agreed the emperor.

The fat eunuch treasurer took a few steps towards the throne and whispered into the emperor's ear.

'Ah, yes, thank you, Timothy.'

Andronicus looked at Count Michael sternly.

'We have heard disturbing news from our dear cousin Arcadius Drogon, the Governor of Magnesia who has been waging an unceasing war against the Muslims.'

Count Michael Cosses willed himself not to laugh out loud.

'It appears that the Catalans took him hostage and plundered his treasury, which is *our* treasury.'

There were loud gasps around the chamber.

'The price of hiring heretics, alas,' said Athanasius out loud.

The fat eunuch was looking at Count Michael with disdain, this man without balls, this boy lover who like a worm inside an apple was corrupting the empire from within.

'It is true, highness,' admitted the count. 'The Catalans, having already destroyed two Turkish armies and having relieved Philadelphia, desired payment to avoid having to plunder Count Ioannes Komnenos' lands. They could have plundered Magnesia, highness, but chose not to.'

'No indeed,' seethed the emperor's son. 'Having emptied Governor Drogon's treasury, they finally remembered why they were hired in the first place.'

'I am surprised you are defending their abominable actions,' sneered Timothy, to accompanying nods from the courtiers and their painted wives.

'They are a rough and ready lot, I will concede that,' said the count, 'and in the peace and calm of this court their actions may indeed seem appalling. But in six months they have achieved more than we have done in as many years. I will gladly make allowances for their lack of manners if it means we can reverse the advances the Turks have made in Anatolia.'

He looked directly at the emperor.

'In the spring, highness, we must unite the Catalan Company with General Mouzalon's army and strike against Osman Bey. With him defeated, the empire can finally begin to reclaim the lost lands of your ancestors…'

Andronicus, his head cast down, held up a hand to quieten the count.

'We thank you for your great service against the Turks, Count Michael. And as a reward we are creating you Count of Samos and Count of Bukellarion, with all the attendant privileges accompanying each title.'

Warm applause greeted this pronouncement, Andronicus looking up and smiling in recognition of the affection shown to him by his court. Count Michael forced himself to smile and bow his head, for the titles were worthless. Samos, a naval theme centred around the Aegean island of the same name, had long ceased to be under Roman control. Indeed, the island was actually under Genoese jurisdiction, though the Italians allowed the Turks to use it, for a fee. The inland theme of Bukellarion abutted his own Opsikion Theme but had been overrun by the Turks decades before. It would take a large army to retake it and raising such a force was beyond his own meagre resources.

'I am unworthy of such generosity, highness,' said the count.

'What plans do the Catalans have for the spring?' asked the co-emperor.

'I do not know, highness,' admitted the count. 'I assume they will leave Anaia…'

'They *will* be leaving Anaia,' snapped the co-emperor. 'The Catalans are squatters on imperial land and will be removed once the spring arrives. If we do nothing we set a dangerous precedent.'

'Especially as they are heretics,' added Patriarch Athanasius.

'Heretics who have given the empire invaluable service,' said Count Michael.

Andronicus had had enough.

'All decisions pertaining to the Catalans will be devolved to my son, who on the advice of Treasurer Timothy is the one who wished to hire them in the first place,' said the emperor. 'And now, Count Michael, lion of Anatolia, you may leave us.'

Glad to be given the opportunity to leave the detached, surreal world of the imperial court, the count bowed, turned on his heels and marched from the chamber. Polite applause accompanied him to the doors, which were opened by a pair of Varangians to allow him to exit.

Co-Emperor Michael later visited the imperial treasurer in his sumptuous mini-palace overlooking the blue waters of the Golden Horn, young male slaves in close-fitting garb showing him into one of Timothy's reception rooms. While he waited for the corpulent treasurer to arrive, he was served wine in a silver chalice and offered sweets and pastries on silver plates. As he reclined on the luxurious couch his eye caught the magnificent painted ceiling, which depicted a garden filled with fruit, flowers, birds and beasts, such as peacocks, hares and a lioness playing with her cubs. The detail was amazing. It must have taken weeks, perhaps months, to complete such a work. He wondered how much such beauty had cost the imperial treasury.

The treasurer swept into the room, smelling of expensive perfume, gold rings on his fat fingers and a huge white silk *kabbadion* covering his over-sized body. He bowed deeply to the heir of the Roman Empire.

'Highness, this is a great honour. Can I get you anything?'

Michael raised the chalice to him.

'I have been well taken care of, lord treasurer.'

Timothy flopped down on a second well-stuffed couch, the padding sinking beneath his great weight. As soon as he was seated, slaves rushed forward to serve him a chalice of wine and offer him sweets.

'I will come straight to the point, lord treasurer,' said Michael, 'what is the current state of imperial finances?'

Timothy took a large gulp of wine, his eyes taking a trip over the lithe body of the male slave nearest to him.

'Dire, highness. Revenues from Anatolia have all but dried up, the Genoese charge us exorbitant fees for transporting our exports overseas, and the taxes from our European colonies are low this year on account of the severe winter they, and indeed we, suffered.'

'So, there is little hope we can raise enough money to bribe the Catalans to leave Anaia?' said Michael.

Timothy shook his head, causing his jowls to wobble.

'Perhaps General Mouzalon could evict them with force.'

Michael sniffed at the notion. 'These Catalans made short work of the Turks. I doubt our own troops would fare any better against them. Probably far worse, in fact.'

Timothy was most surprised by the admission, but then the emperor's son had always adopted a more realistic, pragmatic approach when it came to the empire's many shortcomings.

'Would it be so bad for the Catalans to remain where they are, highness?' asked Timothy. 'The city was, after all, a Turkish enclave with little hope of being recovered by the late, greatly lamented Count Komnenos.'

'Therein lies the problem, lord treasurer,' said Michael, greatly appreciating the fine vintage he was drinking, far better than the wine in the palace. 'If we allow the Catalans to remain in Anaia, what is to say they will not expand the territory they control, attract more Catalans to their colours, and declare a Catalan Empire in Anatolia? To tolerate their insolence is to invite the religion of the heretical Bishop of Rome to take root in Asia. Such a thing would be intolerable.'

Timothy nodded. 'Then may I ask how you intend to evict them from Anatolia?'

Michael gave him a sly smile, his brown eyes narrowing.

'Mercenaries fight for pay, lord treasurer, so we must dangle a great sum before their eyes to entice them away from their lair. I want you to scour the city for any source of untapped revenue, and that includes any obscure taxes that have lapsed. I will order General Mouzalon to raid Turkish territory to capture slaves, which can be sold to raise money. He and his men might as well do something aside from sitting on their arses.'

*****

The winter was mercifully milder than the preceding one. The mountains and highland areas were still covered with crisp, white snow, but the winds were gentle and the valleys were mostly free of frosts. The Catalan Company settled into the role of occupiers of Anaia and the surrounding area. Bayezid Islam, cunning individual that he was, sent emissaries to the city to discuss the continuation of trade between Ephesus Neopolis and Anaia. Grand Duke Roger, eager to administer a prosperous and peaceful city rather than a beleaguered metropolis, readily agreed. For his part, Bayezid Islam realised supplies transiting through his port to Anaia would fill his coffers. He promised the grand duke's ships would be able to come and go freely without being molested, subject to the usual docking fees. And should the Catalan Company wish to leave Anaia and journey overseas, he would gladly make Ephesus Neopolis available, again subject to a prior agreed fee.

For Luca, the winter months were an opportunity to get to know Ayna more intimately. Not physical intimacy, for the preceding winter had provided ample chances to explore each other's bodies. Then Ayna had a rudimentary knowledge of Luca's language. Now she excelled in her linguistic expertise. Every morning, Luca was called to the colours to undertake training. Either route marches over the hills behind Anaia or in the valley in which it sat, plus weapons' drills, which included javelin throwing and swordplay.

Training areas were established outside the city where straw targets were arranged in rows and files to replicate enemy troop formations. Other areas were reserved for mounted exercises, in which Bernat's horsemen practised their charges and how to integrate lancers with Melek's horse archers. In the afternoons, Almogavars were free to return to the targets to hone their skills still further, though not if they had been assigned sentry duties. Many chose to do so, turning the training grounds into areas of constant activity from dawn till dusk.

Hector held the spear in front of him. The weapon was for practise, having a blunt end instead of a metal point. But in the right hands it could still inflict a nasty bruise, or worse, on an opponent.

'The point of the spear is fast and lethal,' he said to Ayna, ignoring Luca armed with a sword and shield nearby.

Like many among the Almogavars, Hector had been intrigued by the rise of Luca Baldi, who had saved the life of a Roman princess, seamlessly integrated into the ranks of the Almogavars, and had been responsible for recruiting Muslim horse archers into the Catalan Company. He was viewed by many as a lucky mascot, though Father Ramon believed him to be nothing more than a heretical influence, especially as he taken a Muslim as a lover. That lover now smiled at Hector as the captain showed her how to wield a spear two-handed.

'Now, Ayna,' said Hector, 'you and your heathen barbarians fought at the wall and were soundly beaten. Do you know why?'

'Because you used sorcery against us,' she replied instantly.

He gave her a mischievous grin.

'No, it is because you had no discipline and did not know how to use your weapons correctly. Luca, attack me.'

To reduce the likelihood of injury, Luca was wearing a padded jerkin, which together with his battle experience and youth, made him confident he could overcome the Almogavar captain. He knew a sudden charge by a swordsman stood a good chance of success

387

against a spearman, so he sprang forward. But Hector was too fast, stepping forward and jabbing the end of the spear at Luca's face, who instinctively brought up his shield to block the blow. But it was a feint and Hector delivered the real strike low, hitting Luca in the chest.

'Again,' commanded Hector.

Luca tried to close with his opponent but getting near to a man expert at wielding an eight-foot spear with both hands is difficult. Hector jabbed repeatedly at Luca's chest, face, groin and knees, taunting him with his smile, forcing the Italian to make increasingly desperate attacks. Eventually, Luca, who had been holding his shield directly in front of him, allowed it to swing off to the left, giving Hector his chance. The captain delivered what would have been a fatal blow to Luca's belly, which winded the young Almogavar.

'The spear can overcome a sword and shield if used correctly,' Hector said to Ayna.

Luca down on one knee, trying to catch his breath, wondered how he had lost. Hector helped him to his feet.

'Using a spear one-handed with a shield, though,' continued Hector, 'slows you down, which can be lethal in battle.'

Ayna pointed to Luca's shield. 'But you use a shield.'

'Only as a last resort in a battle. Mostly, it is slung on the back as a defence against arrows, and sword, axe and spear strikes.'

'I want Luca to teach me how to throw a spear and javelin,' she said.

Hector wagged a finger at her. 'We don't throw spears because the spear is your main weapon in battle, against both horse and foot. We throw javelins. I'm sure Luca can teach you how to throw one, as he had the best instructor to show *him* how.'

Who?' asked Ayna.

'Me,' he beamed. 'Well, you stay here so Luca can teach you the rudiments of the javelin. I have to attend a meeting of the captains.'

He tipped his head at Ayna and sauntered off, training spear on his shoulder.

'He likes you,' Ayna said to Luca.

He walked over and kissed her on the lips.

'What's not to like?'

She rolled her eyes.

'You have never talked about why you were in the ranks of the enemy at the wall,' he said.

Her eyes became pools of sadness.

'You never asked me.'

'I am asking you now. If you do not want to tell me, I will understand.'

She stared into the distance, towards the snow-covered hills behind Anaia.

'My family is from Baghdad, or was.'

She looked at Luca, who wore a quizzical expression.

'Baghdad was once a great city in the east, a centre of learning and culture.'

'Was?' he said.

'The Mongols, a barbarous people from a land far to the east, attacked and captured it. They massacred most of the population and destroyed all the great libraries in the city. By the will of Allah, my father, a librarian, had been sent on a mission to translate some ancient manuscripts in the city of Caesarea, to the west of Baghdad. He escaped the massacre.'

'That was lucky.'

'It was the will of Allah,' she said forcefully. 'He met my mother in Caesarea and continued with his work, but the Mongols are a godless people and forbade the worship of Allah in their lands. But my parents continued to follow the true faith in secret.'

She sighed. 'I grew up in the shadow of the Mongols, their ruler suddenly declaring his intention to follow Islam. My father was overjoyed and attended a gathering in the city square of all those who were also Muslims, lured there on the promise of finally being able to practise their faith openly.'

The sadness returned to her eyes. 'But the Mongols are false Muslims and demanded all those in the square swear allegiance to the *khan*, their leader, first and Allah second. All those who refused were murdered.'

'Your father was one of those killed?'

'Yes,' she said softly. 'The Mongols gave my mother his head as a reminder of what happens when anyone questioned their authority. After that she started to lose her mind and so, fearing for her safety, I took her away from Caesarea and we fled to the land of the Turcomans.'

'Where is your mother now?'

Her head dropped. 'When the spirit is dead, the body soon follows, Luca. I believe she died from grief. After her death, I wandered eastern Anatolia, thieving food and sleeping in forests, until I came across the camp of a man descended from the Prophet Himself.'

'Who's the Prophet?' asked Luca.

She gave him a wan smile. 'It does not matter now. Suffice to say, he and his followers welcomed me. They clothed me, fed me and gave me weapons to fight for Allah. When he led us to the Artake Peninsula, the rest you know.'

He took her hand. 'I am glad your prophet led you to me.'

'He was *not* the Prophet, Luca.'

She was about to tell him the story of Muhammad, the true Prophet, but thought it would just confuse him.

'The point is, Luca, I will not give up my faith because your priests command it.'

He laughed. 'They are not my priests, Ayna. You are free to go.'

'What?'

'You are not my slave, Ayna, and if you wish to leave, though it would break me into a thousand pieces, then I will give you money to allow you to go back to your people.'

She cupped his ashen face. 'You are my people now. You, Jordi, Carla and Chana. Even Sancho, though he is like an angry viper. So, I will stay, and you will teach me how to use a spear and throw a javelin.'

Chapter 23

What use are mercenaries with no battles to fight, no enemies to butcher and no lands to conquer? The Catalan Company was based in a land that was now at peace, its depleted and wary enemy locked behind high stone walls, the valleys and hills bereft of the mounted raiders that had previously cowered the inhabitants of beleaguered Tire and Philadelphia. The only horsemen at large in the winter landscape were Bernat de Rocafort's Catalans and the Roman horsemen of Philadelphia. The Almogavars trained and prepared... for what? The outbreak of peace might have been welcome in Constantinople, but a lengthy cessation of hostilities meant potential disaster for the Catalan Company. How would thousands of mercenaries subsist with no wars to fight?

Fortunately, there is always someone to fight, and in the spring the news the Roman emperor had need of the company against the Bulgarians was greeted with relief and joy in Anaia. The Almogavar council reminded Grand Duke Roger that the Romans had been unreliable employers in the past, but a voyage made by the commander of the company to Constantinople in late winter, during which the emperor proved his sincerity by displaying to him chests filled with gold, which were promised to the Catalans, was enough to convince the mercenaries of the Romans' good faith.

It was early March when the whole Catalan Company marched out of Anaia, dozens of Catalan banners flying among their ranks, the children and some of the women riding in wagons in the middle of the column. Grand Duke Roger had sent word to Philadelphia that the company was quitting Anatolia, which was greeted with dismay by the city's residents. The new governor, the son of Count Komnenos, sent a detachment of horse and foot to Anaia to provide

392

the nucleus of the new garrison. In truth, though, he had neither the resources nor resolution to adequately replace the more than six thousand mercenaries that had held Anaia for several months. Everyone knew, though none would say it, that Anaia would fall to the Turks sooner rather than later.

The air was crisp, the day bright but chilly, as the Almogavars tramped through the valley towards the port of Ephesus Neopolis, which would be the point of embarkation for the company. Commercial intercourse between the port and Anaia had carried on almost uninterrupted during the winter months, the Catalans purchasing food and supplies from the Turkish town. Grand Duke Roger had toyed with the idea of marching overland to the Artake Peninsula, and from there using his ships to transport the company to the city of Kallipolis on the Gallipoli Peninsula, where the company would prepare for the war against the Bulgarians. Such a route would entail retracing the company's march to Philadelphia via Soma, which risked being attacked by the forces of both Mehmed Bey and Karesi Bey. However, when the former learned from his spies in Constantinople, who were nothing more than merchants with the ear of the authorities, the Catalans were leaving, he sent orders to Bayezid Islam to make Ephesus Neopolis available to Grand Duke Roger. He sent emissaries to Anaia to report to the relative of the emperor the same, the governor of the port himself more than willing to assist the Christian mercenaries once more. For a price. For his part, Mehmed Bey wanted to do everything in his power to get rid of the Catalans. He could not defeat them on the battlefield, but he could speed them on their way. Roger accepted the offer for the Almogavars and their servants and dependents, though the horsemen of Bernat and Melek would ride north to Artake, it being a major and

393

time-consuming logistical exercise to transport hundreds of horses by ship.

'Where is this Gallipoli Peninsula, father?' asked Jordi, beside him the delightful Chana, her long black hair shining in the morning sun.

'West of Artake,' Sancho told him, his wife walking beside him. 'But we will not be staying there for long. From there we will march north to fight the Bulgarians.'

'Who are they?' asked Luca, spear in hand, javelins in his quiver.

Ayna also carried a javelin, having improved her proficiency with the weapon. Carla and Chana also carried weapons, it being an Almogavar custom for their women to be trained in their use. From bitter experience in Sicily, the Catalans had learned they could only rely on themselves in times of war, and peace for that matter.

'The Bulgarians are a threat to the Romans in Thrace,' said Sancho, 'and have inflicted several defeats on them in recent years, including one suffered by Co-Emperor Michael himself last year.'

'Let us hope his father pays us fully this time,' remarked Carla.

'If he does not, we will march on Constantinople itself,' threatened Sancho. 'But Roger has seen the gold we will receive, so I anticipate no difficulties.'

'Do you trust the Roman emperor, lord?' asked Ayna.

'Trust is an expensive commodity,' he told her. 'Take a look behind you. I do not need to trust anyone when I have five thousand of the best soldiers in the world to call on, to say nothing of Bernat's horsemen.'

'And Melek's riders?' said Ayna mischievously.

Sancho shrugged. 'Them, too.'

He looked at Chana. 'I have no issue with Muslims, or Jews, fighting alongside us as long as they are loyal.'

'Bayezid Islam is not to be trusted,' said Chana in faltering Catalan. 'He is a fat rapist.'

Luca was shocked by her words but the venom in Chana's voice told him her accusation was true. He looked at his friend, who was quaking with anger.

'If there is to be an exchange of hostages, father, I wish to be one, as before.'

'That will not be happening,' said Sancho, 'even though I would gladly gut that fat governor with my own knife. But sometimes, son, the needs of the many outweigh the needs of the few.'

Jordi was kept well away from the governor's castle when the Almogavars reached Ephesus Neopolis, and he and Luca were on the first galley to leave the port.

The voyage to Kallipolis was a delight. The sea was a glittering blue and the gentle spring breezes ensured the hops between islands were smooth and uneventful. After leaving Ephesus Neopolis, the fleet headed north to the Roman island of Chios, a place blessed with many coves and beaches only accessible from the sea. This meant the company, its dependents and the sailors could put ashore each evening safe in the knowledge they would not be attacked by bandits. Chios was nominally under the control of the Roman emperor, but the reality was he had too few soldiers to adequately garrison the many islands he still possessed in the Aegean. The sea was a playground for pirates, but they stayed clear of such a large and powerful fleet, and so the only ships the Catalans saw were trading vessels and the occasional war galley out of Constantinople.

From Chios the fleet kept on voyaging north to the island of Lesvos, a lush, green place full of fruit trees that the company helped itself to. In addition to the vineyards and olive groves, most of which were abandoned as a consequence of waning Roman power in the Aegean, there were expanses of oak, pine and walnut forests. From there, the fleet sailed north to the west coast of what was now the Karesi Emirate, which meant the majority of the women and children slept on the decks of the ships during the overnight stay. Patrols were mounted up to two or more miles inland from the beach, other parties refilling water bottles from the streams and springs in the area. But Turkish activity was conspicuous by its absence and so the next morning, just after dawn, the ships weighed anchor and set sail for the Hellespont, the narrow channel separating the Anatolian mainland from the Gallipoli Peninsula, which gave access from the Aegean to the Sea of Marmara. Because the strong currents and winds are predominantly from the northwest in the afternoons, the fleet had to wait until early morning to enter the narrows.

The Hellespont was full of vessels, most being Egyptian grain ships taking their cargoes to Constantinople to feed its population. But there were also Roman *dromons* patrolling the passage, complete with terrible tubular weapons that shot fire that could incinerate enemy ships and their crews. The Hellespont was of strategic importance to the very survival of the emperor's capital, and so his naval resources were directed towards keeping the Hellespont free of threats. For the first time since he had stepped foot on Roman soil, Luca was impressed by the display of the emperor's military power.

He sat on the deck of the Catalan *dromon* as a southerly wind filled her sails to propel her and the others in Grand Duke Roger's fleet towards the port of Kallipolis. With him were Ayna, Jordi and

Chana, around them dozens of other Almogavars and their families. The ships were packed to the gunnels, though with favourable winds and the calm seas it had enjoyed thus far, the fleet only spent around ten hours at most in the water daily. The rest of the time was spent ashore, resting and gathering food and water for the next leg of the journey.

'What are you thinking?'

Luca turned away from the shimmering blue sea and the craggy shore beyond to look at Ayna's sensual face.

'I was thinking of my parents. My life in Sicily seems remote now and I often have trouble recalling their faces.'

'You live another life now,' she said.

'As do we all,' chipped in Chana, her head resting on Jordi's shoulder. 'We have no homes to go back to.'

'Jordi has a home,' said Luca. 'He can go back to Catalonia, he and the other Almogavars.'

'The king does not want us back,' muttered Jordi. 'He has cast us adrift.'

'We are all wanderers,' lamented Ayna.

'Do the Jews not have a home?' Luca asked Chana.

'Our home is Israel,' she sighed, 'though you call it the Holy Land. It has been under enemy occupation for hundreds of years. Every Jew dreams of a free Israel. But we are few and our enemies are many.'

She placed a hand over Jordi's heart.

'Here is my home.'

He kissed her on the head.

'What about you, Ayna, what of your homeland?' asked Chana.

'It is ruled by the Mongols,' she spat. 'I will never return while they are there.'

'After we have beaten these Bulgarians,' said Jordi, 'perhaps the emperor will give us land we can call our own.'

They hoped it would not be the Gallipoli Peninsula, the southern part of which was hot, dusty and comprised rugged, rocky terrain with many steep ridges. Fresh water was scarce and the tangle of ravines, gullies and spurs inland from the coast were covered with gorse-like scrub that impeded movement. The city of Kallipolis was situated on a blunt promontory less than a mile in length, with steep cliffs behind. Founded by the Greeks seventeen hundred years before, it was above all a naval base guarding the entrance to the Sea of Marmara. The well-maintained curved stone breakwaters created a harbour that was both large and safe from strong currents. The stone quays were wide and long to allow many vessels to moor in the harbour, and the dockside was filled with large warehouses holding grain and other necessities.

As soon as the Catalan fleet docked, officials sought out the galley of Grand Duke Roger and harangued him with requests. There was no room in the city for thousands of soldiers and their families so they must camp outside Kallipolis, and the governor insisted the Catalans must pay for any food they required, rather than plundering the countryside, which in any case was poor and resembled a land that had already been pillaged. Finally, as a sign of good faith, would the grand duke consider surrendering the company's weapons to soothe the fears of the citizens of Kallipolis? Sancho Rey refused outright to even consider the last demand.

Luca and the other Almogavars marched straight from the harbour out of the city to an area of flat land to the north of the port.

There they pitched their Turkish tents and waited for their orders from the emperor. Several hours later, the company's ships appeared in the sea offshore – the governor had ordered their crews to weigh anchor and leave his harbour on the spurious grounds there was not enough room to accommodate them. To add insult to injury, he then shut the gates of his city, leaving the Almogavars and their dependents to their own devices.

The rising anger of the Catalans was soothed by the arrival of dozens of carts containing food, a gift from Co-Emperor Michael. The mercenaries were cheered further when it was revealed Michael himself was giving a lavish feast in honour of the company's achievements, to be held in the city of Adrianople some one hundred miles to the north. The city, a major Roman stronghold, would be the launch point for the campaign against the Bulgarians. A great army was being assembled near the city, and the Catalan Company would be the élite corps of that army. And it would have joint commanders: Co-Emperor Michael and the new Caesar of the Empire: Roger de Flor.

'What is a Caesar?' Jordi asked his father standing near the campfire, over which was cooking a delicious lamb stew, Ertan sprinkling the mouth-watering broth with herbs.

Sancho did not know, either, but the man standing next to him certainly did. Dressed in a magnificent red surcoat, mail hauberk and burnished helmet sporting a large red plume, Leo Diogenes was the scion of a great Roman family hundreds of years old. He commanded the *Paramonai* – the 'Watchmen' – the unit that guarded the imperial family. The Varangians guarded the emperor himself, but the *Paramonai* were responsible for keeping members of the imperial family from harm. What is more, the *Paramonai* were recruited from

399

noble Roman families rather than foreign mercenaries. But like many units in the imperial army, it was a shadow of the formation that had marched at the head of Roman armies in the empire's heyday.

Leo, helmet in the crook of his arm, flashed a smile at those gathered round the fire waiting for their meal.

'Hundreds of years ago,' he said in fluent Italian, 'when the world was ruled from Rome, the emperor was called "Caesar". Now it means one who is a member of the imperial family and who is looked on with great affection by the emperor himself. It is a great honour.'

Luca and Jordi were underwhelmed. What were foreign titles to them? However, after being frozen by iron stares from Sancho, they both stood and pretended to be interested. Chana and Ayna remained seated, unimpressed by the handsome peacock in front of them.

'Co-Emperor Michael,' continued Leo, 'wishes to invite Grand Duke Roger, his senior commanders and those who have distinguished themselves in last year's campaign to a great celebratory feast, to be held at the city of Adrianople. To the number of three hundred.'

Luca frowned. 'Why three hundred?'

'That was the number of Spartans who held the pass at Thermopylae in Greece against thousands of invading Persians hundreds of years ago. The Battle of Thermopylae is remembered still, just as the campaign of the Catalan Company against the Turks last year will be remembered by future generations.'

Luca, Sancho and Jordi had no idea who the Spartans were, or indeed who the Persians were. But Ayna did.

'I am Persian, and in my culture the battle is also celebrated. As a great Persian victory against the Greeks. The Spartans at Thermopylae were wiped out to a man.'

Leo's smile faded as he looked down his nose at the sultry infidel beauty who dared to speak in his presence. She was obviously some sort of slave and he was amazed the Almogavars allowed her to speak in their presence with her seditious tongue, much less to sit with them. But then, he had heard they were uncouth barbarians. His eyes avoided her to settle on the ample breasts of Chana.

'Which brings us to why we are here,' said Sancho. 'God alone knows why, but Princess Maria has specifically requested you two,' he pointed at Luca and Jordi, 'should attend the banquet at Adrianople.'

Jordi looked at his friend and they both grinned like small children.

'It would be a travesty if the heroes who rescued the princess were not present,' smiled Leo.

'Stew ready,' said Ertan in pigeon Italian.

'You have a Turkish slave to cook your food?' said Leo.

'He is not a slave,' replied Luca. 'He stays with us because he wants to.'

'We are company of equals,' stated Jordi proudly, prompting Chana to smile at him.

'Well, we have better things to do than stand here and debate the rights and wrongs of slavery,' said Sancho. 'We should return to Grand Duke Roger to finalise the arrangements regarding who will be attending the banquet.'

'I have a question, lord,' said Ayna.

Sancho and Leo looked at her, the latter frowning with annoyance.

'Well?' snapped Sancho.

Ayna stood and looked directly at the Roman aristocrat.

'You say this banquet is to be held in the city of Adrianople?'

'What of it?'

'I have been told the city will be the place where the war against the Bulgarians will be launched.'

'What does a Persian woman know of war and strategy?'

'She wonders why if the Catalan Company will be a part of that war, only a small part of it is going to Adrianople to eat a meal.'

Luca and Jordi laughed but Sancho was appalled by her behaviour.

'We have no time for this. We must go, lord.'

'Gladly,' sniffed Leo Diogenes.

'Don't forget to save me and Carla some stew,' said Sancho as he and the Roman noble departed.

'I do not trust that Roman,' hissed Ayna.

'He is a snake,' added Chana.

But the snake was all charm and smiles when dealing with the leaders of the Catalan Company, minus Bernard de Rocafort who was having problems arranging the transportation of his horses across the Hellespont. In his absence, Sancho led three hundred Almogavars, escorted by the same number of *Paramonai* and a handful of Catalan horsemen riding with Grand Duke Roger, from the Gallipoli Peninsula north towards Adrianople. He left Hector behind to command the Almogavars, much to his annoyance.

Sancho made it a point of honour for the Almogavars to cover the hundred miles between Gallipoli and Adrianople in as short a time as possible. As a result, the Catalan foot soldiers, carrying only water bottles and bread and dried figs in their food bags, covered over thirty miles a day, arriving at Adrianople on the morning of the fourth day after setting out. Leo Diogenes, who had difficulty reconciling the Almogavar victories with their peasant-like appearance and manners, complimented Sancho Rey on the discipline and stamina of his soldiers. For their part, Luca and Jordi were relishing the opportunity to fill their bellies with rich Roman food and see Princess Maria again.

Adrianopolis was a high-walled metropolis located in a fertile plain at the confluence of the Hebrus and Tonsus rivers, the waterways running along the southern and western sides of the city. On the green stretch of land between the wide rivers and the white city walls were pitched a mass of round tents – evidence of the gathering army earmarked for war against the Bulgarians. Grand Duke Roger instructed Sancho to pitch the tents of the Almogavars with the rest, but Leo Diogenes insisted the Catalans march into the city where they would be lodged in the palace. Enclosed within its own walls, the palace was a large structure comprising a domed hexagonal hall, off which were corridors leading to sleeping quarters, guard rooms, kitchens, chapels, offices and slaves' quarters. The semi-circular palace portico was paved with alternating red and white marble slabs, and around the palace were stables, storerooms, barracks, bathhouses, armouries and forges.

Luca, Jordi and the rest of the Almogavars spent the remainder of the day resting in the barracks that had been emptied so they could be lodged in the palace. A mass of servants was ferrying vast quantities of food, wine and beer to the palace kitchens, and Co-Emperor Michael made available a similar number of slaves to attend to the needs of the Almogavars. The Catalans ate and slept well that day, waking refreshed and eagerly anticipating the lavish banquet that was to begin at noon.

Before then, Luca and Jordi took the opportunity to walk the palace walls, feeling under-dressed in their functional attire compared to the red-uniformed guards wearing mail and helmets and carrying teardrop-shaped red shields sporting rampant gold lions. Their idle chatter was interrupted by a broad-shouldered officer of the Varangian Guard in a red scarlet cloak, his two-handed axe in one hand, the other resting on the hilt of his sword in its red scabbard adorned with gold decoration.

'I have a message for you both,' he said in Italian. 'Princess Maria invites you to meet with her before you attend the banquet.'

They were both flattered and beamed with delight, but Jordi remembered that time was pressing and if they met with the princess they might be late for the banquet. If they were, his father would be angry.

'Perhaps we might meet the princess later.'

The officer took two paces to stand in front of them.

'It is considered the height of bad manners to slight the princess.'

'Of course we will meet with her,' smiled Luca. 'Lead and we will follow.'

'What about the banquet?' said Jordi.

'I doubt we will be missed,' said Luca. 'Anyway, it is highly unlikely they will run out of food or drink before we arrive.'

'That's true.'

The officer led them from the battlements and out of the palace, saying little as he paced towards a grand mansion surrounded by a pristine white stone wall, the entrance to which was guarded by more Varangians.

'I thought the Varangians never left the emperor's side,' said Luca.

'The emperor assigned the princess her own Varangian detachment following the attempt on her life, which I believe you are acquainted with,' replied the officer, accepting the salute of the sentries at the single gate giving access to the grounds of the mansion.

The gardens surrounding the mansion were a sign of the owner's prestige and wealth. Elaborate fountains ornamented with sculptures were surrounded by lawns, flowers and trees, predominantly conifers and cypress. There was also an aromatic garden growing cassia, frankincense, myrrh and saffron. And flowers from the gardens – lilies and roses – were spread around the mansion for their pleasant aroma.

The princess was waiting for them in one of the reception rooms, standing and smiling when they were shown into her presence. She was dressed in a full length purple silk dress with long sleeves. Only members of the imperial family were permitted to wear purple garments due to the expensive process of making the dye from molluscs. Luca suddenly felt ashamed by the basic apparel he wore and cast his eyes down.

'It gladdens my heart to see you both alive and in one piece after your heroics in Anatolia,' she said. 'Please, sit.'

She extended an arm to two couches, Luca and Jordi doing as instructed. The Varangian Guard officer took up position by the door behind the two couches.

'I have taken a keen interest in your progress since our last encounter in Constantinople,' she told them, walking to an ornate silver jug on a wooden cabinet, filling two silver chalices with wine. She nodded to the officer, who walked over, took the chalices and handed them to Luca and Jordi.

The two Almogavars waited until the princess had reclined on her own couch opposite them before toasting her. They took small sips, not wishing to look uncouth in her presence.

'Do not stand on ceremony,' she told them. 'Empty your vessels. You have earned it my brave young warriors.'

They needed no second prompting, emptying their chalices. Luca felt calm and relaxed. Very relaxed.

'You have both covered yourselves with glory,' she said softly. 'I prayed for your safety during your campaign last year and God clearly heard my prayers.'

Luca smiled. His eyelids suddenly felt heavy, and his legs felt numb. The chalice fell out of his hand and his arms flopped down by his side. He saw Jordi slump back on the couch, his chalice clattering on the marble-tiled floor. He tried to rise but his limbs would not obey his brain. He felt as though he was being pulled down a long tunnel, the room and the princess vanishing into the distance as the darkness overtook him and he fell into unconsciousness.

'I want them both taken back to Gallipoli,' Maria told the officer. 'And they are to arrive unharmed. I hold you personally responsible.'

The officer observed the sleeping Almogavars.

'They might have to be bound. When they wake up they will be mighty angry.'

'They will not wake up for two days at least,' she said. 'I will give you the sleeping draft I slipped into their wine. Small doses will keep them sedated during the journey.'

'May I ask a question, highness?'

'You may ask.'

He cast a disparaging nod at the two slumbering Almogavars.

'Why are you devoting so much time to saving these two wretches, highness? Your nephew, now he has agreed a cessation of hostilities with the Bulgarian king, will soon be marching to Gallipoli to destroy the Catalan mercenaries. They will die anyway.'

'Perhaps, but they saved my life and so it is only right and Christian that I do the same. You have your orders, so carry them out.'

The spears and javelins of the Almogavars had been stacked in their barracks, along with their shields, swords and daggers, for no weapons were allowed in the great domed dining hall. Most of the Catalans sat on benches at tables at right angles to the top table where their captains sat alongside Grand Duke Roger, soon to be made Caesar when the emperor arrived in the city, and Co-Emperor Michael. Great quantities of wine were brought from the kitchens after a dour priest had blessed the assembly and the co-emperor. When he had departed, the hall was filled with excited chatter as Almogavars boasted about their sexual and martial prowess to each other. As the wine flowed and tongues loosened, Roger sat back in his ornate wooden chair and reflected on his good fortune, and that of the company he had founded.

'We have finally found a home,' he said to Sancho. 'Now we can begin to plan for the future, instead of living hand-to-mouth at the behest of kings and princes.'

407

Sancho was admiring the silver chalice inlaid with gold he was holding in his hand.

'Living in Artake and then Anaia has given me a liking for living in a house instead of a tent, I will not lie.'

Roger raised his chalice to him.

'Well, then. Let us raise a toast. To the future.'

'To the future.'

They touched chalices and drank the fine wine, while in front of them hundreds of Almogavars were getting very drunk.

'Where is your son and the Black Sheep?' asked the soon-to-be Caesar.

Sancho shrugged. 'Called away on some important business involving Princess Maria, or so I was informed.'

'How marvellous it is, Sancho,' waxed Roger, 'that a poor shepherd from Sicily and your son should be personal friends of a Roman princess. God smiles on them and us, my friend.'

Sancho nodded politely. Roger was obviously drunk and intoxicated with the idea he was to be made Caesar, which Leo Diogenes had informed him was a title of great importance in the Roman Empire. But Roger was welcome to the company of emperors, patriarchs, princesses and nobles. His long experience in Sicily had taught him such individuals used those lower ranking than themselves like throw-away tools: usable one minute; discarded the next.

Co-Emperor Michael next to Roger suddenly rose from his chair, prompting the fledgling Caesar to do likewise.

'Nature calls,' smiled Michael.

Sancho also rose to his feet out of respect, and out of the corner of his eye saw a familiar figure – the thin eyebrows and sharp

408

nose of Arabates, the treacherous Alan mercenary who had deserted the Catalan Company outside Philadelphia. The Alan saw the Almogavar looking at him and smirked, and Sancho felt a chill shoot down his spine. He turned to Roger, only to see his commander and friend die at the hands of a figure behind him who drew a razor-sharp dagger across his throat in a lightning-fast motion. Grand Duke Roger died instantly, his blood-stained corpse collapsing back down on the chair, the seat next to him vacant after Michael's departure. The sickening truth hit Sancho like a war hammer.

'Treachery,' he screamed, grabbing the knife he had been using to cut chunks of cheese.

He stiffened when a blade was thrust into his back, instinctively spinning and slashing the edge of the knife across the windpipe of the man who had been tasked with killing him. The servant-cum-assassin had not expected to be attacked and registered shock as his throat was lacerated, causing him to drop his own weapon and stagger back in shock.

The Almogavars fought like rabid animals, using anything to hand – knives, benches, platters for shields, overturned tables – to fight off the assassins in their midst. But Arabates and Leo Diogenes had planned their trap well and had not underestimated the fighting ability of the Almogavars. The first part of the plan had been to get the mercenaries drunk. Very drunk. And during their inebriation the hall would slowly fill with more servants – Alans concealing daggers and *Paramonai* with swords beneath their flowing robes. The second part was to ensure Co-Emperor Michael was absent from the hall when the bloodshed began, for he would be leading the army assembled at Adrianople against the remainder of the Catalan Company on the Gallipoli Peninsula. The third part of the plan would be triggered when the co-emperor rose from his chair, which would lead to the upstart mercenary Roger de Flor also standing. The slitting of his throat would be the signal for the killing to begin.

The Almogavars did not die easily. Angel, stabbed repeatedly, his *zamarra* cut to ribbons, killed three before he succumbed to his wounds. Marc managed to grab a sword from a *Paramonai* he had head-butted and fought off half a dozen assailants before he was hit by arrows, Arabates taking no chances, having ordered archers to enter the hall once the slaughter commenced. Biel used a dead Alan as a shield until he was wrestled to the ground and literally hacked to pieces, his head, arms and legs severed from his torso in an orgy of frenzied violence.

Sancho Rey knew he would die but was determined to take Arabates with him. Despite the blood gushing from his back, he tried to reach the gloating Alan leader, scrambling over the table and throwing the contents of a wine jug in the face of an Alan armed with a dagger in front of him. The Alan flinched, allowing Sancho to stab the man in the belly repeatedly, until he keeled over. Sancho stepped over the body but a sharp pain in his back caused him to falter, allowing two more Alans to pounce on him, pinning him to the floor. He grabbed the right hand of one, preventing the blade the Alan was holding going into his eye socket, kicking out at the other assailant and hitting his left ankle with the sole of his boot. The blow caused the Alan to fall across the bodies of Sancho and his Alan comrade, and onto the knife of Sancho Rey. He yelped when the blade went deep into his belly, causing him to drop his own weapon and crawl away.

Sancho grabbed the right arm of the other Alan with both hands, pulled with all his might and lunged with his mouth at the man's throat, locking his teeth into flesh and biting down with all the strength he could muster. His mouth began to fill with blood, but not his own. The Alan made a hideous gurgling noise as his own blood began to seep into his lungs and he began to desperately thrash around as the liquid began drowning him. Sancho kept biting, the pain in his back increasing to resemble a hot poker being driven into his flesh.

Arabates kicked the dying Alan off the body of Sancho Rey, the Almogavar leader trying to rise up when he saw his target standing over him. But he had lost too much blood and his limbs felt like lead weights. The floor around his body was wet with blood. Mostly his own; some belonging to his two assailants. Arabates crouched beside him.

'You and your filthy barbarians are finished. In the morning, we march south to finish off the rest of the Catalan Company. We will kill all the men and enslave the women. Apart from your wife. I will make it my mission to ensure she is paraded naked before the whole army before being raped night and day. And when she can no longer walk from being penetrated so many times, I will skin her alive and send her hide to the emperor as a present.'

Sancho spat a mouthful of blood at the Alan leader, who stood, drew his sword and severed the Catalan's head with a single strike. So died Sancho Rey, his captains, sergeants and the bravest of the Almogavars, along with Roger de Flor, mercenary, admiral and grand duke of the Roman Empire.

And while the cream of the Almogavars was being butchered, a covered wagon guarded by Varangian Guards trundled out of Adrianople on the road heading southeast, towards the coast, specifically the city of Rhaedestus. From there, the unconscious Luca

411

Baldi and Jordi Rey would be loaded on a *dromon* and shipped south to the Gallipoli Peninsula, to be unceremoniously dumped on a beach so they could be found by their fellow Almogavars. Princess Maria doubted they would live long after, not with her nephew leading a great army south to wipe out the remainder of the Catalan Company. But she comforted herself with the thought that at least her two young rescuers would die with swords in their hands facing an enemy across the battlefield, rather than being killed like animals in a slaughterhouse.

To be continued…

Historical notes

The reader may have noticed that though 'The Black Sheep' is set in the Byzantine Empire at the beginning of the fourteenth century, there is no mention of 'Byzantine' in the text. This is because the title Byzantine Empire entered common usage in the eighteenth and nineteenth centuries, having first been coined in the sixteenth century. Those who were citizens of what today we call the Byzantine Empire called themselves Romans. This was because they traced their lineage back to the founding of the city of Constantinople by the Roman Emperor Constantine in 330AD, though it would be more accurate to describe the event the renaming of the city of Byzantium by the emperor. Byzantium was originally a Greek colony founded in 667BC (though the precise date is contested). The city of Constantinople remained mainly Greek speaking until the Byzantine Empire fell to the Ottoman Turks in 1453.

Constantinople grew in size and importance under Roman rule, its population reaching one million people by the sixth century AD. What we would call the Byzantine Empire reached its height in the same century, with lands in southern Spain, North Africa, Syria, Judea, Anatolia, Greece, the Balkans, Italy, Sicily and Sardinia. But ruling such a large empire placed enormous strains upon the army and imperial finances, which in themselves sparked a series of crises in the empire. These crises were made worse by external threats, chief among them being the followers of the religion of Islam. The result was a prolonged struggle between Muslim rulers and Byzantine emperors in what became known as the Arab-Byzantine Wars between the seventh and eleventh centuries. In these wars the Byzantine Empire lost lands in Syria and North Africa, though its control over Anatolia (the area inhabited by modern-day Turkey) ensured it could still raise substantial numbers of soldiers for the imperial army.

A greater threat to the empire's very existence was the appearance of the Muslim Seljuk Turks in the eleventh century. Originating in the steppes of Central Asia, the Seljuks established a huge empire covering an area encompassing modern-day Iraq, Iran, Afghanistan, Turkmenistan, Uzbekistan and Syria. It was inevitable that the Seljuks would look west to the rich lands of Byzantine Anatolia, and the decisive clash occurred at the Battle of Manzikert in 1071, which was a crushing Seljuk victory. In the years afterwards, the Byzantine Empire lost its Anatolian heartlands. This led to internal revolts against what was seen as corrupt and profligate emperors, which further weakened the empire. In addition, and to compound the Byzantine Empire's problems, the Catholic west viewed the rulers of Constantinople as no longer capable of protecting Christian pilgrims to the Holy Land, and as well as being weak and vulnerable.

The fracturing of the Seljuk Empire by the Mongols in the thirteenth century resulted in the establishment of a number of independent emirates throughout Anatolia, all of them Muslim and all competing with each other. These kingdoms were not states in the modern sense of the word, but rather areas controlled to varying degrees by what were in effect warlords. By the year 1300, there were nearly 20 such emirates in Anatolia, plus those cities and areas still controlled by the Byzantines in western Anatolia. Some of those *emirs* feature in 'The Black Sheep', among them Karesi Bey, one of the most powerful, and Mehmed Bey, both of whom would live another 20 years after the events portrayed in this book.

By this time the Byzantine Empire was a shadow of its former self, though ironically its rapid decline was nothing to do with Islam or Mongols but rather Catholic crusaders.

In 1204, when Pope Innocent III preached the Fourth Crusade, he called for an attack on Egypt. The French nobles who made up most of the 15,000-strong crusader army, however, made an alliance with Venice and attacked Constantinople instead. They were excommunicated by a livid Pope Innocent, but this did nothing to divert them from their objective, storming the city on 12 April. It was the first time in its 900-year history that Constantinople's walls had been breached. The Byzantine emperor, Alexius V, was captured and executed and a new Latin Empire of the East proclaimed, Baldwin I being its first ruler. Constantinople was emptied of its treasures, which were shipped back to Western Europe (visitors to Venice can still see some of the loot taken in the Fourth Crusade, such as the four fourth-century bronze horses currently residing in St Mark's Cathedral, which originally stood in Constantinople's Hippodrome).

In the aftermath of the fall of Constantinople, the Byzantine Empire fractured into several different kingdoms. They included the Despotate of Epiros and the Empire of Nicaea (based in western Anatolia), and it was the Nicaeans who restored the Byzantine Empire, or Roman Empire as they would have termed it, in 1261 when Emperor Michael captured Constantinople from the Latins. Unfortunately, the wealth and soldiers of what had been the Nicaean Empire was transferred to the city and its European possessions, and much money was spent restoring Constantinople to its former glory. This proved to be an impossible task but it did have two unfortunate consequences. First, Anatolia was stripped of soldiers, which allowed the Turks to make further inroads into imperial territory. Second, imperial finances became severely strained.

By the beginning of the fourteenth century, therefore, the Byzantine Empire was a pale shadow of its former self. A stark indication of its parlous state was the number of troops it could field. In the early tenth century, for example, Byzantine armies typically numbered around 90,000 men. By the end of the twelfth century, the figure had dropped but was still a respectable 50,000 troops making up the main field army. By the time General George Mouzalon had lost the Battle of Bapheus to Osman Bey in July 1302, the Byzantine field army totalled 2000 men. There were other soldiers garrisoning the empire's towns and cities, of course, which added together produced a substantial number of troops, but such a paltry field army could never hope to reclaim lands lost to the Turks in Anatolia. Indeed, it appeared that Constantinople itself might once again succumb to enemy spears. It was a mixture of hope and desperation that made the emperor, Andronicus II, turn to a mercenary band that had won victory after victory against the French in Sicily during the so-called War of the Sicilian Vespers (1282–1302), which had just ended.

'The Black Sheep' is a work of fiction, but contemporary accounts of the Catalan Company in Anatolia in 1303–04 resemble an embellished medieval epic. What is certain is that in every encounter with the Turks, the Spanish mercenaries were entirely successful against superior odds.

Trying to work out how the Catalan mercenaries, and specifically their infantry arm, the Almogavars, defeated both European knights and Muslim horse archers with apparent ease is difficult. In 'The Black Sheep', I have surmised it was a combination

416

of mobility and firepower that gave them battlefield success. The average Almogavar wore no body armour, his only protection being a helmet and a small round shield. To loiter on a battlefield where thousands of enemy soldiers were armed with Christian crossbows or Turkish recurve bows would be to invite certain slaughter. But the Almogavars were equipped with both javelins and spears, the logical conclusion of such a weapons combination being that they used the former before delivering the coup de grâce with the latter, their attacks delivered at speed to increase shock effect and literally shatter formations. They must have also cooperated closely with their horsemen on the battlefield, which would have secured the Almogavars' flanks in combat, as well as undertaking general reconnaissance duties.

Today, the exploits of the Catalan Company in the service of the Byzantine Empire are largely forgotten. 'The Black Sheep' is an attempt to throw some light on a long-lost Medieval adventure, now buried in the mists of time.

It is a story that deserves to be kept alive.

Made in the USA
Monee, IL
09 April 2021